PAST IMPERFECT

PAST IMPERFECT

Julian Fellowes

WINDSOR
PARAGON

First published 2008
by Weidenfeld & Nicolson
This Large Print edition published 2009
by BBC Audiobooks Ltd
by arrangement with
The Orion Publishing Group

Hardcover ISBN: 978 1 408 45926 3
Softcover   ISBN: 978 1 408 45927 0

British Library Cataloguing in Publication Data available

Printed and bound in Great Britain by
CPI Antony Rowe, Chippenham and Eastbourne

To Emma and Peregrine
without whom nothing at all
would ever get written

Damian

Damian

ONE

London is a haunted city for me now and I am the ghost that haunts it. As I go about my business, every street or square or avenue seems to whisper of an earlier, different era in my history. The shortest trip round Chelsea or Kensington takes me by some door where once I was welcome but where today I am a stranger. I see myself issue forth, young again and dressed for some long forgotten frolic, tricked out in what looks like the national dress of a war-torn Balkan country. Those flapping flares, those frilly shirts with their footballers' collars—what were we thinking of? And as I watch, beside that wraith of a younger, slimmer me walk the shades of the departed, parents, aunts and grandmothers, great-uncles and cousins, friends and girlfriends, gone now from this world entirely, or at least from what is left of my own life. They say one sign of growing old is that the past becomes more real than the present and already I can feel the fingers of those lost decades closing their grip round my imagination, making more recent memory seem somehow greyer and less bright.

Which makes it perfectly understandable that I should have been just a little intrigued, if taken aback, to find a letter from Damian Baxter lying among the bills and thank yous and requests for charitable assistance that pile up daily on my desk. I certainly could not have predicted it. We hadn't seen each other in almost forty years, nor had we communicated since our last meeting. It seems

3

odd, I know, but we had spent our lives in different worlds and although England is a small country in many ways, it is still big enough for our paths never to have crossed in all that time. But there was another reason for my surprise and it was simpler.

I hated him.

A glance was enough to tell me whom it was from, though. The writing on the envelope was familiar but changed, like the face of a favourite child after the years have done their unforgiving work. Even so, before that morning, if I'd thought of him at all, I would not have believed there was anything on earth that would have induced Damian to write to me. Or I to him. I hasten to add that I wasn't offended by this unexpected delivery. Not in the least. It is always pleasant to hear from an old friend but at my age it is, if anything, more interesting to hear from an old enemy. An enemy, unlike a friend, can tell you things you do not already know of your own past. And if Damian wasn't exactly an enemy in any active sense, he was a former friend, which is of course much worse. We had parted with a quarrel, a moment of savage, unchecked rage, quite deliberately powered by the heat of burning bridges, and we had gone our separate ways, making no subsequent attempt to undo the damage.

It was an honest letter, that I will say. The English, as a rule, would rather not face a situation that might be rendered 'awkward' by the memory of earlier behaviour. Usually they will play down any disagreeable past episodes with a vague and dismissive reference: 'Do you remember that frightful dinner Jocelyn gave? How did we all survive it?' Or, if the episode really cannot be reduced and detoxified in this way, they pretend it never took place. 'It's been far too long since we met,' as an opener will often translate as 'it does not suit me to continue this feud any longer. It was ages ago. Are you prepared to call it a day?' If the recipient is willing, the answer will be couched in similar denial mode: 'Yes, let's meet. What have you been up to since you left Lazard's?' Nothing more than this will be required to signify that the nastiness is finished and normal relations may now be resumed.

But in this case Damian eschewed the common practice. Indeed, his honesty was positively Latin. 'I dare say, after everything that happened, you did not expect to hear from me again but I would take it as a great favour if you would pay me a visit,' he wrote in his spiky, and still rather angry, hand. 'I can't think why you should, after the last time we were together, but at the risk of self-dramatising, I have not long to live and it may mean something to do a favour for a dying man.' At least I could not accuse him of evasion. For a while I pretended to myself that I was thinking it over, trying to decide, but of course I knew at once that I would go, that my curiosity must be assuaged, that I would deliberately revisit the lost land of my youth. For, having had no contact with Damian since the summer of 1970, his return to my conscious mind inevitably brought sharp reminders of how much my world, like everyone else's world for that matter, has changed.

There's danger in it, obviously, but I no longer fight the sad realisation that the setting for my growing years seems sweeter to me than the one I now inhabit. Today's young, in righteous, understandable defence of their own time, generally reject our reminiscences about a golden age when the customer was always right, when AA men saluted the badge on your car and policemen touched their helmet in greeting. Thank heaven for the end of deference, they say, but deference is part of an ordered, certain world and, in retrospect at least, that can feel warming and even kind. I suppose what I miss above all things is the kindness of the England of half a century ago. But then again, is it the kindness I regret, or my own youth?

'I don't understand who this Damian Baxter *is* exactly? Why is he so significant?' said Bridget as, later that evening, we sat at home eating some rather overpriced and undercooked fish, purchased from my compliant, local Italian on the Old Brompton Road. 'I've never heard you talk about him.' At the time when Damian sent his letter, not all that long ago in fact, I was still living in a large, ground-floor flat in Wetherby Gardens, which was comfortable, convenient for this and that, and wonderfully placed for the takeaway culture that has overwhelmed us in the last few years. It was quite a smart address in its way and I certainly could never have afforded to buy it, but it had been relinquished to me by my parents years before, when they had finally abandoned London. My father tried to object, but my mother had rashly insisted that I needed 'somewhere to start,' and he'd surrendered. So I profited from their generosity and fully expected not only to start, but also to finish, there. In truth, I hadn't changed it much since my mother's day and it was still filled with her things. We were sitting at her small, round breakfast table in the window as we spoke, and I suppose the whole apartment could have seemed quite feminine, with its charming pieces of Regency furniture and a boy ancestor in curls over the chimneypiece, were my masculinity not reasserted by my obvious and total lack of interest in its arrangements.

At the time of the letter incident, Bridget FitzGerald was my current . . . I was going to say 'girlfriend' but I am not sure one has 'girlfriends' when one is over fifty. On the other hand, if one is too old for a 'girlfriend,' one is too young for a 'companion,' so what is the correct description? Modern parlance has stolen so many words and put them to misuse that frequently, when one looks for a suitable term, the cupboard is bare. 'Partner,' as everyone not in the media knows, is both tired and fraught with danger. I recently introduced a fellow director in a small company I own as my partner and it was some time before I understood the looks I was getting from various people there who thought they knew me. But 'other half' sounds like a line from a situation comedy about a golf club secretary, and we haven't quite got to the point of 'This is my mistress,' although I dare say it's not far off. Anyway, Bridget and I were going about together. We were a slightly unlikely pair. I, a not-very-celebrated novelist, she, a sharp Irish businesswoman specialising in property, who had missed the boat romantically and ended up with me.

My mother would not have approved, but my mother was dead and so, in theory, out of the equation, although I am not convinced we are ever

7

beyond the influence of our parents' disapproval, be they dead or alive. Of course, there was a chance she might have been mellowed by the afterlife, but I rather doubt it. Maybe I should have listened to her posthumous promptings, since I can't pretend that Bridget and I had much in common. That said, she was clever and good-looking, which was more than I deserved, and I was lonely, I suppose, and tired of people ringing to see if I wanted to come over for Sunday lunch. Anyway, whatever the reason, we had found each other and, while we did not technically live together, since she kept on her own flat, we'd jogged along for a couple of years quite peaceably. It wasn't exactly love, but it was something.

What amused me with reference to Damian's letter was Bridget's proprietorial tone when referring to a past of which, almost by definition, she could know little or nothing. The phrase 'I've never heard you talk about him,' can only mean that, were this fellow significant, you would have talked about him. Or, worse, you *should* have talked about him. This is all part of the popular fantasy that when you are involved with someone it is your right to know all about them, down to the last detail, which of course can never be. 'We have no secrets,' say cheerful, young faces in films, when, as we all know, our whole lives are filled with secrets, frequently kept from ourselves. Clearly, in this instance Bridget was troubled that if Damian were important to me and yet I had never mentioned him, how much else of significance had been kept concealed? In my defence I can only say that her past, too, like mine, like everyone's in fact, was a locked box.

Occasionally we allow people a peep, but generally only at the top level. The darker streams of our memories we negotiate alone.

'He was a friend of mine at Cambridge,' I said. 'We met in my second year, around the time when I was doing the Season at the end of the Sixties. I introduced him to some of the girls. They took him up, and we ran about together in London for a while.'

'Being *debs' delights*.' She spoke the phrase with a mixture of comedy and derision.

'I am glad my early life never fails to bring a smile to your lips.'

'So what happened?'

'Nothing happened. We drifted apart after we left, but there's no story. We just went in different directions.' In saying this I was, of course, lying.

She looked at me, hearing a little more than I had intended. 'If you do go, I assume you'll want to go alone.'

'Yes. I'll go alone.' I offered no further explanation but, to be fair to her, she didn't ask for one.

I used to think that Damian Baxter was my invention, although such a notion only demonstrates my own inexperience. As anyone knows, the most brilliant magician in the world cannot produce a rabbit out of a hat unless there is already a rabbit *in* the hat, albeit well concealed, and Damian would never have enjoyed the success that I took credit for unless he had been genuinely possessed of those qualities that made his triumph possible and even inevitable. Nevertheless, I do not believe he would have made it into the social limelight as a young man, in those days anyway, without some help. And I was the one who gave it. It was perhaps for this reason that I resented his betrayal quite so bitterly. I put a good face on it, or I tried to, but it still stung. Trilby had turned traitor to Svengali, Galatea had destroyed Pygmalion's dreams.

'Any time on any day will be convenient,' the letter said. 'I do not go out now or entertain, so I am completely at your disposal. You will find me quite near Guildford. If you drive, it may take ninety minutes but the train is quicker. Let me know and I will either arrange directions or someone can meet you, whichever you prefer.' In the end, after my fake prevarication, I wrote back suggesting dinner on such and such a day, and named the train I would catch. He confirmed this with an invitation for the night. As a rule I prefer, like Jorrocks, to 'sleeps where I dines,' so I accepted and the plan was settled. Accordingly, I passed through the barrier at Guildford station on a pleasant summer evening in June.

I looked about vaguely for some Eastern European holding a card with my name mis-spelled in felt tip pen but instead of this, I found myself approached by a uniformed chauffeur—or rather someone who looked like an actor playing a chauffeur in an episode of *Hercule Poirot*—who replaced his peaked cap after introducing himself in low and humble tones, and led the way outside to a new Bentley, parked illegally in the space reserved for the disabled. I say 'illegally,' even though there was a badge clearly displayed in the window, because I assume these are not distributed so that friends may be met off trains without their getting wet or having to walk too far with their luggage. But then again, everyone deserves the odd perk.

I did know that Damian had done well, though how or why I knew I cannot now remember, for we shared no pals and moved in completely different circles. I must have seen his name on a *Sunday Times* list or maybe in an article on a financial page. But I don't think, before that evening, I understood quite *how* well he had done. We sped through the Surrey lanes and it was soon clear, from the trimmed hedging and the pointed walls, from the lawns like billiard tables and the glistening, weeded gravel, that we had entered the Kingdom of the Rich. Here there were no crumbling gate piers, no empty stables and lodges with leaking roofs. This was not a question of tradition and former glory. I was witnessing not the memory but the living presence of money.

I do have some experience of it. As a moderately successful writer, one rubs up against what Nanny would call 'all sorts,' but I can't pretend this was ever really my crowd. Most of the so-called rich I know are possessed of surviving, not newborn, fortunes, the rich who used to be a good deal richer. But the houses I was passing belonged to the Now Rich, which is different, and for me there is something invigorating in their sense of immediate power. It is peculiar, but even today there is a snobbery in Britain when it comes to new money. The traditional Right might be expected to turn up their noses at it I suppose, but paradoxically, it is often the intellectual Left who advertise their disapproval of the self-made. I do not pretend to understand how this is compatible with a belief in equality of opportunity. Perhaps

11

they do not try to synthesise them, but just live by contradictory impulses, which we all do to some degree. But if I may have been guilty of such unimaginative thinking in my youth, it is gone from me now. These days I unashamedly admire men and women who have made their pile, just as I admire anyone who looks at the future mapped out for them at birth and is not afraid to tear it up and draw a better one. The self-made have more chance than most of finding a life that truly suits. I salute them for it and I salute their bejewelled world. Of course, on a personal level it was extremely annoying that Damian Baxter should be a part of it.

The house he had chosen as a setting for his splendour was not a fallen nobleman's palace but rather one of those self-consciously moral, Arts and Crafts, rambling warrens that seem to belong in a Disney cartoon and are no more convincing as a symbol of Olde England than they were when Lutyens built them at the turn of the last century. Surrounding it were gardens, terraced, clipped and criss-crossed with trim and tended paths, but seemingly no land beyond that. Damian had not apparently decided to adopt the ancient model of imitation gentry. This was not a manor house, nestling in the warm embrace of farming acres. This was simply the home of a Great Success.

Having said that, while not traditional in an aristocratic sense, the whole thing had quite a 1930s feel, as if it were built with the ill-gotten gains of a First World War profiteer. The Agatha Christie element provided by the chauffeur was continued by the bowing butler at the door and even by a housemaid, glimpsed on my way to the pale oak staircase, in her black dress and frilly apron, although she seemed perhaps more frivolous, as if I had suddenly been transported to the set of a Gershwin musical. A sense of the odd unreality of the adventure was, if anything, confirmed when I was shown to my room without first having met my host. There is always a slight whodunnit shiver of danger in this arrangement. A dark-clad servant hovering in the door and muttering 'Please come down to the drawing room when you are ready, Sir,' seems more suited to the reading of a will than a social call. But the room itself was nice enough. It was lined with pale-blue damask, which had also been used to drape the high, four-poster bed. The furniture was stable, solid English stuff and a group of Chinoiserie paintings on glass, between the windows, was really charming, even if there was the unmistakable tinge of a country house hotel, rather than a real country house, about it all, confirmed by the bathroom, which was sensational, with a huge bath, a walk-in shower, shiny taps on tall pipes coming straight up out of the floor, and enormous towels, fluffy and brand new. As we know, this kind of detail is seldom found in private houses in the shires, even today. I tidied myself up and went downstairs.

The drawing room was predictably cavernous, with a vaulted ceiling and those over-springy carpets that have been too recently replaced. Not the shagpile of the minted club owner, nor the flat and ancient rugs of the posh, but smooth and sprung and *new*. Everything in the room had been purchased within living memory and apparently by a single purchaser. There was none of the ragbag

13

of tastes that country houses are inclined to represent, where the contents of a dozen homes, the amalgamated product of forty amateur collectors over two or three centuries, are flung together into a single room. But it was good. In fact, it was excellent, the furniture largely from the early years of the eighteenth century, the pictures rather later, all fine, all shining clean and all in tip-top condition. After the similar experience of my bedroom, I wondered if Damian had employed a buyer, someone whose job was just to put his life together. Either way, there was no very tangible sense of him, or any other personality really, in the room. I wandered about, glancing at the paintings, unsure whether to stand or sit. In truth it felt forlorn, despite its splendour; the burning coals in the grate could not dispel the slightly clammy atmosphere, as if the room had been cleaned but not used for quite a while. And there were no flowers, which I always think a telltale sign; there was nothing living, in fact, giving a staleness to its perfection, a kind of lifeless sterility. I could not imagine that a woman had played much part in its creation, nor, God knows, that a child had played any part at all.

There was a sound at the door. 'My dear chap,' said a voice, still with the slight hesitance, the suspicion of a stammer, that I remembered so well. 'I hope I haven't kept you waiting.'

There is a moment in *Pride and Prejudice* when Elizabeth Bennet catches sight of her sister who has returned with the dastardly Wickham, rescued from disgrace by the efforts of Mr Darcy. 'Lydia was Lydia still,' she comments. Well, Damian Baxter was Damian still. That is, while the broad

14

and handsome young man with the thick curls and the easy smile had vanished and been replaced by a hunched figure resembling no one so much as Doctor Manette, I could detect that distinctive, diffident stutter masking a deep and honed sense of superiority, and I recognised at once the old, patronising arrogance in the flourish with which he held out his bony hand. I smiled. 'How very nice to see you,' I said.

'Is it?' We stared at each other's faces, marvelling simultaneously at the extent, and at the lack, of change that we found there.

As I looked at him more closely I could see that when he had talked in his letter of being 'a dying man,' he had been speaking the literal truth. He was not just old before his time but ill, very ill, and seemingly past the point of no return. 'Well, it's interesting. I suppose I can say that.'

'Yes, you can say that.' He nodded to the butler who hovered near the door. 'I wonder if we might have some of that champagne?' It didn't surprise me that even forty years later he still liked to wrap his orders in diffident questions. I was a veteran witness of this trick. Like many who try it, Damian imagined, I think, that it suggested a charming lack of confidence, a faltering but honourable desire to get it right, which I knew for a fact he had not felt since some time around 1967 and I doubt he knew much of it then. The man addressed did not seem to feel any answer was required of him and I'm sure it wasn't. He just went to get the wine.

Dinner was a formal, muted affair in a dining room that unsuccessfully crossed William Morris and Liberty's with a dash of the Hollywood hills. High, mullioned windows, a heavy, carved, stone

15

chimneypiece and more of the bouncy carpet added up to a curiously flat and unevocative result, as if a table and chairs had unaccountably been set up in an empty, but expensive, lawyer's office. But the food was delicious, if quite wasted on Damian, and we both got some fun out of the Margaux he'd selected. The silent butler, whom I now knew as Bassett, hardly left us for a minute and, inevitably, the conversation played out before him was desultory. I remember an aunt once telling me that when she looked back to the days before the war, she was astonished at some of the table talk she'd witnessed, where the presence of servants seemed to act as no restraining force at all. Political secrets, family gossip, personal indiscretions, all came bubbling forth before the listening footmen and must presumably have enlivened many an evening in the local pub, if not, as in our more greedy and salacious times, their published memoirs. But we have lost that generation's sublime confidence in their own way of life. Whether we like it or not—and I do like it really—time has made us conscious of the human spirit in those who serve us. For anyone born since the 1940s all walls have ears.

So we nattered on about this and that. He asked after my parents and I asked after his. In actual fact my father had been quite fond of him but my mother, whose jungle instincts were generally more reliable, sensed trouble from the start. She, at any rate, had died in the interim since we last met and so had both of his, so there wasn't much to be said. From there, we discussed various others of that mutual acquaintance of long ago, and by the time we were ready to move on we had covered an impressive list of career disappointments, divorces and premature death.

At last he stood, addressing Bassett as he did so. 'Do you think we could have our coffee in the library?' Again he asked softly, as a favour that might be denied. What would happen, I wonder, if someone so instructed should take the hesitant question at face value? 'No, Sir. I'm afraid I'm a bit busy at the moment. I'll try to bring some coffee later on.' I should like to see it once. But this butler knew what he was about and went to carry out the veiled command, while Damian led the way into the nicest of the rooms that I had seen. It looked as if an earlier owner, or possibly Damian himself, had purchased a complete library from a much older house, with dark, richly shining shelves and a screen of beautifully carved columns. There was a delicate chimneypiece of pinkish marble and in a polished steel basket a fire had been lit for our arrival. The combination of flickering flames and gleaming leather bindings, as well as some excellent pictures—a large seascape that looked like a Turner and the portrait of a young girl by Lawrence among them—gave a warmth notably lacking elsewhere in the house. I had been unjust. Obviously it was not lack of taste but lack of interest that had made the other rooms so dreary. This was where Damian actually lived. Before long we were equipped with drinks and cups of coffee, and alone.

'You've done very well,' I said. 'Congratulations.'

'Are you surprised?'

'Not terribly.'

He accepted this with a nod. 'If you mean I was

always ambitious, I confess it.'

'I think I meant that you would never take no for an answer.'

He shook his head. 'I wouldn't say that,' he said. I wasn't completely sure what he meant by this but before I could delve he spoke again. 'I knew when I was beaten, even then. When I found myself in a situation where success was not a possible outcome, I accepted it and moved on. You must grant me that.'

This was nonsense. 'I won't grant you that,' I said. 'Or anything like it. It may be a virtue you achieved in later life. I cannot tell. But when I knew you your eyes were much larger than your stomach and you were a very poor loser, as I should know.'

Damian looked surprised for a moment. Perhaps he had spent so much of his life with people who were paid, in one way or another, to agree with him that he had forgotten not everyone was obliged to. He sipped his brandy and after a pause he nodded. 'Well, be that as it may, I am beaten now.' In answer to my unasked question he elaborated. 'I have inoperable cancer of the pancreas. There is nothing to be done. The doctor has given me about three months to live.'

'They often get these things wrong.'

'They occasionally get these things wrong. But not in my case. There may be a variant of a few weeks, but that's all.'

'Oh.' I nodded. It is hard to know how to respond suitably to this kind of declaration because people's needs can be so different. I doubted that Damian would want wailing and weeping or suggestions of alternative cures based

18

on a macrobiotic diet, but you never know. I waited.

'I don't want you to feel I am raging at the injustice of it. My life has, in a way, come to a natural conclusion.'

'Meaning?'

'I have, as you point out, been very fortunate. I've lived well. I've travelled. And there's nothing left in my work that I still want to do, so that's something. Do you know what I've been up to?'

'Not really.'

'I built up a company in computer software. We were among the first to see the potential of the whole thing.'

'How clever of you.'

'You're right. It does sound dull, but I enjoyed it. Anyway, I've sold the business and I will not start another.'

'You don't know that.' I can't think why I said this, because of course he did know exactly that.

'I'm not complaining. I sold out to a nice, big American company and they gave me enough money to put Malawi back on its feet.'

'But that's not what you're going to do with it.'

'I don't think so, no.'

He hesitated. I was fairly sure we were approaching what they call the 'nub' of why I was here, but he didn't seem able to progress things. I thought I might as well have a shot at moving us along. 'What about your private life?' I ventured pleasantly.

He thought for a moment. 'I don't really have one. Nothing worthy of the name. The odd arrangement for my comfort, but nothing more than that for many years now. I'm not at all social.'

19

'You were when I knew you,' I said. I was still transfixed by the thought of the 'odd arrangement for my comfort.' Golly. I resolved to steer clear of any attempt at clarification.

There was no further need to keep things moving. Damian had got started. 'I did not like the world you took me into, as you know.' He looked at me challengingly but I had no comment to make so he continued, 'but, paradoxically, when I left it, I found I didn't care for the entertainments of my old world either. After a while I gave up "parties" altogether.'

'Did you marry?'

'Once. It didn't last very long.'

'I'm sorry.'

'Don't be. I only married because I'd got to that age when it starts to feel odd not to have married. I was thirty-six or -seven and curious eyebrows were beginning to be raised. Of course, I was a fool. If I'd waited another five years, my friends would have started to divorce and I wouldn't have been the only freak in the circus.'

'Was she anyone I knew?'

'Oh, no. I'd escaped from your crowd by then and I had no desire to return to it, I can assure you.'

'Any more than we had the smallest desire to see you,' I said. There was something relieving in this. A trace of our mutual dislike had surfaced and it felt more comfortable than the pseudo-friendship we had been playing at all evening. 'Besides, you don't know what my crowd is. You don't know anything about my life. It changed that night as much as yours. And there is more than one way of moving on from a London Season of forty years

20

ago.'

He accepted this without querying it. 'Quite right. I apologise. But, truly, you would not have known Suzanne. When I met her she was running a fitness centre near Leatherhead.' Inwardly I agreed that it was unlikely my path had crossed with the ex-Mrs Baxter's so I was silent. He sighed wearily. 'She tried her best. I don't want to speak ill of her. But we had nothing at all to hold us together.' He paused. 'You never married in the end, did you?'

'No. I didn't. Not in the end.' The words came out more harshly than I intended but he did not seem to wonder at it. The subject was painful for me and uncomfortable for him. At least, it bloody well should have been. I decided to return to a safer place. 'What happened to your wife?'

'Oh, she married again. Rather a nice chap. He has a business selling sportswear, so I suppose they had more to build on than we did.'

'Were there any children?'

'Two boys and a girl. Though I don't know what happened to them.'

'I meant with you.'

He shook his head. 'No, there weren't.' This time his silence seemed very profound. After a moment he completed the thought. 'I can't have children,' he said. Despite the apparent finality of this statement there was something oddly unfinal in the tone of his voice, almost like that strange and unnecessary question mark that the young have imported from Australia, to finish every sentence. He continued, 'that is to say, I could not have children by the time that I married.'

He stopped, as if to allow me a moment to

21

digest this peculiar sentence. What could he possibly mean? I assumed he had not been castrated shortly before proposing to the fitness centre manageress. Since he had introduced the topic, I didn't feel guilty in wanting to make a few enquiries, but in the event he answered before I had voiced them. 'We went to various doctors and they told me my sperm count was zero.'

Even in our disjointed, modern society, this is quite a taxing observation to counter with something meaningful. 'How disappointing,' I said.

'Yes. It was. Very *disappointing*.'

Obviously I'd chosen badly. 'Couldn't they do something about it?'

'Not really. They suggested reasons as to why it might have happened, but no one thought it could be reversed. So that was that.'

'You could have tried other ways. They're so clever now.' I couldn't bring myself to be more specific.

He shook his head. 'I'd never have brought up someone else's child. Suzanne had a go at persuading me but I couldn't allow it. I just didn't see the point. Once the child isn't yours, aren't you just playing with dolls? Living dolls, maybe. But dolls.'

'A lot of people would disagree with you.'

He nodded. 'I know. Suzanne was one of them. She didn't see why she had to be barren when it wasn't her fault, which was reasonable enough. I suppose we knew we'd break up from the moment we left the surgery.' He stood to fetch himself another drink. He'd earned it.

'I see,' I said, to fill the silence, rather dreading what was coming.

22

Sure enough, when he spoke again his tone was more determined than ever. 'Two specialists believed it might have been the result of adult mumps.'

'I thought that was a myth, used to frighten nervous, young men.'

'It's very rare. But it can happen. It's a condition called orchitis, which affects the testicles. Usually it goes away and everything's fine, but sometimes, very occasionally, it doesn't. I didn't have mumps as a boy and I wasn't aware I'd ever caught it, but when I thought it over, I was struck down with a very sore throat a few days after I got back from Portugal, in July of nineteen seventy. I was in bed for a couple of weeks and my glands certainly swelled up, so maybe they were right.'

I shifted slightly in my chair and took another sip of my drink. My presence here was beginning to make a kind of uncomfortable sense. In a way I had invited Damian to Portugal, to join a group of friends. God knows, in the event it was more complicated than that but the excuse had been the party was short of men and our hostess had got me to ask him. With disastrous results, as it happens. So, was he now trying to blame me for being sterile? Had I been invited here to acknowledge my fault? That as much harm as he had done to me on that holiday, so had I done to him? 'I don't remember anyone being ill,' I said.

He did, apparently. 'That girlfriend of the guy who had the villa. The neurotic American with the pale hair. What was her name? Alice? Alix? She kept complaining about her throat, the whole time we were there.'

'You have wonderfully perfect recall.'

23

'I've had a lot of time to think.'

The image of that sun whitened villa in Estoril, banished from my conscious mind for nearly four decades, suddenly filled my brain. The hot, blond beach below the terrace, drunken dinners resonating with sex and subtext, climbing the hill to the haunted castle at Cintra, swimming in the whispering, blue waters, waiting in the great square before Lisbon Cathedral to walk past the body of Salazar . . . The whole experience sprang back into vivid, technicoloured life, one of those holidays that bridge the gap between adolescence and maturity, with all the attendant dangers of that journey, where you come home quite different from when you set out. A holiday, in fact, that changed my life. I nodded. 'Yes. Well, you would have done.'

'Of course, if that were the reason, then I could have had a child before.'

Despite his seriousness I couldn't match it. 'Even you wouldn't have had much time. We were only twenty-one. These days every girl on a housing estate may be pregnant by the time she's thirteen, but it was different then.' I smiled reassuringly, but he wasn't watching. Instead, he was busy opening a drawer in a handsome *bureau plat* beneath the Lawrence. He took out an envelope and gave it to me. It wasn't new. I could just make out the postmark. It looked like 'Chelsea. 23rd December 1990.'

'Please read it.'

I unfolded the paper gingerly. The letter was entirely typed, with neither opening greeting nor final signature written by hand. 'Dear Shit,' it began. How charming. I looked up with raised

24

eyebrows.

'Go on.'

> Dear Shit, It is almost Christmas. It is also
> late and I am drunk and so I have found the
> nerve to say that you have made my life a
> living lie for nineteen years. I stare at my
> living lie each day and all because of you. No
> one will ever know the truth and I will
> probably burn this rather than send it, but
> you ought to realise where your deceit and
> my weakness have led me. I do not quite
> curse you, I could not do that, but I don't
> forgive you, either, for the course my life has
> taken. I did not deserve it.

At the end, below the body of the text, the author
had typed: 'A fool.'

I stared at it. 'Well, she did send it,' I said. 'I
wonder if she meant to.'

'Perhaps someone else picked it up from the
hall table and posted it, without her knowledge.'

This seemed highly likely to me. 'That would
have given her a turn.'

'You are sure it is a "her"?'

I nodded. 'Aren't you? "My life has been a living
lie." "Your deceit and my weakness." None of it
sounds very butch to me. I rather like her signing it
"a fool." It reminds me of the pop lyrics of our
younger days. Anyway, I assume the base deceit to
which she refers comes under the heading of
romance. It doesn't sound like someone feeling let
down over a bad investment. That would make the
writer female, wouldn't it? Or has your life steered
you along new and previously untried routes?'

25

'It would make her female.'

'There we are, then.' I smiled. 'I like the way she cannot curse you. It's quite Keatsian. Like a verse from 'Isabella, or The Pot of Basil': "She weeps alone for pleasures not to be." '

'What do you think it means?'

I wasn't clear how there could be any doubt. 'It's not very mysterious,' I said. But he waited, so I put it into words. 'It sounds as if you have made somebody pregnant.'

'Yes.'

'I assume the deceit she refers to must be some avowal of a forever kind of love, which you made in order to get her to remove her clothing.'

'You sound very harsh.'

'Do I? I don't mean to. Like all of us boys in those days, I tried it often enough myself. Her "weakness" implies you were, in this instance, successful.' But I thought over Damian's original question about the letter's meaning. Did it indicate that he thought things were not quite so straightforward? 'Why? Is there another interpretation? I suppose this woman could have been in love with you and her life since then has been a lie because she married someone else when she'd rather have been with you. Is that what you think it is?'

'No. Not really. If that's all she meant, would she be writing about it twenty years later?'

'Some people take longer than others to get over these things.'

' "I stare at my living lie each day." "No one will ever know." No one will ever know what?' He asked the question as if there could be no doubt as to the answer. Which I agreed with.

I nodded. 'As I said, you made her pregnant.'

He seemed almost reassured that there was no other possible meaning, as if he had been testing me. He nodded. 'And she had the baby.'

'Sounds like it. Though that in itself makes the whole affair something of a period piece. I wonder why she didn't get rid of it.'

At this, Damian gave his unique blend of haughty look and dismissive snort. How well I remembered it. 'I imagine abortion was against her principles. Some people do have principles.'

Now it was my turn to snort. 'I'm not prepared to take instruction from you on that score,' I said, which he let pass, as well he might. The whole thing was beginning to irritate me. Why were we making such a meal of it? 'Very well, then. She had the baby. And nobody knows that you are the father. End of story.' I stared at the envelope, so carefully preserved. 'At least, was it the end? Or was there some more? After this?'

He nodded. 'That's exactly what I thought at the time. That it was the start of some kind of . . . I don't know . . . extortion.'

'Extortion?'

'My lawyer's word. I went to see him. He took a copy and told me to wait for the next approach. He said that clearly she was building up to a demand for money and we should be ready with a plan. I was in the papers a bit in those days and I'd already had some luck. It seemed likely that she'd suddenly understood her baby's father was rich, and so now might be the moment for a killing. My offspring would have been about twenty then—'

'Nineteen,' I said. 'Her life was a living lie for nineteen years.'

He looked puzzled for a moment, then he nodded. 'Nineteen and just starting out. Cash would have come in very useful.' He looked at me. I didn't have anything to add since, like the lawyer, I thought this all made sense. 'I would have given her something.' He was quite defensive. 'I was perfectly prepared to.'

'But she didn't write again.'

'No.'

'Perhaps she died.'

'Perhaps. Although it seems rather melodramatic. Perhaps, as you say, the letter got posted by accident. Anyway, we heard nothing more and gradually the thing drifted away.'

'So why are we discussing it now?'

He did not answer me immediately. Instead, he stood up and crossed to the chimneypiece. A log had rolled forward on to the hearth and he took up the tools to rectify it, doing so with a kind of deadly intensity. 'The thing is,' he said at last, speaking into the flames but presumably addressing me, 'I want to find the child.'

There didn't seem to be any logic in this. If he'd wanted to 'do the right thing,' why hadn't he done it eighteen years before, when there might have been some point? 'Isn't it a bit late?' I asked. 'It wouldn't have been easy to play dad when she wrote the letter; but by now the "child" is a man or woman in their late thirties. They are what they are, and it's far too late to help shape them now.'

None of this seemed to carry any weight whatever. I'm not sure he even heard. 'I want to find them,' he repeated. 'I want you to find them.'

It would be foolish to pretend that I had not by this stage worked out that this was where we were

28

headed. But it was not a task I relished. Nor was I in the least sure I would undertake it. 'Why me?'

'When I met you I had only slept with four girls.' He paused. I raised my eyebrows faintly. Any man of my generation will understand that this was impressive in itself. At nineteen, which is what we were when we first came across each other, I do not believe I had done much more than kiss on the dance floor. He hadn't finished. 'I knew all four until well into the early 1970s and it definitely wasn't one of them. Then you and I ran around for a while, and I kept myself fairly busy. A couple of years later, when that period had come to an end, we went to Portugal. And after that I was sterile. Besides, look at the writing, look at the paper, read the phrases. This woman is educated—'

'And histrionic. And drunk.'

'Which does not prevent her being posh.'

'I'll say.' I considered his theory some more. 'What about the years between the end of the Season and Portugal?'

He shook his head. 'A few, mainly scrubbers, and a couple left over from our times together. Not one who had a baby before that summer.' He sighed wearily. 'Anyway, nobody lives a lie who hasn't got something to lose. Something worth holding on to, something that would be endangered by the truth. She wrote to me in 1990 when the upper and upper middle classes occupied the last remaining bastion of legitimate birth. Anyone normal would have let the secret out of the bag long ago.' The effort of saying all this, plus the log work, had depleted what remained of his energy and he sank back into his chair with a groan.

29

I did not pity him. Quite the contrary. Suddenly the unreasonableness of his request struck me forcibly. 'But I'm not in your life. I am nothing to do with you. We are completely different people.' I wasn't insulting him. I simply could not see why any of this was my responsibility. 'We may have known each other once, but we don't now. We went to some dances together forty years ago. And quarrelled. There must be others who are far closer to you than I ever was. I can't be the only person who could take this on.'

'But you are. These women came from your people, not mine. I have no other friends who would know them, or even know *of* them. And in fact, if we are having this conversation, I have no other friends.'

This was too self-serving for my taste. 'Then you have no friends at all, because you certainly can't count me.' Naturally, once the words were out I rather regretted them. I did believe that he was dying and there was no point in punishing him now for things that could never be undone, whatever he or I might wish.

But he smiled. 'You're right. I have no friends. As you know better than most, it's not a relationship I could ever either understand or manage. If you will not do this for me I have no one else to ask. I cannot even hire a detective. The information I need would not be available to anyone but an insider.' I was about to suggest he undertake the search himself, but looking at his shaking, hollow frame, the words died on my lips. 'Will you do it?' he asked after a brief pause.

At this point, I was quite sure that I really didn't want to. Not just because of the prickly, time-wasting and awkward nature of the quest, but because the more I thought about it, the more I knew I didn't want to poke around in my own past, any more than his. The time he spoke of was over. For both of us. I had hardly kept up with anyone from those days, for reasons which involved him, as he knew, and what was there to gain by rootling around in it all? I decided to make a last attempt to appeal to his better nature. Even people like Damian Baxter must have a little. 'Damian, think. Do you really want to turn their life upside down? This man, this woman, they know who they are and they're living their life as best they can. Will it help to find they're someone different and unknown? To make them question, or even break with, their parents? Would you want that on your conscience?'

He looked at me quite steadily. 'My fortune, after death duties, will be far in excess of five hundred million pounds. My intention is to make my child sole heir. Are you prepared to take the responsibility for denying them their inheritance? Would you want *that* on *your* conscience?'

Naturally, it would have been *jejune* to pretend that this did not make all the difference in the world. 'How would I set about it?' I said.

He relaxed. 'I will present you with a list of the girls I slept with during those years, who had a child before April 1971.' This was again impressive. The list of girls I had slept with during the same period, with or without children, could have been contained on the blank side of a visiting card. It was also very precise and oddly businesslike. I had thought we were engaged in some sort of philosophical exchange but I saw now

31

we were approaching what used to be called 'brass tacks.' He obviously sensed my surprise. 'My secretary has made a start. There didn't seem much point in your getting in touch if they hadn't had a baby.' Which was of course true. 'I believe the list is comprehensive.'

'What about the girls you slept with who did not bear children at that time?'

'Don't let's worry about them. No point in making work.' He smiled. 'We've done a lot of weeding. There were a couple of others I slept with who did have an early child but, in the words of the Empress Eugénie's mother when challenged over her Imperial daughter's paternity, *les dates ne correspondent pas*.' He laughed, easier now that he saw his plan would come to fruition. 'I want you to know that I have taken this seriously and there is a real possibility that it could be any one of the listed names.'

'So how do I go about it?'

'Just get in touch. With one exception, I've got the present addresses.'

'Why don't you ask them to have a DNA test?'

'That sort of woman would never agree.'

'You romanticise them in your dislike. I suspect they would. And their children certainly would when they found out why.'

'No.' He was suddenly quite firm again. I could see my comment had annoyed him. 'I don't want this to be a story. Only the true child must know I'm looking for them. When they have the money it will be their choice to reveal how or why they got it. Until then, this is for my private satisfaction, not public consumption. Test one who isn't my child and we will read the story in the *Daily Mail* the following week.' He shook his head. 'Maybe we should test them at the last, but only when you have elected which of the said progeny is probably mine.'

'But suppose one of the women had a baby without anyone knowing and put it up for adoption?'

'They haven't done that. At least, the mother of my baby hasn't.'

'How do you know?'

'Because then she wouldn't have stared at her lie every day.'

I had nothing further to say, at least until I'd thought about it all some more, which Damian seemed to understand and did not wish to challenge. He pulled himself unsteadily to his feet. 'I'm going to bed now. I haven't been up as late as this for months. You will find the list in an envelope in your room. If you wish, we can discuss it some more tomorrow morning before you go. At the risk of sounding vulgar, as you would say, you'll also find a credit card, which will cover any expenses you care to charge on it during your enquiries. I will not question whatever you choose to use it for.'

This last detail actively annoyed me as it was deliberately phrased in a manner designed to make me think him generous. But nothing about this commission was generous. It was a hideous imposition. 'I haven't agreed yet,' I said.

'I hope you will.' He was at the door when he stopped. 'Do you ever see her now?' he asked, confident that I would require no prompting as to the object of his enquiry. Which was correct.

'No. Not really.' I thought for a painful moment.

'Very occasionally, at a party or a wedding or something. But not really.'

'You aren't enemies?'

'Oh, no. We smile. And even talk. We're certainly not enemies. We're not anything.'

He hesitated, as if he were pondering whether to go down this path. 'You know I was mad.'

'Yes.'

'But I want you to understand that I know it, too. I went completely mad.' He paused, as if I might come in with some suitable response. But there wasn't one. 'Would it help if I said I was sorry?' he asked.

'Not terribly.'

He nodded, absorbing the information. We both knew there was nothing further to add. 'Stay down here as long as you like. Have some more whisky and look at the books. Some of them will interest you.'

But I wasn't quite finished. 'Why have you left it until now?' I said. 'Why didn't you make enquiries when you first got the letter?'

This did make him pause and ponder, as the light from the hall came through the now open door and deepened the lines of his ravaged face. Presumably he asked himself the same question a thousand times a day. 'I don't know. Not completely. Maybe I couldn't bear the thought of anyone feeling they had a claim against me. I didn't see how I could find and identify them without giving them some power. And I'd never really wanted a child. Which is probably why I wouldn't listen to my wife's pleadings. It wasn't one of my ambitions. I don't think I was ever naturally paternal.'

'Yet now you are prepared to give this unknown stranger enough money to build a small industrial town. Why? What's changed?'

Damian thought for a moment and a tiny sigh made his thin shoulders rise and fall. The jacket, which must once have fitted flawlessly, flapped loosely around his shrivelled frame. 'I'm dying and I have no beliefs,' he said simply. 'This is my only chance of immortality.'

Then he was gone and I was left to enjoy his library alone.

TWO

I have never been a good judge of character. My impressions at first meeting are almost invariably wrong. Although, human nature being what it is, many years had to pass before I could bring myself to admit it. When I was young I thought I had a marvellous instinct to tell good from bad, fine from shoddy, sacred from profane. Damian Baxter, by contrast, was an expert at assessment. He knew at once I was a patsy.

As it happens, we had both gone up to Cambridge in September 1967, but we were in different colleges and we moved in different crowds, so it was not until the beginning of the summer term of 1968, in early May I think, that our paths first crossed, at a party in the Fellows' Quadrangle of my college, where I was no doubt showing off. I was nineteen and in that heady stage of life for someone like me, at least for someone like me *then*, when you suddenly realise that the world is more complicated than you had supposed, that there is in fact a vast assortment of people and opportunities on offer, and you will not be obliged to continue forever in the narrow channel of boarding school and county, which was all that my so-called 'privileged' upbringing had yielded thus far. I would not say that I was ever antisocial but nor would I claim much social success before that time. I had been rather overshadowed by handsome and witty cousins, and since I possessed neither looks nor a trace of charisma to offset this, there wasn't much I could do to make my presence felt.

My dear mother understood my predicament, which she was obliged to witness silently and painfully for years, but found there was little she could do to remedy it. Until, seeing the burgeoning confidence that admission to university had brought, she decided to take advantage of it to promote a spirit of adventure within me, providing introductions to London friends with suitably aged daughters. Surprisingly perhaps, I had followed her lead and begun to construct a new social group for myself, where I would have no more depressing comparisons to contend with and where I could, to an extent anyway, reinvent myself.

It would seem odd to today's young that I should have allowed myself to be so parentally steered, but things were different forty years ago. To start with, people were not then afraid of getting older. Our strange, patronising culture, where middle-aged television presenters dishonestly pretend to share the tastes and prejudices of their teenage audience in order to gain their trust, had not arrived. In short, in this as in so many areas, we did not think in the way that people think today. Of course, we were divided by political opinions and class and, to a lesser extent than now, religion, but the key difference, from today's viewpoint, is not between the Right and the Left, or the aristocratic and the ordinary, but between the generation of 1968 and the people of four decades later.

In my world, parents in the early Sixties still arranged their children's lives to an extraordinary extent, settling between themselves when parties would be given and at which houses during the school holidays, what subjects their offspring would study at school; what careers they should pursue after university; above all, what friends they would spend time with. It wasn't, on the whole, tyrannical but we did not much challenge our parents' veto when it was exercised. I remember a local baronet's heir, frequently drunk and invariably rude, and for these reasons beguiling to me and my sister and repulsive to our parents, who was actually forbidden entry to our house by my father, 'except where his absence would cause comment.' Can such a phrase really have been spoken within living memory? I know we laughed about this rule even then. But we did not break it. In short, we were a product of our backgrounds in a way that would be rare today. One hears people wonder about the collapse of parental authority. Was it deliberately engineered as the right-wing press would have us believe? Or did it just happen because it was right for the time, like the internal combustion engine or penicillin? Either way, it has vanished from whole chunks of our society, gone, like the snows of yesteryear.

37

At any rate, to resume, that spring there was a drinks party in the Fellows' Quadrangle to which I'd been invited for some reason. I cannot now say if it was an official function or a private bash, but anyway there we all were, feeling clever and chosen, and probably still enjoying the college's reputation for being 'rather smart.' How pitiful such mini-vanities seem, viewed from the tired vale of the middle years, but I don't believe there was much harm in us, really. We thought we were grown up, which we weren't, and posh, which we weren't very, and that people would be glad to know us. I say this although, after my painful youth, I still preserved that all too familiar blend of pride and terror, that is so characteristic of the late teens, when nose-in-air snobbery goes hand in hand with social paranoia. Presumably it was this contradictory mixture that made me so vulnerable to attack.

Oddly enough, I can recall the precise moment when Damian entered my life. It was fitting because I was talking to Serena when he appeared, so we both met him together, simultaneously, on the instant, a detail that seems much more curious on reflection than when I was living it. I don't know why she was there. She was never a college groupie. Perhaps she was staying with someone nearby and had been brought. At any rate I won't find the answer now. I didn't know Serena at all well then, not as I would later, but we'd met. This is a distinction lost on the modern world, where people who have shaken hands and nodded a greeting will tell you they 'know' each other. Sometimes they will go further and assert, without any more to go on, that so-and-so is 'a friend of mine.' If it should suit the other party they will endorse this fiction and, in that endorsement, sort of make it true. When it is not true. Forty years ago we were, I think, more aware of the degree of a relationship. Which was just as well with someone as far beyond my reach as Serena.

Lady Serena Gresham, as she was born, did not appear to suffer from the marbling of self-doubt that afflicted the rest of us and this made her stand out among us from the start. I could describe her as 'unusually confident,' but this would be misleading, as the phrase suggests some bright and brash self-marketeer, the very last description she would merit. It just never occurred to her to worry much about who or what she was. She never questioned whether people would like her, nor picked at the thing when they did. She was, one might say nowadays, at peace with herself and, in the teenage years, then as now, it made her special. Her gentle remoteness, a kind of floating, almost underwater quality, took possession of me from the first time I saw her and many years would pass before she did not pop into my defenceless brain at least once every half an hour. I know now that the main reason she seemed remote was because she wasn't interested in me, or in most of us for that matter, but then it was pure magic. I would say it was her dreamy unattainability, more than her beauty or birth or privileges, though these were mighty, that gave her the position she enjoyed. And I know I am not alone in thinking of 1968 as the Year of Serena. Even as early as the spring, I felt myself lucky to be talking to her.

As I have said, her privileges were great, if not unique, as a member of the select, surviving rump

39

of the Old World. At that time, self-made fortunes were usually much smaller than they would be decades later and the very rich, at least those people who 'lived rich,' still tended mostly to be those who had been even richer thirty years before. It was an odd era for them, poor devils. So many families had gone to the wall in the post-war years. Friends they had dined and danced and hunted with before 1939 had tumbled down in the wreckage of their kind and it would not be long before most of the fallen had been engulfed by the upper middle class, never to regain their lost status. Even among those who had kept the faith, still in their houses, still shooting their own pheasants, there were many who gloomily subscribed to the philosophy of *après moi le déluge*, and regularly vans would chug away, out through the gates towards the London auction houses, bearing the treasures that had been centuries in the assembling, so the family could stay warm and have something decent to wear for one more winter.

But Serena was not afflicted by these pressures. She and the rest of the Greshams were part of the Chosen (very) Few and lived much as they had always lived. Perhaps there were only two footmen where once there had been six. Perhaps the chef had to manage on his own and I do not believe Serena or her sisters enjoyed the services of a lady's maid. But otherwise not much had altered since the early 1880s, apart from their hemlines and being allowed to dine in restaurants.

Her father was the ninth Earl of Claremont, a mellow, even charming, title and when I knew him, as I would do later, he was himself a mellow and charming man, never cross because he had never been crossed and so, like his daughter, very easy to be with. He too lived in a benign mist, although, unlike Serena, he was not a creature of myth, a lovely *naiad* eluding her swain. His vagueness was more akin to *Mr Pastry* . Either way, he never had much grasp of hard reality. Indeed, at times it felt as if the family's soothing title had generated a placid sense of unquestioning acceptance in the dynasty, for which I now think, looking back, they were to be envied. I did not at that time believe that loving came easily to any of them, certainly not 'being in love,' which would have involved far too much disruption, with its horrid, sticky threats of indigestion and broken sleep, but they did not hate or quarrel either.

Not that acceptance of their lot was very difficult. By dint of judicious investment and far-sighted marriage, the family had more than survived the rocky seas of the twentieth century thus far, with large estates in Yorkshire, a castle somewhere in Ireland, which I never saw, and a house on Millionaires' Row, the private road running parallel to Kensington Palace, which was then considered quite something. These days, eastern potentates and people who own football clubs seem to have snapped up those vast edifices and made them private again, but at that time they had mostly fallen into embassies, one by one, with scarcely a family left. Except, of course, for the Claremonts, who occupied number 37, a lovely 1830s stone wedding cake, a shade too near Notting Hill.

As if this were not enough, Serena was also very beautiful, with thick, russet hair and a complexion

41

lifted straight from a Pre-Raphaelite painting. Her features added to her gift of serenity, of real grace, which is an unlikely word to use of a girl of eighteen, but in her case a truthful one. I do not know exactly what we talked about, either at that party in Cambridge or at the many gatherings and house parties where we would meet over the next two years, sometimes art, I think, or maybe history. She was never much of a gossip. This was not a tribute to her kindness so much as to her lack of interest in other people's lives. Nor would there have been talk of a career, although she is not to blame for that. Even in the late Sixties, serious professional ambition would have marked her out uncomfortably among her contemporaries. That said, I was never bored in her company, not least because I must have been in love with her even then, long before I would acknowledge the fact, but the hopelessness implicit in loving such a star would have been all too obvious to that bundle of insecurities I call my unconscious mind and I shied away from certain failure. As anyone would.

'Can I talk to you?' said a deep, pleasant voice, just as I was approaching the punchline of a story. We looked up to find we had been joined by Damian Baxter. And we were glad of it which, to me now, is the strangest detail of all. 'I don't know anyone here,' he added with a smile that would have melted Greenland. My impressions of Damian have been so overlaid by what came after that it is hard for me to dredge up my early feelings, but there's no doubt that he was wonderfully attractive in those days, to men, women and children alike. Apart from anything else, he was so handsome, in a healthy, open-air sort of way, very handsome really, with bright, almost unnervingly blue eyes and thick, dark, wavy hair, worn long and in curls, as we all wore it then. He was fit, too, and muscular but without being sporty, or, worse, *hearty*, at all. He was just redolent of both health and intelligence, an unusual combination in my experience, and he looked as if he slept ten hours every night and had never tasted alcohol. Neither of which would be borne out by the facts.

'Well, now you know us,' said Serena and held out her hand.

I need hardly say that of course he knew exactly who we were. Or rather, who she was. He gave himself away later that evening, when we ended up squashed into a corner table in a dubious and rather cramped restaurant off Magdalene Street. We had picked up a couple of other students when the drinks party disbanded but Serena was not with us. It would have been unusual if she had been. It was rare for her to drift into that kind of easily accessible arrangement. She usually had a good, if unspecified, reason for not joining in.

The waiter brought the obligatory, steaming plates of *boeuf bourgignon*, with its glutinous and shiny sauce, that seemed to be our staple fare. This is not a criticism of the eaterie in question, more an acknowledgement of how and what we ate then, but I must not be ungrateful. Mounds of glazed stew, with rough red wine, was a big leg up, considering what had been on offer ten years before. There is, and should be, worthwhile debate about the merits of the changes the last four decades have brought to our society, but there can be few who do not welcome the improvement of

English food, at least until the raw fish and general undercooking that arrived with the celebrity chefs of the new century. There is no doubt about it that when I was a child the food available to the general British public was simply pitiful, consisting largely of tasteless school dinners, with vegetables that had been boiling since the war. Occasionally, you might find something better on offer in a private house, but even smart restaurants served fussy, dainty platefuls, decorated with horrible rosettes of green mayonnaise and the like, that were more trouble in the eating than they were ever worth. So when the bistros began to arrive, with their check tablecloths and melting candles pushed into the necks of green wine bottles, we were glad of them. A decade later they had become a joke, but then they were our salvation.

'Have you ever been to Serena's house in Yorkshire?' Damian asked. The other two looked puzzled, as well they might, since there had been no mention of Yorkshire or of the Claremont dynasty at any part of the conversation.

This should have set off a thousand flashing bells, but, like the fool I was, I made nothing of it. I simply answered the question. 'Once, but just for a charity thing a couple of years ago.'

'What's it like?'

I thought for a moment. I hadn't retained any very precise image. 'A Georgian pile. Very grand. But pretty.'

'And big?'

'Oh, yes, big. Not Blenheim. But big.'

'I suppose you've always known each other?' Again, as I would come to recognise, this was a clue, had I the sense to read it. From long before that evening Damian had a fiercely romantic view of the golden group from which he felt excluded, but which he was determined to enter. Although, looking back, even in 1968 it was a slightly odd ambition, especially for someone like Damian Baxter. Not that there weren't plenty who shared it (and plenty who still do), but Damian was a modern creature, motivated, ambitious, strong— and if I say it of him it must be true. He was always going to find a place in the new society that was coming. Why did he want to bother with the fading glories of the blue bloods, those sad walking history books, when, for so many of those families, as with the potato, the best was already in the ground? Personally, I think he must have been cut dead at some gathering in youth, in front of a girl he fancied perhaps, snubbed, ignored and insulted by a drunken toff, until he fell into the cliché'd but very real goal of: *'I'll show you! Just you wait!'* It has, after all, been the spur of many great careers since the Conquest. But if this was the case, I never knew the incident that triggered it. Only that by the time we met, he had developed a personal mythology about the British aristocracy. He saw all its members as bonded together from birth, a tiny, tight club, hostile to newcomers, loyal to the point of reckless dishonesty when defending their own. There was some truth in this, of course, a good deal of truth in terms of attitude, but we were no longer living under a Whig oligarchy of a few thousand families. By the 1960s the catchment area, certainly for what remained of London Society, was far wider than he seemed aware of and the variety of types within it was much greater. Anyway, people are people, whoever they may be, and no world is as neat as he would have it.

'No. I haven't known her long at all, not properly. I might have met her a few times over the years, at this and that, but we only really talked for the first time at a tea party in Eaton Square a month or two ago.'

He seemed amused. 'A tea party?' It did sound rather quaint.

The tea party had, in fact, been given by a girl called Miranda Houghton at her parents' flat on the north side of Eaton Square. Miranda was the god-daughter of my aunt or of some friend of my mother's, I forget which. Like Serena, I'd seen her from time to time but without either of us making much of an impact; still, it qualified me for her guest list when the whole business began. These parties were one of the early rituals of the Season, even if, when recording it, one feels like an obscure archivist preserving for posterity the lost traditions of the Inuits. The girls would be encouraged to invite other would-be debutantes to tea, usually at their parents' London homes, thereby forging useful friendships and associations for the larks to come. Their mothers would obtain lists of who else was doing the whole thing from the unofficial but widely recognised leader, Peter Townend, who would supply them free of charge and gladly, to those he considered worthy, in his gallant but doomed attempt to stave off the modern world for as long as might conceivably be possible. Later these same mothers would require of him other lists of supposedly eligible men and he would produce these too, although they were required more for drinks parties and dances than the teas, where men were few and normally, as in the case of me and Miranda, actually knew the hostess. Very little, if any, tea was provided or drunk at these gatherings and in my experience the atmosphere was always slightly strange, as each new arrival hesitantly picked their way across the floor. But all the same we went to them, me included. So I suppose we were committed to the coming experience from comparatively early on, whatever we might afterwards pretend.

I was sitting in the corner, talking about hunting to a rather dull girl with freckles, when Serena Gresham came in and I could tell at once, from the faintest *frisson* that went through the assembled company, that she had already earned a reputation as a star. This was all the better managed as no one could have been less presumptuous or more softly spoken than she. Happily for me, I was near the last remaining empty chair. I waved to her and, after taking a second to remember who I was, she crossed the room and joined me. It is interesting to me now that Serena should have conformed to all this. Twenty years later, when the Season had become the preserve of exhibitionists and the daughters of *parvenu* mothers on the make, she would not have dreamed of it. I suppose it is a tribute to the fact that even someone as seemingly untrammelled as Serena would still, in those dead days, do as she was told.

'How do you know Miranda?' I asked.

'I don't, really,' was her answer. 'We met when we were both staying with some cousins of mine in Rutland.' One of Serena's gifts was always to answer every question quickly and easily, without a trace of mystery, but without imparting any information.

47

I nodded. 'So, will you be doing the whole deb thing?'

I do not wish to exaggerate my own importance, but I'm not convinced that before this she had fully faced the extent of the undertaking. She thought for a moment, frowning. 'I don't know.' She seemed to be looking into some invisible crystal ball, hovering in mid-air. 'We'll have to see,' she added and, in doing so, gave me a sense of her half-membership of the human race that was at the heart of her charm, a kind of emotional platform ticket that would allow her to withdraw at any moment from the experience on hand. I was entranced by her.

I outlined a little of this to Damian as we ate. He was fascinated by every detail, like an anthropologist who has long proclaimed a theory as an article of faith, but only recently begun to discover any real evidence of its truth. I suspect that Serena was the first completely genuine aristocrat he had ever met and, perhaps to his relief, he found her to be entirely undisappointing. She was in truth exactly what people reading historical novels, bought from a railway bookshop before a long and boring journey, imagine aristocratic heroines to be, both in her serene beauty and in her cool, almost cold, detachment. Despite what they themselves might like to think, there are few aristocrats who conform very satisfactorily to the imagined prototype and it was Damian's good fortune, or bad, that he should have begun his social career with one who did so perfectly. It was clear that for him there was something wonderfully satisfactory in the encounter. Of course, had he been less fortunate in his introduction to that world he might have been luckier in the way things turned out.

'So how do you get on to the list for these tea parties?' he asked.

The thing was, I liked him. It feels odd to write those words and there have been times when I have quite forgotten it, but I did. He was fun and entertaining and good-looking, always a recommendation for anyone where I'm concerned, and he had that quality, now dignified with the New Age term of Positive Energy, but which then simply indicated someone who would never wear you out. Years later, a friend would describe her world to me as being peopled entirely by radiators and drains. If so, then Damian was King Radiator. He warmed the company he was in. He could make people want to help him, which alchemy he practised, most successfully, on me.

As it happened, in this instance I could not deliver what Damian was asking for, as he had really missed the tea parties. These little informal gatherings were very much a preliminary weeding process, when the girls would seek out their playmates for the coming year within the overall group, and by the time of our Cambridge dinner the gangs were formed and the cocktail parties had already begun, although, as I told him, the first I was due to attend was not in fact a deb party as such, but one of a series given by Peter Townend, the Season's Master of the Ceremonies, at his London flat. It may seem strange to a student of these rites to learn that for the last twenty or thirty years of their existence they were entirely managed by an unknown northerner of no birth and modest means, but the fact remains that they were.

49

Naturally, Damian had heard the name and almost immediately, with his hound-like scent for quarry, he asked if he might tag along, and I agreed. This was distinctly risky on my part as Townend was jealous of his powers and privileges, and to turn up casually with a hanger-on, was to risk devaluing the invitation, which he would certainly not take kindly. Nevertheless, I did it and so, a week or two later, when I parked my battered green mini without difficulty in Chelsea Manor Street, Damian Baxter was sitting beside me in the passenger seat.

I say Peter was jealous of his role and so he was, but he was entitled to be. From a modest background, with which he was perfectly content, and after a career in journalism and editing where his speciality was genealogy, he had one day discovered his personal vocation would be to keep the Season alive, when Her Majesty's decision to end Presentation in 1958 had seemed to condemn the whole institution to immediate execution. We know now that it was instead destined to die a lingering death, and maybe simple decapitation might have been preferable, but nobody knows the future and at that time it seemed that Peter, single-handedly, had won it an indefinite reprieve. The Monarch would play no further part in it, of course, which knocked the point and the stuffing out of it for many, but it would still have a purpose in bringing together the offspring of like-minded parents, and this was the responsibility he took on. He had no hope of reward. He did it solely for the honour of the thing, which in my book makes it praiseworthy, whatever one's opinion of the end product. Year by year he would comb the stud books, Peerage and Gentry, writing to the mothers of daughters, interviewing their sons, all to buy another few months for the whole business. Can this really have been only forty years ago? you may ask in amazement. The answer's yes.

Peter's own gatherings were not to select or encourage the girls. That had all been done some time before. No, they were basically to audition those young men who had come to his attention as possible escorts and dancing partners for the parties to come. Having been vetted, their names would either be underscored or crossed off the lists that were distributed to the anxious waiting mothers, who would assume that the cads and seducers, the alcoholics and the gamblers and those who were NSIT (not safe in taxis) would all have been excised from the names presented. They should have been, of course, but it was not entirely plain sailing, viz. the first two young men to greet us as we pushed into the narrow hall of the squashed and ill-furnished flat, at the top of a block built in the worst traditions of the late 1950s. These were the younger sons of the Duke of Trent, Lord Richard and Lord George Tremayne, who were both already drunk. A stranger might have thought that since neither was attractive or funny in the least, Peter would not deem them ideally suited to the year ahead. But this would be to ignore human nature and it was not really his fault that there were those he could not exclude. Certainly, the Tremayne brothers would enjoy a kind of popularity, somehow acquiring the reputation for being 'live wires,' which they were not. The fact is their father was a duke and, even if he could not have held down the job of a parking

51

attendant in the real world, that was enough to guarantee their invitations.

We moved on into the crowded, main room, I hesitate to call it the drawing room, since it had many functions, but that was where we found Peter, his characteristic cowlick of hair falling over his crumpled, pug-like face. He pointed at Damian. 'Who he?' he said in a loud and overtly hostile voice.

'May I introduce Damian Baxter?' I said.

'I never invited him,' said Peter, quite unrelenting. 'What's he doing here?' Peter had, as I have said, made a decision not to pass himself off as a product of the system he so admired and in a moment like this I understood why. Since he had not posited himself as an elegant gentleman, he did not feel any need to be polite if it did not suit him. In short, he never disguised his feelings, and over the years I came both to like and to admire him for it. Of course, his words may read as if his anger was directed towards the unwelcome guest, when it was instead entirely meant for me. I was the one who had broken the rules. In the face of this attack I'm afraid I foundered. It seems odd, certainly to the man I am today, but I know I was suddenly anxious at the thought of all those treats, which I had planned for and which were in his gift, slipping away. It might have been less troublesome if they had.

'Don't blame him,' said Damian, seeing the problem and moving quickly in beside us. 'Blame me. I very much wanted to meet you, Mr Townend, and when I heard he was coming here I forced him to bring me. It's entirely my fault.'

Peter stared at him. 'That's my cue to say you're

welcome, I suppose.'

His tone could not have been less hospitable but Damian, as ever, was unfazed. 'It's your cue to ask me to leave if you wish. And of course I will.' He paused, a trace of anxiety playing across his even features.

'Very smooth,' said Peter in his curious, ambiguous, almost petulant way. He nodded towards a bewildered Spaniard holding a tray. 'You can have a drink if you like.' I do not at all believe he was won over by Damian's charm, then or later. I would say he simply recognised a fellow player who might be possessed of great skill and was reluctant to make an enemy of him on their first encounter. As Damian moved away, Peter turned back to me. 'Who is he? And where did he pick you up?' This in itself was curiously phrased.

'Cambridge. I met him at a party in my college. As to who he is,' I hesitated. 'I don't know much about him, really.'

'Nor will you.'

I felt rather defensive. 'He's very nice.' I wasn't quite sure how or why I'd been cast as protector, but apparently I had. 'And I thought you might like him, too.'

Peter followed Damian with his eyes, as he took a drink and started to chat up a wretched overweight girl with a lantern jaw, who was hovering nervously on the edge of the proceedings. 'He's an operator,' he said and turned to greet some new arrivals.

If he was an operator, the operation bore fruit almost immediately. This would not have surprised me much further on in our acquaintance, as by then I would have known that Damian would

53

never be so idle as to waste an opportunity. He was always a worker. His worst enemy would concede that. In fact, he just did. Damian had, after all, made it into Peter's sanctum without any guarantee of a return engagement. There was no time to be lost.

The awkward lantern-jawed girl, whom I now recognised gazing up at Damian as he showered her with charm, went by the name of Georgina Waddilove. She was the daughter of a city banker and an American heiress. Quite how Damian had selected her for his opening salvo I am not entirely sure. Perhaps it was just a warrior's sense of where the wall might most easily be breached and which girl was the most vulnerable to attack. Georgina was a melancholy character. To anyone who was interested, and there were not many, this could be traced to her mother who, with an imprecise knowledge of England and after a courtship conducted entirely during her husband's posting in New York after the war, had been under the illusion at the time of her wedding that she was marrying into a much higher caste than was in fact the case. When they did return to England, in late 1950, with two little boys and a baby daughter, she had arrived in her new country with confident expectations of stalking at Balmoral and foursome suppers at Chatsworth and Stratfieldsaye. What she discovered, however, was that her husband's friends and family came, almost exclusively, from the same prosperous, professional money-people that she had played tennis with in the Hamptons since her girlhood. Her husband, Norman (and perhaps the name should have given her a clue), had not consciously meant to deceive her but, like many Englishmen of his type, particularly when abroad, he had fallen into the habit of suggesting that he came from a smarter background than he did and, far away in New York, this was only too easy. After spending nine years there he came almost to believe his own fiction. He would talk so freely of Princess Margaret or the Westminsters or Lady Pamela Berry, that he would probably have been as surprised as his listeners to discover that everything he knew of these people he had gleaned from the pages of the *Daily Express.*

The net result of this disappointment was not, however, divorce. Anne Waddilove had her children to think about and divorce in the 1950s still exacted a high social price. Norman had made quite a lot of money, so instead she resolved to use it to correct for her offspring the deficiencies and disappointments of her own existence. For the boys this meant good schools, shooting and proper universities, but from early on she was determined to launch her daughter with a dizzying season that would result in a dazzling marriage. Grandchildren would then follow, who would do her Royal stalking by proxy. So did Mrs Waddilove plan the future of the wretched Georgina, condemned to live her mother's life and not her own from more or less the moment the child could walk. Which may explain the parent's blindness to a simple truth, so clear to the rest of the world, that Georgina was hopelessly unsuited to the role expected of her. Good-looking and poised as Anne Waddilove was, she had not anticipated that nature would play a joke on her in giving her a daughter who was as plain as a pikestaff, fat as a barrel and *gauche* to boot. To make matters worse,

Georgina's shy nervousness invariably gave a (false) first impression of stupidity, nor was she at all, by choice, gregarious. Since she wasn't in line for a major inheritance—the presence of two boys in a family generally knocks that on the head—the match Mrs Waddilove had dreamed of seemed what can only be described as highly unlikely by the time Georgina had completed her first few weeks as a debutante.

I have to say that when I got to know her I liked Georgina Waddilove and, while I cannot pretend to a romantic interest in her at any point, I was always happy to sit next to her at dinner. She was knowledgeable about films, one of my interests, so we had plenty to talk about. But there was no escaping the fact that she did not appear destined for success in the harsh and competitive arena her mother had chosen. There was something almost grotesque in watching her lumpen frame wandering, sad and alone, through ballroom after ballroom, decked out in the girlish fashions of the day, her hair sewn with flowers, her frock made of lace, when all the time she resembled nothing so much as a talking chimp in an advertisement for PG Tips tea. I'm sorry to say that she became, if anything, a comic figure among our crowd and, older as I am now and less impervious to others' suffering, I very much regret this. It must have caused her great pain, which she concealed, and the concealment can only have made it sharper.

Was it an instinct for this that took Damian straight to her side, when shining beauties of high rank stood about Peter's drawing room, laughing and chatting and sipping their drinks? Was it as a fox might scent a wounded bird that Damian surveyed the crowd, locating the ugliest, most awkward girl there, and made for her like a missile? If so, his tactic was completely successful and a few days later he dropped by my rooms to show that the morning's post had brought his first stiffy, a thick white card bearing the proud, engraved name of 'Mrs Norman Waddilove, At Home,' who was inviting him to attend a cocktail party 'for Georgina,' on the seventh of June, by the Dodgem Track at Battersea Fun Fair. 'How can she be "at home" by the Dodgems?' he said.

Battersea Park has altered its position in London in the decades since the war. It has not moved physically, of course, but it is an entirely different place today from the scene of so many childhood memories of half a century ago. Built by the Victorians as a pleasure ground for the local *bourgeoisie*, with sculpted rocks and fountains and gentle paths by swan-stocked lakes, the park had cheerfully run to seed by the 1950s and had become instead important to a whole generation of children as the site of London's only permanent fun fair. Erected in 1951, as part of that icon of lost innocence, the Festival of Britain, the fair flourished into the Sixties, when newer forms of entertainment began to steal its thunder. A tragic accident on the Big Dipper in 1972 hastened the inevitable and two years later came closure. The dear, old fun fair, grey and grubby and downright dangerous as it had become, was swept away without a trace, like the hanging gardens of Nineveh.

It is more beautiful today, its ponds and waterfalls and glades restored, than when I first walked there, clutching the hand of an aunt or a nanny and begging to be allowed one more ride before we went home, but it is not more beautiful to me. Nor am I alone in this rose-tinted memory and, in fact, nostalgia was already beginning to envelop the place by 1968 as we, the children who had felt sick from too much candy floss when the fair was at its height, were now in our late teens and early twenties, and for this reason it was a clever choice by Mrs Waddilove as a venue for her party. Georgina, as I have said, was not popular and she might easily have had to endure the humiliation of a sparsely attended gathering had it been held in one of the Park Lane hotels or in the coffee room of her father's club, when half the guest list might easily have chucked. The casualness of the young, as they abandon their social commitments for something more recent and more enticing, was horrible to adults then. These days parents are inclined to shrug and roll their eyes at their children's unreliability, but not to take it very seriously. I don't suggest the phenomenon is new, chucking, dodging, gatecrashing and the rest, but in 1968 nobody saw the funny side. However, on this occasion Battersea Fun Fair appealed and everyone turned up.

I was quite late arriving, as it happens, so the hubbub of chatter was what guided me through the fair and past the stalls, until I came to a temporary white-painted wicket fence, where two officials guarded the entrance and a large card on a blackboard stand announced that the Dodgems were 'closed for a private party.' This ensured some glares from would-be customers, which Georgina's guests affected to ignore, but these

58

disgruntled few did not spoil things. Whatever they may pretend, the privileged classes, then and now, enjoy a bit of envy.

Some of the girls were already in the cars, shrieking and laughing and spilling their wine, as their boyfriends-for-the-night posed and preened, banging and whacking into the cars of others. Nowadays there would be signs requesting that glasses should not be taken on to the track, or there would only have been plastic cups anyway, but I do not recall anyone concerning themselves with such things as slippery surfaces or broken glass. There must have been plenty of both. A marquee with an open side had been erected to accommodate the other guests who were already well away. I looked round for Georgina, hoping to find her at the centre of a grateful crowd, but as usual she was standing alone and silent near the champagne table, so I saw the chance to fetch a drink and simultaneously greet my hostess, killing two birds with one stone.

'Hello,' I said. 'This all seems to be satisfactorily rowdy.'

She smiled wanly. 'Are you going to have a go?'

'Oh, I think so.' I smiled gamely. 'What about you?' But she did not seem to hear my question, her eyes fixed on the track itself, and I could now make out a car with the distinctive figure of Damian crouched over the controls. His co-pilot appeared, from a distance anyway, to be rather an unlikely one. Her face was almost concealed by a curtain of curls, but I could see how calm she was, and unattached. She did not shout like the others, but merely sat there, like some stately princess forced to endure the indignity of a peasant's ferry in order to get to the other side.

Georgina turned. 'What's your dinner in aid of?'

I was nonplussed. 'What dinner?'

'Tonight. Damian said he couldn't come to the Ritz with us because he'd pledged himself to you.'

I realised at once the significance of this, that poor Georgina had already fulfilled her function in Damian's life by getting him started and could now be dispensed with. The doomed girl had yielded to his flattery and friendly charm, and opened the door for him into this world, but now, having gained entry, he had no compunction in leaving her to her own devices. So Georgina's dream of having this new and glamorous companion sitting next to her at the dull, staid dinner that would have been arranged by her mother for a favoured few was to be shattered. As to the fib that had got him out of it, I blush to say I covered for him. In my defence, this was not really by choice but entirely in obedience to natural impulse. When any woman talks of a man's excuse to another man, he is somehow bound to support the fiction as part of a kind of race loyalty. 'Robert says you're having lunch with him next week' forces any male to respond with something along the lines of 'I'm looking forward to having a good catch-up,' even if it's the first he's heard of the plan. Often, afterwards, a man may chastise the friend or acquaintance who has brought this about. 'How dare you put me on a spot like that?' Even so, it is against male nature to speak the truth. The alternative would be to say, 'I have never heard of this lunch. Robert must have a mistress.' But no man can utter these words, even when he is entirely on the side of the woman being lied to. I smiled at Georgina. 'Well, it's just a dinner for a few of us. It's not at all crucial, if you really need him.'

She shook her head. 'No, no. I don't want to mess things up. Daddy was annoyed when I asked him, anyway. That's why I didn't invite you,' she added lamely. 'He thinks we're too many as it is.' Too many duds, I thought, and not enough possibilities. But then, Damian would not qualify in this group. Mrs Waddilove was not in the market for an adventurer.

'Who's coming?'

'I wish you were,' she muttered obediently. 'But as I say, it's not a big party.' I nodded. Having paid lip service to form, she listed half a dozen names. 'Princess Dagmar. And the Tremayne brothers, I think, but there may be a problem.' I bet there will be, I thought. 'Andrew Summersby and his sister.' She ticked off these people in her head, although the list carried her mother's fingerprints, not her own. 'That's about it.'

I glanced over to where the lumpen, red-faced Viscount Summersby stood glumly nursing his drink. He had apparently abandoned any efforts at conversation with his neighbours. Their state was no doubt the more blessed. Meanwhile, in front of him, his sister, Annabella, was shrieking and shouting as she tore round the track, a pale and lean companion trembling beside her. Her tight cocktail frock, raided from her mother's post-war wardrobe, seemed to be bursting at the seams as she wrenched the wheel this way and that. Annabella Warren was not a beauty any more than her brother but, of the two and if forced to choose,

61

I preferred her. Neither was an enticing prospect for an evening's entertainment, but at least she had a bit of go. Georgina, following my gaze, seemed silently to agree. 'Well, good luck with it,' I said.

The dodgem cars had stopped and the drivers and passengers were being forced from their vehicles by the waiting crowd of guests surrounding the track, anxious for their turn. They had a distinctive look, those girls of long ago, racing across the metal, bolted floor to squeeze into the dirty and dented cars awaiting them, part 1950s Dior, part 1960s Carnaby Street, acknowledging the modern world but not yet quite capitulating to it. In the forty years that followed, that decade has been hijacked by the voice of the Liberal Tyranny. Theirs is the Woodstock version of the period—'if you can remember the Sixties, you weren't really there,' run the smug and self-regarding phrases—and they have no conscience in holding up the values of the pop revolution as the whole truth, but they are either deceiving or deceived. What was genuinely unusual about the era for those of us who were around at the time was not a bunch of guitar players smoking dope and wearing embarrassing hats with feathers, and leather singlets lined with sheepskin. What marked it apart from the other periods I have lived through was that, like Janus, it faced both ways.

One part of the culture was indeed about pop and drugs and happenings, and Marianne Faithfull and Mars Bars and free love, but the other, if anything far larger, section of the community was still looking back to the 1950s, back towards a traditional England, where behaviour was laid down according to the practice of, if not many centuries, at least the century immediately before, where everything from clothes to sexual morality was rigidly determined and, if we did not always obey the rules, we knew what they were. It was, after all, less than ten years previously that this code had reigned supreme. The girls who wouldn't kiss on a first date, the boys who were not dressed without a tie, those mothers who only left the house in hat and gloves, those fathers wearing bowlers on their way to the city. These were all as much a part of the sixties as the side of it so constantly revived by television retrospectives. The difference being that they were customs on the way out, while the new, deconstructed culture was on the way in. It would, of course, prove to be the winner and as with anything it is the winner who writes history.

A great fashion then was for adding false hair, in ringlets and falls, to dramatise a hairstyle. They were intended to look real but only with the reality of a costume in a play, that could be discarded the following day with no loss of face. So a girl might appear on Monday night with curls to her shoulders and at Tuesday lunch with an Eton crop. The idea was really to use hair like a series of hats. In this one disguise, perhaps alone among their habits and unlike the wig wearers of today, there was no intention to deceive. The vogue was further enhanced by the practice of depositing these 'pieces' at the hairdresser's a day or two in advance, where they would be rollered and treated and even sewn with flowers or beads, before the whole elaborate coiffure would be pinned to the owner's head in the afternoon before a party. The style reached its apogee when the dances began, but even in the early stages, during the first cocktail parties, it seemed a parable of the unreality we were all participating in, as the debs would alter their appearance almost completely, twice or three times a week. Partygoers would see a stranger approach, only to discover, as they drew near, the face of an old friend peeping out. So it was, on this particular evening, that I suddenly recognised the sedate highness in transit, riding in the seat next to Damian, was none other than Serena Gresham, who climbed out of the car, as cool as a cucumber, and walked over to where I was standing. 'Hello,' she said.

'Hello. How are you getting on?'

'I'm shaken to pieces. I feel like a cocktail ready to be poured.'

'I was going to ask if you wanted another go, with me.'

'Not likely,' said Serena. 'What I do want is another drink.' She looked around and had secured a new glass of champagne before the offer to help her was even out of my mouth.

Leaving her surrounded by would-be gallants, I wandered over to the Dodgem track, where the cars were already fully occupied. Then I heard my name called and I looked round to see Lucy Dalton waving at me. I walked over. 'What is it?' I said.

'For Christ's sake get in.' Lucy patted the battered, leather seat beside her. 'Philip Rawnsley-Price is coming this way and my bottom will be quite bruised enough without that.' Behind me I could hear the man shouting for us to clear the track. 'Get in!' she hissed. So I did. It wasn't a complete reprieve. Before we could set off, Philip, ignoring the shouts of the operator, had strolled across between the now moving cars—in those days, you understand, 'Health and safety,' as a phrase, had yet to be invented.

'If you're avoiding me, you can give up now,' he said to Lucy with a leer that I assume was supposed to be sexy. 'We're destined to be together.' Before she could think of a suitable wisecrack, there was a harsh and sudden jolt. We had been hit broadside by one of the Tremayne brothers with his cackling companion beside him and, with dislocated backs, we were flung into the tangled maelstrom. Philip laughed and moved lazily back to the edge.

Lucy Dalton will figure at some length in these pages and deserves an introduction, although she was not essentially, I think, a complicated character. Like Serena, she was the recipient, unearned, of most of this world's blessings but at a (slightly) more modest level, which had divorced her a little less from the ordinary human experience. It is always hard for outsiders to perceive the differences in status and possession within an envied, privileged group, but these distinctions exist, whichever ivory tower one is dealing with. Champion footballers, all richer than Midas, know well who, within their crowd, merits envy and who should be pitied. Film stars can easily distinguish among themselves the careers that are going nowhere and the ones that have years more to run. Of course, to most of the public the very suggestion that this millionaire is less to be envied than that one seems pretentious and isolationist, but the gradations are meaningful to the members of these clubs and, if one is to attempt to understand what makes any world tick, they have a part to play in that. So it was with us. The Season in the 1960s, even if the concept was already embattled, still involved a narrower group than it would do today, if anyone were foolish enough to attempt its revival. Looking back, we were a halfway house between the genuinely exclusive group of the pre-war years and the anything-goes world of the 1980s and after. There were certainly girls included who would not have made the grade in the days of Presentation, but they were still made to feel it and the inner crowd was mostly drawn from the more traditional recruiting grounds. Within this set, then, the different levels of good fortune were clear to see and to appreciate.

Lucy Dalton was the younger daughter of a baronet, Sir Marmaduke Dalton, whose ancestor had received his title in the early nineteenth century, as a reward for pretty routine service to the Crown. The family was still possessed of a substantial estate in Suffolk but the house itself was let in the 1930s and had been a girls' prep school since the war. I would say the Daltons themselves were fairly happy in the dower house, from which, above the trees, they could just about glimpse the scene of their former splendour, albeit surrounded by prefabricated classrooms and pitches for the playing of lacrosse. In other words, it wasn't ideal.

As a citizen of the modern world, I am now, in late middle age, fully aware that Lucy's upbringing was privileged to an extreme degree. But most humans only compare themselves with people in similar circumstances to their own and I would ask the reader's tolerance when I say that, given the times, to our gang her origins did not seem so remarkable. Her family, with its minor title, in their pleasant dower house, lived much as we all lived, in our rectories and manors and farmhouses, and the important distinction, or so it seemed to us, was between those who lived normally and those who lived as our people had lived before the war. These survivors were our battle pennants, our emblems of a better day, our acknowledged social leaders. With their footmen and their stately drawing rooms, they seemed in magic contrast to our own lives, with our working fathers and our mothers who had learned to cook . . . a bit. *We* were the normal ones, *they* were the rich ones, and it was many years before I questioned this. In my defence, it's a rare individual who grasps that their own way of life is extravagant or sybaritic. It is always those much richer than oneself who deserve these sobriquets, and I would say that Lucy never thought of herself as much more than reasonably lucky.

At any rate, to me she was a cheerful soul, pretty but not beautiful, funny but not fascinating. We'd met when we found ourselves in the same party for a charity ball the year before and so, when the Season started and we discovered we were both to be part of it, we naturally gravitated towards each other as one is drawn to any friendly, familiar face in a new and faintly challenging environment. To be honest, I believe I might have been rather keen on her if I had been more careful at the start, but as it was I missed my chance if there was one, by allowing us to become friends—

almost invariably the antidote to any real thoughts of romance.

'Who is this fellow you've wished on us all?' she said, steering wildly to avoid another merry prang from Lord Richard.

'I don't know that I've wished him on anybody.'

'Oh, but you have. I saw four girls writing down his address before he'd been here twenty minutes. I assume he's not sponsored by Mr Townend?'

'Hardly. I took him along to one of Peter's things last week and I thought for a moment we were going to be thrown out.'

'Why did you "take him along?" Why have you become his promoter?'

'I don't think I knew that I had.'

She looked at me with a rather pitying smile.

Probably it was a half-subconscious desire to bury my lie to Georgina by making it true that prompted me to organise a group for dinner as the party began to thin out, and later that evening about eight of us were climbing down the treacherous basement stairs of Haddy's, then a popular spot on a corner of the Old Brompton Road, where one could dine after a fashion as well as dance the night away, and all for about thirty shillings a head. We often used to spend whole evenings there, eating, talking, dancing, although it is hard to imagine what the modern equivalent of this sort of place might be, since to manage all three in a single location seems impossible now, given the ferocious, really savage, volume that music is played at today anywhere one might be expected to dance. I suppose it must have begun to get louder in the discotheques after I had ceased to go to them, but I was not aware of the new fashion until perfectly normal people in their forties and fifties adopted it and started to give parties that must rank among the worst in history. Often I hear the notion of the nightclub, where you sat and chatted while the music played, spoken of as belonging to the generation before mine, men and women in evening clothes sitting around the Mirabelle in the 1930s and '40s, dancing to Snake Hips Johnson and his orchestra while they sipped White Ladies, but like so many truisms this is not true. The opportunity to eat, talk and dance was available to us and I enjoyed it.

Haddy's did not really qualify as a nightclub. It was more for people who couldn't afford to go to proper nightclubs. These places, Haddy's, Angelique's, the Garrison, forgotten names now but full every night then, provided a simple service, but as with all successful innovations they filled a need. The dinner would belong to the recently arrived style of *paysanne* cooking, but this predictable repast would be combined with the comparatively new invention of dancing, publicly, not to a band but to records, presided over by some sort of disc jockey, a job description then only in its infancy. The wine was rarely more than plonk, certainly when we young ones were paying, but the bonus was that the owners did not expect to sell the table much more than once throughout the evening. Having eaten, we sat drinking and banging on about what preoccupied our adolescent troubled minds into the small hours, night after night, without, as far as I remember, the smallest problem with the management. They cannot really have been businessmen, I'm afraid. No wonder their establishments did not stand the test of time.

69

That particular evening, for some strange reason, Serena Gresham had joined us among the rest, tagging along when I told her where we were going. I was surprised because usually she would listen politely to the plan, make a little *moue* of regret with her mouth and wish aloud she could have come. But this time she thought for a moment and said 'all right. Why not?' It may not seem a very enthusiastic response, but at the sound of her words songbirds rose in flight in my heart. Lucy was there, trying and failing to escape Philip, her nemesis, who had proposed himself after her car had left. Damian came, of course, and a new girl, whom I had not met before that evening, a ravishing, Hollywood-style blonde with little to say for herself, Joanna Langley. I say I did not know her, but I had heard of her as being very rich, one of the richest girls of the year, if part of the new post-Presentation crop. Her father had founded a sales catalogue for casual clothing or something similar, and while the money ensured that no one was rude to her face, things were not quite so pleasant behind her back. Personally, I liked her from the start. She was sitting on my left.

'Are you enjoying it?' she asked as I sloshed some wine into her glass.

I wasn't sure if she meant the dinner or the Season, but I assumed the latter. 'I think so. I haven't done much yet, but it seems a nice crowd.'

'Are you?' This came from Damian, further down the table. I could see he was already training his headlamp glare on to Joanna. Like me, he clearly knew who she was.

She was a little startled, but she nodded. 'So far. What about you?'

70

He laughed. 'Oh, I'm not part of it. Ask him.' He indicated me with a jocular flick of his chin.

'You're here, aren't you?' I replied rather crisply. 'What other qualification do you think we have?' Which was dishonest, but I didn't worry much, as I knew nothing would dampen his ardour.

'Don't let him mislead you.' Damian had brought his gaze back to Joanna. 'I'm a perfectly ordinary boy from a perfectly ordinary home. I thought it would be fun to see it for myself, but I'm not part of this world at all.' It was carefully measured, like everything he said, and I can understand now what it was intended to achieve. It meant that every girl at that table would at once feel protective of him and none of them, or their friends, would ever be allowed to accuse him of pretending to be something he was not. His apparent modesty would give him permission to take and take, but never to feel any responsibility to a world he had declared he did not belong to and to which he owed nothing. Above all, it washed over their defences. From then on they were not afraid of being used by such a man. How could they be when he said himself he had no ambition? We had not even ordered before he was writing down his address for Joanna and two of the other girls present.

I note I have stated that Damian was 'of course' with us. Why was it so understood that he would be? At this early stage of his London career? Perhaps because I had begun to reckon his gifts. I looked down the table to where he sat, with Serena on one side and Lucy on the other, making them both listen and laugh but never overplaying his hand with either, and I understood then that he was one of those rare beings who can fit seamlessly into a new group until, before much time has passed, they seem to be an integral, a founder, member of it. He joked and ribbed, but frowned a little, too. He took them seriously and nodded with concern, like someone who knew them well, but not too well. In all the time I knew him, he never made the classic *parvenu* mistake of lapsing into over-familiarity. Not long ago I was talking to a man before a shoot. We had got on well at dinner the night before and he, supposing, I imagine, that we were now friends, began to poke me jocularly in the stomach as he joshed me about my weight. He smiled as he said it and looked into my eyes, but what he saw there cannot have encouraged him as I had decided, on that instant, I would never seek his company again. Damian made no such error. His approach was relaxed and easy but never egregious or impertinent. In short, it was carefully thought out and well delivered, and that evening gave me one of my first opportunities to witness the skill with which he would land his quarry.

The dinner was finished, the girls' uneaten stew had been carried away, the lights had been lowered a few degrees and couples around the room were beginning to take to the floor. Nobody from our group had ventured forth yet, but we were nearly there and, during a slight lull in the conversation, I heard Damian turn to Serena. 'Do you want to dance?' he suggested, almost in the tone of a shared joke, a funny secret only fully understood by the two of them. It was beautifully done. They were playing some record we all liked,

72

was it *Flowers in the Rain?* I forget now. At any rate, after a fractional pause she nodded and they stood. But next came the wonder. As they passed by my end of the table I heard him remark quite casually: 'I feel such a fool. I know you're called Serena and I remember where we first met, but I never got your surname. If I leave it much longer it'll be too late to ask.' Like a conman or a courtier he waited, just for a second, to see if his ploy would work. Did he breathe more easily when she gave no indication that she knew what he was up to?

Instead, she smiled. 'Gresham,' she whispered gently and they stepped on to the floor. I watched this in amazement and is it any wonder? Not only did Damian know her name long before that night, and where her family lived, and almost certainly the acreage. I would guess he could have listed the dates of every Earl of Claremont since the title was created and probably the maiden names of every Countess. I caught his eye across the room. He knew I had heard the exchange and I knew he knew. But he made no acknowledgement of the fact that I could have shown him up and spoiled his game. This is the kind of high-risk strategy in a career of social mountaineering that must surely almost merit admiration.

Lucy was watching me watching him, a small smile on her lips. 'What's so funny?' I said.

'I have a feeling that until tonight you thought you were Damian's patron, when we must both suspect you will be lucky to find yourself his chronicler by the time the Season is done.' She watched the couple on the floor and grew more serious. 'If you want to stake your claim in that

73

department, I shouldn't leave it too long.'

I shook my head. 'He's not her type. Nor am I, no doubt. But he isn't.'

'You say that because you idolise her and consider him inferior in every way. But these are the views of a lover. She won't think that herself.'

Now I studied them. The music had become slow and smoochy, and they were swaying from side to side in that stepless dance we all did then. I shook my head again. 'You're wrong. He has nothing that she wants.'

'On the contrary, he has exactly what she wants. She won't be looking for birth or money. She's always had plenty of both. I doubt she's very susceptible to looks. But Damian . . .' as she spoke, her eyes focused again on the dark head, taller than most of the men dancing near him. 'He's got the one quality she lacks. That we all lack, if it comes to that.'

'Which is?'

'He belongs to the present century. He will understand the rules of the Game as it will be played in the future, not as it used to be played in the days before the war. That could be very reassuring.' At this precise moment Philip leant over her with an optimistic offer but Lucy turned him down, nodding at me. 'He's already asked me and I've said yes.' She got to her feet and I escorted her obediently to the floor.

Lucy

THREE

The list, which I found lying on the pillow when I went up to my bed, was not long. But it still included some surprises. There were five names and all of them, it seems, had slept with Damian before he had been sterilised *en vacances* under the hot Portuguese sun. They had also all given birth to a child within the dictated time span. Lucy Dalton was there, I was a little sad to see. I had hoped for better from her, since she had been one of the first to see through Damian's disguise. Joanna Langley's inclusion surprised me less. I had been aware of a romance between them at the time and they seemed to me well matched. I'd wondered then why nothing came of it. No doubt I was about to find out. I was not expecting HRH Princess Dagmar of Moravia to figure among the notches on Damian's bedpost, nor the red-faced, loud, man-eater of the day, Candida Finch, whom I wouldn't have thought his type at all. Heavens. There was no denying that he got about a bit. Terry Vitkov, on the other hand, was a routine entry on many lists of that year's conquests, including mine. An American adventuress from the Middle West, she had less money than she liked to suggest and only came to London after exhausting the social possibilities of Cincinnati. Her sexual mores, which would prefigure the next decade rather than, like most of the girls, harking back to a time before our own, ensured that she would be made welcome. At any rate by the boys.

Each name was neatly typed. Next to it was the

woman's current, married surname and, where clarification was needed, the name of the husband. After that came the name, sex and birth date of the child in question with a brief note of any other children in the family. Finally, there was a column of addresses, in some cases two or even three, with telephone numbers and e-mail contacts, although somehow I didn't imagine much of this was going to be accomplished via the Internet. A covering note at the top, 'as far as we have been able to ascertain, the details are as follows,' meant that I could not be wholly confident about the information and some of the entries were much fuller than others, but most of it looked pretty accurate to me. I no longer ran into any of them, but the little that I did know tallied with the contents of the sheet. Behind the paper, held to it with a small clip, was an envelope. This turned out to contain, as promised, a platinum credit card made out in my name.

I breakfasted alone, with what seemed like every newspaper in the known world neatly arranged at the other end of the long table. The butler asked if he might pack, or was there some reason for him to delay this? There wasn't. He bowed, thrilled with my permission to be of use, but before he left the room to carry out his task he spoke: 'Mr Baxter wonders if you might have time to look in on him before you leave for the station.' I can recognise an order when I hear one.

Damian's bedroom was in a different part of the house from the one I had occupied. A wide gallery from the top of the staircase led towards a pair of double doors, standing half open. I heard my name called as I lifted my hand to knock and found

78

myself in a light, high chamber, lined with panelling painted in a soft *gris Trianon*. Perhaps I had been expecting some dark, magician's lair but no, this was clearly the other place, along with the library, where Damian actually lived. A large Georgian mahogany four-poster stood against a tapestry-hung wall, facing a carved rococo chimneypiece, which was in turn surmounted by one of the many Romneys of the lovely Lady Hamilton. Three tall windows looked out across the gardens to what I saw now was a kind of mini-park, with a tidy and impressive display of, I am sure, rare trees. There were inlaid chairs dotted about, and a desk, and little tables piled with books and precious things, and a rather beautiful day bed, of the type that is called a *duchesse brisée*, with a folded rug at the end, waiting to make its master comfortable. The whole effect was charming and delicate and curiously feminine, the room of a finer spirit than I would have credited him with.

Damian was in the bed. I did not see him immediately as the shadow of the canopy blurred him for a moment, hunched and crunched up as he was against the pillows, surrounded by letters and another mass of newspapers. I could not help but feel it would be a black day for the local newsagents when Damian shuffled off his mortal coil. 'You found the list,' he said.

'I did.'

'Were you surprised?'

'I knew about Joanna. At least I suspected it.'

'Our main thing was over long before. But I slept with her one last time the night she got back from Lisbon. She came round to my flat. I suppose

79

she wanted to see if I was all right.'

'I'm not surprised.'

'We went on from there.'

'But hadn't you already got the mumps?'

'I didn't develop a sore throat until a few days afterwards and, anyway, apparently you store a certain amount of whatsit, which isn't affected.'

'A little too much information.'

'As you can imagine, I am by this point the world's greatest living expert.' He gave a wry chuckle. He was wonderfully unbowed by the whole thing. 'What about the rest of them?'

'Well, even I slept with Terry and I'm not exactly surprised by Candida, though I wouldn't have thought she was your type. But I didn't suspect the other two.'

'I suppose you're disappointed in your old pal, Lucy.'

'Only because I thought she disliked you as much as I did.' This made him laugh for the first time that morning. But the effort was painful and we had to wait for a second while he recovered.

'She was only attracted to people she disliked. All the others she turned into friends. Including you.' This was probably true in its way, so I didn't interrupt him. 'Do you see any of them now?'

It was strange to hear him talk so breezily, when I considered how it had all ended. 'Not really. One bumps into people. You know how it is. They all married, then?' It seemed odd, suddenly, that I didn't know.

'Yes, for better or, in some cases, very much for worse. Candida's a widow. Her husband was killed in 9/11. But I'm told they were happy before that.'

Moments like this, when friends from a

different era of your life are suddenly forcefully connected to the modern world, can be quite shocking. 'I'm sorry. Was he American?'

'English. But he worked for some bank that had its New York office on one of the top floors. It was his bad luck that he was summoned to a meeting there on that day.'

'God, how awful. Any children?'

'Two with him. But he couldn't be the father of the baby I'm interested in. The boy was eight when they married.'

'I remember she was a single mother. Very courageous.'

'For a peer's niece in 1971? You bet. But she *was* courageous. She was a bit rough but she was punchy. That's why I liked her.' He paused, a slight smile pulling at the corners of his mouth. 'Were there any names missing that you expected to find?'

We stared at each other. 'Not when the list isn't complete.'

'What do you mean?'

'It's only the girls who gave birth within the time limit.'

Damian nodded. 'Of course. That's right. No, in any other sense it's not complete.' But he didn't elaborate and I so didn't want him to. 'You got the card?'

'Yes. Though I don't think I'll need it.'

'Please don't be English and silly.' He sighed. 'You have no money. I have so much that if I spent a million pounds a day for the rest of my life I wouldn't dent it. Use the card. Have some fun. Do what you like with it. Take it as your payment. Or my thanks. Or my apology, if you must. But use it.'

'I don't have "no" money,' I said. 'I just don't have as much money as you.' He did not trouble to confirm this and I did not protest further, so I must have been convinced.

'Do you have any preference as to where I should begin?' I asked.

He shook his head. 'None in the least. Start where you will.' He paused to take a breath. 'But please don't delay more than you have to.' His speech was coarser and more rasping than it had been the previous evening. Was this usual in the mornings? I wondered. Or is he getting worse? 'Of course, I don't want to hurry you,' he added. What made this poignant, even to me, was his striving to achieve a kind of light courtesy, like something out of a Rattigan comedy. 'Anyone for tennis?' he might have said in just such a tone. Or, 'Who needs a lift to London?' It was brave. I don't deny that.

'I imagine it must take some time,' I said.

'Of course. But no more time, please, than it has to take.'

'Suppose I can't find any evidence either way?'

'Eliminate the ones it cannot be. Then we'll worry about who's left.'

There was logic in this and I nodded. 'I still don't know why I'm doing it.'

'Because if you refuse, you'll feel guilty when I die.'

'Guilty for the child, maybe. Not about you.' I wouldn't describe myself as a harsh person in the normal way of things, and I do not completely understand why I was so harsh with him on that morning. The crimes I held against him were old crimes by then, forgotten, or if not forgotten then irrelevant, even to me. That said, he seemed to understand.

My words had died away in the silence between us, when he looked at me quite steadily. 'I have never had a friend in all my life I cared for more than I cared for you,' he said.

'Then why did you do it?' He misjudged me if he thought these nice, saccharine sentiments would somehow cancel out the memory of his behaviour on the worst evening of my, and I would hope anyone's, life.

'I'm not entirely sure.' He seemed to lose himself in thought for a while, concentrating his gaze on the view beyond the windows. 'I think I have suffered since I was a child from a kind of claustrophobia of the heart.' He smiled. 'The truth is I was always uncomfortable with any kind of love. Most of all when I was the recipient.'

Which is how we left it.

It may sound as if I had been obsessed with all these people, and mainly with Damian, since I had walked off the last dance floor over forty years before, but I had not. Like anyone else, I'd spent the time between dealing with the bewildering illogicality of my life and it had been many years since I had taken the time to consider the way I was, the way we all were. The world we lived in then was a different planet, with different hopes and very different expectations and, like other planets, it had simply drifted away in its own orbit. I glimpsed a few of the girls, now lined and greying matrons, from time to time, at a wedding or a charity function, and we smiled and talked of their children and why they'd left Fulham, and whether Somerset had proved a success, but we did not tear at the changes in the world around us. I had abandoned that world completely in the years immediately after Portugal and, even after it was all forgotten, I never really went back in. Now, when I thought about it, there were some characters from that time I regretted. Lucy Dalton, for example, had been a great ally of mine. Indeed, it was she who sealed my commitment to the Season. I didn't like her husband, it is true, and I suppose that's why we drifted apart, but now that seemed a feeble reason to lose a friend and I decided on the spot to begin my investigations with her. The sheet told me she had moved to Kent, not far from Tunbridge Wells, so it would not be difficult to call her and ask myself for lunch, on the pretext of being 'in the area.'

*   *   *

I say my commitment had been 'sealed' by Lucy for the simple reason that it was at her invitation I attended Queen Charlotte's Ball, then the official launch of the dances and the central ceremony of the whole business. Not to be there meant one was not quite a full player but I had made no plans to go since I had not originally aimed at full membership. In fact, the ball wasn't far off when, to my surprise, I received a card from Lady Dalton asking me to join their party. I rang her daughter before I answered. 'We were taking my cousin, Hugo Grex, but he's chucked,' said Lucy without any prevarication. 'Don't worry if you can't come, but say now so we can find someone else. Almost everyone who wants to is already going.' It was not the most flattering invitation known to man but I was quite curious and I had begun to feel that, when it came to the Season proper, if I was going to do it I might as well *do it.*

'No. I'd like to come. Thank you.'

'Write to Mummy or she'll think you're odd. Then she'll tell you where to be and when. You know it's white tie?'

'Absolutely.'

'See you then if not before.' She had rung off.

Perhaps because I had not originally intended to be at the ball it came as something of a revelation later that day, to discover that Damian Baxter was already going. In those days students at Magdalene, and in many other colleges no doubt, were not provided with anything so simple as a bedsit. Instead, every student had a sitting room as well as a bedroom, which required a certain spread in the accommodation. That year my rooms were to be found in an old converted cottage, which had been swallowed by the new 1950s quadrangle built round it on the other side of Magdalene Street from the college itself. They were rather charming apartments and I still remember them with affection, but they were in separate parts of the building, so it was a surprise to walk back into the sitting room, having gone to my bedroom for a book, to find Damian standing by the chimneypiece, warming his legs in front of the gurgling gas fire. 'I gather you're going to Queen Charlotte's with the Daltons,' he said. 'I don't suppose there's any chance you could put me up? I really don't want to struggle back here after that one.'

'How do you know?'

'Lucy told me. I said I was in the Waddilove

party, so she told me she was going to ring you. I'm rather jealous.' Now, there was a good deal of information in this statement. More, possibly, than he knew. But then again, perhaps not. Clearly, he had been determined to go to the ball and knowing and I am sure nursing the captive Georgina's crush on him, he had seen that as a route. But what he was also telling me was that he had been Lucy's first choice as a replacement when her cousin had dropped out. I was only the fallback, and he wanted me to know it.

'You never said you were going.'

'You never asked.' He pulled a slight grimace. 'Georgina Waddilove. Yikes.' We shared a smile, which was shamefully disloyal on my part. 'Where are you hiring your white tie?'

'I've got my own,' I said. 'Inherited from a cousin. I think it still fits. Or it did when I went to a hunt ball last Christmas.'

He nodded a little grumpily. 'Of course you've got your own. I wasn't thinking.' The mood had altered slightly. He sipped the sour white wine I had provided him with. 'I don't know why I'm going, really.'

'Why *are* you going?' I was genuinely curious.

He thought for a moment. 'Because I can,' he said.

The history of costume is, as we know, a fascinating subject in itself and I find it interesting that I will almost certainly live to see the death of one outfit, at least, that was significant enough in its heyday, namely White Tie. From early in the nineteenth century, thanks to Mr Brummell, until the middle of the twentieth, it was the male costume of choice for any Society evening, the club colours of the British aristocracy. When, in the late 1920s, the Duke of Rutland was asked by his brother-in-law if he *ever* wore a dinner jacket he thought for a moment. 'When I dine alone with the Duchess in her bedroom,' he replied.

Of course, it was a surprise to some that it survived the war, since six years of dinner jackets and uniforms might have killed it off, but Christian Dior's revival of an almost Edwardian style of dress, with his bustles and corsets and paddings and linings, had launched a fashion for sumptuous evening clothes that made the short, dull dinner jacket seem quite inadequate as a pair. Then, in the summer of 1950, the Countess of Leicester gave a ball for her daughter, Lady Anne Coke, at Holkham, which was attended by the King and Queen. The following morning yielded two discoveries. The first was a waiter who had fallen into the fountain and drowned, the second that white tie for men was definitely back. Of course, what Dior and so many others failed to understand was that white tie was not just a costume, it was also a way of life, and it was a way of life that was already dead. White tie belonged to the ancient bargain between the aristocrat and those less fortunate that they would spend much of their day in discomfort in order to promote a convincing and reassuring image of power. After all, splendour and glamour had been inextricably linked to power for centuries, until the comparatively recent appearance of Government by the Drab. Before the first war, among the upper classes, five or six changes a day, for walking, shooting, breakfast, lunch, tea and dinner, were *de rigueur* at any house party and three at least were necessary for a day in London. They observed these tiresome rituals of dress for the simple reason that they knew once they stopped looking like a ruling class they would soon cease to *be* a ruling class. Our politicians have only just learned what the toffs have known for a thousand years: Appearance is all.

Why, then, did it die so suddenly? Because they stopped believing in themselves. It was not just the loss of the valet that was to prove fatal to the costume; it was a loss of nerve that gripped the Establishment in 1945, and would continue to undermine their confidence until, by the end of the Seventies, for all but a few their role in our National life, and with it the point of their white tie, was gone. My generation saw the last of it. When I was eighteen, all hunt balls were still white tie, as well as all the May balls at Cambridge and the Commem Balls at Oxford. A few coming-out parties still tried for it and one event where it was worn without dispute was Queen Charlotte's Ball. Now, when, apart from a state banquet at Buckingham Palace or Windsor, or something rich and rare at one of the Inns of Court, it has almost vanished, it seems strange to think that forty years ago we still got enough use out of our tails for it to be worth owning them.

Queen Charlotte's Ball was not a private party. It was a large-scale charitable event and, as such, did not conform to the normal rules. To start with, it was what was then called a dinner-dance, meaning that we were to eat there and so we would assemble much earlier than usual. Dinner-dances, in those pre-breathaliser days were thought by some to be rather common, I forget

88

now why, perhaps because they had an air of a night out 'at the club' in some Imperial outpost, but on this particular evening there was a ceremony to be got through that was considered sufficient to justify it. The plan was to gather at the Daltons' London flat in Queensgate, to make sure that the group was all present and correct, and then to move on to Grosvenor House almost immediately.

I rang the bell at the Daltons' front door, the buzzer (for we already had those) admitted me and I knew their flat was on the ground floor, so there was no long climb ahead. The front door must once have been the door into the dining room, when the newly built house had been home to a prosperous late-Victorian family, but by the 1960s that dining room had been carved up into an entrance hall and a medium-sized drawing room. A few good things, as is the wont of such families, had been spared for the flat, in case we might mistake their rank, and what looked like a Laszlo of Lucy's grandmother, painted as a girl of nineteen, stared down glassily from above the chimneypiece, which, owing to the division of the room, was awkwardly off centre. The oddness of proportion was enhanced by the fashion, then prevalent, for blocking grates with large flat sheets of hardboard, often, as in this case, with an electric fire placed in front. I cannot think of any vogue in my entire life more guaranteed to kill a room stone dead than this blanking of the fireplace, but we all did it. Like the hideous enclosing of banisters on a staircase, which one found in almost every house divided into flats, it was supposed to make the space look modern and streamlined. It failed.

'There you are.' Lucy kissed me briskly. 'Are you dreading it?' There were four other girls in the room and, counting Lucy, all five were dressed entirely in white, a survival of the custom of wearing white for a girl's first presentation at Court before the war. It had not, of course, been continued in the last period of Royal Presentation, which had taken the form of garden parties, and the girls would then wear pretty, summer dresses and wide-brimmed hats, but with the end of that and the installation of Queen Charlotte's as the official start of the Season, the white rule had been revived. They wore long, white gloves, too, but instead of the Prince of Wales feathers that decorate the heads of both mothers and daughters in all those pre-war photographs by Van Dyck or Lenare, this year, at least, white flowers were worn in the hair, tiaras not being considered proper for unmarried girls. Lady Dalton, I was pleased to see, sported rather a good one, which flashed its fire round the room as she walked towards me, smiling pleasantly.

'You are kind to come,' she said, holding out her own gloved hand.

'You're very kind to ask me.'

'Lord knows what we'd have done if you'd said no,' added a bluff, soldier type, whom I took, correctly, to be Sir Marmaduke. 'Flag down a bus and just collar someone, I suppose.' One often suspects that a late invitation signifies that a certain scraping of the barrel has gone on. But it is a little depressing to be told it.

'Pay no attention,' said his wife firmly and led me away to where the other young stood. The party was more of an age mixture than usual as most of the mothers and fathers of the girls, if not the boys, were to be with us for the evening, so I met a couple of pleasant enough bankers and their wives, together with a rather pretty, Italian woman, Mrs Wakefield, married to Lady Dalton's cousin, who'd come up from Shropshire to begin the launch of her youngest daughter, Carla. We moved on to the girls themselves. Among them was a plain and russet-faced character, Candida Finch, whom I'd already met. To be honest, I had found her a bit uphill, but we were programmed in those days to make conversation with anybody nearby and so I fell into the small talk demanded of me without much hardship, naming mutual acquaintances, reminding her that we had both been at this drinks party and that one, although we had never spoken more than a few words to each other before now. She nodded and answered, civilly enough but, as always with her, too loudly, too aggressively and, every now and then, with a sudden, stentorian laugh that made you jump out of your skin. Of course, now I can see that she was very angry at what had happened to her life, but one can be so blind and so heartless in youth. I looked at the grown ups sipping their cocktails at the other end of the room.

'Is your mother here?'

She shook her head. 'My mother's dead. She died when I was a child.' This was, of course, rather more than I had bargained for and her voice, as she said it, was raw. I muttered vaguely about being sorry and how I must have muddled her with someone else as I thought I'd seen a photograph of them together in a magazine. This time she spoke with considerably more authority. 'You mean my *step*mother. No. She is not here. *Thank God.*' There was no mistaking the tone and the expletive at the end was presumably intended to bring me, and anyone standing near us, up to date with the way things were between them. I wonder sometimes why people can be so anxious to share their unsatisfactory domestic situation with strangers. It must be because it is often the only arena where they have the power to say what they think of the people concerned and there is some satisfaction in that. Anyway, I grasped the situation. It was not, after all, a very unusual one.

As I later learned, Candida's was a sad story. Her mother had been the sister of Serena Gresham's mother, Lady Claremont, making the girls first cousins, but Mrs Finch had died in her thirties, I don't think I ever knew what of, and her widowed husband, already rather looked down on in the family, had proceeded, once his tears were dry, to make what was referred to as an 'unfortunate' marriage to a former estate agent from Godalming, saddling Candida with an unhelpful stepmother, whom incidentally she detested, and the Claremonts with a nearly-sister-in-law from hell. To make matters worse, when the girl was in her early teens, the father, Mr Finch, had also died, of a heart attack this time, leaving Candida entirely in the clutches of his widow, to whom he had left every penny of what remained of his fortune, as well as custody of his daughter. At this point her aunt, Lady Claremont, had stepped in and tried to take the reins. But Mrs Finch from Godalming was no pushover. She was deaf to any advice on schooling and it was only with the greatest difficulty that her permission had been gained for Candida to do the Season, for which, so one gathered, Lady Claremont was footing the bill. Obviously, all this placed the girl in an invidious position, which one might have sympathised with more, had it not been reflected in her loud and awkward manner. Nor was she helped by her appearance, with her dark, unruly, frizzy hair somehow compounding the complexion of a navvy. She had freckles, too, and a nose straight out of Pinocchio. All in all, Candida Finch had been dealt a tough hand.

'Right. Time to leave, everyone.' Lady Dalton clapped her hands firmly. 'How are we going? Who's got a car?' Some of the fathers drained their double martinis and held up their hands.

One detail of the different world I once inhabited that is not often referred to, but which affected every minute of almost every day, was the traffic. That is to say, there wasn't any. Or none to compare with today's. The cars one encounters now midmorning on a normal weekday in London would only have been seen at six o'clock on a Friday night in late December, as people were leaving town for Christmas. The whole business of parking being impossible simply hadn't started. The time you allowed for a journey was the time it would take. London, or the London most of us occupied, was still small and it was rare that one left more than ten minutes before any appointment. In terms of the general stress of being alive, I cannot tell you what a difference it made.

Another contrast with today concerned the area we lived in. To start with, in London, the upper middle, and upper classes had not yet strayed from their traditional nesting grounds of Belgravia, Mayfair and Kensington—or Chelsea, if they were a bit wild. I remember my mother driving me past a very pretty Georgian terrace on the Fulham Road, before one gets to the football ground. I admired the houses and she nodded. 'They're charming,' she said. 'It's such a pity no one could ever live here.' And if Fulham was outside the pale, Clapham, or worse, Wandsworth, had no hold in their lives or on their mental map whatever, other than as the place where their daily lived, or where one might get glass cut or rugs mended or find a cheaper saleroom. This would soon change when my own generation started to marry and the gentrification of the south bank of the Thames would begin. But in the late Sixties it had not quite happened yet. I remember distinctly driving with my parents to have dinner with some impoverished friends of theirs, who, *faute de mieux*, had bought a house in Battersea, just at the dawn of the new era. As my mother carefully read the scribbled directions to my father at the wheel and the location of our destination became ever clearer, she looked up from the paper. 'Have they lost their minds?' she said.

One must remember that, until the middle Sixties at any rate, there was fairly cheap housing to be found in any part of the city, so there was no pressing need to move out. One might not occupy a palace but that didn't mean one couldn't stick around. We lived at one time on the corner of Hereford Square and, behind the west side, if you can believe it, lay a small field where someone kept a pony. In the corner of this was a cottage, probably originally part of some stabling arrangement, and in my mid-Fifties childhood it was lived in by a not-very-successful actor and his potter-wife. They were delightful and we saw a lot of them but they must have been as poor as church mice. Still, there they were, living in a cottage on the corner of a fashionable square. The next time I entered that building was thirty years later. It had been rented by a Hollywood star who was shooting a movie at Pinewood. Recently it retailed for seven million. The result of the property boom was not just the dispersal of people from their home territory, but the end of the 'mix' in London's population. Struggling painters and penniless writers no longer live in the mews cottages in Knightsbridge or behind Wilton Crescent, where they would once rub shoulders with countesses and millionaires in the local shops and post office. Teachers and poets and professors and explorers and seamstresses and political subversives have all been driven away. They have been replaced by bankers. And we are the poorer for it.

The Great Room at Grosvenor House was an appropriate setting for the formal opening race of the Season. It twinkled with that now distinctive, self-important, 1960s, sub-deco glamour, so memorably christened 'Euro-Splendour' by Stephen Poliakoff. One came through the hall of the hotel on to a kind of gallery, where a wide, aluminium-balustered staircase within the room itself led down towards the gleaming floor below. At the sight of it I was suddenly glad that I had come. It was early June, and a warm night, too warm for the boys' comfort, really, as our tails in those days were made from woollen cloth, but there is something about a party on a warm summer night that always seems to promise much. Usually more than it delivers.

Some years later, before the end of it all, the Season would have to take account of the exam year and cater for career girls sitting their A levels and the like, but not then. For such a consideration to have been raised by anyone in 1968 would have been regarded as quirky, eccentric and very middle class. Looking back, I realise there was hardly a parent there who thought their daughters' future would be anything more than an extended repeat of their own present. How can they have been so secure in their expectations? Didn't it occur to them that more change might be on its way? After all, their generation had lived through enough of it to push the world off its axis.

I stood for a moment against the balustrade. There was something very seductive about looking down from above on a ballroom apparently filled with flower-decked swans. At that moment, whatever the rights and wrongs of the ritual, I confess I was happy to be part of it, as Lucy and I descended together, smiling and nodding in the way one does. From across the room, Serena gave me a slight wave, which was gratifying. 'Whose table is she on?' I asked.

Lucy followed my gaze. She did not need to be told whom we were discussing. 'Her mother's. She's the one in blue. The couple talking at the end look like the Marlboroughs and I'm pretty sure the fat one next to Lord Claremont is a princess of Denmark. I seem to remember she's one of Serena's godmothers.' I decided not to push in.

Lucy stopped. 'There's your friend, making hay while the sun shines.' A few yards ahead of us Damian was joking merrily with Joanna Langley.

I wasn't going to let her get away with that. 'Your friend, too, I gather,' I said sharply, which earned me an apologetic glance.

Watching the gossiping couple, somewhat sourly, was the tragic figure of Georgina Waddilove. Pitiful Georgina. The style that was so becoming to almost all the others did not show her to much advantage and she resembled nothing more than an enormous, white blancmange. The flowers sewn on to a mountain of artificial ringlets battened to her head looked like scraps of torn paper caught in a tree. I walked up to where Damian was standing. 'Have you brought your stuff here?'

Damian nodded. 'It's all in the cloakroom.' He smiled at Joanna. 'He's putting me up for the night.'

'Don't your parents have a place in London?' By such questions Joanna would occasionally give herself away. At least she would signify that she was not a founder member of this set-up. I am confident, even at this distance, that there was no malice in her, far from it, but she had not learned to spare someone's feelings by avoiding any subject that might prove delicate. This was partly because, despite her great expectations, she was not really interested in money. If the reason Damian's parents did not have a London home was because they could not afford one, she would not have thought any the less of them for that. Which is to say she was possessed of a larger generosity of spirit than most of us. Damian, as usual, was unfazed.

'No, they haven't,' he said, without further qualification. I had not yet noticed it in him, but he never gave out any information about himself unless asked a direct question. Even then it was carefully rationed.

'I think we'd better sit down.' Georgina had clearly had just about enough of Damian's being cornered by Miss Langley, as she would have put it.

I smiled at the object of her irritation. 'Are you in this party?'

'With *my* mother? Of course not.' Joanna shook her head, laughing, and I found myself watching the movement of her lips. To me, her beauty had a mesmerising perfection, as if one were standing close to a celluloid icon projected on to an invisible screen. 'You don't think she would have missed out on the chance of hosting a dinner of her own?' She nodded at a point further up the room and I could see an eager, bustling, little woman, wearing a good deal of jewellery, who was staring anxiously in our direction. 'Better go.' She sauntered away.

'I suppose you're going, too,' said Damian, 'Think of me.' The last was added in an annoying half-whisper, just audible enough for Georgina to have caught it, although I am not sure that she did.

'You didn't have to be in this group. You could have had my seat if you hadn't taken the first offer.' I made no attempt to prevent Lucy hearing this, nor had I intended to, so Damian was able to direct his answer at her.

'To quote Madame Greffulhe: "*Que j'ai jamais*

98

su." ' Lucy laughed. But by now people really were starting to sit down, and so we set out on the journey back to her mother's table.

'Who's Madame What-Not?' I asked.

'Marcel Proust used to go to her parties, when he was young. Years later, they asked her what it was like having such a genius in her salon, and she replied: *"Que j'ai jamais su!"* '

'If only I'd known.'

'Precisely.'

I was silent, wondering how Damian knew these things. How did he know Lucy knew them? I learned later it was one of his gifts. Like a squirrel, he would seek out and store any unlikely tidbit, in this case the startling news that Lucy Dalton read Proust, and he would save it for a time when it could be used to create an instant, magic bond that would exclude the others present, making him and whoever his target might be into a cosy club of two. I have seen the trick employed by others, but seldom to such effect. He never misjudged the moment. Lucy smiled. 'Please don't tell me you're surprised.'

'I am a bit.' I looked around at the chattering, giggling throng, pulling their chairs up to the tables with their shining, white cloths. 'I doubt that most of this lot read Proust.'

'If they did, they wouldn't tell you. The men here will exaggerate what they know. The women will conceal it.' I hope these words would not be true now, but I'm afraid they were true then.

She enjoyed my wrong-footed silence, until I was the one to break it. 'I thought you didn't like him,' I said, which seemed a non sequitur, but wasn't.

She shrugged. 'I don't much. Who told you I'd asked him first?'

'He did. Why? Was it a secret?'

'No.' She looked at me. 'I'm sorry. I should have invited you before him. I must have assumed you'd already be going.'

I nodded genially. 'That's all right. Don't apologise. Why shouldn't you ask him first? He's much better looking than I am.' Which annoyed her as I intended that it should, but the opportunity for rebuttal was gone. We were back with their party and Lady Dalton was pointing us to our allotted chairs. I had been placed between Carla Wakefield and Candida.

During the first course I talked to Carla about whom we both knew and where we'd both studied, about our plans for the summer and the sports we enjoyed, until the half-eaten salmon was taken away and the inevitable chicken was brought in and I turned to my other neighbour. I could see at once that more of the same would not quite answer.

'You're very good at this, aren't you?' she said and, while it was not exactly voiced in a hostile manner, it wasn't all that friendly, either.

'Thank you,' I replied. She had not, of course, meant it as a compliment, but by taking it as one I hadn't left her any room for manoeuvre. She glowered at her plate. I tried a more honest approach. 'If you don't enjoy it, why are you doing it?' I asked.

She stared at me. 'Because my aunt arranged the whole thing before I was given a choice. Because she is the only relative I have who cares whether I live or die. Most of all, because I don't

100

know what else to do.' As usual, when discussing her family arrangements she spoke with a kind of ill-repressed fury. 'My stepmother has had charge of me since I was fourteen, and as a result of her bizarre requirements when it comes to female instruction, I am uneducated, untrained and completely unequipped for any productive work. Now I am supposed to "make a life for myself," whatever that means. My cousin Serena tells me that things would improve if I knew more people in London. I do not dispute this—only these are not the sort of people I want to know more of.' With a dismissive snort she indicated the body of the room.

It did seem very hard to have lost both parents by the time she was eighteen, even if Oscar Wilde would have thought it careless. 'Where were you at school?'

'Cullingford Grange.'

I had vaguely heard of it. 'Isn't that in Hertfordshire?'

Candida nodded. 'It's the kind of place where they worry if you're reading too much, instead of being out in the nice fresh air.' She rolled her eyes at the strangeness of her stepmother's choices. 'I could recite the rules of hockey in my sleep, but unfortunately nothing was taught about literature, mathematics, history, art, politics or life.' I believed her because her account was only too familiar.

I think, I pray, I come from the last generation of the privileged to pay no attention to the education of their daughters. Even in 1968 there were women's colleges at Cambridge and Oxford, but they were, as a rule, filled with the daughters

101

of the *bourgeois* intelligentsia. Posh girls were an oddity and indeed almost the only one I can remember from my own year left after one term to marry a man with a castle in Kent. There were exceptions, but these generally came from families who were known to cherish an eccentric tradition of educating their women, rather than from the run-of-the-mill squireachy. For the rest, parents would scrimp and save to send the boys to Eton or Winchester or Harrow, while their sisters were put into the charge of some alcoholic, Belgian countess, whose main instruction was not to bother the parents.

After leaving, a girl might spend a year at a finishing school where she could polish her languages and her skiing, then another year would pass in coming out, after which she would get a job arranging flowers in the boardroom or cooking lunches for directors or working for her father, until she had discovered Mr Right who, with any luck, would be the heir to Lord Right. And that would be that. Hopefully, the Hon. John Right would be right for Mummy and Daddy, too, since they, like their own parents, would expect to approve the choice. Our mothers may not have been pushed into their marriages in the Thirties and Forties, but they had certainly been kept out of any marriages their parents disapproved of. We all had stories of aunts and great-aunts who had been sent to study painting in Florence, or to live with a grandmother in Scotland, or to improve their French at some mountainous chateau in the Swiss Alps, to break them of a bad love habit and, lest those Barbara Cartland addicts think differently, usually it worked.

102

I do not mean to imply that all who followed this path were wretched. Lots of them were as happy as clams. They spent the early years of marriage in some part of London their mothers found unlikely, then, if they'd chosen well, they might move into the big house on their father-in-law's estate ('Fizzy and I were just *rattling around* and we thought it was time to let the kids have a go'). For some the father proved stubborn and wouldn't move out, and for most there wasn't a house to inherit, so the young couple would generally buy a cottage or a farmhouse or, if things were going *really* well in the City, a Queen Anne manor house in Gloucestershire or Oxfordshire or Suffolk. After that, he would shoot and complain about politics, they'd both ski and worry about the children, and she would work for charity, entertain and, if things were going *less* well in the City, sell artificial jewellery to her captive friends. Until the children grew up and it was time first to downsize and then to die. All of which, lest we forget and before we feel too sorry for them, was a lot better than scratching for a living in the dirt of the plains of Uzbekistan.

But where did it leave someone like Candida Finch? She was obviously clever but her appearance and her manner would not help to offset her lack of qualifications to say the least. Nor would I have thought there was any certainty of a husband coming up on the next lift. And there wouldn't be much money. What were her options? 'Do you know what you'd like to do?' I asked.

Again, she rolled her eyes in exasperation. 'What *can* I do?'

'I asked what would you *like* to do.'

103

This was enough to soften her a little. It was, after all, a genuine enquiry. 'I think I might have liked to work in publishing, but I have no degree. And before you suggest I take one now, we both know that won't happen. It's too late and I've missed it. I thought I might squeeze a few quid out of a godparent and push into a vanity publishing firm, but they'd have to accept they'd lose every penny, and all to buy me the right to talk about publishing at dinner parties. Which is the most I'd achieve.'

'Be careful you're not determined to fail in order to annoy your stepmother. It doesn't sound to me as if she'll care much either way.' I nearly didn't say this, since our very brief acquaintance did not at all justify it, but she laughed.

'Well, that's true anyway.' Her voice was warmer than it had been. 'You know, you really *are* quite good at this.'

When dinner was over, by some pre-arranged signal the white-clad debutantes slipped away, leaving the tables occupied only by the parents, the young men and the odd non-deb girl, glum and in colour. It was time for the ceremony that we had come for and while I would not pretend to the ecstasy of anticipation that gripped the mothers throughout the room, the rest of us were quite curious. First, an enormous cake, literally six or seven feet high, was wheeled out on to the centre of the dance floor. Next the Patroness of the Ball arose from her chair with sober grandeur and walked across to stand next to it. I seem to remember that this was always Lady Howard de Walden, but maybe I'm wrong, maybe it alternated with the Duchess of Somewhere. Either way, she was a heavyweight in the scales by which these things are weighed. I don't actually think the whole thing would have worked if she were not. As it was, her rigid upright posture and the confident dignity of a crowned monarch, which a lot of those women seemed to possess quite naturally then in contrast to so many of their daughters, gave the exercise a certain credibility even before it had begun. The band struck up and we looked towards the head of the staircase, where the Girls of the Year stood lined up in couples, side by side, poised, waiting. Then, slowly, they began to descend at a measured pace, as solemnly as if they were serving at a Pope's funeral.

Down they came, the lights playing on the white flowers among their gleaming curls, on their long white gloves, on the white lace and silk of their dresses, on their shining, haughty, hopeful faces. Once they had reached the bottom, each pair advanced to where the Patroness stood, dropped into a deep Court curtsey, and moved on. They were not all presented to absolute advantage. Georgina looked like Godzilla in a shroud as she lumbered down towards terra firma. But for most of them there was something almost ethereal in their uniformity. Sixty versions of the Angel of Mons coming down to ease the pain of those beneath.

It may, of course, be with the wisdom of hindsight, but I am fairly sure it was at that precise moment that I first became aware that what we were witnessing did not have long to live. That there would not be many more generations taking part in this performance or, indeed, anything like it. That our parents' dream of somehow rescuing enough of the old, pre-war world for their children to live in, was a chimera, that I was, in short, witnessing the start of the finish. Funnily enough, and you probably will not believe me, it was an impressive sight. Like all disciplined, synchronised movement, the procession was commanding in its execution, as on and on they came, pair after matched pair, gliding down, curtseying low, moving on. All before a giant cake. Yet it was not ridiculous. It probably sounds ridiculous in the telling. Absurd. Even laughable. I can only say that I was there and it was not.

The display was done. The girls were blooded, their status as this year's debutantes confirmed and it was time for the dancing to begin. To counter their former solemnity, the band now played a tune at the top of the hit parade of the day, *Simple Simon Says*, one of those rather exhausting songs, which is full of uninvited instructions for the listener, 'Put your hands on your head, shake them all about,' and so on, but, although almost definitively naff, it was quite a good icebreaker. Lucy was already dancing with one of the other men in the party, so I made the offer to Candida and we walked together on to the floor. 'Who's that man you were talking to, before dinner?' she asked. I did not need to follow her eye-line to know the answer.

'Damian Baxter,' I said. 'He's up at Cambridge with me.'

'You must introduce us.' It was at this moment that I first encountered a particularly terrifying part of Candida's repertoire. Whenever she spotted someone she thought attractive there would ensue a kind of manic, as she thought

106

flirtatious, ritual rather like a Maori dance of welcome, where she would roll her eyes and snicker and rock back and forth with a kind of shouted laugh more suited to a thirsty bricklayer than a young girl coming out. In fairness, I suppose it must have achieved her immediate ends reasonably often, since there could be no doubt as to what was on offer and we were not spoiled for choice in those days, but I do not think, as a routine, it was ever very conducive to long-term commitment, and in fact earned Candida a reputation, by the end of the Season, of being something of a bicycle. I was never treated to this display head on, as she was not at all interested in me, but even for a witness from the stalls it was pretty unnerving.

Following her hungry glance, I looked back to where Damian was standing at the centre of a small but admiring crowd. Serena Gresham was there, laughing, with Carla Wakefield and a couple of girls I did not recognise. Georgina was hanging back in her usual position of resentful witness to the fun of others. I saw now that Andrew Summersby was one of the party and Mrs Waddilove was busily, but ineffectually, trying to draw him into conversation; or, more to the point, she was trying to involve him in a conversation with her own daughter. But neither would play due, I would imagine, to a complete lack of interest on both sides. A friend of mine from Atlanta always called this kind of social interchange 'Pumping Mud.' They were watched from the other side of the table by an older woman, presumably another of Mrs Waddilove's guests, but I did not recognise her. She was an odd

107

specimen, even in that company. Her face was that of a snobbish, Dutch doll, while the weird combination of her unlikely near-black hair, more Benidorm than good old British, with a pair of piercing pale-blue eyes flecked with shades of green and amber, made her look more than slightly mad, half Lizzie Borden, half stoat. She stood very still as she listened to the conversation limping along, but her stillness held a kind of inner threat of danger, a beast of prey, motionless but waiting to spring. 'Who's that standing opposite Mrs Waddilove and Andrew Summersby?'

Candida tore her eyes away from feasting on Damian and glanced across. 'Lady Belton. Andrew's mother.' I nodded. I might have guessed since I could now see that his sister, Annabella Warren, was among the girls in the Waddilove group. I looked back at *Madame Mère*, as she stood surveying the troops. I had heard of Lady Belton but I had not seen her before that night. One glance was enough to endorse the truth of her reputation.

The Countess of Belton was not generally liked, probably because she was not at all likeable. She was stupid, snobbish to the point of dementia and inexplicably arrogant. Admittedly, she was not vain, nor was she extravagant, but she took this to such a degree that it ceased to be a virtue. In fact, that night she was dressed in what looked like the window display of a Sue Ryder shop in West Hartlepool. Later I would come to know and loathe her, but despite all this, in a funny way I cannot quite explain at this distance, she did have something. Perhaps her absolute refusal to bend to her own times gave her a sort of moral conviction.

Certainly she stands out vividly in my memory among the mothers of that year, although I had not then met her beleaguered husband, who always seemed to find an excuse to stay away, and I had only chatted, and not much more, to Lord Summersby, the dull and lumpen eldest son and heir. But even without all this information I saw at once that Georgina's mother was too obvious and her ambition was not realistic.

Watching her flash her smiles between them all and attempt to ensnare her daughter's interest, Candida spoke my thoughts. 'Dream on, Mrs Waddilove.'

She was right. This was a hopeless fantasy. It was quite clear to the most casual observer that Lady Belton's prejudices would never favour a match with the likes of the Waddiloves, however happy she was to dine and drink through that night at their expense. She wouldn't have dreamed of it, even if the girl had been pretty. That is unless a sum of money had been involved that was roughly equivalent to the combined African National Debt. As for the boy, I already suspected he was incapable of independent thought, in which I would be proved right. But anyway, the sad truth is that Georgina was not the type to inspire reckless love.

We danced on. Like the well-mannered chap I was then, I partnered my hostess, Lady Dalton, a custom universally observed in those days but almost abandoned now. To me, there was always something faintly comic in the practice, as one steered these middle-aged women around the floor, she wishing it were a foxtrot, you longing for it to end, one's hand resting lightly on the stiffened stays that were usually detectable beneath the fabric of the evening gown, but, funny as I found it, I am not glad the tradition of dancing with one's friends' parents has gone. It made a kind of bridge between the generations in our increasingly fragmented society and I suspect we can use all the bridges that are going. 'Do you know what you're planning to do when you leave university?' she said genially, as we stumbled around in our unsyncopated way.

I shook my head. 'Not really. Not yet.'

'There isn't a preordained pattern to be followed?'

Again I answered in the negative. 'There's no estate to come, or family business to swallow me up.'

'What does your father do?' At the time, in the late 1960s, this question would have bordered on impertinence, since the smart English had not yet abandoned their pretence that one's professional activity was of minor, and then only personal, interest. But of course Lady Dalton was engaging in research.

'He's a diplomat. But the Foreign Office isn't looking for my type any more, even if I wanted to follow him.' Which was more or less true. Had I been an exceptional candidate it might have been different, but for the more regular intake the Foreign Office, always a kingdom of its own in Britain, had decided at some point in the sixties that the day of the gentleman ambassador was over, that henceforth the role must be downgraded socially in order, I imagine, to be taken more seriously by the post-war intelligentsia. Either that, or it was a way of shifting their political loyalties.

Forty years later, the results of the policy have been mixed, especially since it has not been adopted by the rest of mainland Europe. The British ambassador these days is generally regarded as rather an oddball in the world's capitals, both by the international brigade and by the Society of whichever city they find themselves in. One would have thought this might have diminished our backstairs influence. But perhaps that was what they were after.

Lady Dalton nodded. 'It's going to be so *very* interesting, seeing which directions you all go in.' With that the music ended and I walked her back to the table. She was a nice woman and we were friendly for as long as our paths were to cross, but from that moment she had entirely lost interest in me.

Some time around one in the morning the band leader approached the microphone, instructing us to take our partners for the gallop, and by this sign we knew the evening was nearly done. As always, surveying the modern generation, it seems perfectly incredible that we, who were after all simultaneously participating in the swinging sixties, still ended a good many parties with this period romp, but we did. Unlike the Scottish reels that were also part of most of the parties, the gallop was only ever the last dance of the event and it was really just an excuse to show how drunk you were. You seized some luckless girl and raced back and forth across the floor, bumping around, vaguely in time to some loud, rum-ti-tum music, falling over, shouting and generally demonstrating that you were a very good sport. Needless to say there was a rather desperate quality to it, even a sort of lonely sadness, as one watched those shrieking girls up from the country, their ringlets collapsing, their dresses frequently torn, their make-up vanishing beneath a sheen of red jowls and sweat. At any rate for good or ill we, the merrymakers of 1968, danced it and with that, Queen Charlotte's Ball was over for another year.

My parents' flat was to be found on the ground floor of a tall house in Wetherby Gardens, a street that runs between South Kensington and Earl's Court. In those days this was roughly like passing from heaven into hell and it was an important detail to my mother that the flat was considerably nearer the former than the latter. Now, naturally, either end would command a price beyond rubies. Again, much like the Daltons' London home, the former dining room of the Victorian family for whom it was built had been carved into drawing room, hall and, in our case, kitchen. What had presumably been some sort of library had become a small, dark and rather poky place to eat in, and what must have been a charming morning room, overlooking the small garden attached to the flat and, beyond it, the very large communal garden shared by the block, had been split into two bedrooms, with some unsatisfactory jiggling of the paper wall to get one half of a double door and a reasonable proportion of window into each. Like so many of their generation, my parents were curiously accepting about their accommodation. When, later, in the Seventies and Eighties, we all started pulling down walls and moving bathrooms and converting attics, they watched in semi-horrified wonder, my father, particularly, believing that if God had wanted that shelf in a different

112

place He would have arranged it and who was he to interfere with Providence? It's odd, really, when one thinks how their eighteenth- and nineteenth-century ancestors thought nothing of pulling down ancient family houses to build something more voguish in their place. Maybe it was to do with rationing or making do during the war.

I was already in bed and asleep when I was summoned back to the surface by the repeated ringing of the doorbell. For a while this took the form of a church bell being rung, for some strange reason, by William Ewart Gladstone, but then I woke up and the ringing continued.

Damian was hugely apologetic. 'I'm so sorry. I should have asked for a key. Then I thought you'd probably be going on with the rest of us.'

'Where?'

He shrugged nonchalantly. 'Round and about. We looked into the Garrison for a drink and then we went to get a sandwich and a cup of coffee from that hut on the other side of Chelsea Bridge.' As it happens, we would do this quite often as the year wore on, boys and girls in evening dress, queuing at dawn behind the bikers for a bacon butty from the little wooden kiosk in the shadow of the great power station. They were nice people, those motorcycle men, and friendly as a rule, amused rather than affronted by our pampered appearance. I wish them well.

'Was that the end of it?'

Damian smiled. 'Not quite. We wound up at the Claremonts' house.'

'On Millionaire's Row.'

'Next to Kensington Palace.'

I nodded. 'That's the one,' I said. How cool and

ordered he looked. He could have been about to go out, rather than coming in after what could only be described as a *long* night. 'You have been busy. How did you manage that?'

He shrugged again. 'Serena suggested it and I didn't see why not.'

'Did you wake up her parents?'

'Not the mother. Her dad came down and asked us not to make too much noise.' He looked round the drawing room vaguely.

'Would you like a drink?'

'Just one, maybe. If you'll join me.'

I poured out two glasses of whisky and water. 'Do you want any ice?'

'Not for me.' He was learning fast.

'What happened to Georgina? Was she with you?'

He could barely suppress a laugh. 'No, thank the Lord. We didn't even have to lie. They were dropping off Lady Belton and Andrew at their flat, and Mrs Waddilove wouldn't let Georgina escape.'

There was something slightly unsatisfactory in this. 'Poor Georgina. I'm afraid she's a bit in love with you.'

This time he did laugh. 'There are many who must carry that burden.' It seemed to me, in that moment, that to have this kind of self-confidence at the age we then were must be a kind of Paradise. He mistook the envy in my eyes for a trace of disapproval and hurried to reassure me. 'Come on. I chummed her to Queen Charlotte's. I'll always be friendly when we meet. You can't expect me to marry her because she was the first to ask me to her party.'

Which, of course, I could not and would not.

'Just be nice to her,' I said. Then I took him down the passage and showed him into what was usually my own, cramped bedroom. But my parents were in the country and I had chosen to sleep in theirs. 'Was it what you expected?' I asked, as we were about to close our respective doors. 'Or did you disapprove?'

'I don't know what I expected.' Damian thought for a moment. 'And I'm in no position to disapprove of anything.' He paused. 'One thing I do notice and even perhaps envy.' I waited. 'You all belong to something, even if it's hard to define quite what. Contrary to myth, you don't necessarily all know each other and you certainly don't all like each other. But you do have some sort of group identity, which I don't share.'

'Perhaps you will.'

He shook his head. 'No, I won't. But I don't think I'd want to. Not for much longer, anyway. I have a suspicion that before we're finished I'll be the one who belongs to something. And you won't.'

Which, of course, is exactly what happened.

FOUR

I cannot tell you with any real exactitude whether it made me laugh or cry when I heard, late in 1970, that Lucy Dalton was going to marry Philip Rawnsley-Price. I do remember it came as something of a shock. It was not only his awkward and unsubtle courtship, of her and every other girl who would stop to listen, that made him so

115

unsatisfactory a character. He was born unsatisfactory. He had one of those flat faces, like a carnival mask that had been dropped in the road and run over by a heavy lorry. His skin was sallow, verging on olive, but this did not, as it might have, give him an exotic quality. Rather, he resembled an ailing Mediterranean lift attendant, with round, moist eyes resting in a pool of wrinkles, two fried eggs in fat. After what seemed a very short engagement I was invited to the wedding and I went, but it was a restrained and slightly bewildering affair. Lady Dalton was not her usual, cheery self, as she kissed and handed us down the line, and while all the usual forms were observed— the ancient village church, the marquee on the lawn, the plates of unappetising nibbles, the rather good champagne—none of it seemed to be celebrated with much brio. Even the speeches were pretty formulaic, the only memorable bit being when Lucy's aged uncle forgot what he was doing and addressed us as 'fellow members,' though quite what he thought we were fellow members *of* was never revealed.

Obviously, all of the above became comprehensible when Lucy was delivered of a baby girl early the following year. I saw the couple for a bit after that, kitchen suppers with other girls like her and boys like me, but long before the *Sloane Ranger Handbook* had given that tribe a name and an identity. In my day they were just the girls in pearls and we were the chinless wonders. But I never thought much of Philip, even after the dancing was done and we had all begun to grow up a little. He was one of those who manage to combine almost total failure with breathtaking

116

arrogance and in the end life gently separated us. Besides, they had enthusiastically embraced the Sixties (which, as we know, largely took place during the Seventies) and like many others had to find ways of dealing with the disappointment that set in once it had become clear that the Age of Aquarius was not going to happen after all. They moved out of London while Philip went through a series of jobs or, as he would put it, careers, the last of which, I now learned, was some sort of farm shop that he and Lucy had opened in Kent. By that stage catering, 'hospitality,' sportswear and, I think, a variation of property development had all played their part, so it was hard to feel optimistic in the long term and I was curious to learn if the number on the list still worked, when I rang her for the first time in, I should imagine, at least thirty years. But Lucy answered and, after our initial joshing, I explained that I was going to be in her neighbourhood the following week and I thought it would be fun to look in and catch up. There was a slight silence at the proposal. Then she spoke again. 'Of course. How lovely. What day were you thinking of?'

'Up to you. I'll fit my other stuff round whenever you're free.' Which was unfair of me, but I suspected that if I had been specific it would have been the one day she couldn't manage. This way there was no alternative but to give in gracefully.

'Don't expect much to eat. I'm no better in the kitchen than when we last met.'

'I just want to see where you live.'

'I'm flattered.' She didn't sound very flattered but even so, the Thursday after that, I found myself bowling through the Kent lanes on my way

117

to Peckham Bush.

I followed the directions, through the centre and out the other side, until eventually I turned into a gap between two high hedges and drove down a bumpy track into a former farmyard. Large signs pointed me to a brightly lit shop and showed me to a car park with a surfeit of empty spaces, but the old, red-tiled farmhouse lay a little beyond this commercial centre, so I stopped outside that instead. I wasn't out of the car before Lucy emerged. 'Well, hello,' she said. We had not seen each other, as I have explained, for many years, and it is only by such long gaps that we can chart the cruelty of time as well as, in this case, disappointment.

Things were not always so for her. In what I now see was the restrained manner of the days of our youth, she had been a modest darling of the media in her way, an early 'It Girl,' a precursor of the celebrity culture that was soon to overwhelm us. The point was that, unlike most of the girls, she had embraced the trendy Swinging Sixties to quite a degree, if not so fiercely as to frighten the mothers. She wore miniskirts that were slightly shorter and eyeliner that was slightly blacker, and she would give quotes to make journalists laugh. She would praise 'those darling train robbers' or declare Che Guevara the world's sexiest martyr. Once she was asked for her happiest moment and she replied it was when P. J. Proby split his jeans which made a headline in the *Evening Standard*. It was soft rebellion, drawing-room subversion, an endorsement of every value that would destroy her kind, but done with a cheeky grin. It played well and raised her profile and, during the Season,

118

there had been model shoots and photographs on those feature pages in the *Tatler*, that read today like a message from the Land that Time Forgot: 'This Year's Debs,' 'Fashions to Watch,' 'The Young Trendsetters,' and so on. Lord Lichfield asked to take her picture and was accepted, and I distinctly recall some now forgotten television 'personality' (a concept so new as to be barely dry) inviting her on to his show. She declined, of course, at the insistence of her mother, but even the request had given her a certain cachet.

Of all this fun and bubble there remained not a trace in the sad, tired face before me. She still wore her shoulder-length hair loose, but the bounce had gone, and it was lank, thin and greying. Her clothes, which had once been racy, were now just old: old jeans, old shirt, old scuffed shoes. They covered her nakedness and that was all. Even her make-up was no more than a tired acknowledgement that she was female. She nodded towards the house. 'Come in.'

After this beginning it was almost a relief to see that time had not converted her to domesticity. In fact, it looked as if a terrorist bomb had just exploded in the hall, blowing every possession of the family into a new and illogical place. There is a kind of messy house that cannot quite be explained by the laziness of the occupants; where a sort of anger, a protest against the values of the world, seems to be involved in its brand of farrago, and I would pay Lucy the compliment of thinking this was one of them. The whole place seemed to have been decorated in the very worst years of the 1970s, with bold, depressing designs in brown and orange, framed posters of over-praised films and a

119

good deal of cane and Indian weave. The kitchen was predictably pine-slatted with terracotta, tiled surfaces, the grouting blackened with filth. Its walls were lined with lots of shelves supporting a jumble of non-matching mugs, pictures of the children, ornaments won at long-ago fairs, pages of magazines torn out for some lost reason. And dirt. Lucy looked around, seeing it all with fresh eyes, as one does when a stranger arrives. 'Jesus. I'm afraid we're in rather a pickle. Let me give you a drink and we'll get out of here.' She fished about in the large refrigerator, found a huge, half-empty bottle of Pinot Grigio and, grabbing two cloudy, furry-looking glasses from beneath the sink, led the way into what must have been the parlour of the farmer's wife who lived here once, so tidily, before the world turned upside down.

If anything, the drab, disintegrating chaos was even more dispiriting than in the other rooms I had passed through, with tired, crocheted rugs strewn over the lumpy, disconnected chairs and sofas, and a bookshelf made from planks of wood and bricks. Quite a nice portrait of a young woman in the 1890s hung skew-whiff above the chimneypiece, making an improbable status statement from another time and another place. Two invitations and a bill were jammed into its chipped frame. Lucy followed my eyes. 'My mother gave me that. She thought it might help make the room more normal.' She leant forward and straightened it.

'Who is it?'

'My great-grandmother, I think. I'm not sure.' For a second I thought of that earlier Lady Dalton, coming in from riding, dressing for luncheon,

120

deadheading the roses. What would she make of her role in this dustbin?

'Where's Philip?'

'In the shop, I'm afraid. He really can't leave it. I'm going to give you some lunch, then we'll walk over together.' She sipped her wine.

'How's the shop going?' I grinned brightly. In fact, I could feel myself consciously trying to inject a perky quality into my speech, though whether I was attempting to cheer her up, or myself, I could not tell you.

'Oh, all right,' she smiled vaguely. 'I think.' Obviously yet another of Philip's ventures was about to bite the dust. 'The thing is, a shop ties one down so much. Before we started I thought it would be friends coming in all the time for a chat, and having cups of tea and baking cakes and things, but it isn't. One just stands there, hour after hour, talking to complete strangers who never know what they want. And by the time you pay for everything, you know, the stock and the people who help and so on, there's only about threepence left.' She pronounced 'threepence' in the old way: 'Thruppence.' For a moment, I felt quite nostalgic.

'What will you do if you pack it in?'

She shrugged. 'I'm not sure. Philip's got some idea about renting paintings to people.'

'What paintings? To which people?'

'I know,' she acknowledged my query disloyally. 'I don't understand it, either. He thinks there might be quite a lot of money in it, but I can't see how. Are you OK with pasta?'

I followed her back into the germ-rich kitchen and watched her take small bowls filled with leftover, dark, half-eaten things out of the fridge.

121

She set about shuffling plates and banging saucepans together as she organised our feed. 'How's your mother?' I asked.

Lucy nodded ruminatively, as if somehow this question had already been the subject of a long consideration. 'Fine. Good.' She looked across at me. 'You know they sold Hurstwood?'

'No, I didn't. I'm sorry.'

She shook her head firmly from left to right. 'Don't be.' She wasn't having any of that. 'Best thing that could have happened.' Having rapped this out as severely as a Tsarist ukase to get the point of no regret across, she allowed herself to relax and elaborate. 'It was about four years ago and of course it was terribly boo-hoo when it was going on, but there was no alternative. Not when Daddy did the sums. And the bonus is that they're completely free now, for the first time in their lives. Johnny was never very interested in taking over, so it really is . . .' She hesitated, trying to find a word she had not already employed that would support her argument effectively. She failed. 'It's fine.'

This phenomenon, where the losers in a revolution try to demonstrate their support for, and approval of, the changes that have destroyed them, always fascinates me. I suppose it is an offshoot of the Stockholm Syndrome, where kidnap victims start to defend their captors. Certainly, we've seen and heard a lot of it over the past few decades, especially among those toffs who are determined to show they are not being left behind. 'We mustn't cling on to the past,' they say cheerily, 'we have to move with the times.' When the only movement possible for them, once all

122

their values have been denigrated and destroyed, is down and out. 'Where are they living?' I asked.

'Quite near Cheyne Walk. They've got a flat in one of those blocks.'

'And Johnny and Diana? What happened to them?' I had got to know Lucy's brother and sister as the Season went on, not all that well, but enough to smile and kiss when we met.

'Johnny's got a restaurant. In Fulham. At least, he *had* a restaurant in Fulham. When I last spoke to him it sounded as if it was all going a bit off *piste*. But he'll be OK. He's always full of ideas.'

'Is he married?'

'Divorced. Two boys, but they live with his ex quite near Colchester, which is a bit trying. Mummy made a terrific effort at the beginning. But you know what it's like, it meant hours on the train for the kids and all they ever wanted to do when they got to her was go home. So she's slightly given up at the moment, but she says it'll be much easier when they've grown up a bit.' Lucy brought over the unappetising plates of yellow-grey pasta, smeared with what looked like the guts of a rabbit, and laid mine reverently before me. The world-weary bottle of Pinot Grigio was back in play.

'What was his wife like?' I lifted my fork without enthusiasm.

'Gerda? Rather dull, to be honest, but not horrible or anything. She wasn't someone you'd know. She's Swedish. They met at Glastonbury. I quite liked her, actually, and the whole split was very civilised. They just didn't have anything in common. She's married to a neurosurgeon now, which seems to be much more the ticket.'

'What about Diana?' I always thought Lucy's

elder sister was the more beautiful of the two. She looked like a young Deborah Kerr and, unlike her more frenetic sibling, she had a sort of serenity unusual in someone of her age. We all thought of her as quite a catch and, to her mother's unfeigned delight, she'd been heavily involved with the heir to a borders earldom when I knew them, though I had heard since that this hadn't, in the end, come off. I noticed the question had penetrated Lucy's armour slightly and I understood before I was told that all was not well here either. Time, it seemed, had been unkind to all the Daltons. 'I'm afraid Diana's *not* too good just now. She's divorced as well, but hers was pretty grim.'

'I know she didn't marry Peter Berwick.'

'No. More's the pity, though I never thought I'd say it. He was always so stuck up and tedious when they were going out, but now, glimpsed across the chasm of the years, he seems like Paradise Lost. Her husband was American. You wouldn't know him either. Nor would I, if I didn't have to. They met in Los Angeles and he keeps promising to go back there, but he hasn't so far. Worse luck.'

I had a sudden, vivid memory of Diana Dalton laughing at a joke I had told her. We were next to each other in the dining room at Hurstwood, before going on to a ball somewhere nearby. She was drinking at the time and did a massive nose trick, right into the lap of the Lord Lieutenant, seated blamelessly on her other side. 'Did she have any children?'

'Two. But of course they're grown up now. One's in Australia and the other's working on a kibbutz near Tel Aviv. It's annoying because since she's been in the Priory the whole thing has landed on me and Mummy.'

One more sentence and I would have cried. Poor Lady Dalton. Poor Sir Marmaduke. What had they done to merit this annihilation by the furies? When I last saw them they were model representatives of the class that had run the Empire. They managed their estates, played their part in the county, frightened the village and generally did their duty. And I knew too well they had dreamed of a future for their children that would have consisted of much the same. Certainly their reveries bore no resemblance to what had actually come to pass. I thought of Lady Dalton at Queen Charlotte's, gently probing me about my prospects. What splendid marriages she had planned for her two daughters, pretty and funny and well-born as they were. Would it have damaged the universe if just one of her wishes had come true? Instead, in forty years the entire Dalton edifice, centuries in the building, had come crashing down into the street. Their money was gone, and what little was left would soon be gobbled up by a feckless son and a reckless son-in-law. That's if the Priory fees didn't drain the pot dry before then. And the crimes that merited this punishment? The parents had not understood how to manage the changes the years would bring, and the children, all three of them, had believed the siren song of the Sixties, and invested everything in the brave new world they were so mendaciously promised.

There was a noise at the door. 'Mum. Have you got it?' I looked up. A young woman of about twenty was standing there. She was tall and would have been quite good looking, had she not been encased in an angry mist, irritated and impatient, as if we were needlessly keeping her waiting. Not for the first time I was struck by the phenomenon, another by-product of the social revolution of the last four decades, whereby parents these days frequently belong to an entirely different social class from their children. Obviously, this was Lucy's daughter, but she spoke with a south London accent, harsh and unlovely in its delivery, and her plaited hair and rough clothes would have told a stranger of long, hard struggles on an under-supported housing estate, not weekends with her grandfather, the baronet. Having known Lucy at roughly the same age, I can testify that they could have come from different galaxies for all they shared. Why don't parents mind this? Or don't they notice it? Isn't the desire to bring up your young with the habits and customs of your own tribe one of the most fundamental imperatives in the animal kingdom? Nor is this restricted to any one part of our society. Everywhere in modern Britain parents are raising cuckoos, aliens from a foreign place.

The newcomer paid no attention to me. She was obviously solely concerned in obtaining an answer to her query. 'Did you get it, Mum?' The words hung sharply in the air.

Lucy nodded. 'I've got it. But they only had it in blue.'

'Oh, no.' I write 'Oh, no,' but, in truth, it was much nearer 'ow now.' She sounded like Eliza Doolittle before Higgins has taken her on. 'I wanted the pink one. I told you I wanted the pink one [i.e. Oi wan'ed ve pink wun].'

Lucy's even, patient tone never wavered

throughout. 'They didn't have any left in pink, so I thought blue was better than nothing.'

'Well, you were wrong.' The girl flounced off, sighing and stamping her way upstairs.

Lucy looked at me. 'Do you have children?'

I shook my head. 'I never married.'

She laughed. 'Not quite the same thing these days.'

'Well, I haven't.'

'They drive you completely mad. But of course one couldn't do without them.'

I felt I could do without the recent exhibit pretty easily. 'How many have you got?'

'Three. Margaret's the oldest. She's thirty-seven and a farmer's wife. Then there's Richard, who's thirty and trying to get into the music business. And that one. Kitty. Our surprise.'

Needless to say, the eldest was the object of my special interest. 'And Margaret's marriage has turned out well?'

Lucy nodded. 'I think so. Her husband's not very exciting, to be honest, but nobody's perfect and he is quite . . . steady. That seems to be what she wants.' Thank heaven for small mercies, I thought. 'They've got four children and she still runs her own business. I can't imagine how she manages, but she has sixty times as much energy as any of the rest of us.' An image of Damian hovered over the table.

'They're quite spaced out, then. The children.'

'Yes. Mad, really. Just when one thinks the days of bottle warmers and carting cots round the country are over they begin again. For twenty years, whenever we loaded the car for a weekend away, we looked like refugees trying to get out of

127

Prague ahead of the Russians.' She laughed at the memory. 'Of course, I never meant to start quite so early, but when Margaret—' She broke off, her laugh tapering to a nervous little giggle.

'When Margaret what?'

Lucy gave me a shy glance. 'People don't mind these days so much, but she was already on the way when we got married.'

'I hate to shock you, but most of us had worked out that few healthy babies are born at five months.'

She acknowledged this with a nod. 'Of course. It's just one didn't talk about it then. It all got lost in the wash.' She thought for a moment, then looked up at me. 'Do you ever see anyone from those days? I mean, what brought on this sudden interest?'

I shrugged as nonchalantly as I could manage. 'I don't know. I looked at the map and saw I was passing your front door.'

'But whom do you keep up with?'

I shook my head. 'I'm in a different crowd now. I'm a writer. I get asked to publishers' parties and PEN quiz nights and the Bad Sex Awards. My days of making small talk with countesses from Cumberland are done.'

'Aren't everyone's?'

'I still shoot occasionally. When I'm asked. That's when some red-faced major comes staggering across the room and says "Weren't we at school together?" or "Didn't you come to my sister's dance?" I never get over it. I'm always shocked into silence that I could belong to the same generation as this boring, bibulous old fart.' She did not answer, sensing my evasion. 'I do run into some familiar faces occasionally. I saw Serena at a charity thing not long ago.'

This seemed to confirm an unraised issue. 'Yes, I thought you might have stayed in touch with Serena.'

'But I haven't. Not really.' She raised an eyebrow quizzically and so, to move things on, I volunteered: 'As a matter of fact I saw Damian Baxter quite recently. Do you remember him?'

The last question was redundant. She had changed colour. 'Of course I remember him. I was there, remember.'

I nodded. 'Of course you were.'

'Anyway, even without that nobody forgets the Heartbreaker of the Year.' This time her laugh had a slightly bitter twinge. 'I gather he's terribly rich now.'

'Terribly rich and terribly ill.'

Which sobered her up. 'I'm sorry. Is he going to be all right?'

'I don't think so.'

'Oh.' This information appeared to put her bitterness back into its cage, and she became more philosophical. 'It used to make me laugh to think how our mothers steered us away from him. Had they but known at the time, he was almost the only man we ever danced with who could have kept the show on the road. Did he marry?'

'Yes, but not for long and no one you'd know.'

She absorbed this. 'I was terribly keen on him.'

I found myself becoming rather irritated by my own apparent ignorance. 'You wouldn't have known it,' I said.

'That was only because you were starting to hate him by that stage. I'd never have dared tell you.

Are you disappointed in me?'

'A bit. You always pretended to dislike him as much as I did. Even before. Even when he and I were friends.'

She passed easily over my contradiction. 'Well . . .' Her voice had now progressed through philosophical to wistful. 'It was a long time ago.' Then, as if ashamed of her momentary retreat, she rallied. 'I'd have married him if he'd proposed.'

'What would your mother have said about that?'

'I wouldn't have cared what she said. In fact, at one point I thought I was going to have to force him.' This was accompanied by a little, indignant puff. I looked at her, waiting for an explanation. She smirked. 'When I started Margaret I wasn't *completely* sure whose she was.' Naturally, this almost made me cry out. Could I have scored a goal with the very first kick? It was with some difficulty that I kept quiet and let her finish her story. 'I wasn't really going out with Damian at that stage, but then there was a moment, one afternoon in Estoril.' She gave an embarrassed giggle. 'You were all on the terrace and I sneaked off, and . . .' I suppose I must have looked disapproving in some way as she gave a little, comic snort. 'It was the Sixties! Did we use the term "Wild Child"? Had it been invented by then? I can't remember. Anyway, I suppose I was one. It's funny, because Margaret is *much* the straightest of my children. The only one who's straight at all, really.'

This was a familiar situation to me. 'Our parents used to talk about the problem child in any family,' I said. 'Now, it seems to be more the norm to have one child who isn't a problem. If you're lucky.'

Lucy laughed. 'Well, that's Margaret in this house. It's odd, when you think of it, because we had quite a scare with her when she was little.'

'What sort of scare?'

'Heart. Which seems so cruel for a child, doesn't it? She developed something called familial hypercholesterolaemia.'

'Blimey.'

'I know. It was about a month before I even learned to say it.'

'It trips off your tongue now.'

'You know how it is. At the start you can't pronounce it and by the end you're qualified to open a clinic.' She vanished momentarily into that never quite forgotten, terrible episode in her life. 'Funny. I can almost laugh about it, but it was unbelievably ghastly at the time. It means you're making far too much cholesterol, which eventually gives you a heart attack and kills you. Of course, nowadays no sentence is complete without that word but then it was foreign and frightening. And apparently it had always been more or less a hundred per cent fatal. The first doctor who diagnosed it in Margaret, at some hospital in Stoke, thought it still was. So you can imagine what we went through.'

'What were you doing in Stoke?'

'I can't remember now. Oh, I think Philip had an idea of reviving a china factory. It didn't last long.' I'd had another glimpse of the tangled odyssey that was Philip's non-career. 'Anyway, my mother turned up and scooped us off to a specialist in Harley Street and the news improved.'

'So it was treatable by the time Margaret had it?'

She nodded, reliving her relief. 'Completely, thank God. But only just. Literally, it had all changed something like four years before. It took us ages to get over the shock. We were both in the grip of terror for months. I remember getting up one night and finding Philip bending over her cot and crying. We never talk about it now, but whenever I get cross with him I secretly think of that moment and forgive him.' She hesitated, contradicted inwardly by the Spirit of Honesty. 'Or I try to,' she added. I nodded. I could easily see why. The Philip who wept for his innocent child in a darkened nursery sounded not only much nicer but a thousand times more interesting than the ballroom show-off I had known. Lucy was still talking. 'What we couldn't understand was that we kept being told it was completely hereditary, but neither of us had any knowledge of its occurring in our families. We questioned our parents and so on, but there was no clue. Still, as I say, Mummy found us a wonderful doctor and once we'd nailed it properly it came right.' She paused. I would guess she didn't venture into this territory very often. 'I always think that Margaret's passion for normal, ordinary life was probably fostered by that early threat of losing it. Don't you agree?'

Obviously, this entire speech went straight to the heart of the case that had brought me to Kent, but before I could say another word I was aware of a presence in the door. 'Hello, stranger.' The battered, bloated figure of a man who bore only the slightest resemblance to the boy I had known as Philip Rawnsley-Price was standing there. In our salad days Philip had resembled a young and much better-looking, cheeky-chappy actor called

Barry Evans, famous then for a film, *Round the Mulberry Bush*, in which he represented those of us who wanted to be trendy but didn't quite know how, a large group at any time, which ensured his popularity. Sadly, his stardom didn't last and the former actor was found dead in the company of an empty whisky bottle at the age of fifty-two, having spent the previous three years driving a taxi in Leicester. I seem to recall there was some pressure on the police to investigate the circumstances of Evans's death, involving, as they did, cut telephone wires and other peculiar details, which naturally gave his relatives concern, but the police could not be bothered. A decision that might, I imagine, have been different had the unfortunate Mr Evans died at the peak of his fame.

Looking at Philip, framed in the doorway, it was hard not to feel at that moment, that the fate which had engulfed him was almost as bad. He wore ancient, stained cords, scuffed loafers and an open-necked check shirt with a worn, frayed collar. Old clothes were obviously a family uniform. Like me, he had put on weight and his hair was thinning. Unlike me, he had developed the mottled red face of a drinker. More than anything it was the sagging, tired look about those poached-egg eyes, so characteristic of the born privileged who fail, that gave him away. He held out his hand with what he imagined to be a roguish grin. 'Good to see you, old chap. What brings you to this part of the forest?' He took hold of my fingers and gave them the ruthless, wince-making squeeze that such men use in a vain attempt to persuade you they are still in charge. Lucy, having waxed so lyrical about him, now seemed put out to be interrupted.

'What are you doing here? We were coming over as soon as we'd finished lunch. Who's in the shop?'

'Gwen.'

'On her own?' Her voice was sharp and admonitory. And it was directed to include me. It was obviously her deliberate intention to show me that her husband was an incompetent fool. One minute earlier we had been swept up in the moving pathos of the tear-drenched daddy, but now it was apparently necessary for Lucy to point out that things had not gone wrong in their lives because of *her*. On the face of it this behaviour was of course illogical and contradictory, but among these people it is not uncommon. Their marriage had clearly reached that stage where she, and probably he, could be generous and gallant about the other when they were apart, but the actual physical presence of their partner would set their teeth on edge. This emotional conundrum often occurs in a culture where divorce is still seen as essentially giving in. Even today, the upper and upper middle classes find personal unhappiness, at any rate the admission of it, tedious and ill-bred, and they must always talk in public, or to close friends for that matter, as if everything to do with their family situation were going tremendously well. Maintaining the legend is the preferred option for most of them, as long as nobody is in the room whose presence undermines the performance. They generally adhere to this, right up to the moment of blow-up. It can be quite odd for members of this social group, as their circle will often contain many couples who appear to be perfectly content, until a call out of the blue, or a

scribbled line in a Christmas card, will suddenly announce the divorce.

Philip nodded in answer to her harsh interrogation. 'She can manage. Nobody's been in for more than an hour.' There was a kind of resigned hopelessness in this simple account of the state of his business. In the area of his professional activity Philip had lost the energy required by pretence. He could just about stand behind the counter, but to talk up his drudgery would have been too exhausting. He picked a spoon off the counter and started to feed himself out of the pasta pot. 'Lucy tells me you're a writer now? What have you written that I might have read?'

Naturally, this was a defensive attempt to diminish me and my activities, but I do not believe it was malicious. He suspected, rightly, that I was judging him, so he was showing that he reserved the right to judge me. Anyone of my kind and my generation who has chosen to make their living in the Arts will be familiar with this treatment. In our youth the careers we had decided on were considered completely mad, by our parents and by our friends, but as long as we were struggling our more sober contemporaries were happy to encourage and sympathise and even to feed us. The trouble came when we arty folk achieved any kind of success. Then the idea that we should be making money or, worse, making more money than our adult and sensible acquaintance, was akin to impertinence. They had chosen the boring route in order to be secure. To have achieved security but to have enjoyed jokes and larks along the way was little short of irresponsible and deserved to be punished. I smiled. 'Nothing, I should think. Since

135

if you had read anything by me I have no doubt you would have made the connection.'

He raised his eyebrows at Lucy, comically signifying, presumably, that I was a touchy artist who must be humoured. 'Lucy's read some of your stuff. I gather she thinks very highly of it.'

I did not point out that this remark meant his earlier question had been entirely redundant. 'I'm glad.' My words fell into a silence and we sat for a moment. There was an inertia in the room and we all three felt it. This often happens when old friends get together after an interval of many years. Prior to the meeting they imagine that something explosive and fun will come out of it, but then they are usually faced by a lacklustre group, in late middle age, who have nothing much in common any more. For better or worse, the Rawnsley-Prices had negotiated their journey, I had travelled mine and now we were just three people in a very dirty kitchen who didn't know each other. Besides, I needed further information before my pilgrimage could be considered complete and I wasn't going to get it while Philip was with us. It was time to break up the group. 'Can I see the shop?' I said. There was a pause, with a sense of the unspoken in the air. I assume this was simply Philip's male need to present himself as my equal in terms of worldly success which, modest as mine has been, might prove hard when I had actually seen the business. Or maybe it was Lucy's sudden realisation that for the same reason I was not going to take away from our day spent together the idea that everything was going swimmingly. It is an unspoken ambition for most of us that our contemporaries should see us as

136

successful, but in Lucy's case she was about to be denied it.

After a pause, Philip nodded. 'Of course.'

It will come as no surprise that the farm shop was a hopeless place. Fittingly, I suppose, it was housed in a former cattle shed, which had been converted quickly and with insufficient money. There was a cheery, if forced, optimism in the inevitable pine counters and shelves. Above them, brightly coloured cards in *faux*, red, giant handwriting proclaimed the scintillating array of produce on offer: '*Fresh* vegetables!' they shouted. '*Home made* Jams and Jellies!' But in that yawning, unpeopled space they took on a dismal, pathetic quality, like someone eating alone in a paper hat. The floor was cheap and the ceiling had not been properly finished and, as I could have predicted, the whole place was full of items no one in their right mind would ever want to buy. Not just tinned pâté made from wild boar or goose wings, but gadgets to prevent wine losing its flavour in the fridge and woolly things to wear inside your boots while fishing. Christmas stocking presents to be bought and given by someone who knows nothing about it. The meat counter looked particularly unattractive, even to a carnivore like me, and seemed actively to repel further investigation. A single customer was paying for a cauliflower. Other than that the place was deserted. We looked around in silence. 'The trouble is all these shopping malls—' Philip drawled the word in a bad, American accent, trying to convert his pain into a joke. 'They're building them everywhere. It's impossible to match the prices without going broke.' I hesitated to

137

mention that they seemed to be going broke anyway. 'We keep being told that everyone's environmentally conscious nowadays, that they care about where their food comes from, but . . .' He sighed. What might have been intended as an ironic shrug just turned into a sad sag of his shoulders. I freely confess I felt tremendously sorry for him in that moment. Whether or not I used to dislike him, I had after all known him for a very long time and I did not wish him ill.

It is a fact that in the brutal periods of history, what changes is not the cutting edge of every new market, or the ambition that drives a new factory owner or a new hostess, or a new conquest from the performing stage, or a new triumph in a political drawing room. All that is constant. It is the level of coasting that goes on behind the bright and harsh façade that is different. In a gentle era— and my youth was passed in a fairly gentle era— people of little ability could drift by in every class, at every level of society. Jobs were found for them. Homes were arranged. Someone's uncle sorted it out. Someone's mother put in a word. But when things get tough, when, as now, the prizes are bigger but the going is rougher, the weaklings are elbowed aside until they fall back and slip over the cliff. Unskilled workers or stupid landowners alike, they are crushed by a system they cannot master and find themselves ejected on to the roadside. Just such a one was Philip Rawnsley-Price. Subconsciously, he thought his *braggadocio* would carry him through, that he had the charm and the connections to make it work, however he might choose to live his life. Alas, his connections were the wrong connections and his charm was non-existent, and now he was in his late fifties there was no one left alive who cared much whether he swam or sank.

I had never taken to Philip when we were young, but I pitied him now. He had been defeated by our 'interesting times' and he would not rise again. A hand-to-mouth existence lay ahead, of inheriting a cottage from a cousin and trying to rent it out, of hoping he would be remembered when the last aunt bit the dust, of wondering if his children might manage a little something for him on a regular basis. That was what he had to look forward to and it was anyone's guess whether Lucy would hang around to share it. It rather depended on what alternatives presented themselves. All this we both knew as we shook hands awkwardly outside. 'Come back and see us again,' he said, knowing that I never would.

'I will,' I lied.

'Don't leave it so long the next time.' And he was gone, back to his vacant counters and his empty till.

Lucy followed me to the car. I stopped. 'Did you ever get to the bottom of Margaret's condition?' She looked at me, puzzled, for a moment. 'You said it was hereditary but there was no trace of it on either your side or Philip's.'

'That was the thing. Of course I had the most nerve-racking suspicions. I kept thinking I ought to be poring through Damian's medical records . . .'

'But you didn't.'

'No. I was about to confess and suggest it, with a sinking heart as you can imagine, when we found out that Philip's aunt, his mother's eldest sister, had died of it, the very same thing, in childhood.

139

And his mother never knew. Nor did either of her siblings. You can imagine how it was in those days.' She gave a little grimace. 'They were all just told that our Father in heaven had taken their sister because he loved her. Basta.'

'How did you find out?'

'Total luck. My ma-in-law was talking to *her* mother, who must have been about a million by then, and for some strange reason she told her all about Margaret. We'd never explained to Granny what was wrong, because we didn't want to worry her. At any rate this time she finally learned the truth, and right away she started weeping like a fire hydrant and it all came pouring out.'

'Poor woman.'

'Yes. Poor old thing. Of course she blamed herself and it more or less finished her off. We all told her that it wasn't her fault, that it wasn't a killer any more and so on, but I don't think it made much difference.' She smiled sadly. 'So the mystery was solved. The tragic thing was that the aunt could so easily have been saved with the right drugs but it happened in the twenties, when it was a question of hot drinks and cold compresses and having your tonsils out on the kitchen table. Anyway, as I say, Margaret's been fine ever since.'

'Were you at all sorry?'

This time she was genuinely bewildered. 'About what?'

'That she was definitely Philip's and not Damian's.' This was unkind of me, since it would hardly help her to dwell on heaven, trapped, as she was, in an outer circle of hell.

But Lucy only smiled and, just for a second, the minxish child-woman she had once been, looked

140

out from behind her wrinkles. 'I'm not sure. Not at the time, because the whole drama had been explained and that was *such* a relief. Later, maybe. A little. But please don't give me away.'

We'd kissed and I was back in the car, when she tapped on the window. 'If you see him . . .'

I waited. 'Yes?'

'Tell him I remember him. Wish him luck for the future.'

'That's the point. I don't think he's got a future. Not a very long one, anyway.'

This made her silent and, to my amazement, I thought for a second she was going to cry. At last she spoke again, with a softer and more gentle voice than I had heard from her since my arrival. Or indeed, ever. 'All the more so, then. Give him my best love. And say that I wish him nothing but good things. Nothing but good, good things.' She stepped back from the vehicle and I nodded. Her simple encomium spoke more for Damian's treatment of her than I would have credited him with.

The interview was over. I put my foot on the accelerator and started on the road back to London.

Dagmar

FIVE

Her Royal Highness Princess Dagmar of Moravia, despite her name, was a mousy, timid, little character. She had an apologetic, poignant manner, as if she were aware of always being disappointing, which I am sorry to say was usually true where we were concerned, because we all wanted to like her more than we did. You will probably not believe me, or put it down to excessive snobbery on my part, but the tiny Princess and her enormous mother, the Grand Duchess, were immensely impressive to us all in those dim and distant days. Nobody could believe more firmly than I in the miracle of constitutional monarchy, but the years of constant exposure in every branch of the media has inevitably resulted in a certain devaluation of Royal blood, as the public came to realise that for the most part these men and women, often pleasant, sometimes intelligent, occasionally physically attractive, are no more remarkable than any other person one might stand behind at the grocer's or the bank. Only Her Majesty, by never being interviewed, by never revealing an opinion, has retained a genuine mystery. Of course, we the public love to conjecture what her response to something might be. 'She must hate this,' we say. Or 'How pleased she will be about that.' But we do not know and it is our own ignorance that fascinates us.

If you can imagine it, forty years ago, we had that fascination for virtually anyone with genuine Royal blood in their veins. I don't just mean snobs.

Everyone. Because we knew nothing, we wondered about everything and the glamour Royals brought into a social gathering is quite unparalleled today. No film star at the peak of her success can confer anything like the excitement of finding Princess Margaret among the dancers in a ballroom in the Fifties or Sixties. Or at a cocktail party, to walk in and discover a ducal cousin of the Queen chatting in the corner was to know that *this* was the place to be tonight. In my own youth, in 1961 to be exact, my school once bussed all the boys, plus thirty musical instruments, for a bumpy hour across Yorkshire so that we could solemnly stand on the grass verge at the side of the road and cheer the cars carrying the wedding party of the Duke of Kent from York Minster to the bride's home at Hovingham. Six hundred boys, however many buses, a brass band specially rehearsed, all in order to watch some cars that did not stop nor even, as I remember, slow down. Perhaps the bride and groom did a little, at least my image of the young Duchess is in focus, but not the others. The band played, we waved and feverishly shouted our hip-hip-hoorays, the cavalcade shot past, blurred faces in Molyneux and Hartnell, and then they were gone. The whole thing took five minutes from start to finish, if that. Then we climbed back into the buses and returned to school.

So it was that even a member of a minor, deposed Royal house seemed to confer a favour on every invitation they accepted in those dead days, and Dagmar was no exception. Her dynasty, the Grand Ducal House of Moravia, was not in fact very ancient. It had been one of those invented families, installed by the Great Powers in different

Balkan states as the Turkish Empire gradually disintegrated throughout the second half of the nineteenth century. During those years, German and Danish, and in some cases local, princes were pushed on to thrones in Romania and Bulgaria, in Montenegro and Serbia, in Albania and Greece. Just such a one was the mountainous and modest state of Moravia, which bordered on almost all of the above. The Turkish governor having finally retreated in early 1882, a minor princeling of the House of Ludinghausen-Anhalt-Zerbst was selected, largely on the basis of his being a godson of the then Prince of Wales. Whether or not his selection reflected the British Prince's close friendship with the boy's mother at the time of his birth I could not say, although Lord Salisbury was asked by Marlborough House, as a personal favour, to suggest Prince Ernst for the post, thereby signalling our government's approval. Since the territory was not much larger than the estate of an English duke, and considerably less profitable, it was not thought that a kingly crown would be appropriate and at the Settlement of Klasko, in April 1883, the area was solemnly proclaimed a grand duchy.

It must be said that the wife of the new Grand Duke was not enthusiastic. Until then, she had been having quite a jolly time between their home in Vienna and a sporting estate in the Black Forest, and after two years she was still writing to a friend that she thought she lacked an important requirement for the job, namely the smallest desire to remain in Moravia, but the couple persevered with some success. Their new country's good fortune was to be located at a sensitive crossroads of many of the trade routes. This ensured invitations to every Royal fête around the world, as well as cheering offers for their daughters' hands in marriage, and before very long a Russian grand duchess, an Austrian archduchess and a princess of Borbon-Anjou had all begun life in the airless, cramped nurseries of the hideously uncomfortable palace in the capital of Olomouc, a building not much larger than the dean's residence in the close at Salisbury and a lot less manageable to run.

Surprisingly, perhaps, Grand Ducal Moravia made it as far as the Jazz Age, but the forces of Stalin, coupled with a swelling resistance to the monarchist solution, proved the undoing of the dynasty. By 1947 it was over and the ex-reigning Moravian family had taken up residence in a five-storey house in Trevor Square, a pleasant enough location and very convenient for Harrods.

But even easy shopping could not revive the spirits of the defeated Grand Duke and in a matter of months he had given up the unequal struggle. It was at this point that his son, having assumed the grand ducal title, the last of his family to do so, and released perhaps by the demise of his august papa, made a spirited decision that would vastly diminish his chances of regaining the throne of his forebears and vastly increase his chances of living well in the interim. With the dignified, if pained, acceptance of his widowed mother, a princess of a cadet branch of the Hohenzollerns, he contracted to marry the only daughter of a businessman from Leeds, one Harold Swindley, who had made a fortune in self-catering, package holidays. In the following three years, two children had arrived to

148

bless this most sensible of unions, the new, so-called Crown Prince Feodor and his sister, the Princess Dagmar.

But for us, and even more for our parents, the Fall of the House of Moravia was still pretty recent and even the elevation of Miss Marion Swindley could not dim the lustre of a genuine crown. Only twenty years had passed since their deposition when Dagmar arrived at our parties. Besides, the Communist regime that replaced them was not popular, the family was still on the guest list at Buckingham Palace and there was talk at the time of a restoration coming in Spain. In short, forty years ago the Royalist cause didn't seem hopeless by any means.

The new Grand Duchess had delivered. The Swindley money may not have been particularly fragrant but, for the first years of the marriage at least, there was quite a lot of it. And she learned her part pretty well until, like every fervent convert, she was soon *plus Catholique que le Pape*. Admittedly, she was not by any standards a beauty but, as the Dowager Grand Duchess was once heard to sigh when watching her daughter-in-law stump across a drawing room looking like a Marine in training, 'Oh, well. One can't have *everything*,' and nobody could say she was not impressive. Her size alone guaranteed that. Nor was she a fool, having inherited more from her (discreetly invisible) father than she might care to admit in terms of solid, common sense.

For all the bowing and ma'am'ing that still went on in those days, the Grand Duchess understood that no throne awaited her timid daughter in the post-war world. She also knew that she had not anticipated the drain on her capital made by a husband who wished to live *en prince* but did not intend to do a day's work, nor earn a single penny. She was, at heart, a sound northern lass and well aware that no fortune can hope to survive when the expenses are limitless and the income nil, and she was anxious to see the girl settled as well as might be, before the gilt had quite gone off the gingerbread. So she decided that, even though British princesses by that stage never 'came out' in any normal way and only occasionally appeared at the parties of special friends, nevertheless Dagmar would participate fully in the whole year-long business. The girl would thereby build a position for herself in British Society and, with any luck, land one of its prizes. The Grand Duchess also accepted—unlike many, if not most, Royals—that she would have to put her hand in her pocket to achieve this. By 1968, when the Grand Duke had been spending like a sailor for a quarter of a century, this could not have been as easy as it was once, but she had bitten off the mouthful and she fully intended to chew it. I am happy to say I was on the list to be invited.

The inspiration for the party was the Duchess of Richmond's Ball, that famous 1815 gathering, given in Brussels on the very eve of Waterloo, and it was held at the Dorchester in Park Lane. Today, one thinks of the hotel as the haunt of film stars and merchants from the East, but in those days it played quite a major part in what was still referred to as 'Society.' On the night in question we came in, I think, by the ballroom entrance at the side, situated on Park Lane itself, and the theme of the evening was quite clear the moment one stepped

150

inside, into that long, rather low, hall. Liveried footmen stood to attention, all modern signs, 'Exit' and the like, had been hidden behind greenery and there were candles everywhere. None of these last details would be legal today, of course, but nobody cared then. In truth, the party seemed to have taken over most of the ground floor of the hotel. It can't have, really, can it? But that's what it felt like on the night. Of course, we didn't arrive much before eleven, having eaten our dinners elsewhere, and the champagne that greeted us, held out by the white-wigged flunkeys, was not by any means the first drink of the evening. One has to remember that in the late 1960s, while nobody suggested that it was a good idea to drive a car when plastered, it was still long before such considerations had begun to shape our social life. 'Which of you is drinking tonight?' would have bewildered the couple arriving at a dinner, since the answer would invariably have been 'both.' For this reason no hostess scrupled to ask various friends to provide dinners for her guests before a ball.

Later in the Season, when more dances were given in the country, this would entail putting them up for the night, and essentially meant throwing a house party for strangers, who would drunkenly rattle around the countryside in their cars at all hours. But in London the thing was more easily managed. Sometimes you were flattered to receive an invitation to join the dinner provided by the parents of the deb of the evening, but this didn't happen (to me, anyway) all that often and usually a pleasant little postcard would drop through the letter box, saying that the writer believed you were going to the dance being given for So-and-So and she would be 'terribly pleased if you would dine here first.' At the end of which dinner, fairly far gone or at least merry, we would cheerfully climb into our vehicles and head off for the location of the party proper. This system had obvious advantages. The bonus for the young was that the dances went on forever, because they didn't really get going much before eleven. While the benefit for the old was plain economy. The parents of the girl in question usually had to hire the place, at least in London, and even in the country marquees would be expected unless the house was vast. Then there was the music, as well as a pretty good breakfast at the end of the event, but by adopting this system the hosts were spared the additional burden of dinner and wines for three or four hundred young and hungry people. No wonder the custom cheered the fathers up no end.

Having taken in the thoroughness of the arrangements, I made my way into the ballroom and here the illusion was impressive. At that time it was customary for a limited number of the older generation to be invited to these gatherings. They would be drawn from the godparents of the debutante, as well as from the relatives and close friends of her parents, and as a rule they would fringe the proceedings, chatting in some other drawing room, watching the children dancing, occasionally venturing on to the floor to demonstrate an adapted foxtrot or quickstep, before retiring fairly early for the night. They were not expected to participate as full guests since, as we all know, the sight of dancing parents is torture for the young and always was. All this was especially true of costume parties, which are rather a bore for anyone out of their thirties, and the adults would simply arrive in evening dress, occasionally with some gay little gesture, worn as a brooch or a hair ornament. None of which applied to this particular event. I do not know if it was respect for the Grand Duchess or terror (probably the latter), but every single attendee, old and young, was in costume. As a particularly witty detail, or possibly after an instruction from on high, several of the mothers and fathers had deliberately chosen outfits of a slightly earlier date than those worn by their offspring. Men in wigs and ruffles, women in high-piled, powdered hair and beauty spots, from the 1780s or '90s, gave us all the sense that we were indeed back in the Regency and this was the older generation of the day, frowning and disapproving of modern youth. It always amuses me that this particular era, redolent as it is of Versailles and Queen Marie-Antoinette, is such a favourite costume theme with toffs. They seem to have forgotten that it did not as a whole turn out well for the privileged classes, so many of whom would leave their heads, and no doubt wigs, in the basket below the guillotine.

'What have you come as?' Lucy was dressed in a Jane Austen, white frock, high-waisted and pure, with a ribbon round her throat and her artificial ringlets sewn with tiny, white silk roses. She looked artful rather than innocent, but charming nonetheless.

'I'm a hussar,' I replied slightly indignantly, 'I should have thought it was obvious.'

'The trousers are wrong.'

'Thank you for that.' The trousers *were* wrong,

as it happens, but the rest of the outfit was perfect, bright scarlet, heavily braided, with a fur-edged jacket slung between my left shoulder and my right armpit. I thought I looked fabulous. 'They're only wrong for 1815. They would be right by 1850. Anyway, it was the best I could manage. It was too late to find anything in London, so I had to raid the costume store of Windsor Rep.'

'It looks like it.' She stopped and stared round the room, which was beginning to fill up. 'Where was your dinner?'

'Chester Row. The Harington-Stanleys.'

'Any good?'

'Well, the food was like a shooting lunch that had been brought up to London in a rusty cake tin, but it was quite fun apart from that. What about you?'

She grimaced. 'Mrs Vitkov. With a group to meet her daughter, Terry. At that new French place in Lower Sloane Street.'

'The Gavroche?'

'That's it.'

'Lucky you.'

She gave me what used to be called an old-fashioned look. 'Have you met Terry Vitkov?'

'Not yet.'

'Don't.'

'Where are they from? The Balkans?'

'Cincinnati. And believe me, Miss Terry is a piece of work.' She stopped and nodded with a tight smile. 'Careful. That's her.' I turned to look. I could see at once that we needn't have worried and that Terry Vitkov was quite happy to be the subject of our discussion. She looked as if she were more than used to being the centre of attention.

She was a good-looking girl. Indeed, she would have been very good-looking if it were not for a certain prominence of nose and chin, faintly suggesting a Man-in-the-Moon profile, which, combined with the intensity of her piercing and heavily made up eyes, gave her the air of a prisoner on the run, desperately searching the room for either an enemy or an escape route. Tonight she appeared to be dressed as a Regency courtesan, rather than a great-lady-from-times-gone-by, like every other woman there. Indeed, she was more or less the only person in the ballroom, who would patently *not* have figured on the guest list of the real Duchess of Richmond. She walked up to us and we were introduced.

'Lucy's been telling me all the dos and don'ts for getting on in London.' She spoke with a breathy urgency, the voice of one determined to make every human interchange register. I could see at once that despite her flashing frequent smiles, designed no doubt to suggest a spirit of girlish, flirtatious fun and displaying thereby a set of admirably white, if rather large, teeth, Terry Vitkov took herself tremendously seriously.

'I don't think I've covered them all, have I?' said Lucy laconically.

Our companion was already training her searching gaze on the other guests. 'Which one is Viscount Summersby?' she asked.

Lucy checked the ballroom. 'Over there. With the blonde girl in green, next to the big looking glass.'

Terry sought him out. Her shoulders sagged. 'Why do they always have to look like the man from Pest Control?' She sighed. 'Who's that one?'

155

A tall and handsome young man flashed her a smile as he passed.

'Don't bother. No money. No prospects.' Lucy clearly understood her companion's priorities. 'Of course, he's clever and he's headed for the City. He may make something of himself.'

But Terry shook her head. 'That takes twenty years and by the time they've got there they're ready to trade you in for a younger model. No. I want some money from the outset.'

I nodded, sagely. 'But not Lord Summersby.'

She smiled. 'Not until I know I can't get something better.' What made this amusing, of course, was that she meant it.

We had been moving slowly in a rather sloppy presentation line and by now had nearly reached our hosts, who stood, all four together, posed against a rich curtain erected as a kind of screen for the purpose. The Grand Duke cut a melancholy figure. He was a slight and pasty-looking creature anyway, especially when placed at the side of his massive spouse and, in truth, I do not believe I ever heard him say an interesting sentence. He wore his elaborate costume, which I took to be that of the Duke of Richmond, with an air of surprise, as if he had been put into it while under sedation. Perhaps he was. His son, dressed as an officer of the guard, stared straight ahead stiffly. He could have been posing for an early daguerreotype, when you had to keep your head still for four or five minutes until it was done. His bland, mottled face exuded an air of bored and generalised geniality.

The daughter, Dagmar, technically of course the Star of the Night, looked frightened and if anything a little drab. She was a tiny creature, literally no more than five feet tall and, while one is always being told that Queen Victoria was four foot eleven and managed to run an Empire, still for most of us it is very, very small and means you spend your whole life looking up. Standing there in the shadow of her mother, to paraphrase Noël Coward, she looked like the Grand Duchess's lunch. Dagmar wasn't what you would call plain, even if her sallow mini-face was hard to define or at least to categorise. She wasn't exactly pretty either, but her large eyes were arresting and she had a soft, moist, trembling mouth, usually half open and quivering and seeming to suggest she was always on the verge of tears, which, in a way, touched your heart. But she never appeared to have any idea of how to present herself. Her hair, for instance, was very dark and straight and, with imagination, it might have been effective. But it just hung there, as if it had been washed in a hurry and left to dry. I really did think something might have been made of her on the night of her own ball, but as usual nobody had tried. The dress was from the correct period but it was dull, and only faintly enlivened with a thin blue sash beneath her modest bosom. To be honest, she looked as if she had taken five minutes to get ready for a game of tennis, and so fragile that one good, strong puff of wind would carry her out of the window and down Park Lane in an instant.

Which could not be said of her mother. I cannot be sure, to this day, whether the Grand Duchess was intending to impersonate the original Duchess of Richmond. It would seem logical, given the wording of the invitation, but the costume she had

157

chosen was more suitable for a great empress, Catherine the Great maybe, or Maria Teresa, or any other absolute female monarch. Acres of chiffon blew softly this way and that, while a river, a torrent, of purple velvet, embroidered in thick, gold thread, cascaded from her more than ample shoulders to the floor and lay there in massive hillocks and dunes, its ermine trim forming a kind of plinth to set off the huge, majestic figure above. Her bosom, like a rock shelf beneath the sea, was ablaze with diamonds and a sparkling crown-like tiara rose from her lightly sweating brow. I suppose the display was all that remained of the Moravian crown jewels, either that or they had been rented from the Barnum Brothers for the night. This was a scene-stealing one-woman show and none of the others got a look in, least of all the wretched Dagmar who, knowing her mother, must have expected something of the sort. At any rate, while the crowds spun, buzzing, round her mama, she didn't seem unduly put out, unlike the Grand Duke and the Crown Prince who both looked as if they were aching to go home. We were announced.

'Good evening, Ma'am.' I bowed and she accepted my obeisance gracefully. I moved on to her husband. 'Your Royal Highness.' I bowed again. He nodded vacantly, his mind probably on some long-ago Court reception in dark and dusty Olomouc. Leaving him to dream alone, I passed into the body of the room. Looking back, I think that evening was when I first understood what I have now come to recognise all around me, viz. that when it comes to aristocrats, or even royalty, most of the members of those worlds (who have not moved away from the whole performance

158

entirely, that is) fall into separate, apparently similar but in fact quite disparate, groups. The first, made familiar by a million lampoons, have a clear understanding that the world of their youth and their ancestors has changed and will not be coming back, but they continue to mourn it. The cooks and the valets, the maids and the footmen who made life so sweet will never again push through the green baize door, busy with the tasks of the day. The smiling grooms who brought the horses round to the front at ten, the chauffeurs washing their gleaming vehicles, standing in deference when one strolled into the stable yard, the gardeners ducking out of sight at the sound of a house party's approach, all that army dedicated to their pleasure have left for other climes. These people usually know, too, albeit half subconsciously, that the deference they still receive within their social circle is somehow thin and even false, compared to the real respect accorded to their parents and grandparents, when high birth had solid accountable value. They know these things, but they do not know what to do about them, other than to weep and live out their lives with as much comfort as they can muster.

Into this category one could squarely place the last Grand Duke of Moravia. There was something in his aimless and depressive grace that told of his awareness of the truth. 'Don't blame me,' he seemed to be saying. 'I understand this is absurd. I know you have no reason to bow and scrape before me, that the game is over, that the band has played, but I have to go through the forms, don't you know? I have to look as if I take it seriously or I would be letting other people down.' This was the text permanently hovering in the air above him. Of course, the same group boasts a nastier version. 'It may be over,' they flash from their pitiless eyes, 'but it isn't quite over for *me!*' and they toss their heads and prey on their rich, social-climbing acolytes and sell the last of their mother's jewels, that the show may struggle on for a few more years at least.

But the other category in this group is different from these and, as a type, is largely undetected by the general public. These men and women also have the status that pertains to them from the old system and they enjoy it. They like the rank and the history that supports them. They are glad to be seen as part of the inner circle of aristocratic Britain. They make sure that one member at least of the Royal Family is present at every major bash they throw. They dress, at least the men dress, to please the diehards. They shoot, they fish, they know their historic dates and other people's genealogy. But all the time they are pretending. Far from being bewildered as to the workings of the new and harsher century, they understand precisely how it turns. They know the value of their property, just as they knew it would regain it. They fully grasp the intricacies of the markets, how and what to buy, what and when to sell, how to achieve the right planning permissions, how to manipulate the payments from the EU farming policy, in short, how to make the estate, and their position, pay.

They decided long ago that they did not want to belong to some fading club, endlessly nostalgic for better days that will never come again. They wanted to retake a position of influence and even power and if it was not, after the 1960s, to be overtly political power then so be it, they would find another route. They are fakes, really. Despite their lineage, despite their houses and their jewels and their wardrobes and their dogs, despite their mouthing the traditional prejudices of their class, they no longer think like most of their own kind. They belong to today and tomorrow, far more than to yesterday. They have brains and values as tough as any hedge fund manager's. But then again, they would argue that they are only being true to their own race, truer than the defeatists, because the primal job of any aristocrat is to stay on top. Bourbon or Bonaparte, king or president, the real aristocrat understands who is in power and who should be bowed to, next.

Of course, forty years ago much of this was hidden from us. The old world had taken a swingeing blow during and after the war from which it was deemed unlikely to recover. Everyone lamented the end in unison and it was only much later that we began to realise we were not all in the same boat as we had thought, and that some families had not, after all, trodden the same downward path, whatever they may have said at the time. In many cases it was my own generation, debutantes then, with brothers at university or just starting out in the city, who began secretly to reject the notion of going down with the ship and started looking about for ways to get back to dry land. These would prove the survivors, and this group was the one to which the Grand Duchess of Moravia, in contrast to her fatalistic spouse, was drawn, even before it was truly formed. She wanted to create a beachhead within the new world, from which to re-launch the family. I liked her for it.

The music was starting now, a group had taken up their positions on the modest stage and were performing cover versions of the current top ten. They were not, I think, a very famous group, but at least they had been on television, which seemed considerably more exciting then than it does now, and couples were drifting on to the floor at the end of the long chamber. The ancient parents, sitting in their costumes on sofas against the wall, were less helpful to this part of the evening and several of them, sensing it, rose and moved towards the doorway leading to the sitting-out rooms and the bar. Lucy and I walked forward. As we did so there was a slight murmur of jostling admiration and I caught a glimpse of Joanna Langley surrounded by her customary group of admirers. She was brilliantly dressed as Napoleon's sister, Princess Pauline Borghese. Her costume, unlike mine or most of the others, was new, copied, presumably for the occasion, from a portrait by David. Of course, the Princess would have been an unlikely guest at a ball given by her brother's arch enemies and anyway, Joanna's modern, celluloid beauty made her unconvincing as a period piece, but she was a joy to look at all the same.

The group shifted a little and I was surprised to see the familiar figure of Damian Baxter standing next to her. As I watched, he leaned in and whispered into her ear. She laughed, nodding a hello to me as she did so and thereby drawing me to Damian's attention. I walked over. 'You never said you were coming to this,' I said.

'I wasn't sure I would, until this afternoon. Then

162

I suddenly thought "what the hell," got on a train and here I am.'

'You never said you'd been invited.'

He fixed me with a look, the corners of his mouth twitching. 'I wasn't.'

I stared at him. Did I feel a slight trace of Baron Frankenstein's terror, when his monster first moved of its own volition? 'You mean you've gatecrashed,' I said. He smiled covertly by way of an answer.

Lucy had been listening to this. 'How did you get your costume at such short notice?' And what a costume. In contrast to mine, with its wrong trousers and slightly rubbed sleeves, Damian looked as if the outfit had been made for him by a master tailor. He was not an officer, as most of the men in the room had chosen to be, but a dandy, Beau Brummell or Byron or someone similar, with a tightly fitting tailcoat hugging his torso, and buckskin breeches and high, polished boots to show off his legs. A dazzling cravat of white silk was wound round his neck and tucked into the brocade waistcoat beneath. Lucy nodded at me. 'He had to go out to Windsor Rep and that was what they came up with.'

Damian looked at me. 'Poor you. Never mind.' Any notion I'd cherished of looking rather good withered and died, as Damian chattered on in his light, unconcerned way. 'I got a friend to sort one out at the Arts Theatre, in case I wanted to come. She managed to get it ready in time and that's what decided me.' I'll bet she did, I thought. Some wretched girl, pricking her fingers to the bone, standing over the washing machine at midnight, burning her hand on the iron. I'll bet she did. And what would be her reward? Not to be loved by Damian. Of that I was quite sure.

Today, pushing into such a function would be a good deal harder than it was forty years ago. The endless security consciousness of the present generation, to say nothing of their self-importance, ensures guards and lists and ticking and 'please bring this invitation with you' to every gathering more exclusive than a sale at Tesco. But it was different then. There was a general supposition that people who hadn't been invited to something did not, as a rule, try to attend it. In other words, what the gatecrasher of those days relied on, what he or she required, was only nerve, nothing more, which, naturally, Damian had in plentiful supply. But I had less than he and I did not want to be seen chatting to someone who might be thrown out at any moment. I despise myself now when I think of it, but I took Lucy's arm and steered her on to the floor.

'You can't keep a good man down,' said Lucy cheerily. But I wasn't inclined to see the funny side. Drowning in my youthful egotism, I could only fear that Damian's appearance might in some way damage me.

He, needless to say, was enjoying himself enormously. I could see at once that, like a child who will be naughty until it is smacked or a gambler who must play until he loses, Damian had to promote his uninvited appearance until somehow the law enforcers registered it. He danced first with Joanna, as if to announce his arrival. He was the best-looking man in the room and she was the best-looking woman in Europe, so they made quite a pair. Other couples turned to

164

watch them and admire, parents glanced over and asked each other about the glorious duo. A little while later, the ball now well and truly under way, the band announced an eightsome reel. It may seem curious to a modern reader that we should have danced a Scottish reel in the middle of a perfectly normal party, not at some Caledonian festival or even a Burns Night in Kircaldy, but we did. In fact, we danced it at most of the parties that year and, with the steps demanding a less cluttered and less crowded floor, it was a sure way to be noticed, so it came as no surprise to see Damian walking forward to take his place in one of the sets with Terry Vitkov on his arm. She gleamed and beamed, this way and that, clearly enjoying her newly found status as troublemaker, as she leaned proudly on the arm of the rebel. I wondered later whether it was at this particular party that Damian's own position began to shift from social observer (or climber, depending on your generosity of vision) to subversive. From admiring student to hostile agent. Am I jumping the gun and did it remain in the balance that night? Or had he already decided he hated us all?

Watching them take their places, waiting for the chord that would start us off, it struck me then that he and Terry were rather a good pair. Both outsiders in their different ways, both with everything to gain from the future and nothing to lose with the vanishing past. I assumed she had money—she did, but less than I thought at the time—just as I assumed that Damian would make money—again, I was right. He did. And much more than I thought at the time. Might they not combine and conquer the world? They were both

165

adventurers. Why should they not join forces?

I was partnering a rather dull girl from somewhere near Newbury and now we set off, marching round in our hand-held circles. Glancing across, I was momentarily impressed by the skills Damian had already acquired in this, so recently foreign, territory. He knew the steps and performed them well; he took his turn in the centre of the ring without a trace of self-consciousness, holding himself erect, executing the different parts of the reel with a degree of grace and dignity I could not have claimed for myself. He chatted to the girls around him and to the other men, part of their crowd now, part of their world, after only a few cocktail parties and dances. We had almost forgotten that we did not know him.

After that the pop group resumed, but Damian showed no sign of flagging. He danced with plenty of the girls, Lucy Dalton and a raucous, ruddy-faced Candida Finch among them. He was about to dance with Georgina Waddilove, who would certainly have betrayed her country to make him stay by her side, but in that instant, just as the music started he seemed to get a stitch and beg her, instead, to join him in a drink. I lost sight of him as they drifted away together into the room serving as a bar. It is hard, looking back, to state with any accuracy my precise feelings at that stage towards this cuckoo I had brought into the nest. As I have said, I'd begun to suspect he had an agenda more complicated than I had first understood, but I still admired his chutzpah, and never more so than when he returned to the ballroom that evening. Somehow, while he was away, a happy

166

conjunction had allowed him to achieve what he came for. To my amazement and the admiration of all those present who knew he was there illegitimately, he reappeared in the open doorway leading the hostess, at least the girl who but for her indomitable mother should have been the centre of the evening, Princess Dagmar herself, onto the dance floor. It was a slow number. The lights were lowered, the band strummed away and, in full view of her guests, Dagmar slipped her arms round the interloper and pressed her tiny face into his chest. Lightly caressing her lank hair as they smooched, Damian noticed me watching him from across the floor. He caught my eye. And winked.

The trouble, which I suppose we all knew would come in the end, happened at the breakfast and in a way it was a miracle it was delayed until then. The custom, at every private dance, was to provide breakfast towards the finish, starting usually at about half past one or so. These repasts varied in quality and were sometimes, frankly, not worth waiting for but the Grand Duchess had clearly invoked the old proverb of 'in for a penny, in for a pound' and laid on the best the hotel was capable of, which was very good indeed. We waited in a group, rather than a queue, ready to help ourselves to eggs and bacon and sausages and mushrooms, all laid out before us in silver chafing dishes.

Damian was standing a little ahead of me. He appeared to have resigned his charge of Dagmar, who was nowhere to be seen, but moved on to the equally great, or greater, prize of Serena, who was as animated as I had ever seen her, laughing and chatting, and leaning her head close to his. I remember I was surprised at the time to register how well they appeared to know each other. She had come as Caroline Lamb dressed as a page, taken from the famous portrait by Thomas Phillips and, of course, the trim tailoring of her velvet coat, displaying, as it did, her wonderful legs in stockings and knee breeches, made all the other girls present look stuffy and dowdy by comparison. Damian, at her side, was a convincing Byron and perhaps that had been the original idea behind his costume. In fact, they could almost have planned it, they made so well-matched a pair. Serena was not as beautiful as Joanna Langley—no woman was—but she had a fineness of feature that offset it. In short, they looked wonderful together and once again Damian found himself the cynosure of all eyes. 'Excuse me, Sir, but do you have an invitation?' The voice, loud and with a trace of a Midlands accent, transcended the chatter and hung like a seagull in the air above us.

The question had come so entirely out of the blue that it succeeded in silencing everyone present. I saw one girl stop dead, half a fried egg hanging from a spoon until it slipped and fell back on to the plate beneath. A suited man, presumably a manager or something similar, was standing next to Damian. He was standing too close, impertinently close. So close that he was obviously using his closeness to express that he belonged there, in this room, in this hotel, but that in his opinion Damian Baxter did not. Of course, the truth was more complicated. Most of those present knew that Damian did not have an invitation, but he had been present at the party for so long by that stage that for the majority this argument seemed to have become semantic. He had not created a

168

disturbance, he had not got drunk, he had not been rude, all the things that people dread from gatecrashers had simply not happened. Besides, he knew many of the other guests. He had come as a friend and chosen the correct costume. He had danced and talked and even partnered the girl whose ball it was, for heaven's sake. What more did they want? The answer to this was, apparently, proof of an invitation. He blushed, something I do not believe I ever saw him do again. 'Look,' he said softly, laying a placatory hand gently on the man's grey, worsted sleeve.

'No, Sir. *You* look.' If anything the voice was getting louder and word had spread. Couples drifted into the breakfast room from the dancing next door to see what was going on. 'If you do not have an invitation I must ask you to leave.' Ill-advisedly, after shaking Damian's hand away, he tried to take hold of his elbow, but Damian was too quick for him and almost danced backwards to free himself. At this moment Serena, alone in that company decided to intervene. In my craven silence I admired her enormously.

'I am perfectly happy to vouch for Mr Baxter, if that would make any difference.' Judging by the man's expression it did not look at first as if it would. 'My name is Lady Serena Gresham, and you will find it on the guest list.' Now, what was peculiarly interesting about this was Serena's mention of her rank, something she would normally never have done; not if it meant having her tongue torn out. It is hard to understand for those who were not there, but the years of the 1960s were an odd, transitional period when it came to titles. I mean, of course, real titles, hereditary titles. Because at that precise moment of our history nobody quite knew what their future might be. An unspoken agreement between the parties not to create any more of them seemed to have been reached in about 1963 and the belief at that time, certainly outside aristocratic circles, was that the world was changing into a different place and that, among these changes soon, perhaps very soon, the status of a life peerage would far exceed that of an inherited one. In short, that the prominence of the ancient, great families would be vastly diminished in favour of the new people on their way up. But alongside this official doctrine (promoted by the media at the time and still touchingly upheld today by a few politicians and the more optimistic worthies of the Left), there was nevertheless a sneaking suspicion that despite confident pronouncements from the pundits on the subject, this would not prove quite true and that a historic name would continue to have muscle in modern Britain. It was not unlike Mr Blair's attempt to rebrand the country Cool Britannia. There was a period when everyone thought it might work, then a second chapter when the media would insist the experiment was working even though we all knew it wasn't and finally a universal acknowledgement, from Left and Right, that it had been a ridiculous and colossal failure.

But, at the time this contradictory attitude towards hereditary rank meant that as a weapon, titles had to be used circumspectly and that all public display was self-defeating. Just as anyone who shouts 'Do you know who I am?' at a hotel or airline employee immediately forfeits what little advantage they might possibly have gained from their position.

Forty years later all this has altered. After half a century, while a life peerage is a perfectly respectable honour, it is only really meaningful in a political context. In smart society it has failed to garner any real aura or kudos beyond that of a knighthood. Mrs Thatcher tried to acknowledge this with a few hereditary creations in the early 1980s, but she was not supported and after that the nobility remained shut, despite continuing to dominate the social pyramid unchallenged. In fact, when toffs *are* given life peerages they tend to wear them lightly as if anxious to show that they do not take their new rank seriously. 'We're just the day boys,' said one to me recently. Obviously, the old system should either be reopened or abolished, since the present situation should be judged untenable in any democratic society, but there is little sign of reform. Instead, today, up and down the land the descendants of some lucky mayor or banker in the Twenties, reign graciously over us, while the great of our own day, often with far more significant achievements than the forebears of the grandees present, give place and sit forever below the salt.

The point is that today Serena would never question the advantage of her position and using it in this context would almost certainly work. But in those days, forty years ago, it was an act of bravery for her to hold it up and risk a potshot. She was right to be diffident, since it was clear her intervention wouldn't do the trick. The man stared at her officiously. 'I'm very sorry, Your Ladyship,' he started, 'I'm afraid—'

'This is absolutely ridiculous!' Dagmar's shrill

cry rang out across the room. One of her striking and even poignant qualities was the absolute Englishness of her voice, making her foreign name and rank feel even stranger. And it was not just English, but a sound from the England of sixty years before, the voice of a miniature duchess opening a charity bazaar in 1910. She strode towards the table, pushing the crowd apart as she came, like a Munchkin general. 'Of course Damian does not have to go!'

This complication really flummoxed the man. 'But Her Royal Highness asked most particularly—'

'Her Royal Highness doesn't know anything about it!'

'Oh, I think I *do!*' The vast bulk of the Grand Duchess was now added to the mix. The guests fell back as she swept majestically through the room, a re-enactment of Sherman marching through Georgia, scorching the earth on her journey, accompanied by, interestingly, Andrew Summersby, who hovered beside her like a small and ugly tug in the shadow of an ocean-going liner. 'I'm very sorry, Mr Baxter, I am sure you did not mean to offend in any way.' She paused for breath and I saw Damian try to cut in, presumably with a view to improving his chances, but she was not interested in a dialogue, only in a statement of policy. 'However, I feel there are rules in these things and they must be adhered to.' She smiled to sugar the pill. 'We can't risk Society crashing down about our ears. I hope you won't think too harshly of me.'

'No, indeed,' said Damian waggishly, still hoping to regain his balance.

'But Damian *was* invited!' The cry came from a hideously embarrassed Dagmar. Naturally it made an interesting contribution to the argument. The crowd's eyes swung towards her, like the audience of the tennis match in Hitchcock's *Strangers on a Train*. 'I invited him!' I am sure everyone present knew this was a lie, but it was a gallant and generous lie, and it sent her higher in the estimation of her guests, most of whom were not particularly fond of her before that night, despite their readiness to take full advantage of her hospitality. I say this so you may know that her intervention did achieve some good. As an argument against her mother's decision it was of course completely fatuous.

'Excuse me, my dear, but Mr Baxter was *not* invited. Not by you. And, more to the point, not by *me*.' The Grand Duchess's tone brooked no argument. She had not finished. 'This was something he made quite clear within earshot of Lord Summersby, who was good enough to bring it to my attention. I would go so far as to say that Mr Baxter was *boasting* of his lack of invitation.' The shade of the Grand Duchess's face was darkening and it was not a becoming alteration. Coupled with the primary colours of her costume, she was beginning to resemble a blow-up Santa Claus hovering between the buildings in Regent Street at Christmas; but, as always with her, there was a quality to be reckoned with. I especially enjoyed a slight flavour of Eastern Europe in her voice as her rage intensified, as if her duty towards her people—subjects in a country which, lest we forget, she had never even visited—had somehow infused her with a new and different past, washing away her healthy, early years in West Yorkshire and making her Moravian in spite of herself.

Her words had naturally revealed who was to blame for the incident, which I would like to describe as 'horrid,' but which had, of course, completely *made* the party for most of those present. The sneak responsible was none other than Andrew Summersby. I would guess that this public unveiling was not part of his original plan and he looked uncomfortable as the eyes of the company now turned upon him. He hesitated for a moment before making the decision, which I cannot blame him for, given his situation that, having been uncovered, he had better brazen it out.

Until this point he'd been hovering at the back of the proceedings, but now he strode forward. 'Come on,' he said, laying hold of Damian by the upper arm, rather like someone making a citizen's arrest, which I suppose he was doing, and attempting to guide him away.

In one swift move, and to the amazement of us all, Damian again got free, this time with a thousand times more fury than he had vented on the hotel employee when the man had tried something similar. 'Take your hand off me this instant,' he snarled. 'You stupid, ridiculous *oaf* !' Obviously, Andrew was not expecting anything of this sort when he had first decided to betray the uninvited guest, least of all from someone whom he judged to be far beneath him in God's scheme of things. Andrew unquestionably was an oaf, and a *very* stupid one, but few people would then have called him such to his face and he was quite unprepared for it. To be honest, I think he just wanted to have a go at Serena or one of the other girls who had been hovering around Damian all evening and he'd got jealous. I'm quite sure nobody was sorrier than he that the whole situation seemed to be spiralling out of control.

He was dressed, like some of the others, as a Death's Head hussar, with tight, in his case unbecoming, trousers, and a coat slung across his back, all of which may have fatally impeded his movement, but he couldn't back out now. He lunged forward, making a second attempt to grip the miscreant's arm. Once more, Damian was too quick for him, stepping back in a sort of pirouette, like Errol Flynn in a Warner Brothers romance, and before anyone could stop him he had swung the full force of his right fist into a punch that met Andrew's nose with a loud and sickening crunch. Several of the girls screamed, particularly the nearest, one Lydia Maybury, whose white, organza frock, charmingly cut on the bias and embroidered with lilies of the valley, was copiously sprayed with a mixture of gore and snot from Andrew's smashed proboscis. He himself looked so startled, so astonished by the unbelievable course events had taken, as if the sea itself had suddenly come rushing in through the ballroom windows, that he stood for a moment in a trance, staring through sightless eyes, stock still, blood spouting from his nostrils, before staggering backwards. Watching this, but paralysed with a kind of ecstatic horror, none of us thought to catch and save him, and instead he collapsed full length on to the breakfast buffet, pushing it over as he fell, showering himself and the bystanders with hot plates and sausages and jugs of orange juice and bacon and toast and

175

burners and scrambled eggs and mustard and cutlery and all. The crash was like the Fall of Troy, echoing through the hotel passages, frightening the horses, wakening the dead. It was succeeded by complete and total silence. We all stood there, rabbits caught in the headlights, stunned, amazed, hypnotised, watching the bloody, breakfast-decorated body of the fallen Viscount. Even Dagmar was as still and as silent as a statue.

Then Damian, with one of those gestures that made me forgive him more, and for longer, than I should have done, took hold of the Grand Duchess's hand, hanging limply by her side as she stood witness to the ruin of a party that had cost a large percentage of her annual income. 'Please forgive me for making such a mess, Ma'am,' he raised her unresisting hand to his lips, holding it there for a second, with exquisite elegance, 'and thank you so much for what, until now, has been an enchanting evening.' So saying he released her fingers, bowed crisply from the neck like a lifelong courtier, and strode out of the chamber.

I need hardly add that once the story had gone round London, and with the sole exception of the ball given by Lady Belton for Andrew's sister, Annabella, before very long Damian had received invitations to every other major event of that Season. This was not because of any increased approval on the part of the mothers, all of whom were more terrified than ever that Damian Baxter would ensnare one of their sacred children.

It was at the absolute and unbending insistence of the girls themselves.

SIX

The Grand Duchess had been right to make her investment, even if things did not quite turn out as she had wished. In 1968 the family had just enough money and just enough status for Dagmar to have landed a big—or a biggish—fish. That she did not, I attributed at the time to her setting her sights too high and thereby missing whatever chance there might have been of something decent. As I would discover, I was not completely right in this analysis, but I suspect that even so, like many of rank or fortune, Dagmar had grown up with unrealistic expectations. To begin with she had no clear idea of how pallid she really was. She could always assemble (then, anyway) a crowd who would conceal her shyness from herself and she did not seem to appreciate that she would have to make more of the running if things were to go her way. All this the Grand Duchess knew and, in the nicest possible way, she tried to encourage her daughter to make what hay she could before the sun went in completely, but like most young women, Dagmar did not listen to her mother when her mother said things she did not want to hear.

Part of the problem lay in her curious inability to flirt. Faced by a man, she would alternate between nervous giggling or complete silence, her huge semi-tearful eyes wide open, fixed on her partner, while he would flounder in his desperate attempts to find some topic, any topic, that would elicit a vocal response. There wasn't one. Eventually this helplessness provoked a protective

177

instinct in me, and while I never exactly fancied Dagmar, I began to dislike anyone who made fun of her or, as I once heard, imitated her sad, little laugh. On one occasion, I had to take her away from Annabel's when her date excused himself to go to the loo, before apparently running up the steps back to street level and jumping into a taxi. She cried on the way home and of course I had to love her a little bit after that.

To correct a popular misconception, I must point out that by my time the London Season was no longer, as it had once been, much of a marriage market. The idea was more to launch your young into a suitable world where they would thenceforth live and in due course find friends, and after a few years a husband or wife. Few mothers wanted this achieved before their sons and daughters had reached their middle twenties at the earliest, but Dagmar's case was different, as the Grand Duchess knew. They were selling a product in what promised to be a falling market and there was no time to be lost. We all thought at one point she had a reasonable chance of Robert Strickland, the grandson and eventual heir to a 1910 barony, awarded to a Royal gynaecologist after a tricky but successful birth. Robert didn't have much money and there was neither land nor house, but there was something and he was a kind fellow, if hardly the life and soul of the party. He worked in a merchant bank and had the supreme merit, certainly where the Grand Duchess was concerned, of being slightly deaf. Unfortunately, just as he was coming to the boil Dagmar fluffed it, Robert interpreting her nervous giggle as a lack of interest in his hinted-at proposal, and it was not repeated. By the end of that summer he was happily engaged to the daughter of a Colonel in the Irish Guards. There would be no other opportunities at that level.

Even so, everyone was a little taken aback to read in the gossip columns in the late autumn of 1970 that she was engaged to William Holman, the only child of an aggressive *parvenu* from Virginia Water. When I knew him William was about to be 'something in the City,' an all-purpose phrase beloved of our mothers. He had been a hanger-on at some of the dances in our year, wearing and saying inappropriate, desperate things, according to our youthful, shallow, snobbish yardsticks, and was not taken seriously by anyone. I suppose, looking back, he was quite clever and perhaps he did seem to be going somewhere. It just wasn't evident to us that it was somewhere very nice. I missed the wedding. I think I had double booked it with a weekend in Toulouse. But apparently it was perfectly all right, if a bit rushed. They were married in an Orthodox church in Bayswater and the reception was held at the Hyde Park Hotel. The groom's parents looked ecstatic and the bride's were at least resigned. In the last analysis Princess Dagmar of Moravia was married, and to a man who could pay the bill for dinner and manage something more than a basement flat. As the Grand Duchess might have remarked, and probably did in the privacy of her bathroom, it was better than nothing. She was also presumably aware that there were other factors at work, rendering the ceremony welcome. Six months later the Princess was delivered of a son, a healthy boy and not noticeably premature.

For obvious reasons I didn't see much of Dagmar after the Portuguese holiday, and once I'd missed her wedding we lost touch completely. I didn't like William and he couldn't see the point of me, so there was not much to build on. To be fair, he did do well, better than I had anticipated, eventually making chairman of some investment trust, and being rewarded with both millions and a knighthood from John Major. When I read about him in the papers, or glimpsed him across the room at some function, I was amused to note that he had become a convincing version of what he had hankered for all those years ago, with suits made by some award-worthy cutter behind the Burlington Arcade and all the loudly mouthed prejudices to match. Someone told me he hunted now and was even a good shot, which made me rather jealous. It never ceases to amaze me the way real money continues to ape the habits and pastimes of the old upper class, in a day when they could afford to call a different tune. This was not widely true during the seventies, but once Mrs Thatcher was on the throne, secret longings for gentility resurfaced in many a breast. Before long, every City trader exchanged his red braces for a Barbour, and was shooting, fishing and stalking like a middle-European nobleman, while the clubs in St James's, once desperate for new applicants, had pleasure in re-establishing their waiting lists and toughening again the criteria for membership.

One sign of all this that the sociologists seem to have missed was that from the eighties onwards, the upper middle and upper classes resumed a different daily costume from those beneath them in the ancient pecking order, which was definitely a return to the way things used to be. A unique phenomenon of the 1960s was that we all dressed in the new, outlandish modes, quite irrespective of background, perhaps the only time in the last thousand years when most of the nation's youth wore versions of the same costume, though it seems a pity we should choose as our badge of unity those terrible hipsters and kipper ties and velvet suits and bomber jackets and all the other horrors on display. Hideous as the fashions were, nobody was immune. The Queen's skirts leaped above her knee and, at the Prince of Wales's inauguration at Carnarvon Castle, Lord Snowdon appeared in what looked like the costume of a flightdeck steward on a Polish airline. But by the 1980s the toffs were tired of this unsuitable disguise. They wanted to look like themselves again, and gradually first Hackett's and later Oliver Brown and all those others who recognised this secret longing and aspired to supply it, appeared in the high street. Suddenly posh suits were once more of a recognisably different cloth and cut, while country clothes, tweeds and cords and all the rest of that tested uniform, pulled themselves from the dusty wardrobes where they had lain unloved since the 1950s. The toffs were visually different again, a tribe to be known once more by their markings, and it made them happy to be so.

That said, for those of us who witnessed what seemed then to be the end of everything, the 1970s had first to be negotiated before matters would start to improve. Much that was teetering came crashing down and there were dark days to be gone through. It seems strange to write it now, when all is changed, but to us, then, Communism was here to stay. In fact, most of us privately, if silently, believed that world Communism would eventually be the order of the day and we set about enjoying ourselves with no expectation of a long future for our way of life, dancing to the band on the increasingly steep deck of the *Titanic*. The sixties had come and gone by that stage, with their promises of free love and hair-worn flowers, but these attractive notions did not, in the event, compose the legacy of that troubled era. The trail that was left was not of peace and rose buds, but of social breakdown, and certainly some people who lost their currency value in those bleak years, never regained it.

So it wasn't a complete surprise when I dialled Dagmar's number and asked for the Princess, to be told that 'Lady Holman' was in the drawing room. I had prepared what I intended to say. My excuse was a charity ball that I'd been given to chair for Eastern European refugees. Some years before I'd written a moderately successful novel set principally in post-war Romania, which had inevitably taken me into this territory, and I was quite interested by what was happening in that stormy land. At last a voice came on the line. 'Hello?' she said. 'Is it really you?' She was still the diffident Dagmar of old, but somehow she sounded even more meek. I explained about the cause. 'I'm supposed to come up with some ideas for the committee and I immediately thought of you.'

'Why?'

'Wouldn't a Balkan princess look rather relevant? So far, all I've got is two actors from a soap opera, a TV chef whom no one's heard of and a bunch of dowagers from Onslow Gardens.'

She hesitated. 'I don't really use that name now.' There was a sorrow in her voice, though whether it was a momentary stab of nostalgia or a general critique of her present existence I could not, of course, tell.

'Well, even if you're listed as Lady Holman, everyone will know who you are.' One says these things and I said this, although, as is often the case in such circumstances, I did not believe it to be true.

'Well . . .' She paused awkwardly. I had hoped that William's success in the City would have bolstered her confidence, but the reverse seemed to have happened.

'Can we discuss it? I'm going to be driving very near you next week. Could I possibly look in?'

'When?'

Once more, as with Lucy Dalton, I sensed a trapped animal searching for a route out, scanning the net for a possible tear, which I firmly closed off with my next speech. 'It entirely depends on you. I've got some stuff to do in Winchester but I can easily fit it round your diary. What day would suit best? It'd be such fun to see you again after all these years.'

She was enough of a lady to know when she was caught. 'Yes, it would. Of course it would. Why not come for some lunch next Friday?'

'Will William be with you?'

'Yes. He doesn't really like my entertaining when he's not here.' This sentence had escaped her mouth before she fully grasped its ugly, bullying significance. The words seemed to reverberate down the line between us. After a silent pause she attempted to round off its sharp edges: 'He gets so jealous when he finds he's missed seeing people he likes. I know he'd love to catch up with you.'

'Me, too,' I answered, because I had to. I was not quite clear how I would carry out my mission if William was too controlling to allow us a moment together, but there was nothing I could do about that. 'I'll be with you on Friday, just before one.'

Bellingham Court was a real house. It was about five miles from Winchester and not perhaps quite far enough from the motorway, but it was a genuine Elizabethan schloss, with high mullioned windows and corbelled ceilings and panelled great chambers and whispering passages, a thoroughly satisfactory ego-puffer of a place. As I turned in through the neatly painted gates, and drove down the long, tended and impeccable drive, it was easy to see it had been the subject of a recent, and massive, restoration programme. I parked in the wide forecourt, bordered by two broad, shallow parterres of water, edged in new and expensively carved stone, and before I had time to ring the bell the door was opened by a middle aged woman in sensible shoes, whom I took, correctly, to be the housekeeper. She led me inside.

The money here was not comparable to Damian's Croesus-like hoards. The Holmans were very rich, that was all, not super-duper-Bill-Gates-unbelievably rich. Just rich. But they were rich enough, by heaven. The hall was large, stone-flagged, and off-white, with a dark, carved screen at one end and some wonderful furniture. These items had been selected as contemporary with the house, which I later discovered was not the theme in the other downstairs rooms, the designer having decided that Tudor artefacts are easy to admire but hard to live with. The style had therefore been confined to the hall, with a few pieces in the library. There was in this a kind of premeditation, a sort of thought-out pattern that, just as in Damian's Surrey palace, was oddly undermining to any sense of country living. Proper country houses have a kind of randomness, objects and furniture are deliberately thrown together, survivals of many other houses, which have somehow all ended up there in a kind of *chic* higgledy-piggledy. Nor is this a skill unknown to many designers who, given ample time and money, can rustle up a house that looks as if the family have owned it since 1650, when in fact they moved in the summer of the previous year. But here, at Bellingham, this casual, comfortable elegance had not been achieved. In fact, there was a slightly disconcerting quality to the whole house that I cannot exactly describe, as if it had been prepared for an elaborate party to which I had not been invited. Had I been told it had been dressed for a photo shoot and I wasn't to touch anything, it would not have surprised me. The pictures were almost all large, full, or three-quarter-length portraits, over-cleaned and a little too shiny. They had a foreign feel to them and I squinted at some of the name plaques on the most important ones, as I passed. 'Frederick Francis, 1st Grand Duke of Mecklenburg-Shwerin, 1756–1837' said one, while another announced 'Count Felix Beningbauer gennant Lupitz, 1812–1871, and his son, Maximilian.'

'You see we are very pro-Europe in this house.'

The voice startled me and I looked up to see a tiny figure standing at the far end of the hall, looking more like a boy scout on bob-a-job week than a princess in late middle age. Of course, I knew it was Dagmar because her stature meant it had to be, but I could not at first find her in the face I was presented with. Her hair was grey, though as flat and lank as it had always been, and at last I recognised her wobbling, tremulous, anxious lips, but not much else of her youthful appearance had survived. Her eyes were still huge, but sadder now and, despite our luxurious setting, it seemed to me that for her, life had been a bumpy ride. We kissed, a little gauchely, two strangers pecking at each other's cheeks, before she led me into the main drawing room, a fine, light chamber, but again with a synthetic air. It was the perfect mixture of Colefax chintz and antiques, Georgian this time, beautifully chosen as individual items but with no coherence as a whole. There was more of the splendid, European parade on the walls.

I indicated a couple of them. 'I don't remember you having all these in Trevor Square. Or were they in storage?' We knew, without saying, that they formed no part of the provenance of Squire William de Holman.

She shook her head. 'Neither.' Now, at last, she was beginning to come back to me. The moist half-open mouth had firmed up a bit, but she still had that odd, discordant, tearful note in her voice, a faint, sad scrape of the vocal cords grinding together, that reminded me of the girl she had once been. 'William has scouts in all the auction houses, and whenever there is a picture coming up with the faintest connection to me he bids for it.'

186

She did not elaborate on quite what this told us about her husband. No more did I.

'Where is he?'

'Choosing some wine for lunch. He won't be long.'

She poured me a drink from a supply concealed in a large, carved, rococo cupboard in the corner which I saw, to my amusement, contained a small sink, and we talked. Dagmar was more aware of what I had been doing with my life than I anticipated and she must have noticed how flattered I was when she spoke of one particular novel that had barely broken the surface of the water. I thanked her. She gave a little smile. 'I like to keep up with the news of the people I knew then.'

'More than with the people themselves?'

She shrugged lightly. 'Friendships are based on shared experience. I don't know what we would all have in common now. William isn't very . . . nostalgic for that time in his life. He prefers what happened later.' Which did not surprise me. If I were him, so would I. 'Do you see anyone from those days?' I told her I'd visited Lucy. 'Heavens, you are having a time of it. How is she?'

'All right. Her husband's got another business. I'm not sure how well it's doing.'

She nodded. 'Philip Rawnsley-Price. The one man we were all on the run from and Lucy Dalton ends up marrying him. How peculiar time is. I imagine he's quite different now?'

'Not different enough,' I said ungenerously and we laughed. 'I've seen Damian Baxter, too. Quite recently. Do you remember him?'

This time she let out a kind of giggling gasp that

brought the old Dagmar I had known completely back into the room. 'Do I remember him?' she said. 'How could I forget him when our names have been linked ever since?' My mind running, as it was, on another track, this remark amazed me. Had I entirely missed a romance that everyone else knew about?

'Really?'

She did a double take. Clearly she was puzzled by my slowness. 'You remember my party? When he flattened Andrew Summersby? And added about two thousand pounds to the bill? Which was quite a lot of money then, I can tell you.' But she was not made angry at the recollection. Quite the reverse. I could see that.

'Of course I remember. I also remember your attempts to pretend he'd been invited. I rather loved you for that.'

She nodded. 'It was hopeless, of course.' She smiled like a naughty, little elf at the thought of her long-ago gallantry. 'My mother was still living in some fantasy kingdom in her own head. She thought if she allowed one young man, who had behaved perfectly all evening, to stay on without an invitation, somehow Rome would fall. Needless to say, her intransigence made us ridiculous.'

'You weren't ridiculous.'

She flushed with pleasure. 'No? I hope not.'

'How is your mother? I was always so terrified of her.'

'You wouldn't be now.'

'She's alive, then?'

'Yes. She's alive. We might see her if you've time for a walk after lunch.'

I nodded. 'I'd like that.' There was a lull and I

188

could hear the sound of a bee trapped somewhere against a window, that familiar buzzing thump. Not for the first time I was struck by the strangeness of this kind of talk, with people you once knew well and now do not know at all. 'She must be pleased with the way things turned out for you.' In saying this I was perfectly sincere. The Grand Duchess had been so determined on a sensational marriage for her daughter that William Holman must have been a crushing disappointment, however necessary he was at the time. Little did either she, or we, know that he would deliver a way of life that would far outshine the promises of the eldest sons on offer in 1968.

She looked at me pensively. 'Yes and no,' she muttered.

Before I could comment further, William strode into the room, right hand extended towards me. He was better-looking than I remembered him, tall and thin, and his greying hair giving him a sort of blond, youthful appearance. 'How nice to see you,' he said and I noticed that, unusually after such a time, his voice was more changed than his face. It had become important, as if he were addressing the boardroom of a corporation, or a village hall full of grateful tenants. 'How are you?' We shook hands and exchanged the usual platitudes about Long Time No See, while Dagmar fetched him a drink. He looked down as he took it. 'Isn't there any lemon?'

'Apparently not.'

'Why not?' Given that I was more or less a stranger to him, despite our protestations of delight in each other's company, William's tone to his spouse was oddly and uncomfortably severe.

'They must have forgotten to buy any.' She spoke as if she were locked in a cell with a potentially violent felon and was trying to attract the attention of the guards.

'They? Who are "they"? You mean "you." *You* have forgotten to ask them to buy any.' He sighed wearily, saddened by the pathetic mediocrity of his wife's abilities. 'Oh well. Never mind.' He sipped the drink, wrinkled his nose with displeasure and turned back to me. 'So, what brings you here?'

I explained about the charity, since I was not, naturally, about to go into the true reason. He looked at me with that face of *faux* concern that people use when listening to hard luck stories in the street. 'Of course, this is a marvellous cause, as I said to Dagmar when I first heard about it, and I admire you terrifically for getting involved . . .'

'But?'

'But I don't think it's one for us.' He paused, expecting me to come in and say that of course I understood, but I waited, without comment, until he felt sufficiently wrong-footed to elucidate. 'I don't want Dagmar to be held captive by all that. Obviously, the position of her family was a very interesting one, but it's finished. She's Lady Holman now. There's no need for her to cash in on some bogus title from the past, when she has a perfectly good one in the modern world. This kind of thing, vital as it might be,' he gave a smile but it did not reach his eyes, 'seems to me to take her backwards, not forwards.'

I turned to Dagmar for a comment, but she was silent. 'I don't see her position as bogus,' I said. 'She's a member of a ruling house.'

'An ex-ruling house.'

190

'They were on the throne until three years before she was born.'

'Which was a long time ago.'

This seemed needlessly ungallant. 'There are plenty of people living in exile who look to her brother for leadership.'

'Oh, I see. You think we'll all attend Feodor's coronation? I hope he can get the time off work.' He laughed suddenly, with a kind of sneer in the sound, as he brought his face round to Dagmar's, that she might fully register his contempt. It was intolerable. 'I'm afraid I find all that stuff is just an excuse for a few snobs to bow and curtsey and gee up their dinner parties.' He shook his head slowly, as if he were making a reasonable point. 'They should pay more attention to what's going on around them today.' He sipped his drink to punctuate the finality of his argument. In other words there could be no further discussion on the subject.

I turned to Dagmar. 'Do you agree?'

She took a breath. 'Well—'

'Of course she agrees. Now, when's lunch?' I saw then that the real burden of William's song was that for years he had endured being treated as Dagmar's moment of madness, the shaming *mésalliance* that had overtaken the Moravian dynasty, and now he didn't have to put up with it any more. Things had changed. Today, he was the one with the money, he was the one with the power and weren't we going to know about it. Worse than this, having triumphed, he could no longer tolerate Dagmar having any sort of position of her own. She must have no value at all other than as his wife, no podium where she might shine

191

independent of his glory. In short, he was a bully. I understood now why the Grand Duchess's approval had been equivocal.

Luncheon was a curious event, providing as it did an endless series of opportunities for Dagmar to be publicly humiliated. 'What on earth is this?' 'Is it supposed to taste burnt?' 'Why are we eating with nursery cutlery?' 'Those flowers deserve a decent burial.' 'Shouldn't there be a sauce with this or did you ask for it to be dry?' If I had been Dagmar, I would have stood up, broken a large plate over his head and left him forever. And that was before we got to the pudding. But I know only too well that this kind of wife-battering, for that is what we were dealing with, destroys the will to resist and, to my sorrow, she simply took it. She even gave credence to his complaints by apologising for shortcomings that were entirely fictional. 'I am sorry. It should be hotter than this,' she would say. Or, 'You're right. I should have asked them to seal it first.' The limit came when William took a bite of the little crêpes Suzette that had been brought in and spat it back onto his plate. 'Jesus!' he shouted at the top of his voice. 'What the hell is this made of? Soap?'

'I don't understand you.' I spoke carefully. 'It's delicious.'

'Not where I come from.' He gave a merry laugh, as if we were all enjoying a jolly joke.

'And where do you come from, exactly?' I said. 'I forget.' I stared at him and he held my gaze for a second. Behind his head the housekeeper glanced quickly at a maid who had been helping to serve to check if she'd registered this exchange. I could see them silently acknowledge that they both had. In fact, they were nearly smiling. However, whether or not it was entertaining for the staff to witness the tyrant brought low, it was snobbish and self-defeating of me to do it. William, red in the face with fury, was on the brink of ordering me out of the house, which would have rendered my journey completely pointless. Mercifully, he was never one to allow his anger to undo him. Years of tricky negotiations in the City had made him cleverer than that. And I would guess the thought of the story going round London, coming from someone who was perhaps better known than he (not richer, not more successful, just a little better known) was something he was not prepared to risk. Of course, my chief crime in his eyes wasn't that I had been rude to him and failed to take his part. It was that I seemed to find his wife more congenial and more interesting than he was, which was even worse than my reminding him of the long journey he had traversed since we first met. I knew he made a point of editing every visitor who entered the house, so presumably this kind of challenge seldom, if ever, happened. He was out of practice when it came to being contradicted.

With a deep and deliberately audible breath, he put down his napkin, painstakingly rumpled, and smiled. 'The awful thing is I have to run. Will you excuse me?' I saw, to my amusement, he was trying to be 'gracious.' It was not in his gift. 'I'm at home on Fridays, but it doesn't mean I don't have to work. If only it did. Dagmar will see you off. Won't you, my darling? It's been such a treat to catch up again.' I smiled and thanked him, as if I had not just been instructed to leave, and we both pretended everything was fine. Then he was gone.

Dagmar and I stared at each other, her little, crumpled face and narrow shoulders suddenly making her look like a picture of some starving child in war-torn Berlin. Or Edith Piaf. Towards the end.

'Do you feel like a walk after that?' she said. 'I don't blame you if you want to get away. I won't be offended.'

'Hasn't he just told me to get off his land?'

She made a little pout. 'So?'

'Don't make him angry on my behalf.'

'He's always angry. What's the difference?'

The gardens at Bellingham had been tidied, replanted and restored to an approximation of their Edwardian appearance, with a large walled garden and separate 'rooms' containing statues surrounded by box hedges or roses in neat and tidy beds. It was all very nice, but the park was something more. Survivors of the original build, the giant oak trees, ancient and venerable, gave the whole place a sober beauty, a gravitas lacking in the quaint gardens or the newly refurbished interior. I looked around. 'You're very lucky.'

'Am I?'

'In this, anyway.'

She also stared about her, admiring the stately trees and the roll of the hills surrounding us. 'Yes,' she said. 'I am lucky in this.' We walked on for a bit. 'How was he?' she said suddenly, out of the blue. I did not immediately understand her. 'Damian. You told me you'd seen him recently.'

'Not very well, I'm afraid.'

She nodded. 'I heard that. I was hoping you'd tell me it wasn't true.'

'Well, it is.' Again, we were silent as we crested a

194

shallow slope with a wonderful view across the park towards the house.

'Did you know I was mad about him?' she said.

I was becoming used to surprises. 'I knew you'd had a bit of a walk-out. But I didn't know it was the Real Thing.'

'Well, it was. For me, anyway.'

'Then you were very discreet.'

She chuckled sadly. 'There wasn't much to be discreet about.'

'He talked of you the other day,' I said.

At this, her colour altered before my gaze and she raised a hand to her cheek. 'Did he?' she whispered. 'Did he really?' It was very touching.

I could see we were at last approaching the discussion I had come for, but I wanted to progress it carefully. 'He just mentioned that you and he had been out together a few times, which I hadn't known before.'

Released by the knowledge that somehow she was still alive in Damian's imagination, her words came pouring out. 'I would have married him, you know.' I stopped. This was astonishing. We seemed to have gone from nought to a hundred miles an hour in less than two minutes. Damian had given the impression of a one-night stand, but, for Dagmar it was *Tristan and Isolde*. How often it seems a pair of lovers can be engaged in two entirely different relationships.

She caught my expression and nodded vigorously, as if I were going to contradict her. It was an extraordinary transformation and the first time I had ever seen her take the lead in anything approaching an argument. 'I'd have done it if he'd asked me. I would!'

195

I raised my arms in surrender. 'I believe you,' I said.

Which made her smile and relax again, knowing by my action I was friend not foe. 'My mother would have thrown herself out of an upper window, of course, but I was ready for her. And I wasn't as mad as all that. I knew he'd do well. That was what I loved about him. He was part of the world that was coming.' She glanced at me. 'Not the world we *thought* was coming, all that peace and love and flowers-in-your-hair. Not that. The *real* world that crept secretly towards us through the seventies and arrived with a bang in the eighties. The ambition, the rapacity, I knew that another rich oligarchy would be back in place before I died and I was sure Damian would belong to it.'

A strange feature of growing older is the discovery that everyone who was young alongside you was just as incapable of expressing their thoughts as you yourself were. Somehow, in youth, most of us think that we are misunderstood but everyone else is stupid. I realised, with some sorrow, that I could have been much, much friendlier with Dagmar than I had been, if I'd only realised what was going on inside her little head. 'So, what happened? You couldn't convince your mother?'

'That wasn't the reason. She would have given in if I'd screamed loudly enough. After all, in the end she let me marry William who had no background at all, just because she thought he might make money.'

'What was it, then?'

She sighed, still sorry. 'He didn't want it.' She

frowned, anxious to qualify her statement. 'I mean he liked me a bit and he was quite amused by all the . . . stuff. But he never fancied me. Not really.' Of course, the sad truth was that none of us had fancied her. Not, at any rate, what Nanny would describe as *in that way*, she was too much of a waif, too much the loveless, pitiful child, but at her words I was struck with a wave of pity for our younger selves, bursting with unrequited love, as all we plain ones had been. Aching to tell, somehow believing that if only the object of our passions could be brought to understand the force of our love, they would yield to it, yet knowing all the time that this is not so and they would not.

Dagmar hadn't finished. 'There was a moment when I thought I could have him. At one particular point I thought I could promise him everything he was doing the Season to get. Social . . .' She hesitated. She had been so carried away that it had led her into territory that made her awkward. Her timid diffidence came flooding back. 'You know . . . social whatever . . . I thought he might want it enough to take me as part of the deal.' She looked across. 'I suppose that sounds very desperate.'

'It sounds very determined. I'm surprised it didn't work.' I was. Whether he found her attractive or not, I would have thought the Damian Baxter of those years would have leaped at the chance of a princess bride.

Now it was her turn to look at me pityingly. 'You never understood him. Even before that terrible dinner in Portugal. You thought he wanted everything you had. More than you had. Which he did, in a way. But at some moment during the year we spent together he realised he only wanted it on his own terms or not at all.'

'Perhaps that's what you admire in men. William certainly has it on his own terms.' Which could have been cruel but she did not take it as such.

Instead, she shook her head to mark the difference in her mind between the two men. 'William is a little man. He married me to be a big man. Then, when he had made his own money and bought a knighthood, and generally became, as he thought, big, he didn't want me to be big as well any more. He wanted me to be little, so he could be even bigger.' I cannot tell you how sad these words were, as I listened to her far-back, 1950s Valerie Hobson voice issuing from her minute frame. She looked so breakable. 'He thinks as long as he ridicules my birth and criticises my appearance, and yawns whenever I open my mouth, he can demonstrate that I am the one who needs him and not the other way round.'

'He still buys portraits of your ancestors.'

'He doesn't have much choice. If we waited for his to come up we'd have to live with bare walls.' It was nice to hear her being waspish.

'Why don't you leave him?' It is hard to explain quite why, but this was not as intrusive a question at the time as it seems on the page.

She thought for a moment. 'I don't entirely know. For a long time it was the children, but they're not children now. So I don't know.'

'How many are there?'

'Three. Simon's the eldest. He's thirty-seven, working in the City. Gone.'

'Married?'

'Not yet. I used to wonder if he might be gay. I

wouldn't mind, but I don't think he is. I suspect it's more that he's been put off the institution by his parents' example. Then there's Clarissa, who's happily married to a successful and very nice paediatrician, I'm glad to say, even if William doesn't approve.'

'Why not?'

'He would have preferred a stupid peer to a clever doctor.' She sighed. 'And finally our youngest, Richard, who's only twenty-four and starting out in corporate entertainment.' She paused, reflecting on her own words. 'Don't the young have funny jobs now?'

'Not like our day.'

She looked at me. 'Well, you went into a funny job. None of us thought you'd make a living. Did you realise that?'

'I suspected it. Just as I always expected you to do something surprising.' I only said this to cheer her up, but in a way it may have been true. To me, she had been a bit of a wild card, so retiring, so minor key, with her giggles and her long silences, that I used sometimes to have a sense that there was a completely different person living inside this shy and weeny head, even if I never investigated it at the time. I half expected the day to come when she'd break loose. Somehow it didn't seem possible that she would just slide into that Sloane life of buying school uniforms and cooking for the freezer in some provincial Aga kitchen.

Obviously, Dagmar found the idea of herself as a career girl rather flattering. 'Really? Very few of us did anything very spectacular. Rebecca Dawnay composes film music now and didn't Carla Wakefield open a restaurant in Paris? Or am I muddling her with someone?' She was combing her brain, 'I know one of the London editors is a former deb, but I forget which one . . .' she sighed. 'Anyway, that's about it.'

'Even so.' I had quite recovered from my initial bewilderment at her unfamiliar appearance. Now Dagmar looked like herself again and it brought the memories rushing back. 'Do you remember in Portugal, on the first night? When we took a picnic to that haunted castle on the hill and talked about life? You sounded like someone plotting a breakout. I expect you've forgotten.'

'No, I haven't forgotten.' She stopped walking, as if to punctuate her sentence. 'I think you're right and I was planning something of the kind. But I got pregnant.' We had all known this, of course, in the unspoken way such news was received in those distant days, so I didn't comment. 'William asked me to marry him and, whatever you think of him now, I was pretty relieved at the time I can tell you. Anyway, then Simon arrived and that was that.'

We were nearly back at the house by this time and I needed some answers. 'When did you give up on Damian?'

Her muscles tensed and her face took on the look of a nervous chipmunk. I realised the question, or at least the return to 1968, was not at all easy for her, but there was no way round it. I waited while she composed her reply. 'I gave up on him when he didn't propose to me and William did.' She hesitated. 'The truth is, though I hardly know how to say it,' she blushed again, but clearly she had decided that she was too far in to back out now, 'either of them could have been the baby's father. I was going out with William at the time, but Damian and I slept together on the night we arrived in Estoril. I remember it very well because it was the last time that I thought I just might get him. Then, later that same night, he told me it wasn't going to happen. Ever. That he was fond of me, but . . .' She shrugged and suddenly the lonely, heartbroken girl of forty years before was there, walking beside us in the park. 'After that, when my period was late, I knew that it was either William or the abortion clinic. It's odd to think of it, given how William behaves to me now, but I cannot describe my relief when he did pop the question.'

'I'm sure.' I was.

She gave a sudden shiver. 'I should have worn a jersey,' she said. And then, with a shy glance. 'I don't know why I told you all that.'

'Because I was interested,' I said. Actually, this is quite true. Especially in England. Very few Englishmen ever ask women anything about themselves. They choose instead to lecture their dinner neighbours on a new and better route to the M5, or to praise their own professional achievements. So if a man does express any curiosity about the woman sitting next to him, about her feelings, about the life she is leading, she will generally tell him anything he cares to know.

We were passing the stable block, which was a few hundred yards away from the main house. It was much later, perhaps mid-eighteenth century, and the wall of the yard ended in a rather handsome lodge, built for some trusty steward or perhaps a madly superior coachman. Before we'd gone a few more steps the front door opened and an old woman came out with a wave. She was

201

wearing the tweeds and scarf of a standard County mother. 'Dagmar told me you were coming,' she called over the grass separating us. 'I wanted to come out and say hello.'

I stared at the wrinkled, bony creature walking towards me. Could this really be the majestic Grand Duchess of my youth? Or had her head been transplanted on to another's body? Where was the weight, in every sense? Where were the charisma and the fear she had inspired? Vanished entirely. She approached and I bowed. 'Ma'am,' I murmured, but she shook her head and pulled me towards her for a dry kiss on both my cheeks.

'Never mind all that,' she said gaily and slipped her arm through mine. This simple action in itself was a marker of how much had vanished from the world in the years since we last met. My sentimental side approved it as a friendly and relaxing alteration. But, all things considered, I suspect that more had been lost than gained for both of us. She looked across at her daughter. 'Is Simon here yet? He told me he was trying to be with you for lunch.'

'Obviously he couldn't get away. He won't be long.' Dagmar smiled at her mother, this cosy, easy pensioner who had stolen the identity of the warlord of my early years. 'We've been talking about Damian Baxter.'

'*Damian Baxter.*' The Grand Duchess rolled her eyes to heaven, then smiled at me. 'If you knew the rows we had over *that* young man.'

'So I gather.'

'And now he's richer than anyone living. So I suppose he's had the last laugh.' She paused. 'But anyway, whatever she's told you, it wasn't my fault that it didn't happen. Not in the end. You can't blame me.'

'Whose fault was it?'

'His. Damian's.' Her voice had the finality of the Lutine Bell. 'We all thought he was a climber, an adventurer, a man on the make. And so he was, in his own fashion.' She turned back to me to wave a pointed finger at my nose. 'And you brought him among us. How we mothers used to curse you for it.' She laughed merrily. 'But you see . . .' Suddenly her tone was becoming almost dreamy as she clambered back through the lost decades, searching for the right words. 'He wasn't after what we had. Not really. I didn't see that at the time. He wanted to experience it, to witness it, but only as a traveller from another land. He didn't want to live in the past where he had no position. He wanted to live in the future where he could be anything he wished. And he was quite right. It was where he belonged.' She looked back at her daughter, now walking behind us. 'Dagmar had nothing useful to give him that would make life easier there.' She lowered her voice. 'Maybe if he'd loved her it would have been different. But without love, there wasn't enough in it to tempt him.'

I was struck by Damian's journey in that year of years. At the start he had been thrilled by his first invitation from Fat Georgina. By the end he had turned down the hand of a perfectly genuine princess. Not many can say that. There was a noise of footsteps, and around a laurel-sheltered corner of the drive William came almost goose-stepping towards us in a gleaming new Barbour and spotless Hunter gumboots. He caught sight of me and

203

frowned. By his reckoning I should have been safely back on the road by then. 'Here's William,' I said brightly. His mother-in-law looked at him with disdain and in silence. 'It must have been a relief that he stepped up to the mark when Dagmar needed him.' Obviously, I had spoken without thinking.

She turned a freezing fish eye upon me. 'I do not understand you,' she said coldly. It felt like the return of an old friend.

'I meant if Dagmar was anxious to marry.'

'She was not "anxious" to marry. She just felt that it was time.' Having settled this, the Grand Duchess relaxed and, after her brief outing, vanished back inside the chipper, little pensioner. 'William wanted what Dagmar could bring him. Damian did not. That's all there was to it.' She glanced in my direction. 'I know you didn't like him by the end.' I said nothing to contradict her. 'Dagmar told me about that business in Portugal.' Someone told everyone, I thought wryly. 'But it blinded you to what he was and what he could be. By the time Damian left our life, even I could see he was an unusual man.' I wonder now if she wasn't enjoying herself, discussing these events with someone who had been there when they were all taking place. Especially as I was an old friend, or at least I was a person she had known for a long time, which after a certain point is almost the same thing, and in all probability we would not meet again. I had provided her with an unexpected chance to make sense of those years and those distant decisions. I would guess they were not much talked of in the usual way of things and she wanted to make the best use of me. I cannot otherwise explain her next comment. 'William never had Damian's imagination,' she said. 'Nor his confidence in what the future would bring. Whatever his faults, Damian Baxter was a visionary in his way. William was just a tedious, vulgar social climber.'

'That doesn't mean he didn't love your daughter.' I saw no reason why we couldn't give him the benefit of some doubt.

But she shook her head. 'I don't think so. She made him feel important, that's all. That's why he resents her now. He can't bear the thought that he ever needed her to flatter his little ego.' I said nothing. Not because I disapproved of her disloyalty. If anything, I was honoured by the trust implicit in her indiscretion. But I had nothing I felt I could usefully add. She looked at me and laughed. 'I can't stand him, really. I don't think Dagmar can, but we never talk of it.'

'There's no point. Unless she's going to do something about him.'

She nodded. The rightness of this comment made her sad. In fact, the whole conversation had taken her into a strange, uncharted territory and I could see a light coating of glycerine beginning to make her eyes shine. 'The thing is, I don't know how we'd all manage. He'd find some way to give her nothing if they separate, some shyster lawyer would savage her claims and then what?' She sighed wearily, a hard worker in life's vineyard who deserved more rest than she was getting. There was the distant noise of an engine and her eyes looked up to find it. 'It's Simon, at last. Good.' The distraction had pulled her back from the cliff edge. She was probably already regretting what she had revealed.

A gleaming car of some foreign make was spinning down the drive towards us. As I watched it, I felt a sudden surge of longing. Let this man be Damian's son, I thought. Please. I cared about it in a way I had not cared with Lucy. In their scatterbrained way, the Rawnsley-Prices would shake out some sort of future, juggling Philip's demented schemes, surviving on luck and others' charity, but here, today, I felt as if I had been visiting old friends trapped in some hideous, third world prison for a crime they did not commit. Like all her kind, the old Grand Duchess was more frightened of poverty than it was worth. It would only be comparative poverty, genteel poverty, after all, but at a distance even that seemed unacceptable to her. I suppose she felt she had seen enough change and we must surely forgive her for that. This is always a delicate subject where the British upper classes and most Royalty are concerned, if they are facing poverty when they are used to living well. Most of them dread not only the coming discomfort but the loss of face that attends the loss of income, and they will submit to almost any humiliation rather than have to reduce their circumstance in public. Of course, there is another smaller group among them that doesn't give a damn either way. They are the lucky ones.

I thought again of the delivery from suffering that might be coming down the drive towards us. A quick DNA test and they would all be free of this horrible despot and their miserable existence. Dagmar and her mother and the other children would escape into a new land, where they would do just as they liked, and William would sit alone at his table, grumbling and fuming and insulting his servants to the end of his days. I wondered how we were going to get Simon to agree to a test. Would he worry about William's feelings? Did William have feelings? Dagmar had dropped back to stand by me. Her mother and her husband were a little way in front of us, waiting for the car as it drew nearer. 'It's been so lovely seeing you again,' I said. 'And your much-mellowed mama.' I wanted her to think of me as a friend. Because I was one.

She acknowledged my words with a quick smile, but then grew serious. Clearly, she'd deliberately manoeuvred a last moment with me out of earshot of the others. 'I hope you won't pay too much attention to what I was saying before. I can't think what came over me. It was just self-pity.'

'I won't mention it to anyone.'

'Thank you.' The crease of worry faded away. On the sweep before the house the shiny car had stopped and a man in his late thirties climbed out. He turned with a wave to face us.

And in that moment Dagmar's fate was sealed, as all my fantasies of playing Superman to this lost family came crashing down. But for their ages, he could have been William's identical twin. There wasn't a trace of his mother in him. Eyes, nose, mouth, hair, head, figure, manner, gait, they were like two peas in a pod. Dagmar saw me looking at him and smiled. 'As you can see, he was William's son after all.'

'Clearly.' We had reached my car by this stage and I opened the door.

'So everything worked out for the best,' she said.

'Of course it did. It often does, despite what they tell us on television,' I replied, climbing into the vehicle, taking her better, happier future with me. For a moment it seemed she was going to say something more, but then she thought better of it. So I said it for her. 'I'll give your love to Damian when I see him.'

She smiled. I had guessed right. 'Please do. My best love.' She looked round. 'Are you sure you won't stay and say hello to Simon?'

'Better not. I'm late and he'll be tired. I shall just enjoy you as a loving family group while I drive past.' Dagmar nodded, with a certain irony in her expression. I know she was glad to see the back of me that day and no wonder. I had committed the sin of reminding her of a happier time. Worse, I had made her admit to truths about her present life that she preferred to keep buried even from herself. I had my reasons, but it was cruel all the same.

At any rate, without further protest she stepped back, politely attending my departure, and a moment later I was on my way.

Serena

SEVEN

By the time I had got lost finding the motorway and caught in the evening traffic as I came into London, the whole excursion took longer than I'd planned and I did not arrive home much before eight. Bridget had let herself in some time earlier, and polished off half a bottle of Chablis in the interim. This made her rather sour as she banged around the kitchen making dinner. I cannot now think why I never questioned that she should always cook for me, when she spent her days in an office tussling with important decisions behind a desk, while I lolled around for most of the time, performing needless, invented tasks to fill the daylight hours as I waited for inspiration. In my defence, I don't remember her ever objecting to the arrangement. If it was my turn we went out. If it was her turn she cooked. Sometimes you just accept things.

'Your father rang,' she said. 'He wants you to call him back.'

'What about?'

'He didn't say, but he tried twice and the second time he sounded rather annoyed that you weren't here.'

There was a vague but completely unreasonable reprimand buried in this somewhere. 'I can't manage my day in case my father might ring.'

'Don't blame me.' She shrugged and went back into the kitchen. 'I'm just the messenger.' I was struck, not for the first time, by the tremendous mistake that about half the human race usually

211

finds itself making when it comes to wobbly relationships. The division is not by sex or class or nationality or race or even age, since almost every type is found on both sides of the divide. The mistake is this: When they are in a partnership that is not going well, they attempt to inject a kind of drama into it by becoming moody and critical and permanently not-quite-satisfied. 'Why do you *always* do that?' they say. 'Now, are you listening because you *never* get this right?' Or, 'Don't tell me you've forgotten *again!*'

Not belonging to this team, I find it hard to penetrate their thinking. Do they imagine that by being demanding and edgy and cross, they will force you to work harder to make things better? If so, they are, of course, completely wrong. This kind of talk just gives one permission to go. The more dissatisfied they are, the more their gloom will become a self-fulfilling prophecy. In fact, the first time you hear that put-upon sigh, 'I suppose I'm expected to clean this up,' you know it is simply a matter of time. The irony being that the ones who are truly hard to leave are those who are always happy. To desert a happy lover, to make them unhappy when they were not unhappy before, is hard and mean, and involves guilt of a major kind. To leave a miserable whinger just seems logical.

Of course, this implies it is easy to get up the nerve to end an affair that is past its sell-by date. But for many it is not. They tell themselves they are being nice, or honourable, or adult, in struggling on, but what they are being is weak. I do not mean a bad marriage or when there are children involved. But when we're only talking childless cohabitation it is plain cowardice to settle for failure. The years spent after we have decided that we will not die and be buried next to *this* one, are just wasted, so why do we put it off? Is it misguided kindness or false optimism or because we've taken a villa for the whole of August with the Grimstons and we can't let them down? Or even: Where on earth would I put all this stuff? It doesn't matter. Once the inner voice has spoken and given the verdict, every day spent evading the end is unworthy of you. And when it came to Bridget FitzGerald, I was unworthy.

My father was quite grouchy when he picked up the receiver. 'Where have you been all day?' he said.

'I had to go to Hampshire for lunch.'

'Why, for God's sake?' As any adult child knows, when dealing with an aged parent there is no point in engaging with this stuff.

'You could have rung me on the mobile,' I suggested.

'It's illegal if you were driving.'

'I've got an ear thing.'

'Even so.' Again, silence is the only sensible option. At last, his anger spent, he returned to his topic. 'I want you to come down and see me. There are some things we ought to talk about.' In fact, he lived above London on the map, on the border of Gloucestershire and Shropshire, but my father was of that generation where London was the highest point in Britain. So he went 'up' to London and 'down' to everywhere else. I rather loved him for it. I suppose he went down to Inverness, but I don't remember trying him on this. I cannot ask him now for he has died since I lived through these

213

events. I miss him every day.

Bridget came out of the kitchen, carrying a plate of food on to which she had already spooned a huge helping of some stew and various vegetables. 'I've served it up in the kitchen. I know you don't like me to, but we haven't got all day.'

I always find this kind of talk intensely irritating, draped as it is with self-importance. 'You are quite right,' I said coolly. 'I don't like having a plate piled up with things I have not chosen since I have been out of the nursery for some years. Nor do I see why we haven't got all day. What pressing engagement are we racing to meet?' Having delivered this twaddle, no less self-important than the speech that had provoked it, I sat down at the table.

But Bridget had not quite finished. 'I'm afraid it's very overcooked,' she sighed, as she laid the concoction before me.

It was clearly time to acknowledge that we were having a spat and with that remark she had finally used up the last stock of patience I had kept in reserve. 'I cannot think why, since I was here before eight,' I muttered, deliberately using a harsh and frigid tone to combat hers. 'At what hour were you planning to eat?' She bit her lip and said nothing.

Of course, as I knew well enough, this was a dishonourable dig. Before meeting me, Bridget had generally tucked into her evening feed at about half past six or seven, and she still found my insistence on dining at half past eight or nine not so much unreasonable as weird. This will be familiar to many who have ventured beyond their home pastures to find a mate. Even in this day and

214

age, even after almost everyone, south of Watford anyway, says 'lunch' and when all sorts of foods from avocados to sushi have become ordinary fare, still the time for evening eating can provoke an absolute clash of cultures. To me, early eating can only be explained if food is considered essentially as fuel to strengthen one for the adventures yet to come. So, people will dine at six or six thirty in order to be fuelled by seven, in time to fill the next few hours with fun. This time may be spent in a club or in a pub or keeping fit or studying macramé or learning Mandarin or line dancing or simply watching television while sitting on a sofa. The evening is your oyster and, by eating early, you are free to enjoy every pleasure while it lasts.

The reason this is completely bewildering for the upper middle and upper classes is simply because for them the dinner *is* the pleasure. It is the apex, the core, the point. If the whole business of feeding is over by half past seven, what on earth is one to do until bed? These people don't go to self-help groups, or engage in amateur acting, nor do they study art or quilting, or drop into a bar. This is why any role in local government is so difficult for them. It takes place just when they prefer to be sitting at a table for a very different purpose. For those who cross the great social divide, there can be few habits harder to adjust to, whichever direction they have travelled. Certainly, Bridget had found it difficult and now, here I was, deliberately goading her, insulting her, putting her down. I was ashamed of myself. But not, it seems, sufficiently ashamed to regain my good humour. I stared at the plate. 'And I wish you wouldn't pile it up like that. It's so off-putting.' I whined as I unfolded my napkin. 'I feel like a tramp being fed before retiring to my cubicle in a Rowton House.'

'And I feel like the skivvy serving him,' said Bridget without the trace of a smile, and we let it rest there.

At the time of these events my father lived in a modest village called Abberley, on the Gloucestershire borders. He was eighty-six then and he'd chosen it as his retreat after my mother's fairly early death ten years before. There was no pressing reason for him to go there, since their marriage had largely been spent abroad and the first years of his retirement had been passed in Wiltshire, but I suppose he wanted a change and our family had been based for the latter half of the nineteenth century at Abberley Park, a rather over-christened large house of negligible architectural merit, situated behind a cobbled forecourt, at one end of the main street of the village. It meant little to me, as it had only been a third-rate hotel in my lifetime; still we would visit it occasionally for lunch or tea, and Pa would pretend a kind of nostalgia for the place. This, I suspect, was to encourage me to take an interest in my family's history, but I always found his Turgenev-style melancholy fairly unconvincing. The large, dreary hall and the largish dreary drawing and dining rooms on either side of it were all hideously decorated, and any trace of private life had long since vanished from the atmosphere. My father had no memories of the house anyway, since his grandfather had sold it, after the agricultural depression, in the early years of the twentieth century before he was even born. I suppose the staircase, in slightly crude nineteenth-

216

century baroque, was pretty and the dark, panelled library may once have been nice, but its translation into a bar, complete with upside-down bottles on silver holders, had obliterated its fragile charm. However, the seller-grandfather, plus his wife and various other members of the two preceding generations of our clan, lay in the graveyard of the local church and were commemorated with plaques in the nave, and I imagine this gave my papa a sense of belonging, something neither he nor my mother had ever quite achieved in their previous home.

His life in Abberley was pleasant enough but a bit sad, of course, as all old men living on their own are sad, in a way that old women are not. He had a housekeeper called Mrs Snow, who was reasonably civil and would cook him lunch every day and depart after it was washed up and put away. She would leave his dinner in the fridge, in a terrifying array of dishes covered in cling film, with post-it notes carrying strict instructions: 'Boil for twenty minutes,' 'Put in a pre-heated oven at gas mark 5 for half an hour.' I could never see the point of this, since she wasn't a very good cook, to say the least of it, her repertoire consisting entirely of English nursery food from the 1950s, and he could have bought everything at the local Waitrose. It would have been quicker and easier to prepare, as well as much nicer to eat. But, looking back, I think he rather enjoyed the disciplined activity of unwrapping everything and obeying her iron will. It must have taken up quite a bit of the evening and that would have been a real bonus.

On the day that I went to see him Mrs Snow was preparing our lunch when I arrived, but he told me

217

in dulcet tones, as he poured two glasses of very dry sherry, that she was going to leave us as soon as she had brought in the pudding. In other words she was not going to stay to wash up. 'We'll have the place to ourselves,' he muttered out of the side of his mouth as he led the way to a chair in his chilly and unsuccessful drawing room. Why is it that some people can live in a house for twenty years, yet the furniture still looks as if the removal van has just pulled out of the gates? In this, his last house he had copied a few rooms from earlier homes that my mother had decorated, but he never seemed to find a template for the little, irregularly shaped drawing room, so it just waited, with its magnolia walls and disparate collection of furniture, for an inspiration that never came.

'Good,' I answered, since that was what seemed to be called for.

He nodded briskly. 'I think it's better.' Years in the diplomatic had made him secretive as a rule, in addition to which he shared the usual prejudice of his kind that it was impossible to have any kind of conversation about money, outside the walls of a bank or a brokers', were it not serving one of two purposes. These comprised discussing your future son-in-law's net worth and prospects, and talking about your own will. Since my sister was long married, I gathered at once that the second was what we were in for and so it proved.

We had exchanged bits of family information in a desultory fashion through some unsalted, tasteless shepherd's pie and we were staring at an uninviting plum duff with custard, when Mrs Snow leant round the door in her coat and hat. 'I'll be off, then,' she said to my father. 'I've put coffee in the library, Sir David, so don't let it get cold.' In response to this, he twisted his face into something akin to a wink, signifying that as with all, lonely old people who employ one servant, the relationship was becoming dangerous, and he nodded his thanks. We heard the door bang and he started.

'I had rather a turn the other day and I went to see old Babbage. He's run a few tests and it seems I may be cracking up at last.'

'I thought you said Babbage ought to be struck off.'

'I never did.'

'You said he couldn't diagnose a gunshot wound.'

'Did I?' My father was slightly cheered by this. 'Perhaps I did. Anyway, it doesn't alter much. I'm going some time and it won't be long now.'

'What did he say?'

'Nothing to bother you with.'

'I have driven for two and a quarter hours. I deserve details.'

But he could not break the habits of a lifetime. 'It was all about blood being where it shouldn't be. Revolting stuff that I have no intention of discussing over pudding.' There wasn't much to come back with, so I waited while he got to the point. 'Anyway, I realised that you and I had never had a proper talk about everything.'

How strange death is. It seems to make such nonsense of the years that have gone before. Here was my father about to die, presumably of some form of cancer, and what had been the point of it all? What had it all been for? He'd worked pretty hard, in the way his generation did work, which was different from, and more sensible than ours, with their late starts and long lunches and getting home by half past six. Even so, he had done his best and travelled the world and stayed in horrible hotels, and sat through boring meetings and listened to heads of state lying, and experts making dire predictions that proved quite unfounded; he had studied worthless reports without number, and pretended to believe government spokesmen when they made ludicrous and mendacious claims for their inadequate ministers, and . . . for what? He had no money. Or not what my mother would have called 'real' money. This house, a few shares, one or two nice things left over from his forebears who had lived better than he did, a pension that would perish with him. My sister and I had been given good educations, which must have set them back, but Louise had largely thrown hers away by marrying a very ordinary stockbroker and bringing up three children, all of whom were dull to the point of genius, while I —

'I want you to know what I've arranged, in case you think I've made anything unnecessarily complicated. You're the executor, so you'll have to deal with it if I've made a nonsense.'

I nodded. My thoughts would not get back in their box. Poor old boy. It had been a good life, I suppose. At least that's what people would say when his funeral eventually came to pass. 'He had a good life.' But did he really? Was it a good life? Was it enough? He met my mother towards the end of the war, when she was working for someone in the Foreign Office. He had been seconded to assist with the settlement of Poland and other places where the British would make the wrong decisions, as a preparatory move to taking up his

220

career again when the fighting stopped. They married in 1946, just before he was appointed second secretary to our embassy in Madrid, and, on the whole, they'd been quite happy. I honestly believe that. She liked travelling and the constant relocation of their home had pleased, rather than annoyed her. Once he made ambassador, I would go as far as to say she had a good time and, while he never got one of the really big ones, Paris or Washington or Brussels, still he did get Lisbon and Oslo, both of which they enjoyed, as well as Harare, which proved a lot more interesting than either had bargained for, and not in a good way. But when it was all over they'd come home to a farmhouse which they'd bought near Devizes, and that was it. He'd been knighted before his second-to-last posting and I was glad, as it helped them to feel they had made their mark, which of course they hadn't. It was also probably of mild use in getting them started socially in what was, for them, a brand-new part of England. But I never really understood the compulsion to make their home in the country when neither of them was the type to spend their lives walking dogs and working for local causes. Certainly, they were not at all sporty. My father had given up shooting twenty years before, after he spent four days on a grouse moor in the Borders without hitting a single bird, and my mother never cared much for anything that made her cold.

There is a tyranny that forces people of a certain class to insist they are only happy in the country and it is a cruel one. My parents were among its many victims. As everyone but they could see, their natural milieu was urban. They

221

liked varied and informed conversation. They liked to mingle with different social groups. They liked their gossip from its source. They liked to talk politics and art and theatre and philosophy, and none of this, as we know, is much to be found beyond the city limits. Nor were they big local employers and, since their families had no historic connection with the part of Wiltshire they had chosen, they would never have more than a day pass to the County proper, so their egos were doomed to starvation rations as long as they remained there. In short, there was no real chance for them of happiness, or even entertainment, in that society, not as there would have been in Chelsea or Knightsbridge or Eaton Square but they made do, with introductions and dinners and charity functions and signing petitions about local planning and getting cross about the way the village pub was run and all the rest of it. And then my mother died, which was exactly what my father had never expected. But he showed courage as he packed up his life in Devizes and exchanged it for an equally meaningless one in Gloucestershire, and now here he was, after ten years of non-event, telling me about his own approaching death as we tucked into the disgusting splodge on our plates. I have never felt the ultimate absurdity of most lives more strongly than at that moment.

'It's all written down, so there shouldn't be any confusion,' my father said, producing from somewhere near the table a plastic folder filled with typed sheets. He handed it to me as he stood up. 'Let's go through.'

He led the way into the little library, which he used for most of his daily activities, and as usual I

222

was touched by the sight of it. Unlike the characterless drawing room, the library was an exact reproduction, in miniature, of one my mother had designed for the Wiltshire farmhouse, with walls lined in red damask and fluted bookshelves in a soft dove grey. Even the cushions and lamps had been transferred intact after the move. A portrait of her, rather a good one, painted just after their marriage, in a snappy, 1940s suit, hung over the chimneypiece and my father would glance at it from time to time as he spoke, as if seeking her approval for his decisions, which I imagine was exactly what he was doing.

In front of the green corduroy sofa, a table held a tray made ready by the indefatigable Mrs Snow, with coffee equipment for two. He poured himself a cup, nodding at the folder. 'Funeral, memorial, it's all there. Prayers, hymns, who should do the address if you don't want to, everything.'

'I thought you hated hymns.'

'So I do, but I don't think a funeral is a good place for a "statement," do you?'

'It's your last chance to make one.' Which made him smile. 'I'll do the address,' I said.

'Thank you.' He chuckled gently to cover his emotions. 'I've left this house to Louise, since you got the flat.'

His words were perfectly logical and true but, irrationally, I felt a twinge of irritation. Does anyone ever feel content with the way things are arranged at these times? An only child, perhaps. Never a sibling. 'What about the stuff?'

'I thought you could split it. But I haven't really specified.'

'I wish you would.'

'What? Every teaspoon?'

'Every last teaspoon.' He looked sorrowful at this. He probably wanted to believe that his children got on well, which we did, quite, but we were not really close any more and I knew Louise's über-tiresome husband would push in and make her take anything decent if he weren't stopped now. 'Tom will say that they have children, and I don't, so they must have all the family things. Then there'll be a fight and Louise will cry and I'll shout and Tom will look wounded. That's unless you just write it down in black and white so there's no argument.'

'All right, I will.' He nodded gravely. 'In fact, I tell you what. I'll leave your mother's jewellery to her and you can have the rest of the contents. If you want to give her a stick or two you can. I suppose it'll all go back to her sprogs if you don't have any of your own.'

'I imagine so. It's not going to the cats' home, anyway.'

'I wish you had a family.'

This was a frequent observation and normally I would have fobbed it off with a joke or an exasperated sigh, depending on my state of mind; but given the topic we were discussing, a bit of honesty felt more appropriate. 'So do I, really,' I said.

'You still could, you know. Look at Charlie Chaplin.'

'I don't even need to go back that far.' Why does everyone over fifty still quote Charlie Chaplin in this context? Every day, there is some demented actor in the news, saying what fun it is to be a parent in his seventies, and how it makes every day bright and new. I sometimes wonder how long they can keep up this fantasy before they succumb to rage and clinical exhaustion.

'Of course . . .' He hesitated. 'I don't suppose . . . what's-her-name?'

'Bridget.'

'Bridget. I expect it's a bit late for her.'

Since Bridget was fifty-two, this was almost a compliment. I nodded. 'I expect so. But that doesn't necessarily . . .' It was my turn to tail away. We both knew what I was saying. My father cheered up considerably, which I have to say I found a bit annoying. I'd always known she wasn't his type, even if I'd pushed it to the back of my mind, but he'd been unfailingly polite to her and by that stage she was quite fond of him. It felt unjust to realise that he had secretly been hoping throughout that eventually she would pass on by.

'Oh, I see. Well. You're a dark horse.' He poured himself another cup from the silver pot of lukewarm, brownish coffee'ish liquid left for our delectation. 'Do I know her?'

'There isn't anyone, in particular.' I gave a brisk shake of the head.

'What's the matter?'

I was unprepared for this, both the question and the tone, which was uncharacteristically warm. 'What do you mean?'

'You've been in a funny mood since you got here.' His comment was clearly directed at far more than my relations with Ms FitzGerald. I was taken aback because my father was not much given to introspection, either for himself or with regard to anyone else. When we were young, whenever a conversation at dinner threatened to get

225

interesting he was inclined to cap it with the proto-English imprecation: 'now, don't let's get *psychological.*' I do not mean he didn't appreciate the importance of other people's inner life. He just didn't see that it was anything to do with him. Gossip bored him. He couldn't remember incidents or personalities well enough to savour the punchlines and he used to get quite impatient whenever anyone tried to intrigue him with some local scandal.

In truth, his stance drained my mother, since she was never allowed to discuss the private affairs and theoretical activities of their acquaintance, and this inevitably made their conversation very arid. 'What business is it of ours?' he would say, and she would nod and agree with him, and say of course and how right he was, and thereby be silenced. After I'd grown up, I used to defend her and quote Alexander Pope: 'The proper study of mankind is man' and so on. The fact remained he felt uncomfortable and ungenerous delving into the murky waters of others' personal histories and she gave up trying to change him, retaining these topics to enjoy with her friends and her children. It was all right, but I do give thanks that their later years were spent in the era of television, or the evenings would have been silent indeed. Still, here he was, showing an interest, asking for some sort of private explanation of my mood. It was so rare an event, that I couldn't waste time on prevarication.

'I have a feeling that I want to change my life.'

'What do you mean by that? Get rid of Bridget? Stop writing? Sell the flat? What?'

'Yes,' I said. We stared at each other. Then I

226

thought again. 'Actually, I don't think I want to stop writing.'

'What's brought this on?'

I told him about Damian's request and how I had fared so far. He thought for a moment. 'I quite liked him at the time, until you had your falling-out.' He paused, but I had no comment to make. 'Even so, I'm rather surprised to find he left such a mark on all those lives.'

'Far be it from me to defend him after what he put me through, but he is the only member of that gang who went on to be one of the most successful men of his generation.'

'Yes, you're right. Of course that's right. I wasn't thinking.' My father spoke as one who feels himself justly corrected. 'So, what is it?'

'I'm not completely clear in my own head, but I believe I'm finding it depressing to be obliged to compare what we all thought was coming when we were young with what actually arrived.'

My father nodded. 'To quote Nanny, comparisons are odious.'

'They are also pointless, but that doesn't prevent one from making them.' For some reason, I felt it was important that he understood me. 'It's more than that. I'm not sure what we're all doing with our lives. Damian may have made his mark, but none of the rest of us has.'

'Not everyone can be a world-famous billionaire.'

'Nor should they be, but everyone needs to feel they're part of something worthwhile. That, in the last analysis, their life has some meaning in a larger context. The question is what am I part of? What have I done?'

But he couldn't take this very seriously. 'Don't you think people have been asking themselves that since Chaucer first sharpened his pencil?'

'I think there have been times when the majority felt they belonged to a culture that was working, that they had an identity within a worthwhile whole. "I am a Roman Citizen," "God Bless America," "The man who is born an Englishman has drawn a winning ticket in the lottery of life." All that. People have felt their own civilisation was valuable and that they were lucky to belong to it. I'm fairly sure I believed that too, or something like it, forty years ago.'

'You were young forty years ago.' He smiled. Clearly, he was not very worried by my soul-searching. 'So what are you asking? Do you want to sell the flat? If so, then that's what you must do.'

In a way I could have left then as, if I'm honest, I had really gone down there seeking his permission to do this very thing. I was taken unawares by his swift and open reaction to my complaints, as I had assumed it was all going to take much longer to get his agreement. Because I should be clear, this response on his part was very generous, more generous than an outsider can perhaps immediately appreciate. As I have said, my mother was the one who insisted on their giving me the London flat, thereby cutting down their capital by quite a chunk. He'd resisted it for a time, because he saw their standard of living would suffer, which it did, but he eventually surrendered to her pleading. Now, here I was, proposing to cash in my chips, to pocket the boodle, to take the money and run, and he wanted to make it clear that he did not mind in the least. Some months later I would learn that he'd already known he was much more ill than he had let on and that death could not be long distant, so I suppose he wanted us to be in step at the end, but to me that thought only makes his kindness more moving. 'That's so fantastically nice of you,' I said.

'Nonsense, nonsense.' He shook his head at the very notion. 'Now, what about some more coffee?'

Of course, his instinctive desire to downplay the moment was precisely what made it so poignant. Like too many of his type, my father had an absolute inability to express the love that motivated him, being always far too English to demonstrate his feelings. Even when we were little he hated kissing us goodnight and was visibly thrilled when the custom was allowed to lapse in our early teens. But there was nevertheless a silent unspoken affection in his words at this moment that makes my eyes fill now, months later, when I remember them. 'I don't want you to think it was wrong to give it to me when you did,' I said. 'It provided me with the perfect base, with a tremendous start. I was, and am, incredibly grateful.'

'I know. But because something was right for you then, doesn't mean it's right for you now. If you want to sell it you must sell it.'

'Thank you.'

'And the girl? Isn't it working?'

I couldn't help thinking, disloyally, that Bridget would be ecstatic to hear herself referred to as 'the girl,' however politically incorrect that might sound. She was very good-looking and had the kind of looks that would last, but she was no spring chicken, if not quite yet an old boiler. I wasn't sure

229

how to answer him. 'It's not that, exactly. It works as well as it ever did.'

'But?'

'My problem is that during my searches I've been reminded of what it feels like to be in love. I think I'd forgotten.'

'Again, you are remembering what it feels like to be *young* and in love. Love at nearly sixty, whatever sentimental American films may try to tell you, ain't the same.'

'Maybe not. But I'm fairly sure it's more than I've got now.'

'Then of course you must move on.' He nodded slowly. 'Tell me, do you ever see Serena Gresham in your travels?'

The question came flying out of the blue and almost winded me. On this day my dear old father was full of surprises. Could he really remember Serena? Why would he know what I had felt about her? Unless he'd had some kind of personality transplant? We hadn't mentioned her name in thirty years at least and anyway I would never have given him credit for taking enough interest in my life to notice my romantic sufferings. 'No. At least, barely. Sometimes. At the odd thing in London. That's all.'

'She married, didn't she?'

'Yes.'

'And that was satisfactory?'

'I don't see enough of her to have an opinion. She's got two grown-up children and she's still with him.'

He considered my limp reply for a second. 'I'm not convinced you would have been happy, you know.'

230

This sort of thing is hard to take at any age from any parent, but it came so closely upon one of the kindest gestures he'd ever made that I didn't want to snap. 'I just wish I'd had the chance to find out' was all I said.

'You could never have been a writer. You'd have ended up in the City. To make the kind of money it would have taken to keep her.'

'Not necessarily.' At this he gave a little snort. As always with a father, the assumption of superior knowledge, particularly where it concerned people I had been close to and he barely knew, was infuriating. But again, after the earlier exchange I didn't want a fight. 'Plenty of people nowadays live completely differently from the way they were brought up. You do for a start.'

'Maybe. But my generation wasn't given the option and, believe me, old habits die hard. I should know.' He saw I was struggling not to join battle on Serena's behalf and relented. 'I don't mean I didn't like her, but I just never thought you were suited. For what it's worth.'

'Yes. Well.' I spoke and was silent.

An awkwardness had entered the proceedings. My father was suddenly uncomfortably aware that he had ventured into alien, possibly even hurtful, territory. He smiled jocularly to get things back to normal. 'Well, I hope I'm still around to meet the new girl, when she turns up.'

'So do I,' I said and I meant it. I'm very sorry that he won't be.

We spent the rest of the afternoon discussing his will, which I was now allowed to read. He had, as he said, left his home to my sister and the remainder of his capital was divided between my niece, my two nephews and myself. This wasn't quite fair, in my opinion, since for these purposes Louise and her children should have weighed as one person, but he telephoned his lawyer while I was there and dictated a codicil that gave me the entire contents of the house, so I didn't like to cavil. Then it was done. His requests for the church services seemed gentlemanly. In fact, it was all pretty modest, more of a decorous whimper than a bang.

We were in the kitchen, making a cup of tea prior to my departure, before my father mentioned the state of my life again. Mrs Snow had left the things laid out on the kitchen table, complete with cling-filmed biscuits. Obviously, she didn't believe him capable of instigating even the smallest domestic operation from scratch and she was probably right. 'I don't think Damian is behaving correctly in this,' he said after another silence, as he poured out two cups of builders' brew. 'You'll almost certainly end by disturbing the balance of a perfectly workable life. Some man or some woman will suddenly find themselves a thousand million times richer than their siblings, richer than every relation they have in the world. Their mother will face the task of explaining to her husband that the eldest child is a bastard. It's not going to be easy.'

'And if the money should mean that a life encumbered by poverty might suddenly take wing and achieve great things?'

'You sound like a novel from a railway bookstall.'

'You sound like an officer from Health and Safety.'

He bit into his digestive. Mrs Snow was not a

232

risk taker, with biscuits or anything else. 'Nor do I think it fair for Damian to lay this burden on you. It's not as if he had much credit to call on.'

'No.' But I did not want to pretend that I didn't know why I had been asked. 'Unfortunately there really wasn't anyone else who could have undertaken it.'

'Maybe. But I don't believe he understood what he was exposing you to.'

This was an odd comment, which I had not anticipated. 'Why? What have I been "exposed to"?'

'You've been made to go back into your own past and to compare it with your present. You've been forced to remember what you wanted from life at nineteen, forty years ago, before you knew what life was. Indeed, you must face what you all wanted from life, those silly, over-made-up girls and the vain, self-important young men you ran around with then. Now, thanks to Damian, you must bear witness to what happened to them. To what happened to you. Eventually, in old age, almost everyone with any brains must come to terms with the disappointment of life, but this is very early for you to have to make that discovery. You've been rendered discontented when it's too late, or nearly too late, to fix, but soon enough for you to have many years ahead to live with that discontent. Damian ought to have spoiled his own life, not yours.'

'He doesn't have much of his own life left to spoil.'

'Even so.'

And of course he was right, really.

Is it serendipity? That explanation for those

strange, coincidental happenings that seem, for a moment, to create a sense of planning in our arbitrary lives? Or is serendipity more to do with accidental knowledge of things? Of chance deductions that lead to greater understanding? Either way, I believe it was serendipity that took a hand in the next stage of my Damian-led journey.

We were staying for the weekend, Bridget and I, with a very tiresome architect and his very charming wife at a house he had purchased some years before in Yorkshire. It was an old house, a historical house, a 'great house' in a way and, oh boy, didn't he know it. The architect in question was called Tarquin Montagu. I did not believe that this was a name he, or more probably anyone, would have received at the baptismal font, and I certainly never discovered any link between him and the ducal house of Manchester, a connection that he liked to imply. He came into my life as the husband of a delightful novelist called Jennifer Bond who was also with my publisher. We'd been paired for a book tour one summer a few years before, forging a friendship in the process. I was not then clear about how he came by his money, since he was never associated with any vividly spectacular building, but he lived in a way that Vanbrugh would have envied and some years before our visit he had bought a splendid semi-ruin near Thirsk, called Malton Towers.

A George IV, Gothic confection, abandoned by its family after the war, Malton had followed the sad trail of such places in those years as first a school and then a training college, and after that a home for old people, and I am fairly sure at one point a finishing school specialising in *nouvelle*

234

cuisine. Until finally it achieved a slight, if spurious, fame in the mid 1990s as a 'World Centre' for some later version of Transcendental Meditation, which attracted the members of one of the manufactured Boy Bands of the era. This last incarnation was run by a dubious character who claimed the authority and support of, I seem to remember, the Dalai Lama, but I may be wrong in that. At any rate the day dawned when a red-topped Sunday scandal sheet revealed that he was not, in fact, a philosopher in touch with the higher plane, as his earnest pupils had no doubt assumed, but instead an old fraud from Pinner who had previous form for shoplifting, car theft and making false claims on his insurance. His exposure resulted in a mass exodus of the faithful, shortly followed by that of their non-spiritual leader, and for the next eight years the wind had whistled through the dusty galleries and servants' attics and former drawing rooms of the decaying folly until, at what can only have been the eleventh hour, Tarquin showed up. I am quite sure that from the house's point of view it was a very good thing that he did. Whether it was quite so beneficial to Jennifer's quality of life is rather more open to question.

The continuing craving on the part of the successful to reproduce the lifestyle and customs of the nineteenth-century aristocracy must be trying for our Labour masters. They would deny this, as they deny so many aspects of human nature, but I'm sure it is so. And the life these aspirants choose to ape is from a very specific period. Not for them the casual round of the eighteenth-century aristo, sleeping sitting upright,

235

breakfasting at noon on sticky chocolate before a ride; who wore no uniforms for his sporting or social activities, who dined at five in the afternoon, drank three or four bottles of port a night and frequently, when travelling, shared a bed with his manservant, while his wife might hunker down with her maid. This is not an attractive model for the modern millionaire. Nor, certainly, would they copy the altogether more brutish customs of the sixteenth-century toff, whose personal hygiene, to say nothing of his politics, would make a strong man faint. No, their template was developed by the late Victorians, who had such a talent for mixing rank with comfort: Majesty and deference combined with warmth and draught-free bedrooms, splendour with thick carpets and interlined curtains, where the food is hot, but there are still footmen to serve it.

Sadly, to live like this requires much, much more money than most modern copiers ever imagine. They do the sums and there seems to be enough to bring the house up to date, tidy the garden, hire someone nice to help at table and they begin. Alas, these palaces were designed to preside over thousands of rent-producing acres, to be the window display of huge fortunes in trade and manufacturing, which might have been concealed from Society but, like the mole, were working busily all the while in the dark. Because these houses eat money. They gobble it up, as the rampaging giants of the Brothers Grimm eat children and every other good thing in their path.

When the genuinely, very rich buy these palaces I am sure they enjoy them and, even if they do not often stay long, still the houses are the better for their passing. The trouble comes when they are bought by the not-quite-rich-enough, who think they can just about manage. With these, as a rule, there is a pattern. They make their fortune, such as it is. They buy a castle to celebrate. They restore it and entertain like mad for eight to ten years and then they sell, exhausted by their own poverty and the constant effort to stay afloat. While the County, those families whose fortunes were never deconstructed, and whose houses and pretensions are built on solid rock, smile, occasionally with regret, and move on to the next candidates. Tarquin Montagu was about six years into the process.

Reviewing him now, having not seen him for a while, I feel more sympathy for him than I did. That is to say that I feel some sympathy, when before I felt none at all. At that time, when we were staying with him, he must have been worried that his whole self-ennobling adventure would implode, but it was part of his personality not to admit or ever discuss his fears. He would have seen that as weakness and loss of control. In fact, his main problem was his total inability to relax control under any circumstances. I would go as far as to say that his nature was the most controlling I have ever encountered. This made him not only impossible to entertain, or to be entertained by, but also lonely and desolate, for he could not admit to anyone, least of all his wife, that events were slipping out of his grasp. I had known him as a difficult and rather ill-tempered man, who always found any conversation not centred on him, hard to follow and harder still to contribute to. But I had not fully understood the extent of his mania

237

before we arrived at his house, tired from the long drive, at tea time on that summer Friday. We were normal people. All we wanted was to be shown our room, to have a hot bath and generally to recover in order, like the model guests we were, to come downstairs refreshed, changed and ready to eat, or talk about, whatever our hosts might throw at us.

It was not to be. First, apparently, we had to sit and listen to a history of the house and when Jennifer suggested that we might be more in the mood for this lesson after we had rested, Tarquin replied that he did not judge us yet as 'ready' to see the rooms he had prepared. Naturally, my almost overpowering instinct was to tell him to piss off and drive straight back to London. But looking at Jennifer's tired and harassed face, I suspected this was an option taken by more than one guest before now, so in pity and to Bridget's relief, I allowed myself to be led into the library, to listen to the lecture like a good boy.

'The thing is,' said Tarquin, getting into his interminable stride, 'you have to understand that when Sir Richard decided to rebuild in eighteen twenty-four, he wanted both to be in the height of fashion, but at the same time not to lose the sense of historicity that his ancient blood demanded.' He took a deep breath and looked at us as if waiting for a response though what this might be I could not fathom.

'So that's why he chose Gothic?' I volunteered eventually, wondering if we were ever going to be offered sustenance. I had arrived wanting a cup of tea, but after twenty minutes of this I was ready for whisky, neat and in a pint pot.

Tarquin shook his head. 'No. Not exactly.' The

smugness of his tone was enough to make one seize a chair and smash it over his head, like a cowboy in a Mack Sennett comedy. 'That was why he chose Sir Charles Barry as his architect. Barry was still young then. This was before the old Houses of Parliament burned down. He was known as a designer of churches and a restorer of ancient monuments, not a maker of country houses. To have a servant of God as the master of the works gave the whole project a gravitas that ensured respect from his neighbours.'

'Because he built it in Gothic,' I suggested. I wasn't going to give up easily and my boredom was making me angry. But I felt this was as challenging as I could be while still pretending to listen to Tarquin with respect. In other words I was a living lie.

'No!' he spoke, this time, with a harsh edge to the word. 'The style of the building is not the issue! The style is not important! I am talking of the spiritual background with which he approached the design.'

'In Gothic,' I murmured.

'Can I go to the loo? I'm bursting,' said Bridget and, as so often in the company of women, I wondered why I hadn't thought of that myself.

'Of course,' said Jennifer. 'I'll show you your room.' With a sharp glance at her husband she led the way out, stopping to allow us to take up our cases in the hall. During all of this Tarquin was so annoyed at having his dissertation interrupted that he remained, still and sulking, in the library, watching us in glowering silence as we made our way up the imperial, double staircase.

'God Almighty.' I fell backwards on to the bed,

with a loud sigh, which I rather hoped the retreating Jennifer had caught as she crossed the landing. If she did, it cannot have been a novel experience. 'I don't think I can manage a weekend of this.' The bed itself was a large four-poster, at first sight grand and imposing, but in fact Edwardian export, cheap and clumsily carved, and clearly purchased by the Montagus for the overall effect, not for any intrinsic quality, presumably because they couldn't afford the real McCoy. I had already noticed that the whole house was like this, impressive at a glance but disappointing to any further study, like a lovely stage set to be admired from the stalls but not explored too closely. In fact, the whole thing *was* a stage set, on which Tarquin could play out his personal fantasies of high-born and literate grace. Oi vey.

That night, matters did not improve as we gathered to eat in the gloomy and under-furnished dining room, Bridget shivering beneath her gauzy shawl. A huge Jacobethan table dominated the centre of the room and as we came in I heard Tarquin remonstrate that the places had all been laid at one end, instead of the four of us being ranged around the vast board like the characters in an Addams Family film. That, or a BBC period drama where a combination of modern prejudice and complete ignorance frequently obliges their fictionalised upper classes to adopt inexplicable customs. 'If you're going to give us a sermon, I'd prefer to listen and not just watch your lips move,' said Jennifer, which brought the exchange to an end. We sat, Tarquin, needless to say, as our master at the head. He glanced at us, toying with a bottle of white wine on a coaster in front of him, a slight smile tweaking at the corners of his mouth. 'Give them some of that wine,' Jennifer murmured as she brought round plates of ethnic-looking broth.

'I'm not sure they deserve it,' said Tarquin, continuing to favour us with his twinkling, quirky gaze. 'For better or worse, I've chosen this. It's a fairly unusual Sauvignon, crisp but zingy at the same time, which I tend only to use on very special occasions. Is this one? I can't decide.'

'Oh, just give them some fucking wine,' said Jennifer, voicing accurately my own unspoken response. She sat down heavily on her husband's left, opposite Bridget, with me on her other side, and started to drink her soup. Tarquin did not answer her. Clearly, these rumblings of revolution had been getting more frequent of late. Like an unimaginative king, he was bewildered by the challenge to his authority and could not quite gauge the appropriate response. For a moment he sat in still and sober silence. Then he stood and poured the hallowed liquid into our glasses.

As he did so, I caught Jennifer's eye for a moment but she looked away, not quite ready to acknowledge, as one does in just such a glance, that she was trapped in a ghastly marriage to a crashing bore. I sympathised with her decision, not least because I didn't, for a moment, believe that I knew all the facts. There are many factors in a marriage or in any cohabiting arrangement, and just because someone gets too cross at dinner parties, or hates your best friend, or cannot tell an anecdote to save their life, these are not necessarily faults that outweigh the benefits of the union. That said, Marriage to a Controller is one

241

of the hardest kinds of relationship for the outside witness to understand.

Genuine controllers are anti-life, killers of energy, living fire blankets that smother all endeavour. For a start, they are always unhappy on anyone's territory but their own. They cannot enjoy any party they are not giving. They cannot relax as guests in a public place, because that would involve gratitude and gratitude is, to them, a sign of weakness. But they are intolerable as hosts, especially in restaurants, where their manner to waiters and fellow diners alike poisons the atmosphere. They cannot admire anyone who is more successful than they are. They cannot enjoy the friends of their partner because these strangers may not agree to accept them for the superior being they are. But since they have no friends themselves, it means they must regard any human gathering with suspicion. They cannot praise, because praise affirms the worth of the person to whom it is given and the process of controlling is built on the suppression of any self-worth in whomever they are with. They cannot learn, because learning first demands an acknowledgement that the teacher knows more than they, which they cannot give on any subject. Above all, they are boring. Boring beyond imagining. Boring to the point of madness. Yet I have known women to espouse and move in with such men, clever, interesting women, good-looking, witty women, hard-working and successful women, who have allowed themselves to be taken in and dominated by these tedious, mediocre bullies. Why? Is it sexy to be controlled? Is it safe? What?

'Are there any plans for tomorrow?' Bridget, almost blue with cold by this stage, looked brightly across the table.

'That depends,' said Tarquin.

But Jennifer could not wait to learn what it depended on. 'Nothing until the evening, but then we thought we'd go to a charity fireworks thing at a house not very far from here. We've already got the tickets so we might as well. You take a picnic and there's some sort of concert. It could be fun, as long as it's not raining.'

'Are we to be limited by something so slight as the weather?' Tarquin adopted a dark and supposedly mysterious tone, by which I assume he was attempting to snatch back the conversation, but something in Jennifer's independent response had empowered us, and we carried on as if he had not spoken.

'That'd be lovely,' said Bridget and the matter was settled.

We got through the evening somehow, finishing up back in the library, an apartment that must once have been handsome indeed, with really superb late-Regency mahogany bookshelves, which had somehow survived the depredations of the post-war decades. I was quite surprised that the bogus high priest had not flogged them during his tenure or after his fall. Could the Sunday papers have been unjust? Of course, the original collection of books was long gone and Tarquin had been quite unable to replace it. He had made do with those huge sets, entitled *Stories from the Empire*, or something similar, bound in red artificial leatherette and machine-tooled, but there were lots of them and they did at least fill the

243

space, creating once again a reasonable impression from a distance. 'Where is this house? Where we're going tomorrow?' asked Bridget, before Jennifer returned with a tray of coffee.

Tarquin raised his eyebrows, hesitating for the maximum effect. 'You'll find out.'

My sigh must have been audible.

EIGHT

I don't quite know why, but it was not until we were nearly there that I began to suspect our destination. We turned off the main road at a point I did not at first recognise. When I'd known it the road had not been a dual carriageway and there was no estate of modern housing, with its sickly yellowish street lighting, near the corner. But then, as we came into the village a bell did start to ring. The peripheries might have altered but the main street was much as it had always been, unspoiled and, if anything, improved. The pub was certainly much smarter, catering no doubt for the yuppie weekend trade and not just for the thirsty farm labourers who had crushed into the bar forty years before. We passed it by and, once out of the village, it was no more than five or ten minutes before I could see the familiar little Palladian lodge, and in a loosely stretched-out line of cars we turned through the gates into the drive and enjoyed the comfortable crunch of private gravel beneath the wheels.

But I said nothing. Not even to Bridget, who did not know the place or much about my life when I was a visitor here. My reason was simple: I could not see any profit in reviving the association, given the circumstances of my last meeting, not with Serena but with her parents. I could, after all, be fairly sure they had not forgotten that dinner, since few lives boast many such evenings. Thank Christ. And there was another, weaker motive for my silence, which was that they might have forgotten both the episode and me. My worst nightmare would have been for Tarquin to talk up my acquaintance with the family to gain some local mileage from it among the assembled throng, which he was more than capable of doing, and then for me not to be recognised by any of them. This may seem like vanity. It *was* vanity. But it was also a reluctance to let daylight in on my dreams. Even if my career with the Greshams had ended in disaster, I liked to think that I had been a feature of their lives in that distant era, when they had been so vital a feature in mine. And while logic told me this was unlikely, still I'd preserved the fantasy thus far and I wished to get back into the car at the end of the evening with my chimera intact. Anyway, they would not be there. I was quite sure of that when I thought more about it. They would be in London or on holiday or at any rate somewhere else when the locals and the lesser County invaded their demesne. 'Oh, look,' said Jennifer and there was the house, perched high on its terraces, lording it over the valley beneath, as we made our way down the winding drive. It was lit, rather gracefully, by spotlights concealed in the surrounding shrubs, an innovation since my time, and the shining beams seemed to give the cool grey stone façade a kind of ethereal beauty in the

245

dusk.

'What a fabulous place,' said Bridget. 'What's it called?'

'Gresham Abbey,' said Tarquin, as if the words belonged to him and he was reluctant to allow them free range.

'Is it National Trust?'

'No. Still private. Lord and Lady Claremont.'

'Are they nice?'

He hesitated. 'Nice enough.' Which meant, of course, that he did not know them. 'They're quite old. They're not really out and about much.' As he said it, I found it strange to think of Lady Claremont as 'quite old.' She had been a frightening, powerful, if fundamentally benevolent figure in my youth, elegant, crisp, always competent, always charming, but with a rod of tungsten in her spine. She had not, of course, paid much attention to me as I hung about on the edge of her parties, obediently sitting where I was told, usually in the most junior spot at the table, obligingly talking to my neighbours during dinner, walking with their old relations in the gardens, buying things I did not want at the village fête, reading in the library.

I remember her coming in on me once, as I sat squinting at the page before me in the gathering gloom. She laughed and I looked up as she turned on all the lamps in the room with a single switch. 'You mustn't be too scared to put the lights on,' she said with a brisk smile and went on about her business, and I felt so humiliated that my back started to prickle with embarrassed sweat. Because I suppose I had been too scared to turn them on, or rather I was just hoping that someone else would come to turn them on for me and I wouldn't have to take responsibility for it. But as I say, she was never unkind. Nor was she cross to see me there again and again. Just uninterested.

As we approached the house, we were greeted by the customary cheery gardeners and groundsmen, each equipped with their torches, who waved and signalled and called instructions to each other, until we had been safely routed off the drive and into a large field, where row upon row of cars gave us an idea of the scale of the gathering. 'Will you look at this,' said Bridget, 'there can't be much else happening in Yorkshire tonight.'

'I think you'll find the music is of a very high standard,' said Tarquin in the voice of an ageing geography mistress, which momentarily stifled our good humour. We parked and started to lug the various bits of picnic apparatus out of the car. Tarquin had already taken responsibility for a frightful plastic 'wine carrier' and was legging it towards the gate that would lead us back to the festivities. By parking in the field, we had skirted the house, so the gate in the pretty, iron, sheep fencing led directly into one side of the gardens that stretched away from the back of the abbey in a falling series of terraces, leading down to the distant lake in the valley below. Clearly, taking in the crowd that was already here, Tarquin was determined to find a good spot and he was soon out of sight, leaving us to manage the rest. Bridget followed him with a collection of rugs and cushions, obliging Jennifer and me to carry the long, white cold box between us. We staggered along, nearly tripping on the tufts of cow grass, until we reached the gate.

'Can we stop for a moment?' said Jennifer. Actually, it was quite heavy and the rope handles were cutting into our sissy palms. We leant for a moment against the rail. In the distance we could hear the murmurs and laughter of the crowd, and some sort of canned music was coming out of hidden loudspeakers, Elgar or Mahler, or at any rate an inoffensive choice for those oh-so-British ears. Jennifer broke our silence. 'I think we've got until nine to eat and then the real music starts.' I nodded. 'You are kind to come,' she added in a tone of real gratitude. 'I know we kept saying we'd make a date, but I never thought we would and I do appreciate it.'

'Nonsense. We're loving being here.' But of course it wasn't nonsense and we weren't loving it. I was, as I have mentioned, very fond of Jennifer. There is something about a publicity tour that is so ghastly, and makes one feel so vulnerable, as your book or film or whatever it might be that you are flogging is paraded in front of the public gaze, like a Spartan baby exposed to the cruelties of Mount Tygetus, that a bond is formed with fellow sufferers which is hard to describe to anyone who has not been through it. Like survivors in a lifeboat, I suppose. Selling things is part of the modern world and if you have a product, you have to sell it, but by heaven it's no fun if it does not come naturally to you; and Jennifer, like me, came from a world that was uncomfortable with selling in any guise. Even buying should not be advertised, but professional, or worse, personal, selling can only ever be shameful. This prejudice manifests itself in lots of sharp, spiky comments. 'I saw you on the box with that man who can't pronounce his

Rs. I never watch it normally but the au pair turned it on.' Or 'I heard you on the car wireless being grilled by some angry little northerner. Grim.' Or 'What on earth were you doing on afternoon television? Haven't you got any work to get on with?' And you listen, knowing that this same afternoon programme sells more books than any billboard or advertising campaign in Britain and in fact you're lucky, incredibly lucky, to have been invited on to it.

Of course you want so much to say that. Or at the very least to tell them to grow up or drop dead, or to open their eyes to the fact that the Fifties are over. But you don't. My late mother would have said 'they're just jealous, darling' and maybe they are, a bit, even when they don't know it. But I am jealous, too. Jealous that their living never requires them to make an ass of themselves at the end of the pier at a shilling a go, which is exactly what it feels like most of the time. In any life, in any career, only people who've made the same journey understand each other completely. Mothers want advice from other mothers, not from childless social workers, cancer sufferers need to hear from survivors of cancer, not from the doctors who cure it, even victims of a scandal will only really want to compare notes with some other politician or celebrity who has similarly gone down in flames. This was the bond that Jennifer and I shared. We were published authors of moderate and precarious success, and I valued her friendship. I wanted to please her and for some reason I knew it was important to her that we should come and stay in Yorkshire. I had assumed her urgency was a measure of her love but I suspect, now, that by this stage, it was because very few people would stay, certainly nobody would come twice who didn't need to borrow money, and that the weekends when she was alone with Tarquin were becoming intolerable.

'Is he always like this?' I asked. I felt that her honesty in thanking me for coming merited a bit of straight talking, although, as the words left my mouth I wondered if I hadn't overstepped the mark.

But she smiled. 'Not when he's asleep.' Her expression developed into an ironic laugh. 'I can't decide whether he was the same when we first married and I was so young and so insecure that I mistook his pomposity for knowledge and his patronising for instruction, or whether he's got worse.'

'I think he must have got a bit worse,' I said. 'I'm not sure Helen Keller would have married him if he'd been as he is now.'

She laughed again, but still her laugh was sad. 'I wish we'd had a child,' she said, but then caught my look. 'I know. Everyone thinks it would have solved everything and everyone is wrong.'

'Don't ask me. I'm the sad old bachelor who could never commit.'

'I just think, with him, it would have shored him up. Allowed him that bat squeak of immortality that children bring. Or even if he'd just succeeded at something convincingly. Because he never really has.'

'He lives very well for a failure.'

She shook her head. 'It's all inherited.'

This surprised me. 'Really? I hadn't got him down for a Trustafarian.'

She knew what I was saying and she wasn't offended. 'It's not old money. All that stuff about the Montagus is bollocks. It isn't even our real name. His father arrived from Hungary after the uprising of 1956. He started as a lorry driver, built up a transport business and sold out in the mid Nineties. Tarquin's his only child. He was a lovely man, actually. I doted on him, but Tarquin used to keep him hidden, so none of our friends were allowed to meet him. Now he wants you to think the money is the remains of an ancient fortune, amplified by his own recent success. It's neither. But I expect you knew that.'

I didn't confirm this, as it seemed superior and smug. 'It's rather a romantic fantasy, in a way.'

'It can't last for much longer.' She sighed wearily at the thought of impending collapse. 'The whole thing costs far more than either of us realised and there's very little coming in, now we've tied it all up in the house. I write my books so at least we can eat and go to the theatre, but I'm not sure how long that'll keep us above the waterline. He's a hopeless architect, you know. He gets taken on for particular jobs now and then, when a practice needs some extra help, but nobody ever asks him to stay.'

'Would you?'

This time she laughed out loud. 'Perhaps that's it. Perhaps he's a fabulous architect but anathema to have in the office.'

'So what are you going to do?'

Which made her stop laughing. 'I don't know. Everyone says I should leave him, most of all my mother, which would have astonished her and me if anyone had predicted such a thing twenty years

251

ago, but the odd thing is, in a funny way I do still rather love him. You'll say I'm mad, but I watch him boring everyone to death and trying to control and impress and make people admire him, and I know he's so puzzled and frightened and bewildered inside. He can tell it isn't working, but he just doesn't understand why not. No one comes to stay any more.'

'Except us.'

'Except fools like you. And nobody wants to know us down here. I've seen them literally roll their eyes when we walk into a room. I somehow feel I can't leave him open to attack, when it's so obvious to everyone but him that he can't protect himself.'

As often as I am reminded that love, like everything else in this world, comes in many different shapes and sizes, I can still be amazed by some of the forms it takes. 'I don't think you're mad. It's your life,' I said.

'I know. And it isn't a dress rehearsal. But even if I don't add up to much in the end, the fact is I took him on, nobody forced me, and I have to see it through. I suppose that sounds like a quote from G. A. Henty.'

'It sounds like something only a very decent woman would say.'

She blushed and at that moment Bridget reappeared at the fence. 'Please come. If he doesn't stop talking about the wine we're going to drink I swear to God I'll break a bottle of it over his head.' So saying, she relieved Jennifer of her burdensome share of the cold box and guided us to our site on the top terrace where Tarquin had staked his claim. To a restful mixture of chattering

252

crowd noise, music and Tarquin droning on, we unpacked our food and spread it forth luxuriously upon our waiting, cushioned rugs.

We had nearly finished eating when Tarquin suddenly broke off his current lecture. He had been telling us about the Ptolemaic dynasty of Egypt or some subject equally fascinating, and we had each retreated into a kind of glazed, mental cave of our own making, when his voice altered and took on a nervous edge: 'They're here.'

'Who?' Bridget was keen to support the introduction of any new topic, never mind what.

'The family. The Claremonts.'

As he said their name, I was amazed to find that, like a lyric in a wartime love song, my heart actually skipped a beat. Dear Lord, does there never come a time when we are too old for such foolishness? But when I looked there was no sign of Serena, only an elderly group, all in evening dress; presumably they had enjoyed a smarter, better dinner inside. They glanced benevolently at the crowds enjoying their policies in so pleasant and decorous a manner, and in their midst were two ancient pensioners who seemed to be impersonating the Earl and Countess of Claremont, darling Roo and Pel, as I had never known them well enough to call them, who had once been such a vivid part of my life. I looked at them now, these icons of my youth, confident that they could not see me. Was I avoiding them because the sight of me would make them start and stretch their eyes in horror, or because I could not bear to see that they did not recognise me and I was forgotten? Probably the latter. I was sneakily afraid that if someone had mentioned that one of

253

the hundreds of picnickers was an acquaintance of theirs from four decades before and had thought of them many, many times in the interim, they would have been none the wiser. Not even had I been paraded before them in person.

This deflating suspicion was reinforced by the sad but apparent truth that my Lord Claremont had been more or less exchanged for another man. The handsome, corpulent, sexy, flirty hedonist, with his thick, wavy hair and his wavier smile, had completely vanished and been replaced by a bony, stooped individual. His nose, stripped of its flesh and unsupported by the plump cheeks on either side, had become prominent, hooked like the Duke of Wellington's to whom he was no doubt related in some wise, while his generous lips had been shaved down, as if by a razor, and he had almost no hair left. I would not say he appeared less distinguished. Not at all. This fellow looked like someone who read poetry and philosophy and pondered the great issues of life, while the Lord Claremont of my memories knew how to get a good table at the last minute and where you could find an excellent Château d'Yquem, but not much else. For a moment he glanced my way but of course registered nothing, which was not surprising since, while I knew him in those distant days, he did not know me. Not really. Certainly, he gave little sign of being aware of that awkward, plain young man whose only use was to make up a table for bridge. Even so, looking at this stick-like figure, with a Baron Munchausen outline, I missed the man he had been and it was hard not to feel a pang at the pitiless work of the passing years.

Lady Claremont was less altered. It seems odd

to think of it, but I must have known her first when some of the bloom of youth was still upon her. Serena was the eldest child and her mother had married young so she cannot have been much more than forty-two or -three, when we met. It is always odd for the young grown old to realise how youthful the dominating creatures of their early years must in many cases have been. In those days her haughty, witty confidence was further empowered by her cold beauty and as a result, to me she had seemed formidable. It is true that her looks had largely, though not entirely, disappeared. But I could see, even from a distance, that she had replaced whatever she had lost with other qualities, some more sterling than the earlier version. She glanced our way and for a moment, forgetting everything that had kept me huddled out of her eyeline, I was tempted to signal my presence in some way, but the thought of her ignoring my wave and the fun it would give Tarquin when she did kept me still. Then came the broadcast announcement that told us the concert was about to begin. She looked at her husband, muttering some suggestion, I would assume about returning to their seats and a moment later, with a final, general acknowledgement, the group from the house climbed the stone steps towards the top terrace.

The concert was cheerful rather than profound, a Hungry Hundreds medley of Puccini, Rossini and Verdi, with a bit of Chopin thrown in to make you cry. The lead-up to the interval was the Drinking Song from *Traviata,* which was adequately sung by quite a good tenor from some northern company, and a fat soprano over from

Italy, who was supposed to be much better than him but wasn't. It was an appropriate choice as the throats of the watching hoards were dry as dust by this time, and you could hear the champagne corks starting to pop as the couple trilled the final soaring note. Tarquin, naturally, had provided some rare sustenance, Cristal, or the like, and was lecturing us on how to savour it, when we were interrupted by a man in the neolivery of the modern butler, striped trousers and a short black jacket. There was no mistaking Tarquin as our leader and he went over to him, murmuring in his ear. Tarquin's surprise deepened to astonishment as he pointed me out. 'That's him,' he said, and the man scuttled over towards me.

'Her Ladyship wonders if you and your party would like to join the family after the concert, Sir, to watch the fireworks from the terrace.'

I cannot deny I felt a warm sense of self-justification at his words, as anyone must when they find what they had supposed was a one-way relationship, is in fact reciprocal. I had been forgiven, or at any rate I had not been forgotten. I turned to the others. 'Lady Claremont has asked us up to the house for the fireworks.' Silence greeted this extraordinary development. 'After the music's finished.'

Jennifer was the first to gather her wits. 'How tremendously kind. We should love it. Please thank her.'

The man nodded with a slight inclination of his head, rather than a bow, and pointed towards the steps. 'If you go up to the top there—' He stopped, looking back at me. 'Of course, you'll know the way, Sir.'

256

'Yes.'

'They'll be in the Tapestry Drawing Room.'

'Thank you.' He hurried back to his normal duties. There was silence as the other three stared at me.

'*You'll know the way, Sir?*' For once, Tarquin's determination never to be impressed had deserted him.

'I used to come here when I was younger.'

Tarquin was silent. I knew him well enough by now to understand that he was considering the facts with a view to reimposing his mastery of the situation. So far, the solution had eluded him.

'Why didn't you say?' Jennifer's enquiry was, under the circumstances, a reasonable one.

'I didn't know where we were coming until we got here. We asked but Tarquin wouldn't tell us.' Jennifer threw a swift, admonitory glance at her pensive spouse. 'And I wasn't sure they'd be interested in seeing me again after such a long time. It's true that I used to stay here at one period of my misspent youth, but it was forty years ago.'

'Then she must have very sharp eyes, this "Lady Claremont" of yours.' Bridget spoke in derisive, inverted commas, as she always did when dealing with any part of my past that threatened her. I knew already, without being told, that of all the aspects of this uncomfortable weekend, the present episode would prove the *most* uncomfortable for her. But before we could discuss it further, the orchestra struck up and we were being sprayed with a deeply accessible version of 'Quando M'en Vo' from *La Bohème*, which may be played for laughs in context but is generally more lachrymose in concert and soon had all those MFHs and lifetime presidents of the village flower show committee reaching for their handkerchiefs.

I knew that in fact the Tapestry Drawing Room opened directly on to the gardens above us, but some trace of late-teen diffidence told me that to push in through the French windows with a crowd of strangers was overplaying my hand, so I devised the plan that at the end of the performance we would deposit our debris in the car, to obviate the need to collect it later, and make our way to the front of the house. The programme of events stated clearly that there was a fifty-minute break between concert and fireworks to allow the night to get properly dark, so I knew we had time. In that way we could come into the house via the front door, like normal people, and not be suspected of springing an ambush on our hosts.

I was glad of the decision when we got there, as quite a crowd was arriving and it was clear that the Claremonts had cunningly devised this plan to placate those locals who felt they had a right to be acknowledged by the family without the bore of giving them all dinner. The hall at Gresham was vast and high, stone-floored and with a screen of columns completing the square, behind which a graceful cantilevered staircase rose up to the next floor, its steps so shallow that a woman descending in a long skirt, which for our generation meant evening dress, seemed to float down as if her feet barely skimmed the steps beneath. It was a more awkward progress for men, who had to adjust quickly to the fact that each step taken only brought them about an inch nearer their destination, but for women the effect was like gliding, flying, and quite magical to watch, as I remembered so very well.

The portraits displayed here had been selected by Lady Claremont in a massive re-hang when she and her husband took over the house in 1967, just before my first visit, and which I could see at once had not been altered. They were chosen, as she freely confessed, unashamedly and entirely for their looks, and despite the anguished protests of Lord Claremonts' surviving aunts, those distinguished Victorian statesmen in undertakers' frock coats, those fearsome Georgian soldiers, all red faces and stubborn chins, those wily Tudor statesmen with their shifty eyes and avaricious mouths and generally the uglier members of the family, had been banished to anterooms and passages and bedrooms, except the ones by really famous painters, who had wound up either in the library or hung in fearsome double tiers against the crimson, damask walls of the great dining room. Both these chambers, Lady Claremont had explained to me at the time, were masculine rooms and so needed to be impressive but not pretty. Here, in the hall, charming children from every period were interlarded with handsome, nervous, young men in their Eton leaving portraits, trembling with anticipation at the welcoming life ahead, and lovely Gresham girls, painted on their betrothal to other lordly magnates or as part of some series of Court beauties for King Charles II or the Prince Regent, smiled down on their worshippers beneath. Their shining, gilded frames were set off by the apricot walls and the intricate plasterwork, picked out in varying shades of grey and white, while in the centre of the ceiling hung a

259

huge chandelier, like a shower of glistening raindrops, frozen in their fall by a glance from the Snow Queen.

'How perfectly lovely,' said Jennifer, looking around, provoking a severe look from her husband, which I understood. Anything giving away that they were not regular visitors was to be suppressed. Jennifer grasped this too, of course, but had obviously made the interesting decision not to play along with his self-importance. Bridget, needless to say, was retreating into one of her silent-but-ironic moods, but I couldn't spare the time to administer to it. I was back at Gresham, which I never thought to be again, and I was determined to enjoy it.

The Tapestry Drawing Room was on the corner of the garden front, and the easiest way to reach it was through an oval anteroom at the back of the hall, where facing doors led left, to the dining room, and right, to our destination. It was a lovely place. The walls were lined in a kind of dusty blue moiré, with cream panelling edged in gilt up to the dado, and high panelled doorcases with over-door paintings set into them, taking the cream and gilt on up to the ceiling. Against the huge spaces of blue hung a set of Gobelin tapestries, celebrating a series of victories, achieved, I am pretty sure, by Marlborough. I forget precisely why they were here. Maybe an earlier Claremont had been in part responsible for the great duke's glory; in fact, now I am writing it I think that was why they were upped to an earldom in the 1710s. Beneath our feet was a ravishing Aubusson carpet, with its slight, distinctive wrinkling, and on it sat various magnificent pieces of furniture, most spectacularly a pedestal clock, seven foot high on its plinth, its inlaid case embellished with gilding, which had been presented to the third Earl by the Empress Catherine of Russia in return for some unspecified personal service, which no one had ever convincingly explained. The butler we had spoken to during the interval held a tray of glasses and a couple of maids were wandering about with more wine and bits of food. Lady Claremont, with that amazing eye for detail that had clearly not deserted her, had provided mini-savouries in the form of angels on horseback and tiny, pick-up bits of Welsh rabbit or mushrooms on itsy bits of toast, all of which would be welcome, even after eating dinner.

'There you are. We couldn't believe our eyes when we saw you.' Lady Claremont kissed me swiftly and efficiently on one cheek, not for her the double-kiss import of the 1970s. 'You should have let us know you were coming.' I presented my party, who all shook hands. Jennifer alone thanked her for inviting us and Tarquin tried to start a conversation about the famous clock on which, needless to say, he had a great deal of information at his fingertips. But she had spent a life avoiding just such overtures, and soon gave a nod and a smile to indicate she had heard enough. Then she turned to her ancient neighbour, introducing me. 'Do you remember Mrs Davenport?' Since the woman did look a bit familiar I nodded as I shook her wizened hand. 'He was here all the time at the end of the Sixties,' Lady Claremont explained with a gay laugh. 'We used to feel terribly sorry for him.' She looked at me indulgently and I could sense my throat tightening at the prospect of what was coming next, but nothing could stop her as she looked about to gain the maximum audience. 'He was *so* in love with Serena!'

And she and the said Mrs Davenport laughed happily together at the memory of my roiling misery, which could still keep me awake at nights, and which I had thought private and brilliantly concealed from all but me. I smiled by way of response, to show I too thought it a terrific joke that I had wandered through these same charming rooms with my heart actually hurting in my chest. But her steady, even voice served to calm my remembered pain, as she chatted on about this and that, Serena and the other children, the lovely weather, the ghastly government, all standard stuff for a drinks party at a country house. I was interested that she had not mentioned the event we shared, that made an effective end to those dreams of long ago. Of course, it is a relatively modern American import, the notion that we must 'have these things out,' while the old, English traditions of letting sleeping dogs lie, and brushing things under the carpet, have been spurned. But who gains from this constant picking at the scabs of life? 'We have to talk,' says at least one character in almost every television drama these days, until one longs to scream at the screen, 'Why? Just let it go!' But I was not surprised Lady Claremont had avoided the culture of revisiting old wounds. In a way, her asking me up for a drink was her way of saying, 'It's all right. Like you, we've moved on. After so many years, surely we can have a chat again like normal people without even mentioning it.' And if she had made fun of my love pangs, still I appreciated her courtesy in this.

By the time I'd concluded my ruminations the tide of the party had separated us. Tarquin, having listened to the exchange with glee, could not decide whether to turn our hostess's ribbing into a way to belittle me and thereby derive some fun from my failed romance of long ago, or whether the mere fact that I had been to Gresham sufficiently often for Lady Claremont even to be aware that I was in love with her daughter and to welcome me now as an old friend entitled me to special handling. I left him to his indecisive review. Across the room, Jennifer had unearthed somebody they actually knew and seemed to be chatting quite merrily, and Bridget, as usual making a virtue of being out of her depth, was sulking, so I was essentially alone again in this, the haunting, painful setting of my earlier self.

Clutching my glass, nodding and smiling, I pushed back through the crush into the oval anteroom. We had passed through it quickly on our way in but, as I remembered so well, it was a lovely place, not huge but delicate and inviting, upholstered in a light and feminine chintz, and filled with light and feminine things. In this house it served as the boudoir and Lady Claremont's desk sat against one wall, a beautifully carved *bureau plat*, its surface littered with papers and letters and lists of things-to-do. I looked idly at a set of small Flemish paintings depicting the five senses, painted by David Teniers the younger some time in the 1650s. I had always admired them and I greeted them now like old friends. How delicate they were, how fine the detail, how strange that, since the paint first dried, not one,

263

not two, but twenty generations had been born, had planned, had dreamed, had coped with disappointment and had died. I wandered over to the dining-room doors. They were closed but I turned the handle and pushed one open, startling a maid who was finishing laying the table. 'More than fourteen for breakfast?' I smiled to show that I came in peace.

She relaxed a little, answering in a rich, warm Yorkshire accent, 'We're nineteen tomorrow. And that's with two of the ladies staying in bed.'

'I remember the rule was always that fourteen or under ate breakfast in the small dining room. More than that and it was laid in here.'

I had succeeded in catching her attention. In fact, she was quite curious. She looked at me more closely. 'Did you used to stay here, then?'

'I did. At one time. It's reassuring to know that nothing's changed.' Actually, this was true. It *was* reassuring to find so much was still the same here, in this isolated appendix of my life, when almost everything had changed elsewhere. Although I later learned there was an element of illusion in this and that the estate, along with the country, had taken a downturn during the Seventies, successfully reversed from the mid-Eighties onwards in the hands of a new and gifted manager.

In fact, this happy story was true for many families I had known before their temporary fall. It should have been true for all of them, really, had not too many succumbed to that most dangerous of modern fashions among the born-rich, the desire to prove, to themselves and to everyone else, that their money is a reflection of their own brains and talent. The advantage of this is that it obviates the need to feel grateful to their forebears, or obliged to respect their successful, self-made acquaintance, who might otherwise demand some kind of moral superiority over those whose enviable position owes all to the efforts of others. The disadvantage, of course, is that it is not true. In denial of which, rich but silly aristocrats up and down the land will blithely launch into schemes they do not understand and investments that have no real worth, on the word of advisors without either judgement or merit, until their ignorance inevitably overturns them. I could name at least twenty men of my acquaintance who would be worth many millions more than they are if they had never left their bedrooms and come downstairs. And more than a few who began with everything and ended up with literally almost nothing. In this field I suspect that women, more pragmatic as a rule and less needy of self-worth when it comes to having a 'head for business,' have generally proved more sensible. Certainly, Lady Claremont would never have allowed her dearly loved spouse to get his hands on the wheel, or even near it, when it came to steering the Gresham inheritance.

'Mummy shouldn't have said that. I hope she hasn't driven you in here.' Her voice could always unnerve me. 'If you *were* even a bit in love with me I find it tremendously flattering.' That Serena should be so near to me was a joy, that she should have heard her mother's words was a nightmare, so it was with mixed emotions that I turned to find her looking at me through the door from the middle of the anteroom.

'At the time, I always rather hoped no one had

265

guessed.'

'I didn't at the beginning.'

'Until Portugal.'

'Before. But never mind.' Unsurprisingly, she didn't want to be drawn into that one. 'Of course, Mummy told me afterwards that she knew when you first stayed here, but I suppose one's mother is bound to be more aware of these things.'

'Yours is.' We both smiled. 'It was kind of her not to bring up the whole Estoril thing, seeing it was the last time I saw them.'

'Was it really?'

'I might have glimpsed them across the room at a summer party at Christie's or something, but I haven't spoken to them properly between that night and this.'

She shrugged gently. 'Well, it was ages ago.' I wondered at her. As I have already mentioned, I had run into Serena occasionally over the years, so there was no four-decade gap to be leaped, but the sight of her was always an amazement. To start with, she seemed to have aged one year for every ten that the rest of us had gone through. In fact, she was hardly changed at all. A few fine lines at the sides of her eyes, a shallow crease by her mouth, her hair a slightly paler colour, nothing more. 'Are you all here for the weekend?'

'Most of us. Mummy made it a three-line whip. In case the whole thing went belly-up and we had to save the show. But the organisers were much better this year than last.'

'Is Mary with you? And Rupert?'

'Mary is. She was in the hall when I last saw her. Poor old Rupert's in Washington. He's been posted there for the last three years.'

'Washington? What an honour.'

'An honour and a bore. We're aching for him to get something in Paris or Dublin or anywhere he can get home from for the weekend.'

'What about Peniston? Have you brought him with you?' Serena had two children. The elder, Mary, whom I was doubtless about to see again after many years, was now married to the first secretary in the Washington embassy, Rupert Wintour, and was well on her way to being an ambassadress. When a child, she was ordinary in every way, and horribly like her father to look at, so I confess I suspected her husband's motives when I first heard about the marriage. His father, Sir Something Wintour, was an entrepreneur and his mother a former beautician, so the eldest child of an earl seemed like a suspiciously welcome choice, but once I had met him I felt I'd been unjust to Rupert. He was quite a bright spark. Serena's other child was the essential boy, Peniston, a little younger than his sister, whom I had seen occasionally in their house in Lansdowne Crescent, just as our friendship was petering out.

'Peniston's here but he arrived under his own steam, since he's married and has children of his own. These days I'm a grandmother three times over.'

'I need proof.'

She smiled pleasantly, used to compliments. 'Helena's come with William and the boys. You must say hello. And Anthony. I'm not sure where Venetia's got to. Mummy says she's in New York, but I got a card last week from Singapore. You know what she's like.' She rolled her eyes ceilingwards, with a tolerant laugh. There were

267

three girls, starting with Serena herself and a brother who was, of course, heir to the kingdom. Helena, the second Gresham sister, had married an amiable landowning banking baronet in a neighbouring county, a union that had satisfied her mother, if it did not send her into ecstasies. However the youngest sister, Venetia, had defied the family by accepting the proposal of a pop impresario, an episode I remember only too well. The Claremonts had absolutely refused to countenance it at first. But to everyone's surprise, since she was not seen as particularly strong or rebellious, Venetia had stuck to her guns and in the end they caved in rather than endure the scandal of a wedding without their presence. As my own father used to say, 'Never provide material for a story.' Venetia was the winner in the end. Her husband made an immense fortune in the music industry and now she was richer than, or at least as rich as, any of them but the family exacted its revenge by continuing to patronise her, as if her life had been a trivial and wasteful mass of nothing, up to the present day.

Oddly, the male sibling, Anthony, was the one we all knew least. He came after Serena and before the others. He was still young, not much more than a boy, when Serena and I were running around together, but I can't say that even when he was grown up we were ever much the wiser where he was concerned. He was polite, of course, and pleasant to talk to at dinner or while having a drink before lunch, but he was always curiously opaque. He revealed nothing. The kind of person who, years later, might turn out to be a terrorist or a serial killer, without causing any great surprise. I liked him though, and I will say that he never demonstrated that supremely tedious habit that some people acquire, of loudly advertising to all and sundry the amount of information they are concealing. He hid everything about himself, but without pretence, mystery or conceit.

'So, how are you?' she said. 'Have you got another book out? I shouldn't have to ask. I feel rather feeble, not knowing.' There is a way of enquiring into an artistic career, which may sound or read as generous, but which in fact manages to reduce the value of it almost to nothing. The contempt is contained within its enthusiastic kindness, rather as a little girl's painting will be praised by someone who is hopeless with children. No one can do this better than the genuinely posh.

'There's one coming out next March.'

'You must let us know when it does.' Such people often say this sort of thing to their acquaintance in the media: 'Let me know when you're next on television,' 'Let us know when it's published,' 'Let us know when you're back on *Any Questions*.' As if one is likely to sit down and send off three thousand postcards when a personal appearance is scheduled. Obviously, they understand this will never happen. The message is really: 'We are not sufficiently interested in what you do to be aware of it if you don't make us aware. You understand that it does not impinge on our world, so you will please forgive us in future for missing whatever you are involved in.' Serena did not mean it unkindly, which is the case with many of them, but I cannot deny it is disheartening at times.

Her friendliness continued unabated. 'When did

269

you know you'd be here tonight? You might have given us some warning. You could have come to dinner.' I explained the situation. Serena raised her eyebrows. 'Are they friends of yours? He's acquired the title of Bore of the County, but perhaps we're being unjust.'

'I wouldn't say that.'

She laughed. 'Well, it's nice to welcome you back. Has it changed?'

'Not really. Not as much as most of the rest of my life.'

'A trip down Memory Lane.'

'I'm living in Memory Lane at the moment.' Naturally, this demanded an explanation and I gave a partial one. I did not tell her the reason why I was interviewing all these women from our joint past, only that Damian wanted to check up on what had happened to them and he'd asked me to do it, because he met them all through me in the first place.

'But why did you agree? Isn't it very time-wasting? And you certainly don't owe him a favour.' She raised her eyebrows to punctuate this.

'I'm not completely sure why I'm doing it. I didn't intend to when he made the request, but then I saw that he was dying—' I broke off. She was visibly shocked and I rather regretted blurting it out as I had done.

'Dying?'

'I'm afraid so.'

She took stock, regaining command of herself. 'How odd. You don't think of someone like Damian Baxter as "dying."'

'Well, he is.'

'Oh.' By now she had quite recovered her

270

equilibrium. 'Well, I'm sad. Surprised and sad.'

'I think he was always quite surprising.'

But Serena shook her head. 'I don't agree. He was exciting, but most of what he got up to was not surprising, it was inevitable. It wasn't at all surprising that he gatecrashed the Season so effectively. And it wasn't a bit surprising that he made more money than anyone else in recorded history. I knew all that would happen from the moment I met him. But dying thirty years before his time . . .'

'How did you know?'

Serena thought for a moment. 'I think because he was always so angry. And in my experience people who are angry when young, either explode and vanish or do tremendously well. When I heard he'd gone into the City I knew he'd end up with zillions.'

I could not contain my curiosity, even if it felt like biting down on a loose tooth. 'Did you like him? When all was said and done?'

She looked at me. She knew the significance of the question, despite the years that we had travelled since it had the smallest relevance to either of our lives. On top of which she shared the usual reluctance of her tribe to give emotional information that might later be used in evidence against her. But at last she nodded. 'At one point,' she said. Then she seemed to gather up her carapace from the floor and wrap it firmly round herself once more. 'We really ought to join the others. I think it's about to start.' In answer to her words there was a sudden fizzing roar and through the uncurtained tall windows we could see a rocket darting across the night sky. With a loud bang, it

271

exploded into a wide shower of golden sparks, accompanied by an appreciative 'ooh!' from the watching crowd.

'Is Andrew here?' In common courtesy I could avoid the question no longer. Even so, it felt lumpy, as if it had stuck to my lips.

She nodded. 'He's outside with the children. He always loves fireworks.' Behind her, the anteroom was suddenly filling up again, as some of the contents of the drawing room beyond spilled out to take advantage of another way outside. Serena started towards them. I fell into step beside her as we passed through the open French windows and in a moment we were enveloped in the sudden chill of the now dark, night air. Further along to the right, the rest of the house's guests were emerging from the doors of the Tapestry Drawing Room itself and the wide terrace was already becoming quite crowded. Another rocket, another bang, another twinkling shower, another ooh. 'Andrew, look who's here.'

It is still an offence to me that, of all people on earth, she should have married Andrew Summersby. How could my goddess have married this clottish beast of burden willingly? At least Shakespeare's Titania chose Bottom when she was on drugs. My Titania picked her Bottom when stone-cold sober and with her eyes wide open. Obviously, we all knew that Lady Claremont had propelled her daughter towards it, as in those days she did not question the accepted wisdom that a mother's job was to promote a suitable marriage, and a husband of equal rank and fortune trumped every trick. And obviously we all knew that Lady Belton was pushing from the other side until her shoulder must have been out of joint. But even so, it was hard to understand at the time, and harder still now, looking back. I wondered silently if Lady Claremont, with the different values and awarenesses of the modern world, would have promoted the match quite so furiously today. I rather thought not. But what good are such contemplations? If my grandmother had had wheels, she would have been a trolley car.

Andrew's stupid, bovine face, wider and flatter and redder and, if possible, even more repulsive than when I knew him, turned blankly towards me, with a solemn, self-inflating nod. 'Hello,' he said, without any question or courtesy to mark the gap since we last met.

Bridget had now found her way to us through the crowd and she chose this moment to curl her arm through mine in a deliberately possessive manner, advertising ownership, smiling smugly at Serena as she did so, all of which I found incredibly irritating but I did not show it. 'May I present Bridget FitzGerald?' I nodded towards my companions. 'Andrew and Serena Summers—' I corrected myself. This was wrong. Andrew's father was dead, which I knew. I just wasn't thinking. 'Sorry. Andrew and Serena Belton.' Serena smiled and shook Bridget's hand, but Andrew for some reason looked rather insulted and raised his glance back towards the fireworks. I thought at the time it was because I had got his name wrong, but I have a horrible suspicion, knowing his absolute lack of brain or imagination, that he had objected to being introduced to a stranger of lower rank as anything other than 'Lord Belton.' You may find this suggestion hard to believe, but I can assure you he

273

was not alone among perfectly genuine toffs in this brand of foolishness, which takes the form of imitating the clothes and customs of their fathers from half a century ago and more. This is in the mistaken belief that it is an indicator of their good breeding, as opposed to absolute proof of their idiocy.

Serena continued blithely on, as if his rudeness were quite normal, which I suppose to her it was. 'This is my daughter, Mary. And my son, Peniston.' The introduction was for Bridget's benefit. I smiled and said hello, which greeting was returned by Mary pleasantly, as I willingly concede, and Peniston also held out his hand. They clearly knew who I was, which was pathetically gratifying. Serena smiled too, enjoying the presence of her children. 'When did you last see them?'

'In another lifetime, I'm afraid.' I smiled and shook the young man's hand in my turn. 'I won't mention the girl in sulks over having to wear some party dress she hated, or the boy in blue rompers, peddling his first tricycle round the kitchen.'

'That's a relief,' said Peniston.

'I remember that dress,' said Mary. 'Granny sent it and it was covered in the most hideous smocking, like an illustration from a Jack and Jill reader in the Fifties. I screamed the place down rather than wear it and I would do the same today.' We laughed, and I found myself revising my opinion of Mary, even if her resemblance to Andrew was very off-putting. Through all this, Bridget looked blank and Andrew once again assumed the expression of affront that I could already tell had become habitual. There was no obvious reason for this, although it might have been because the reference to his daughter's tantrums or his heir's rompers, or perhaps to his wife's kitchen, was some piece of iniquitous *lèse-majesté* on my part. I neither knew nor cared.

But the young siblings eased the touchy moment by chatting away about mundane things and Andrew's gaucheness was soon forgotten. Presumably Peniston and his sister often had to perform this service to cover the tracks of their tiresome Papa. I was not, in truth, much disposed to like the new Viscount Summersby, as he now was, since his very name still made me shudder, but even I had to admit he seemed a nice fellow. I can't pretend he was exactly attractive, being overweight and shortish, and if his face was pleasant, it was not good-looking. But then again, my impression of him may be suspect. Most men, or women too for aught I know, have ambivalent feelings towards the children of those they once loved. Particularly if it was not their choice to end the relationship. In a way these boys and girls, symbols of some horrible misjudgement by the gods, should never have been born if things had gone right. Yet it's not their fault, is it? As one usually comes to see in the end. So it was for me, with Mary Wintour and Peniston Summersby. The news of their impending births had cut me like a knife from fore to aft, but of course, presented with this nice man, this agreeable woman, it was quite a different matter, and even I could see it wasn't fair to hate them because their father was a blockhead and their mother broke my heart. There wasn't much of Serena in either of them, to be honest, and even less as they had grown. As a little girl, Mary had been a miniature of Andrew, far more than her brother, but on that night he too looked more like his father, if he looked at all like either. Happily for them and for their prospects, neither seemed to resemble Andrew in charm.

Peniston smiled. 'Granny was frightfully excited when she spotted you. She's terribly proud to know a real novelist. She's read everything you've ever written.'

'I'm flattered.' I was. And astonished. Suddenly it was less extraordinary that I'd been found among the crowd.

'She just loves knowing a writer. Most of her friends have the greatest difficulty reading to the end of a restaurant bill.' A pretty woman in her early thirties had joined us. 'This is my wife, Anne.'

'What he says is quite true. Roo's thrilled you're here. She's got all your books, you know. I expect she's lining them up for you to sign.'

'She has only to ask.' Since Lady Claremont's interest in my work presumably implied an albeit slight interest in me, I was amused that in forty years she had never invited me to a single gathering either here at Gresham or in London, nor made the smallest attempt to re-establish contact. Why was that, if her fascination with my career was so great? At the time, my paranoia immediately attributed the cause to the Estoril evening, but I am fairly sure now that I was wrong. Occasionally one does come across this curious diffidence on the part of the posh and there is nothing sinister or deflating in it. I suppose it is the flip side of their tendency to patronise. They are still marking the absolute divide between their world and yours, but in this case it is demonstrated

276

by a kind of modesty, a tacit recognition that their muscular, social powers may not always impress those who have other choices.'

'You're missing everything.' Andrew's voice cut across our merriment, and we obediently turned our attention back to the fireworks. Fizz, bang, ooh. Fizz, bang, ooh. The display ended with what should have been a very impressive showing of the Gresham crest, a rearing lion holding a flag of some sort. In the event it didn't quite work, as most of the lion's head failed to ignite, rendering the image faintly macabre, but even so it delivered a reasonably big finish. And then it was over, and time for the guests, inside and out, those not staying the night anyway, to make their exit and not to take too long about it. I managed to find our hosts in the throng to thank them and say goodbye.

Lady Claremont was still smiling, with that glint in her eye. 'We must get you down here. If you could ever spare the time.'

'I'm down this weekend, so I must have some time to spare.'

'Of course you are. With those funny people who've got Malton Towers.' The phrase 'those funny people' told me everything I needed to know about Tarquin's chances of ever getting in with the County. 'One of Henry's great-grandmothers grew up at Malton. He used to stay there quite often before the war. But you thought it was ghastly, didn't you?' She looked at her aged husband.

He nodded. 'Coldest bloody house I ever entered. Cold food, cold baths, cold everything. I never had a wink of sleep in all the years I went there.' It was easy to see that his lordship had had about enough of this interminable evening and was more than ready for bed, but he hadn't quite finished. 'They're crackers to have taken it on. Ruined my cousins, ruined every organisation that came after them. And at least my relations had the land, much good did it do them. Your friends have just bought a bottomless pit.' Actually, to me this sounded not only like fairly accurate reporting but also curiously reassuring. It is easy to forget, watching the Tarquins fling every last penny they possess into supporting some pseudo-aristocratic, gimcrack fantasy, that there are still people for whom these are normal houses in which normal lives should be led. If they're uncomfortable then they're uncomfortable and that's that. Never mind the plasterwork or the Grinling Gibbons carving, or the ghost of Mary Stuart in the East Wing. There was a kind of no-nonsense quality to his dismissal of Malton Towers that seemed to earth my own experience of it, releasing me from reverence. At any rate Lord Claremont had said his piece and there didn't seem much point in getting him to elaborate, so I nodded and moved on.

I caught sight of Serena in the hall. She was with her family and talking to Helena, who was looking a good deal older than her older sister. But she was friendly when we met again, kissing me and wishing me well, as I grinned across her at the object of my ancient and unrequited passions. Looking back I cannot quite explain why the sight of Serena that evening, far from making me sad as it might so easily have done, had in fact given me a terrific lift. I felt marvellous, giddy, tight, high, whatever Seventies word is most appropriate, at

278

being reminded of how much I once could love. Still loved, really. A whole set of muscles that had atrophied through lack of use sprang to life again within my bosom. Rather as you are empowered by discovering an ace has been dealt you when you pick up the cards from the baize. Even if you never get a chance to play it, you know that you are the better and stronger for having an ace in your hand.

'It's been so lovely to see you,' Serena said, sounding wonderfully as if she meant it.

'I have enjoyed it.' As I answered her I knew that my tone was strangely steady, almost cold, in fact, when I did not feel cold towards her in the least, very much the opposite. I cannot explain why, except to say that an Englishman of my generation will always protect himself against the risk of revealing his true feelings. It is his nature and he cannot fight it.

Again, she smiled her smile of the blessed. 'We're all fans, you know. We must try and get you down to Waverly.'

'I'd love it. In the meantime, good luck with everything.'

We touched cheeks and I turned away. Stepping out of the front door, I had not gone more than a few paces when I heard Andrew's indignant enquiry. 'Good luck with what? What did he mean by that?' I confess the temptation was too great and I sneaked back, staying out of sight from the front door.

'He didn't mean anything. Good luck. That's all.' Serena's patient and modulated tones dealt with him as one might soothe a frisky horse or dog. 'Good luck with life.'

'What an extraordinary thing to say.' He seemed

to clear his throat to draw her attention to him. 'I'm rather surprised to find him so effulgent and you so welcoming, after everything that happened.'

'Oh, for heaven's sake.' They were alone now, or thought they were, and Serena's tone was less careful. 'Since the evening you speak of we've seen the fall of Communism, the Balkans in flames and the collapse of the British way of life. If we can survive all that, we can surely forget one drunken dinner that got out of hand, forty years ago—' But by then, Bridget was pulling at my sleeve with a funny look, and I had to come away and out of earshot. If Andrew had more to contribute on the subject after Serena's outburst it was lost to me. Not for the first time I wondered at how, among the upper classes particularly but perhaps in every section of society, extremely clever women live with very, very stupid men without the husbands' ever apparently becoming aware of the sacrifice their wives are making daily.

'That was the greatest treat,' said Jennifer, as we nudged our way out of the gates and back on to the main road. 'What luck we had you with us. Wasn't it, darling?'

I didn't expect an answer, as I realised that it was almost physically painful for Tarquin to acknowledge another's superior power at any time. Most of all in his own would-be kingdom. But Jennifer remained looking fixedly at him, driving through the side of her right eye, until he managed a sort of grudging response. 'Good show,' he muttered, or something along those lines. I couldn't really hear.

His envy and Bridget's misery combined to fill the car with a green mist of resentful, hurt rage,

280

but Jennifer wouldn't give up. 'I thought they were so nice. And they're obviously very fond of you.'

'Well, he's *very* fond of them. Or some of them. Aren't you? *Darling?'* Bridget's contribution at moments like this was the vocal equivalent of throwing acid. Of course, as I was forced to realise, the downside of remembering what love *is* came in the form of a clear realisation of what it is *not* and whatever it was that I was sharing with Bridget was not love. I'd seen this coming. I had hinted as much to my dear old Daddy when I went to have lunch with him. But I don't think, before that evening at Gresham, I'd appreciated that the buffers were not only in sight but nearly upon us. In fairness, I cannot blame Bridget for feeling cheesed off. She was an intelligent, attractive woman, and she was obliged to accept that, once again, she had wasted several, long years on a dry well, on a bagless hunt, on a dead end. As I have mentioned, she'd made this mistake before, more than once, which I knew well, and until this very evening I'd always taken her line that the men in question were beasts and cads for not releasing her when they must have known it was going nowhere. Instead, they had, as I thought, strung her along until they had stolen her future and her children, who would never now know life. It was at this point, in that darkened car pushing through the Yorkshire lanes, that I suddenly realised that they had not been cads exactly, simply selfish, insensitive, unthinking fools. As I was. And from tomorrow morning I would be sharing their guilt, in the Sad Story of Bridget FitzGerald.

She didn't speak again until we were in our freezing, damp bedroom. She had started to undress in that angular, vengeful way that I knew so well, talking over her shoulder at me, or through the back of her furious head. 'The whole thing is so ridiculous.'

'What thing? There isn't a "thing".'

'Darn right, there isn't. She's not at all interested in you. Not in the least.' She spoke the words crisply with a vivid, sparky relish, as if Serena's lack of love for me was somehow all her own work, a real achievement to be proud of.

'No. I don't suppose she is.'

'Not in the least.' The repeat was heightened in volume and acerbity. 'Anyone can see that. She could hardly remember who you were.' This was, I thought, a punch below the belt but I decided not to argue. Instead, I settled for looking wounded. I was wasting my time. Bridget, in full flow by now, was unfazed by any perceived sense of injustice. 'She'd never leave him. You can't imagine that she would.'

'No.'

'And if she did? What makes you think she'd ever want to live with a sad, little depressive like you?'

'I don't.'

'Because she wouldn't, you know. You can't believe that would happen in a million light years.'

'Fine.'

'Give up all the privileges? All the profile? Go from Countess of Belton to Mrs *You*? Never.'

For a moment I was going to protest facetiously that she would have been more correctly styled as 'Lady Serena *You*' but thought better of it. I was rather interested by her suggestion that Serena and Andrew had a 'profile.' What did that mean?

What is a 'profile' in this context? I suppose Bridget's rage had now taken on a life of its own and her editing faculties were impeded. 'I dare say it is unlikely,' I said.

'I'll say. That type never do.'

'She's a "type," is she? Well, that's encouraging. I must look out for some more of them.'

'Oh, fuck off.' I cannot complain at this since I deserved it.

But by the time I too had undressed and we were both shivering beneath our inadequate coverings in our ugly carved bed, she had calmed down. Up until now her anger had protected me against feeling guilt, but I was not to get off scot-free. Just before I turned out the light she lowered her book and looked over at me. 'What did I do wrong?' Her voice was quite gentle again and the soft Irish burr that I always found so beguiling gave it a poignancy that reminded me painfully how much I hate to hurt.

I shook my head and gave what I hoped was a warm smile, which in that temperature was quite a challenge. 'It's not your fault,' I answered her in what I felt was a suitably genuine tone. 'You've done nothing wrong. It isn't you, it's me.' As one mouths these oh so familiar sentiments, and this last, hackneyed sentence in particular, one likes to feel that one is expressing a noble and generous sentiment. That you are 'taking the blame' for the failure, 'shouldering the responsibility' and so on. In fact, of course, this is dishonest, as any serial love-rat, to lift a title from the tabloids, could tell you, and we are almost all love-rats at some stage. The phrases are a kind of lazy shorthand, designed to deflect the brickbats hurtling at your head and

283

bring all discussion of the topic to a close as quickly as possible.

Bridget, quite rightly, felt she deserved more than this craven and mendacious reply. 'Please,' she said. 'I mean it.' And her tone was now pulling at my heart strings to an uncomfortable degree. 'Is there anything I could have done that would have made it better?'

I looked at her and decided on honesty. 'You could have been happier.'

She bridled. 'You could have made me happier.'

I nodded with almost military precision. 'Precisely,' I said. And with both of us feeling that her words had put us each inalienably in the right, I turned out the light and we pretended to sleep.

Joanna

NINE

It was the day after we returned from Yorkshire
that I received another call from Damian. I say
'from Damian' but in fact Bassett's modest,
unassuming voice greeted me down the receiver.
'Mr Baxter was wondering . . .' He paused
nervously and I began to wonder what Damian
could be wondering that would give me such
offence, but the answer, when it came, was mild, 'if
you might possibly be able to get down to see him
at all soon.'

I felt I should confess my lack of progress
straight away, not that it was very likely I was
concealing a major find. 'I haven't much to report
yet, I'm afraid,' I said.

But Bassett did not seem to be expecting
anything different. 'Mr Baxter knows that, Sir. He
assumed that he would have heard from you
before now if there was anything to hear. But he
would like to catch up with you all the same.'

Despite Bassett's dulcet tones, there was an
absolute expectation of my agreeing to this
suggestion that triggered an alarm bell in my vitals.
I had the uncomfortable feeling that I had
somehow put myself in Damian's power by
agreeing to his request, that, in short, far from
doing him a favour I had in fact been bought. I was
not being paid, of course, but against my better
judgement I had accepted the insulting credit card
and in a way it made me an employee, which I
should have spotted at the outset. I had broken my
own rule, viz. that if one is bought, let it be for a

high price. This is why no one should ever accept a charity lecture or brief local appearance where a fee is involved, at least in England. The sum is invariably tiny, but the organisers will most definitely feel, once they have pressed a few coins into your hand, that they own you body and soul. If you must do these things, and sometimes one must, then please do them for nothing. Do them out of the goodness of your heart. The money will make no difference to your life, but you will never have to endure the sense of being a purchased hireling, since you retain the whip hand of your generosity. Better yet, donate the fee you might have had to their cause, or to something equally worthy, and add a halo to your head for good measure. But in this instance somehow, by sleight of hand, Damian had tricked me and retained the moral high ground. I was no longer doing a good turn, I was carrying out a commission. It is quite a different matter.

Eventually the plan was settled. I had rather a heavy week coming up, so the decision was made that I would return to Surrey after lunch on the following Sunday. Accordingly, I took the train and was met once more at the station by the flawlessly uniformed chauffeur, but as we arrived at Planet Damian it came as a surprise to see what looked like a village fête going on in the gardens. The cars were parked in a field further down the road, and the booths and general activity were apparently cordoned off from the upper lawn, so the event did not really impinge on the actual house, but even so it was not very compatible with my cherished image of Mr Baxter, being altogether too philanthropic for his tastes. However, in answer to my question as I got out of the car, Bassett confirmed the situation. 'Yes. It's held over two days in the summer, Sir. It's in aid of the local Catholic church, St Teresa's. In Guildford.'

'Is Mr Baxter a Catholic?' The thought had never occurred to me. Not that I mind Catholics. It was just strange to think of Damian subscribing to any religion.

'I believe so, Sir.'

'And does he do this every year?'

'He does, Sir. Since he first came here.' I attempted to conceal my cynical amazement as I was shown directly to the library. When I walked into the room I realised at once why I had been sent for. Damian was dying. He had of course been dying before, when I was last there on the visit that started it all, but one may be dying without having death written all over one's face. This time it was not so much that he had a fatal illness. Rather, at first appearance, he looked as if he were already dead.

He lay back, stretched out, on his daybed, eyes shut. Were it not for the faintest movement of his emaciated chest I would have assumed I had come too late. I suppose I must have appeared shocked, as just at this moment he opened his eyes and let out a rasping, little laugh at my expression. 'Cheer up,' he snorted. 'I'm not quite as bad as I look.'

'That's a relief,' I said. 'Since you couldn't look worse.'

Naturally this bucked him up. He rang the bell by his chair and when the ever vigilant Bassett put his head round the door suggested, in that diffident way of his, that we might have some tea. 'Are you staying the night?' he asked when Bassett

289

had gone off on his commission.

'I don't think so. I was planning to continue the search tomorrow, and I don't believe I should put it off.'

'No. For pity's sake don't put it off, whatever you do.' But he raised his eyebrows to make this reference to his coming demise, into a sort of joke. 'So, how have you been getting on?'

I told him about Lucy and Dagmar. 'They seem very fond of you.'

'Don't sound so surprised.'

Of course, that was the point. I was surprised. But I didn't feel I could word this acceptably so I didn't try. Instead, I repeated their separate messages of goodwill and felt glad I had delivered them faithfully. 'I don't think I was aware how well you knew them.'

'You weren't aware of a lot of things about me.' He waited, perhaps for me to contradict, but I was silent. 'Poor little Dagmar.' He gave a semi-comic sigh, inviting me to join in his contemplation of her hopelessness, but after my recent visit I would have felt disloyal so I resisted. He continued, undeterred. 'She should probably have been born in 1850, been married by proxy to some German grand duke, and just lived out her life observing the rituals. She would have done it very well and no doubt been much loved by all those loyal subjects who would never get near enough to find out how boring she was.'

'She's less boring now,' I said. 'Less boring, less diffident and less happy.'

He nodded, absorbing my report. 'I was surprised when she married him. I thought she'd go for dull and respectable, and end up in a farmhouse in Devon, with a lot of huge, Royal portraits looking out of place and filling the half-timbered walls from floor to ceiling. I never expected her to go for nasty and successful, and end up back in a palace and miserable.'

'Well, she's got the portraits, anyway.'

'Did she tell you she wanted to marry me?' He must have caught my expression on hearing this, as he read it very accurately. 'I'm past being ungallant. I'm nearly dead. At that point you truly can say what you like.' Which, on reflection, I feel is probably true.

'She did, actually.'

'Really?' I could see he was surprised.

'She said she longed for it, but you weren't interested. She said she had nothing to offer that you wanted or needed.'

'That sounds rather peevish.'

'Well, it wasn't. She was very touching.'

He nodded at this, somehow acknowledging Dagmar's generosity with a kinder tone than he had used before. 'I never said she wasn't a nice woman. I thought she was one of the nicest of all of you.' He considered for a minute. 'It was hard for ex-Royals.'

'I agree.'

'It was all right for the ones still on thrones,' he added, thinking more on the topic. 'After all the nonsense of the Sixties and Seventies was over, they were in an enviable position. But for the others it was hard.'

'I suppose you didn't want to take all that on. Not once you knew more about what it would entail.'

'There were lots of things I didn't want to take

291

on, once I knew a bit more about them.' He looked at me. 'If it comes to that, I didn't want to take on your whole world, once I knew more about it.' He returned to the matter in hand. 'But you're quite sure she wasn't my pen pal?'

'I am.'

'And it wasn't Lucy either?' I explained further about the hereditary condition of the daughter. Thoughtfully, he absorbed the detail that ruled him out. 'So, how was she?'

'All right.' I tipped my head from side to side, in that gesture that is intended to signify so-so.

He was quite curious at this. 'You don't seem to be waxing lyrical. I always thought of you two as very thick.'

'Her life is more her own fault than Dagmar's.' The truth is I did feel more tepid about the Rawnsley-Prices. The phrase about people 'making their own bed' is not very meaningful, since we all to some extent make our own beds and have to lie on them. We have no choice. Even so, it does have some meaning. Unlike many people, Lucy had enjoyed real options when young and she seemed, to me anyway, to have chosen none of the more creative or interesting ones.

He spoke my thought. 'Lucy is another Sixties casualty.'

I felt it behoved me to stick up for my old friend a bit. 'She's not as bad as some. At least she's not one of those sad sixty-year-old television executives, wandering around in a leather jacket and talking about the Arctic Monkeys.'

'Maybe. But she assumed that her act as a madcap baronet's daughter, embracing the new values, with a zany, whacky sense of fun would run and run. She was mistaken.' He was right in this so I didn't defend her further. 'Besides, that particular routine is only convincing when the player is young. Zany and whacky at fifty-eight is just tragic.'

'She has our best wishes, though.'

'If you want. She'll survive.' He looked at me as I stared out of the window on to the gathering below.

'Your fête is very well attended, I must say.'

'I can see you're taken aback to find me doing something for charity.'

'I am a bit.'

'You're right. I am not very nice. Not really.' He spoke quite sharply, unwilling to lie, even by being silent. 'But I do approve of these people. I admire their ordinariness. When I was young I couldn't deal with anyone who lacked ambition. I couldn't see the point of a life that just accepted and had no wish to change. I was at ease with people who wanted to be millionaires and cabinet ministers and movie stars. I sympathised with any vaulting goal, no matter how ludicrous. But those with no desire beyond a decent life, a nice house, a pleasant holiday were quite alien to me. They made me uncomfortable.'

'But not now.'

He nodded, endorsing my comment. 'Now, I see the ability simply to embrace life and live it as noble. Not always to drive yourself like an ox through a ploughed field, which is what I used to admire. I suppose, hundreds of years ago, it was the same when people entered convents and monasteries to give their lives to God. I feel these men and women, in just getting on with it, are also

293

in their way giving their lives to God. Even though I don't believe in him.' He stopped to enjoy my amazement. 'I bet you never thought I'd say that.'

I agreed without hesitation. 'Or anything remotely like it.' He laughed and I continued, 'Presumably, this is all reflected in the benefiting Saint, young, innocent and surrounded with pastel-shaded flowers.'

'No. That's the other Saint Teresa. Our one is Teresa of Avila. She spent most of her life empathising with Christ's suffering and having visions of everyone drenched in blood. Then she started a new order and was locked up by the Pope, but she fought like a tigress and won through in the end.'

'You should have told me that straight away. I would have understood her appeal at once.'

This time he laughed out loud and we had to wait for his fit of coughing to subside. By then his mirth had been replaced by something gentler. 'I want you to understand that I have changed. It's important to me.' He was watching my face all the time for the effect of his words, which was quite disconcerting. 'At least, one says that. But one never knows if it is really change that one is experiencing, or simply qualities always present finally making their way to the surface. I do think I'm kinder than I was.'

'That wouldn't be difficult.'

'And less angry.' His words chimed with the dining room conversation in Yorkshire, and I must have somehow acknowledged this in my reception of his comments.

Which somehow he picked up. 'What?'

'Only that I ran into Serena Gresham, or Serena

Belton as she is now, last weekend, and she said something similar. That you were very angry when she knew you, and that angry people tend either to explode or to achieve great things.'

'Or both.' We were interrupted by the arrival of a tray of tea, all laid out like a prop in a Hollywood film, with thin, cucumber sandwiches and a little silver dish of sliced lemon. But I could tell it was all for me. Damian was past eating or drinking anything for pleasure. When Bassett had gone he spoke again. 'You have been combing through the attics. How is she?'

'Pretty well. Andrew as awful as ever.'

'Was he there?' I nodded with a grimace, which Damian echoed. 'I always used to wonder how he would keep up through a family dinner in that house. All of them sparking away like firecrackers and Andrew sitting there like a lump of mud.'

'I think he keeps up by being unaware that he is not keeping up.'

'And her ladyship?'

'More or less unchanged. I'm sad to say jolly old Lord C. has been replaced by a carving, stolen from a tomb in the Capuchin Church in Vienna, but she's much the same as she was.' I told him about Lady Claremont's joke at my expense. It was a risky admission, given what came after my love had been revealed all those years ago, but I was in too deep by now to be careful.

He smiled. 'You should have married her.'

'Don't let's go down that route.' With all that had happened I was no longer surprised that my rage should be as near the surface as it was.

If I expected him to be chastened I was disappointed. 'I just meant that I bet Lady

Claremont would have been better off with you than Andrew.' As usual, he made no reference to his own part in the whole business.

'Or you. Or anyone.'

'No. Not me,' he said flatly.

I couldn't break free of the subject quite yet. Once reopened, the wound felt as if it were freshly cut. 'Why did she marry him? What was she? Nineteen? And she wasn't even pregnant. The daughter came along ten months later and was the spitting image of Andrew, so there was nothing untoward. I just don't get it.'

He nodded. 'It was a different world then. We did things differently.'

'How involved were you? With Serena?' As I spoke, each word was like a lash, leaving a red stripe on my back.

He chuckled. 'What a wonderfully quaint expression. You sound like *Woman's Hour* thirty years ago. In what way "involved"?'

'You know in what way.'

He was silent for a moment. Then he shrugged. 'I was mad about her.'

Had I known this or not? It was so hard to decide, after everything that had happened. To hear him say it was still a kind of shock. Rather like the death of a great friend after a long terminal illness. I drank deeper of the poison. 'Who broke it off?'

I could see I was beginning to annoy him. Once again, we had used up our false friendliness and were getting back to our true feelings for one another. 'I didn't want to spend my life being patronised.' I could see he was back there for a moment, in the place that I had never left. 'I remember once,' he said after a moment, 'when I went to Gresham—'

'You used to go to Gresham?' I couldn't believe it. Where was I all this time? Sleeping in a box in the cellar? Why had I known none of this?

'You know I did. For the dance.' He was right. I did know it. 'She was giving me a lift. So I got myself to their flat. Where was it? Somewhere in Belgravia?'

'Chester Square. And it was a house, not a flat.'

He looked at me, understanding fully the significance of my exact recollection of the detail. 'Anyway, we'd loaded up the cases and then, as we set off, Serena said—' he paused, with a deep sigh, back in that smart little red two-seater that I once knew so well. 'She said, "Now this is going to have to be very carefully stage-managed" and she started to list what I was to do when I got there, how I was to behave, what I should and should not say to her mother when she greeted me, how I should manage her father's questions, what I should mention to her brother and her sisters. On and on she went, and as I listened I thought this isn't for me. I don't want to go somewhere where I'm a liability, where things have to be monitored so my hosts don't regret asking me, where I need to take a course before I can get out of the car, where I'm not a welcome member of the party.' He stopped, out of breath, and waited until he had caught up with himself.

'I can see that,' I said. Which I could.

He looked at me as if he suspected me of triumphing in his confession. 'I didn't face it at the time but, if I'm honest, I think that was when I knew it wouldn't work. Not in the long term.'

'Did you say anything to her?'

The question made him slightly uncomfortable. 'Not then.' He had recovered. 'Later.'

'But it was the end from that moment?' What did I want from him?

'I don't know. I can't remember. The point is I realised that if I ever did marry, I wanted it to be into a family that would hang bunting off the balconies, send up fireworks, take out ads in *The Times*, not roll their eyes in unforgiving silence at my unsuitability. You saw what that guy who married the youngest sister had to go through. He was an unperson by the time they'd finished with him.'

'Did Suzanne's family put out the flags?' This sounds rather unkind and I suppose it was, but I was so filled with jealousy that I felt I could have killed him. I'd say he got off pretty lightly.

His smile became rather wry. 'The trouble was you lot had spoiled me. I didn't like you or your world, and I didn't want what you had, but when I tried to go back to my old crowd I'd lost the taste for their tastes. I had become like mad old Lady Belton, too snobbish, too aware of unimportant differences and needing to be stage-managed, myself.'

'So we repelled you from our world and spoiled you for your own.'

'In a nutshell.'

'Serena must have got married almost straight away? When you and she were finished.'

'Not long afterwards.' He thought about this. 'I hope she's happy.'

I sipped my tea in a vague, and vain, attempt to soothe my troubled spirits. 'Not very, I would

298

guess. But with her kind it's hard to tell.'

Once more he was watching me, with all the care of an anthropologist making a study of a rare and unpredictable beast. 'Are you enjoying it at all? This Proustian return? It's your past as much as mine.'

'Not much.'

'What does your . . .' He hesitated. 'I hate the word "partner." What does she make of it all?'

'Bridget? I don't think she's interested. It's not her scene.' This last was true, but the statement before it wasn't completely. Still, I couldn't be bothered to get into all that. 'It doesn't matter either way,' I continued. 'We've broken up.'

'Oh dear. I hope it's coincidental.'

'Not completely. But it was coming anyway.'

He nodded, insufficiently curious to pursue it. 'So, who's next?'

'Candida Finch or Joanna Langley. Joanna, probably.'

'Why?'

'I always had rather a crush on her.'

He smiled at my revelation. 'Obviously, something we shared.'

'Do you remember the famous Ascot appearance?'

'How could anyone forget it?'

'Were you with her then?' I asked breezily. 'I know you weren't in her party when you got there. Didn't you come with the Greshams?' Another crunch, hard down on that loose and aching tooth.

He frowned, concentrating. 'Technically. But I don't think I was "with" either of them at that stage. That all came later.'

I winced. 'I used to think you and Joanna made

rather a good pair.'

He nodded. 'Because we were both common and on the make? And I wouldn't get in your way?'

'Because you were both modern and in touch with reality, which is more than you could say for most of us. The big learning curve we were all facing wasn't going to be necessary for you two.'

'That's generous.' He acknowledged my courtesy with a polite nod from the neck. 'But we weren't as synchronised as we must have looked from the outside. I was very ambitious, remember.'

'I certainly do.'

My tone was perhaps more revealing than I had intended and it made him flick his eyes up at me. 'And in those early months of the whole thing I still hadn't decided what I did, or didn't, want from all of you. Joanna wanted nothing. Except to escape from her mother and hide. She may not have known it, at least not consciously, not then. But it was in her and of course she found out the truth before very long.'

'As we all know.'

Damian laughed. 'As we all know.'

'And when she did, it was clear you weren't going in the same direction.'

He nodded in acceptance of this, although I could see, each time I interrupted, that it troubled him not to set his own pace. Actually, I fully understand how annoying this can be, those tiresome, unfunny men at dinners who heckle a speaker, destroying the jokes, but not replacing them with anything amusing of their own. Even so, I wasn't prepared to listen to Damian's cleaned-up and sanitised account of these events, without the odd comment. He continued, 'When you do see her and you've finished your snooping, I'm interested to learn what she feels about all that time now. I look forward to hearing when you've tracked her down.'

This was the question that was troubling me. Of all the women on the list she was the one with the least information. 'You haven't given me a lot to go on. To find her.'

Damian accepted this. 'Her name doesn't bring up much on the Internet. The Ascot story, of course, and some other early stuff, but nothing after the divorce.'

'Divorce?'

'In 1983.' I must have looked solemn for a moment. He shook his head, clucking his tongue as he did so. 'Please don't let's pretend it's a shock. The wonder is that they got fourteen years out of it.'

'I suppose so. What was the husband called again? I forget.'

'Kieran de Yong. You'll find there's plenty about him.'

'Kieran de Yong.' I hadn't thought of that name in so long, but it still had the power to make me smile.

Ditto Damian. 'I used to get a glimpse of him at the odd city *feste*, but he always studiously ignored me. And I haven't seen anything of Joanna, in print or person, since they split.' He spoke musingly. 'What do you think his real name was?'

'Not Kieran de Yong.'

He laughed. 'It might be Kieran. But I doubt it was de Yong.'

Now I too was trying to remember those headlines and that curious young man. 'What was he? A hairdresser? A modelling agent? A dress designer? Something that chimed with the *zeitgeist* of the day.'

'I think you'll be surprised. Most people get less from the future than they expected but some people get more. We've got an address for him. They should have given it to you.'

I nodded. 'If they've split up, will he know where to find her?'

'Of course he will. They've got a son.' He paused. 'Or I have. Anyway, even if he doesn't he may provide a lead. In any case I should start with him because we haven't come up with an alternative.'

I was leaving when I had to ask one last question. 'Are you really a Catholic?'

He laughed. I suppose the wording was rather funny. 'I'm not sure what you mean. I was born a Catholic. Didn't you know?'

I shook my head. 'So you "lapsed"?'

'I'm afraid so.'

His answer interested me. 'Why "afraid"? Would you like to believe?'

Damian glanced at me patronisingly, as if I were a child. 'Of course I would,' he said. 'I'm dying.'

The car was waiting patiently outside, but I knew there was a train every twenty minutes and so, with the immaculate chauffeur's permission, I allowed myself a little wander among the stalls of the fête below. I thought about Damian's unexpected words as I looked at these tables of old, unreadable books, at the piles of lamps from all the worst periods, at the cakes and jams, painstakingly made and all soon doubtless to be outlawed by the Health and Safety *Stasi,* at the dolls without their voice boxes and the jigsaws 'missing one piece,' and I, too, felt a kind of comfort and balm in the decency they represented. Naturally, it was very old-fashioned, and I am sure that if a New Labour minister could be offended by the Last Night of the Proms, she would be rendered suicidal by the sight of this comic, uniquely English event, but there was goodness here. These people had worked hard at what I would once have judged as such a little thing, yet their efforts were not wasted on me; in fact, they almost made me cry.

*　　　*　　　*

It is hard to be certain from this distance, but I think I'm right in saying that Ascot came after Queen Charlotte's Ball. I had anyway, as I have said, met Joanna Langley several times before the race meeting, but it was on that day that I suppose we became friends, which even now I like to think we were. It was then that I understood she was a creature of her own era, that she was not, like the rest of us, engaged in some kind of action replay of our parents' youth.

Ascot as a fashionable event is almost finished now. No doubt sensibly, Her Majesty's Representative has decided the meeting would better earn its keep as a day for racing enthusiasts and corporate entertaining. To this end the Household Stand (their sole remaining perk, poor dears, in exchange for all that unpaid smiling and standing) and various other, arcane sanctums were eliminated from the wonderful, new grandstand, and the famous Royal Enclosure is no longer

303

workable in the altered layout. Once the Court felt unwelcome, many of its members found other things to do and after this retreat it followed as the night the day that first the smart set and next the social aspirants, those who do not live and breathe horses anyway, would start to drop away. Soon, most of them will abandon it, I would guess forever, since once British toffs are given permission to avoid a social obligation it is hard to make them take it up again. Some will say it was high time and the racing crowd will be glad that horses have once again become the business of the day. But whether or not we would agree with this now, in the 1960s we enjoyed it like billy-o.

For some reason, that year I had gone with the family of a girl called Minna Bunting. Her father held some position at Buckingham Palace which I cannot now recall, Keeper of the Privy Purse maybe, or at any rate one of those ancient-sounding titles that brought, among other privileges, a place in the Ascot car park reserved for the use of members of the Royal Household. This was, and is, located across the road from the main entrance to the course and has always been considered very smart, despite consisting of a large but unremarkable ashphalt yard, overlooked by the unfragrant main stables and boasting a single loo more properly reserved for the grooms. A sort of disintegrating Dutch barn provided a bit of shelter on one side and a couple of abandoned pony stalls offered some shade on the other. Otherwise it was lines of cars. But the whole arrangement was supervised every year by the nicest group of men you could hope to encounter, which always gave the place rather a lift, and I do know it was considered quite a feather in my cap to be having my picnic lunch there, even if there were moments when the aroma made swallowing hard.

I think Minna and I were fairly keen on each other, in a moderate way, for a brief while back then. I know we went out to dinner a few times and I could not now tell you why this ended. I am often struck by how hard it is to unravel your own motives when you look back on certain incidents or relationships in the dim and distant past. Why this girl failed but that one broke your heart. Why this man made you smile and that one made your spirits sink. They all seem to have been quite nice, friends and enemies and lovers alike, young and pleasant and, to be honest, all much of a muchness from the vantage point of hindsight. What was it about them as individuals that intrigued or bored me forty years ago?

We had finished our lunch and it was time to make our way over the road and on to the course, so we strolled together down the high, laurel-lined path to the entrance. The police were managing the traffic, as they did even then in those comparatively traffic-free days and we were obliged to pause. 'What on earth is going on?' said Minna.

She was right. On the other side of the road, by the main entrance, the gathering of what later came to be called *paparazzi*, was going mad. As a rule there were far fewer of them then, not much more than a handful from the fashion magazines and the odd red top, but the public's taste for what celebrities were wearing was easily assuaged in 1968. On this day, however, you would have thought there was an item of international news being played out before us all. We crossed to the other pavement, passed through the gates and walked into the little courtyard where the disorganised could buy their badges on the day itself, and moved on to the gate into the Royal Enclosure. Something happening at the barrier was what was apparently fascinating the photographers most. Some were resorting to that trick, familiar now but novel in those days, of just holding their cameras above their heads and snapping away blindly, on the off chance that something worth printing might come out.

Armed with our badged lapels and a sense of entitlement, we pushed through the crowd and there was the cause of the riot. Joanna Langley, in an exquisite trouser suit of white lace, a pale hat trimmed with more lace and white flowers setting off her gleaming curls, white gloves on her hands, white bag by her side, was attempting to reason with the bluff ex-soldier in a bowler who sat guard. 'Sorry, Miss,' he said, without malice but without hesitation either, 'no trousers is the rule. And I can't change it. Even if I wanted to. Skirts only. That's what it says.'

'But this is almost a skirt,' replied Joanna.

' "Almost" isn't good enough, I'm afraid, Miss. Now if you'd like to stand aside.' He beckoned to us and we started forward.

'Hello,' I smiled at Joanna, as we drew near. I may not have known her well by that stage, but all our previous encounters had been friendly ones. 'You seem to be making news, today.'

She laughed. 'It's my mother's idea. She's put me up to it. I thought she was wrong, and they were bound to let me in. But it seems not.'

'Come on.' Minna pulled at my arm, anxious to dissociate herself from the media throng. As with all these people, then or now, this is not an affectation. They really hate it.

But I was too intrigued. I couldn't understand what Joanna was saying. If her mother was the one who thought she would be refused entry, how could she have put her up to it? 'Why did your mother want you to be stopped? Is she here?'

Joanna nodded towards a small group beyond the railings. I recognised the anxious, little woman from Queen Charlotte's Ball. She was wearing a tailored, fuchsia suit with a socking great brooch on her bosom. She seemed to be quivering with excitement watching her daughter, nudging her companions, sucking at her lower lip, but oddly she made no attempt to come nearer. 'What's she waiting for?' I asked.

Joanna sighed. 'What they're all waiting for. This.' Before my astonished gaze, she reached up under the tunic of her trouser suit and unfastened the waistband of her trousers. With a graceful movement she extracted first one long, shapely, stockinged leg and then the other, until she was standing there in a white micro-miniskirt, with the trousers making a pool of lace on the ground. Predictably, the frenzy of the photographers knew no bounds. They could have been witnessing the last appearance of Marilyn Monroe, the discovery of Hitler's child, the Second Coming, so excited were they by this *coup de théâtre*. 'I suppose I can come in now,' she said softly to the astonished, bowler-hatted gateman, who could not pretend to be uninterested.

'I suppose you can,' he said and nodded her through.

I was within earshot when Joanna was reunited with her family. 'Well, that was very silly,' she said as she rejoined them.

'Just wait. It'll be all over the evening papers tonight, never mind tomorrow morning.' Her mother spoke in short, sharp, chirrupy bursts, like a hungry bird in a hedgerow.

'I think it was a bloody embarrassment,' said a large man in a thick northern accent.

'That's because you don't know anything.' Mrs Langley always treated the man I came to know as her husband and Joanna's father with an odd and quite unusual mixture of deference and contempt. She needed to keep him in his place, but she also needed to keep him.

'I quite agree. Now, come and buy me some champagne.' Joanna slipped her arm through her father's. She always loved him best and she made no secret of it, but it somehow never empowered either of them to resist her mother's demands. It was an odd, uncomfortable set-up.

We watched them go. 'Do you want a drink?' I wondered.

Minna shook her head. 'Not yet. Not with them.'

It may have been because she heard these words, even if I hope not, but Joanna turned back once more and called, 'Come up to the box for some tea. Number five three one. Come about four and watch the next race.' I waved by way of answer and they were gone.

'We're meeting my father in White's at four,' said Minna.

'I'm sure we can do both if we want to.' We drifted up the steps into that long, faintly lavatorial tunnel at the base of the grandstand, built at such an unfortunate part of the sixties and yet much missed now that it has been swept away despite its replacement being infinitely superior, and we set off on our way through to the back of the building and the Enclosure lawns. It was at precisely that moment I saw Damian loitering in the arch, looking at his race card, with his left arm casually draped round the waist of the girl standing next to him. He was dressed correctly, for my crowd, in a black morning coat and if his costume stood out it was only because it looked as if it had been made for him, not, as with most of us, like a misfit dragged from an upstairs wardrobe, from clothes discarded by forgotten uncles, which our mothers told us, without irony, would be perfectly all right once the sleeves were let down. I was amused to see that his silk hat was old and black, and wondered for a moment where he'd found it. In the great days of racing before the war, there were all sorts of rules about black and grey coats, and black and grey hats, being worn before the Derby or after the Oaks, or some such thing, but by the time I had begun to put in an appearance the matter had been simplified: If you were a toff you wore a black coat and a black hat, and if you were not you wore grey. The only real qualification to this that happened in my time was that after the early Eighties, again if you were posh or trying to be, you didn't take a hat to a wedding at all.

Actually, unlike many modern, sartorial adjustments, this was an improvement, as between the church and the reception there was hardly a moment to wear it and one always ended up abandoning it in a pile behind a curtain, where it was liable to be taken in error, leaving you with an even worse one. The hat did, however, remain compulsory for race meetings and here there was a complication, because there came a point when they stopped making proper silk hats, I imagine for some politically correct, ecological reason, so the struggle was on to get hold of one before they either vanished completely or soared into the thousands to buy. As a result, you could tell the smart people as half the men were wearing hats that had clearly not been either made or bought for them, and were instead relics of dead fathers or grandfathers, or discards from uncles or cousins of their mothers, slightly bashed, slightly rubbed and either too big or too small. My own, courtesy of my dear old dad, balanced on the top of my head like a wobbly 1950s cocktail hat, but I made do.

'Goodness,' I said by way of greeting. 'Wherever I go, there you are.'

'Then you must go to all the right places.' He laughed, as his companion turned at the sound of my voice. It was Serena.

There are few markers of small-mindedness so clear as when people resent their friends becoming friendly with each other. But I am sorry to say that you see it often, a slight biting of the lip when they hear that this couple has met up with that couple and, despite their making the original introduction, they have not been invited. 'We're just *so* grateful to you for giving us the Coopers,' say the happy ones, and they are greeted with a cold smile and a murmured acknowledgement, but nothing more than this. Of course, some people pay no attention to the new amity that has been born over their own dinner table, others have the largeness of spirit to be pleased that their friends like each other, but there is a depressingly sizeable group that can never get over the feeling they have somehow been excluded, left out, ignored, that they are less loved because the love these men and women can give is going to each other and not, as it once did, to *them*. As the thinking world knows, this is an ignoble emotion, diminishing, sad, even pathetic, and should be avoided, certainly in public where it is as attractive as picking one's nose. And yet . . .

If it is bad enough with friends, it is much worse with lovers, or rather with would-be but never-were lovers. To witness someone you have adored unsuccessfully from afar actually fall in love with another of your so-called friends, so that you must watch this warm, well-suited, reciprocal, relationship bloom, in such sharp contrast to the withered, one-sided, bitter thing you cherished in the darkness of your secret thoughts, to stand by and watch all this is very hard. Particularly as you know you demean yourself by giving so much as a tiny clue as to your true feelings. But you lie in the bath or wait in a queue at the post office, and your inner being is hot with anger, boiling with hatred and destruction, even towards those whom, at one and the same time, you love with all your heart. So it was, I blush to admit, with me and Serena, or rather, with me and Damian since he was the author of all my woes.

That arm, so casually laid across the back of her pink Christian Dior suit, his hand lightly resting on the curve where her hip swelled softly down from her waist, that arm was a grotesque, violating betrayal. I'd touched her arm in greeting as people do; I had taken her hand, even brushed her cheek with mine, but all these privileges were available to anyone she had met more than twice. I had never touched her in any way that might imply intimacy. I had touched her as a friendly human being, but never as a man. I found myself wondering what the texture of her skirt must feel like. Was the slight roughness of the weave in the cotton imprinting itself on the edge of his palm and tantalising his fingertips with the almost undetectable movement of her body beneath? Could he feel its warmth? In my mind I could feel it and yet, unlike Damian, I could *not* feel it.

'Any ideas for the two thirty?' said Damian and I woke up.

'Don't ask me,' I said. 'I only ever bet on names that remind me of something else entirely.'

'Wildest Dreams,' said Serena, speaking into my hidden longings. 'Fletcher gave me a list and he was sure about Wildest Dreams. Then he says You'll Be Lucky for the Gold Cup.' Was there no horse running whose name did not encapsulate the hopelessness of my desires?

'Who's Fletcher?' asked Damian.

'Our groom at Gresham.' It was as if that simple sentence, carrying as it did in the few words it was made of the absolute divide between her life and his, flung him away from her side.

'Joanna Langley's waving at us.' He pulled his arm off Serena's flank, and started to walk across the grass towards the group centred on Joanna's miniskirted and lustrous form. I took his place, with Minna still loitering rather discontentedly on my other side.

'Did you see that nonsense at the gate?' Minna was squinting into the sun to get a clearer view of them.

'No, but I heard about it.' Serena smiled. 'It sounded quite funny but I don't really see the point.'

'She'll be all over the papers tomorrow,' I said.

I must have sounded like a complete idiot. 'I know that,' she said. 'But what does she want from it? What does she get out of it?'

'Fame?'

'But fame for doing what? Taking off her trousers? It might make her famous for being famous but what's the point of that?' Serena was bewildered by the choice that Joanna had made at the gate that morning, and as far as I recall, Minna and I just nodded and agreed with her. Perhaps it was what we both thought, or if it wasn't, it was what we all knew we were supposed to think.

The idea of being famous for being famous, a phrase we often used, was a risible and pejorative dismissal in those distant days, but the concept was, of course, a harbinger of our own time. The current fame mania is often mistakenly described as the Cult of Celebrity, but this at least is not new. There were always famous people and they were always interesting to the public. Nor, as again the argument goes today, were they all famous for doing wonderful things. There have always been well-known rakes and showgirls and criminals and worthless stowaways among the great, but as a rule they developed personalities that justified their stardom. What is genuinely new is the Cult of Non-Celebrity, the celebration as if they were

313

famous of men and women who are perfectly ordinary. The oxymoron of the unknown celebrity really is a modern innovation. Maybe it was a sense of this coming fashion, this dawning interest in fame for fame's sake that would inevitably open the gates of Valhalla wider, that prompted the likes of Mrs Langley to exploit its possibilities. But there was a confusion at the core of her planning and that was in her intended audience. She was playing to the wrong gallery. The upper classes have never been attracted by fame. At least, they may sometimes enjoy famous visitors to their galaxy, but they do not see it as an appropriate attribute among their own kind. Even now, they don't need it to stand out in the crowd, and they do not, as a rule, see the point of it for any other reason. Maybe the modern heirs will occasionally employ these vulgar methods to promote their interests, but there still remains a moral obligation, even among this younger, savvier group, to pretend that publicity is invariably demeaning and worthless.

Joanna herself understood this fundamental truth, which her mother had not grasped. She saw that the more she became a darling of the press, the more she was invited on to *Top of the Pops*, or whatever it was in those days, the less welcome she would be in the world to which her mother was so wrong-headedly anxious for her to belong. I am afraid that poor, misguided Mrs Langley genuinely believed that her beautiful daughter was improving her chances of an eligible husband, and a place in Society, by these shenanigans when, in fact, she was diminishing them to the point of invisibility.

I learned this from a conversation I had with

314

Joanna that same day, when I decided to take up her invitation and make my way to the Langleys' box. This decision came after a slight altercation with Minna, and in the end she went off alone to meet her father for tea while I retreated to the door in the wall, guarded like all the Enclosure entrances by those charming chaps in their obligatory bowler hats. My disagreement with Minna cannot have been sinister as I had dinner with them all later that evening, but perhaps it contributed to the end of our mini-romance. I have never been very good at people who cannot step out of their own setting even for a moment, whatever that setting might be.

Once through the door, I was suddenly propelled into the middle of the other Ascot and in some ways flung forward into the future, into our present day. Toughs in shiny suits, or with no jacket at all, jostled past with their women gaily, if sometimes surprisingly, adorned as I pushed on towards the covered escalator that would take me up to the floor where the boxes could be found in this different and even uglier stand. Here and there, dotted about in the crowd, there were fellow Enclosure members battling their way to and fro, and there was some joshing, wolf whistles and the like, to mark the difference in our costumes. This rapids-running element of journeying from the Enclosure to the boxes would in fact continue until the end of fashionable Ascot, but it grew a little less friendly as the years went on. Various politicians of every hue saw class warfare as so important a weapon in manipulating public opinion that they could not resist inflaming it. Even today, we are constantly encouraged to

315

believe in a capitalist economy, but to despise and revile those who profit from it. It is an odd philosophical position, to say the least, a dysfunctional theory that has contributed to a largely dysfunctional society, but as I say, in the 1960s it was only just starting. Breaking down class barriers was still seen as a happy thing then, so the jokes at one's expense were, on the whole, good-natured.

The boxes at Ascot have always occupied a kind of limbo position when it comes to the whole event. There are boxes set aside for major trainers and owners, and of course I do not mean these. Their usefulness is logical and credible, but those people were always present at Ascot as part of the racing fraternity and never because of fashion. They will continue to be at the meetings, long after the *beau monde* has moved on. But for those who only went to Ascot for the fun and frolic, a day out with some horses in the background, the boxes were always faintly unconvincing. To start with it was not necessary to get an Enclosure badge to rent or visit one, and in the old days, when the authorities exerted some control over whom they admitted to the Enclosure, the boxes could become the haven of the socially not-quites, those divorced actresses and grinning, motor dealers who were snubbed by the Old Guard.

The second problem was that most of them were simply minute. You went through a door in a concrete gallery, to be admitted to an itsy-bitsy entrance hall, with a little kitchenette from a 1950s caravan on one side. This led into the space for dining and generally living it up, which was roughly the size of a hotel bathroom, and beyond was the balcony, where two people could just about stand side by side on two or three steps. All in all, the average box was about as capacious and gracious as a lift in Selfridges. But to the mighty ones who are socially insecure, a much larger group than many people realise, they offered a chance to enjoy the race meeting on their own terms, in a place which might be modest but where they were king, instead of spending the day detecting sneers and slights in the behaviour of the Enclosure crowd that surrounded them. I would guess this was the appeal for Joanna's father, and that Alfred Langley was prepared to accompany his wife and daughter, but only on the condition that he could have a box to hide in for most of the day.

Mrs Langley darted up to me, her eyes flicking round the empty room behind my back, checking that nobody more important needed attention. 'Joanna's on the balcony,' she said, 'with some friends.' Then, nervous that she had somehow given offence with this blameless statement, she continued, 'She told us you were coming.'

'I'm afraid Minna had to meet her father in White's, but she sends her love.'

Mrs Langley nodded. 'Sir Timothy Bunting,' she muttered, as if I were unaware of the name of my host.

'Yes,' I said.

She nodded again. There was something shifty about her that her smooth hair and tailored suit and really rather nice diamond brooch could not mask. She was jumpy, like Peter Lorre waiting to have his collar felt in a black-and-white thriller about the mob. As I got to know her better I found this sense of frightened uncertainty never left her.

She couldn't relax, which I suspect was both part of what turned her daughter against her, but at the same time was the root of her power.

Joanna was leaning against the railing when I went out, attended by Lord George Tremayne and one or two other swains, all a little, but not very, drunk, and all holding empty or near-empty champagne flutes, that new glass that had only recently started to replace the gentle, bosom-shaped cup favoured in the previous decade. But then the Langleys were nothing if not up to the minute. That said, it was a lovely day and the sight of Joanna smiling up at me, her face framed with her own golden hair and the white brim of her lace hat, with the wide sweep of the lush green racetrack behind her, was very cheering. 'I came,' I said.

'So you did.' She walked up a step or two and kissed my cheek, then turned back to her companions. 'Push off, will you?' They protested, but she was quite definite. 'Go inside. Get some more to drink and bring me one in a minute.' She touched my sleeve. 'I've got something to tell him and it's private.' Naturally, none of this would have been sayable if she had lived even remotely within the rules of the crowd she was running with, but not for the last time I appreciated that the advantage of not being held captive by the need to observe correct form is that you can often get things done far more efficiently. In other words, they left.

I have already written about her beauty and it is probably true that I place physical beauty too high on my list of desirable attributes, but, in this case, it really was spectacular. No matter how closely one looked, Joanna's face was as near perfect as any I have ever seen not made of plastic, drawn on a page or enshrined on the silver screen. Smooth, evenly coloured skin, without a trace of a blemish; a mouth shaped with the soft curves of a petal, beneath widely placed deep-blue, almost purple, eyes, fringed with thick, long lashes; a statue's nose; and masses of gleaming born-blonde curls framing her cheeks and cascading to her shoulders. She was, as the song says, lovely to look at. 'What are you looking at?' Her voice, with its faint tinge of Essex, caught at my reveries, repeated the phrase and returned me to the present.

'At you,' I said.

She smiled. 'That's nice.' There was, in addition to everything else, something particularly charming in the contrast between her ethereal appearance and her absolute normality, her complete next-doorness which is hard to capture in words but was probably the core of the charm that delivered Charles II to Nell Gwynne, or enabled so many of the cockney Gaiety Girls to marry into the peerage in the 1890s. Her cheeriness was in some way the opposite of vanity, yet not self-consciously modest either. Just perfectly natural.

'What is this private thing you have to say to me? I couldn't be more fascinated.'

She blushed slightly, not an angry red, but with a soft, warm pink diffused evenly across her features, like someone caught unawares in the dawn light. 'It's not really private. That was just to make them shove off.' I smiled. 'But I was sorry you saw all that nonsense at the gate. I don't want you to think badly of me.' Again the direct simplicity of her appeal was both flattering and

319

tremendously disarming.

'I couldn't think badly of you,' I replied, which was no more than the truth. 'And anyway, I am fairly sure the world will be reading about it tomorrow morning, so I will, if anything, feel rather bucked to have been an eyewitness.'

I'm afraid this had not made things better. 'My mum thinks it all helps. To be in the news. To have everyone going on about me. She thinks it makes me . . .' She hesitated, searching for the right word, 'interesting.' Whatever word she had chosen this was clearly a question and a request for help, even if it was not phrased as such.

I attempted to look encouraging and not judgemental. 'To quote Oscar Wilde, the only one thing worse than being talked about is not being talked about.'

She gave a perfunctory laugh, more as a polite recognition that I had said something supposedly funny than because she found it amusing. Then, after a moment, she said, 'Yeah, I've heard that before, but you don't believe it, do you? None of you do.'

The trouble was this was true, really, but I didn't want to be a killjoy, certainly not to kill her joy. Still, she was asking my opinion so I strove to be as honest as I could be. 'It depends entirely what you want to come out of it. What are you striving for? What is your goal?'

She thought for a moment. 'That's the point. I don't know.'

'Then why are you doing the Season? What did you hope to gain when you began?'

'I don't know that either.' She spoke with all the hopelessness of a rabbit caught in a snare.

I understand that, theoretically, Joanna should have been freer than this. Her father was a self-made man, so she had not been brought up within the armed enclave, but in other ways her restrictions were even more severe. It was perhaps the last era when the aristocracy had the power to admit the new rich, or to refuse them entry. Later, when the posh way of life was back in fashion and the dream of joining it began again, the recent rich had far more muscle to push in whether the old world wanted them or not, but in the late Sixties the ex-Ruling Class still maintained considerable sway. I distinctly remember one friend of my mother's threatening a foolish youth, who had made a mess of her flat, uninvited. 'One more example of this kind of behaviour,' hissed the exasperated matron, 'and I will slam the door of every London drawing room in your face!' It was a meaningful threat because, then, it was a real one. In 1968 she could still have delivered. By 1988 those same doors were swinging free. Of course, today they are off their hinges.

To employ a phrase not actually in use for twenty years after this, I decided to cut to the chase. 'It is not complicated,' I said. 'If your mother and you are hoping for a grand marriage to come out of this year, you and she are going the wrong way about it. If you want to be famous and go on television or marry a film producer or a car manufacturer who is looking for a bit of glamour to invigorate his life, you're probably doing exactly the right thing.'

She looked at me. 'It's silly, really.' She sighed. 'You're right. My mum wants me to be Lady Snotty. That's what she dreams of night and day.

That's why it's so sad that she thinks all this stuff is helping when I know, much better than she does, that it isn't.'

'Then make her listen. With a little backtracking, I'm sure you can still manage what she's after and it wouldn't be so reprehensible. As Lady Snotty, as you put it, with your other very considerable advantages you could do a great deal of good if you were so minded.' I know I sounded like a bogus prelate from *Hymns on Sunday*, but at the time I couldn't quite see what else to say. I even think I believed I was telling the truth.

Joanna shook her head. 'That isn't me. I'm not saying I disapprove of it but it's not me. Sitting on committees, cutting ribbons, hosting a bring-and-buy sale to get funds for the new X-ray machine at the local hospital. I mean—' she broke off, clearly afraid she had offended me. 'Don't get me wrong. I think all that's very good. But I just couldn't do it.'

'And your mother wants you to.'

She shook her head. 'Actually, I don't think she's got that far. She just wants me to have a big, posh wedding, with lots of pictures in the *Tatler*. She hasn't thought beyond that.'

'Then why don't you think beyond it for her? Maybe it isn't charity work for you, or standard charity work. Maybe you could get involved with a special school, or local government. All sorts of causes will want you once you have a bit of social muscle. What I'm trying to say is that I'm sure it's achievable.' I had a mental image of the Tremayne brother up in the box above us, happy to marry her, without condition, to get the loot. 'Maybe, if you think of the possibilities you might come round to the idea.' What interests me now, thinking back to this fruitless, pompous and patronising advice, is that it didn't occur to me to suggest that she pursue a career instead of this worthless and really rather immoral plan. Why not? There were working women then, and quite a lot of them. Perhaps it just didn't seem a likely outcome for anyone in my gang, or were we so far out to sea that we had lost sight of land? Whatever the reason, in this, as in so many things, I would turn out to be entirely wrong.

'You sound like Damian,' she said, taking me by surprise.

'Do I?'

'Yeah. He's always telling me to capitalise on my looks. To "go for it," when I don't know what I'm supposed to go for.'

'I wasn't aware that you knew him so well.' Was I fated to be a grudging camp follower, staggering along in Damian's trail?

'Well, I do.' She looked at me with a cool stare that told me everything. And as I returned her gaze I thought of Damian's hand, earlier that very day, resting lightly on Serena Gresham's pelvis, and I wondered what I had done wrong in an earlier life that I should be obliged to hear, in the span of a single afternoon, that Damian had wormed his way into the affections, if not the beds, of these women, both dream goddesses for me in their different ways; that, in short, my toy, my own invention, my action doll was apparently getting all the action. That months, or even weeks, after I had let him into the henhouse, this fox was ruling my roost. Joanna must have seen some of this in my troubled brow. 'Do you like him?' she asked.

323

I realised that this was a proper question and one that I had not addressed until now, and should have. But I chose to answer as if it were neither of these things. 'I'm the one who introduced him to all of you.'

'I know that, but you never sound now as if you like him.'

Was this the moment that I realised I didn't? If so, I did not face it for quite a while after. 'Of course I like him.'

'Because I don't think you've got much in common. He wants to get on, but he doesn't want to fit in, but not like you and not in the way you mean. You think he'll take advantage of the whole thing and keep in with these people, that he'll end up marrying Lady Penelope La-di-da and send his children to Eton, but you're wrong. He can't stand you all, really. He's ready to break out and say goodbye to the lot of you.' There was clearly something in the notion that excited her.

Was this news? I can't pretend I was surprised. 'Then perhaps you should break out together. You seem rather well suited.'

'Don't talk like that.'

'Like what?'

'All toffee-nosed and self-important. You sound like a berk.' Naturally, this silenced me for the next few minutes, while she continued, 'Anyway, Damian and I, we're not well-suited, not deep down. I thought we might be for a bit, but we're not.'

'You both seem to me to be very up to the minute.' For some reason I couldn't stop sounding like the stupid-berk-plonker she'd described. To quote my mother against myself, I was just jealous.

But the comment made her more thoughtful than indignant. 'He does want to be part of today's world,' she admitted, 'like I do. But he wants to dominate it. He wants to bully it, to take over, to push people like you around in it and be the big, bad cheese.'

'And you don't? Not even as a great lady, dispensing warmth and wisdom from the house at the end of the drive?'

Again, she shook her head. 'You keep going on about that, but it's not me. And I don't want to be on television either. Nor married to some big-business boss with a modern flat in Mayfair and a villa in the South of France.' The world she described so accurately in that single phrase was, of course, one she knew well and presumably also despised, along with County Society, the peerage and Damian's imaginative vision of himself as a City whizz-kid, which was impressively ahead of its time.

'There must be something that you do want,' I said.

Joanna laughed again, mirthlessly. 'Nothing I'll find pursuing this game.' She thought for a while. 'I don't mean to be rude'—always a precursor to rudeness of the most offensive sort—'but you lot are all completely divorced from what's going on around you. Damian's right about that. You're just not part of the Sixties at all. The fashions. The music . . .' She paused, shaking her head slowly, dizzy with wonder at our irrelevance.

I felt a little indignant. 'We play the music.'

She sighed. 'Yes, you play the music and you dance to the Beatles and the Rolling Stones, but you're still in evening dress and you're still in some

325

ballroom or marquee, with hot breakfast being served from two o'clock onwards by a line of footmen. That's not what they're singing about. That's not what's happening.'

'I don't suppose it is.'

'The world's changing. And I want to change with it.'

'Darling!' I knew Damian's voice well enough not to need to turn round.

'Talk of the devil,' said Joanna.

Which I completed: 'And there he is.'

Damian came lazily down the steps towards us and enfolded her in a hug when he drew level. 'Come and cheer us up. You've spent long enough with droopy-drawers. He'll start to think he's in with a chance and then there'll be no controlling him.' He winked at me, as if inviting me to share the joke, which had, of course, as we both knew been intended as an insult. Initially, at the start of the Season he had felt the need to defer to me a little, just to make sure that I was still on side, but the need for that was long gone. He was the master now.

'All right,' she said, 'I'll come. But only if you give me a certainty for the next race.' She smiled and started back up the steps towards the door of the box where her fan club hovered.

Damian smiled back at her, his arm still round her waist. 'There's only one certainty for you. And that is me.'

And with a shared laugh they were inside and lost to view.

I have often thought since of my conversation with Joanna on that bright summer's day in our privileged seats above the crowded racetrack. It was perhaps in some ways my closest encounter with the elephant trap of Sixties fantasy, that would swallow so many of my contemporaries in the following decade. Things were changing, it is true. The post-war depression had been shaken off and the economy was booming, and many old values were being rejected. But they would be back, most of them. Not perhaps white tie or taking houses in Frinton for the summer, but certainly those that governed ambition and rapacity and greed and the lust for power. There would be fifteen years or so of chaos, then most of the old rules would be resurrected. Until now, when there is a richer elite buying houses in Belgravia than at any time since the Edwardians. But these were not the changes that Joanna and her ilk expected.

They thought, they *knew*, a world was coming where money would be meaningless, where nationalism and wars and religion would vanish, where class and rank and every worthless distinction between people would drift away into the ether like untrapped steam, and love would be all. It was a belief, a philosophy, that coloured my generation so strongly that many still cannot find the strength to shake it off. It is easy to laugh at these infantile notions, mouthed with increasing desperation by ageing ministers and sagging singers as their pension age approaches. Indeed, I do laugh at them since these fools have apparently lived a whole life and learned nothing. But, even so, I don't mind saying I was touched that day, listening to this lovely, well-intentioned, clever, nice, young woman, sitting in the sun and putting all her bets on Optimism.

Predictably, every paper ran a picture of Joanna Langley removing her white lace trousers to gain entry to Ascot the following day and I seem to remember that either the *Mail* or the *Express* printed a whole series of them, like a literal strip cartoon. And we all joked about it and most of us took her even less seriously than we had before and Mrs Langley's aspirations were crushed still further underfoot. But of course it was soon immaterial. I never did find out whether Joanna tried to talk to her mother about her doubts. If so, it did not have much effect, as the invitation to her coming-out ball in the country, from 'Mrs Alfred Langley' arrived not long afterwards. It was printed on white card so stiff it might have been cut from seasoned oak, with lettering sufficiently embossed to stub a toe. I would guess most people accepted. With the ruthless reasoning of the English, we all expected that a lot of money would be spent on the evening's pleasures and so it would be worth attending, whatever we thought of the daughter. I personally, of course, liked her and I freely confess I was much looking forward to it, and seen from now, when such entertainments are rarer and, to my old and jaded palate, seem pretty indistinguishable, I can only imagine what delights Mrs Langley had ordered for our delectation. I am certain it would have been a night to remember with treats galore.

However, as things turned out we opened the newspaper on a sunny day in early July, to read the banner headline 'LOVE DASH HEIRESS!' and the article below explained that Joanna, only child of 'Travel King, Multi-Millionaire, Alfred Langley,' had eloped with her dress designer,

Kieran de Yong. The couple had not yet married, an added, salacious delight for the journalists of the day, which would hardly merit a mention these days, but they were 'believed to be sharing Mr de Yong's flat in Mayfair.' After Joanna's comment at the races I could not prevent a slightly wistful wince at the final detail.

Two days later another card arrived from Mrs Langley. On it was printed the sober but straightforward information: 'The dance arranged for Miss Joanna Langley will not now take place.'

TEN

To my surprise, and contrary to my jokey and snobbish expectations, Kieran de Yong turned out to have been a busy boy since last we met. The printout filled me in on what he had been up to, during the intervening years and it was almost alarming. He had been twenty-eight when he ran off with 'Joanna, daughter of Alfred Langley, of Badgers' Wood, Godalming in Surrey,' making him nine or ten years older than most of us, and the following year he married her. After which, presumably putting some Langley gold to work, he'd built up a chain of dress shops by the late 1970s called Clean Cut, which I thought quite clever, and there were various photographs of him at 'red carpet' events during this period, clutching Joanna and wearing clothes that were terrible, even by the standards of that terrible time. What kind of blindness struck my generation? What allowed people to leave the safety of their homes wearing white, leather jackets with cowboy studs and fringe, or pale-blue, glistening suits, with black shirts and silver kipper ties? Or Russian peasant shirts or butchered army uniforms? I imagine they must have thought they looked like Elvis or Marlon Brando, when in fact they resembled a children's conjuror on speed.

But de Yong seemingly calmed down during the decades that followed. Later photographs, with assorted models and finally a striking second wife, showed him in clothes that went from first sleek and finally to good. He sold his chain for millions in the Eighties and turned his hand to property, the god of that era, with a huge stake in Docklands, which must have given him sleepless nights at one point before it proved the doubters wrong and came back sevenfold. Other buildings followed, a couple of famous, City landmarks, a resort in Spain, a new town in Cumbria. He had expanded into drug research and manufacture, and his company led the field in work on arthritis and some of the less bewitching forms of cancer, with profits channelled into education and addressing the problems of social mobility, or rather the lack of it, engendered by the fads of the academic establishment. I was impressed that this baby of the Sixties was sufficiently courageous to challenge a group still so completely enslaved by the Sixties message. In short, this was a brave, full life, and a terrifyingly worthy one. My only surprise was that I, and so presumably the general public, had heard so little of him.

I'd never known Kieran de Yong, really. The one occasion on which we met for any length of time was during that same Portuguese house party

330

that still has a habit of revisiting my dreams, but even then we hardly spoke and after everyone was back at home, most of us never wanted to set eyes on any of the other guests ever again. At least I didn't, so it was the worst possible start for a friendship. But at the time I had anyway dismissed him as common and uneducated, dull and faintly embarrassing, with his nightmarish outfits and his sad attempts to be cool. Joanna made things worse by being furiously protective, and her aggression injected the atmosphere with awkwardness whenever they appeared. In my defence, you will agree that it is hard to listen closely to a man with dyed hair, even more so when it's dyed a strawberry blond. But now, staring at this impressive list, I felt thoroughly humbled. What had I done in my life that could even hold a candle to this account? What had my friends done, simply to be worthy of a mention in the same breath?

Of his private life there was little information. He had married Joanna in 1969, so in this case the disputed baby had been born firmly in wedlock and the impending birth had not been the cause of any questionable nuptials. The child was a boy, as I already knew, Malcolm Alfred, but there were no further details of him on the Wikipedia entry. The divorce had come in 1983 and, to be honest, I shared Damian's amazement that it had taken so long. The striking second wife was one Jeanne LeGrange, wed in 1997, whose name suggested a well-travelled, international life and apart from that, nothing. No more mention of divorces, nor more wives, no more children. My main point of interest was that according to Damian's account, Joanna had continued their affair well into her

331

marriage. It seemed to confirm that she married de Yong to escape her mama and not because of an unconquerable love, which did not surprise me, since I had never thought anything else.

Damian's list gave me a number for Kieran's business which, when I first read it, I assumed would take me more or less directly to him, but now I understood the scale of what we were dealing with I wasn't so sure. It seemed rather like telephoning Buckingham Palace and asking to speak to the Queen. But in the event I was put through to his office and eventually to his private secretary with very little fuss, and when I had reached her she was quite polite. I explained I was an old friend from many years before, and, employing a similar device to the one used with Dagmar, I explained that I wanted to come in and talk about a new charity I was involved with that I thought might interest him. She sighed, gently but audibly. I was probably the fiftieth applicant that day. 'Mr de Yong's charity work is handled by a different department,' she said. 'Would you like me to put you through to them?'

I decided to push my luck, since I had no viable alternative, but my confidence in a productive result was waning. 'Well, to be honest, I'd rather talk directly to Kieran, if he's got a spare moment.' I thought the slightly insolent use of his Christian name would make me sound more convincing, but I am not sure this was correct. She hesitated, then asked me to spell my surname once again, and I was put on hold and forced to listen to a rather bad recording of Stravinsky's *Rite of Spring*. This time I wasn't sure what I would do if he didn't want to see me. And in truth, I couldn't imagine

332

why he would. If he had any memory of me at all it would only be the faintest reminder of a rather stuck-up, spotty youth who had snubbed him at every turn. That, and the dreadful evening when we last saw each other. Of course, one of the great pleasures of success, especially when many people have dismissed you and your chances, is to seek out those same ignorami and force them to retract their earlier opinions. To make them acknowledge, in their eyes if not with their tongues, that they were totally and completely wrong about you. That you, in short, have made them look like fools. I could only hope that the idea of my swallowing humble pie would be amusing.

Then, to my surprise, there was a click and Kieran was on the line. 'Good heavens,' he said. 'To what do I owe this unexpected pleasure?' The words may have been trite, but it was easy to tell from their delivery that he had mellowed. His East London accent had softened but not in a pretentious way, and his tone was, given the facts, unexpectedly warm.

'I'm surprised you remember me.'

'Nonsense. I've followed your career with interest. I've even read some of your books.'

I smiled with relief that my task was once more rendered do-able. 'Enough of this love talk,' I said and it was his turn to laugh. But when he asked me what it was about I fumbled as, naturally, I hadn't thought I would be talking so soon to the man in question and my story was not yet quite straight in my head.

Mercifully, he cut through my maunderings with an invitation. His lunches were taken for months to come, but he wondered if I might be free for dinner. 'Or is it difficult for you to get away in the evenings?'

'Not at all, I'm sad to say. What about you?'

'I'm the same.' So a dinner was indeed arranged, which, he suggested, might take place at the Savoy Grill since it was about to close for a couple of years of 'renovation.' This was unless I had an objection. Which I hadn't. Like him, I felt that a famous restaurant of our joint youths that was about to vanish forever seemed like a good, even witty, place to revisit the past. We had a date.

The old Savoy has left us now, that illogically impressive mixture of *Odéon* and *Belle Epoque*, which has been such a beacon in my life from childhood and growing up, when I would be taken for tea by ancient aunts past debbing days, with balls and cocktail parties in the River Room, and through the intervening years, smiling and cheering at weddings and birthdays and every kind of private celebration, right up to the present, when I have served my time at all those festival lunches and award-giving dinners, with their predictable menus and back-slapping, manufactured gaiety. Not long after my dinner with Kieran the new owner closed its doors and auctioned off the contents, and it would be a long, long time before the revelation of the reconceived hotel. And even if the team has recognised the special place the Savoy has occupied in London hearts for over a century, since Richard D'Oyly Carte first dreamed his dream, even if they have tried to serve its history as honourably as they could, still the stamping ground of Nellie Melba and Diana Cooper, of Alfred Hitchcock and the Duchess of Argyll, of Marilyn Monroe and Paul

McCartney, and all the rest of that glittering crew will have joined the palace of John of Gaunt that once stood on the site, and must henceforth trust to history books and memory.

I hadn't visited the Grill for a while and when I got there, it was to find it had already been much altered from the fashionable *rendezvous* of my adolescence that lasted well into my adulthood. In the early Sixties, I used to go regularly with a disreputable cousin of my father's who'd taken a shine to me, and who regarded the place as a sort of private club and would bring the most recent, luckless object of his fancy there for an orgy of oysters and dishonest vows. Naturally, he was a wonderfully dashing role model to an unattractive teenager with bad skin. On leaving the army in his forties, Cousin Patrick chose to live a short-term life, that is, to enjoy himself without putting down any roots or taking on any responsibilities. He was certainly very handsome and very charming, so this was more achievable than it might have been for some. My own mother adored him despite my father's disapproval, but in the end I suppose the latter's strictures about reaping what you sow were proved correct since our cousin's fun-filled years of avoiding commitment left him to face a stroke and early death alone, proving once again, as if we needed any more proof, that we generally end up with lives that are the product of our choices.

Even so, he was an inspiration to me, since he accepted no rules or boundaries and, having been brought up by my very straight and fairly strict pater, this seemed to me like an empowering paradise. I remember once being in a restaurant with him and, finding it difficult to attract the waiter's attention, Patrick reached round and picked up a stand, one of those whatnots that hold mats and menus and salts and peppers, and flung it the entire length of the room. It landed with a crash like a nuclear explosion that silenced the full, chattering space until you could have heard a pin drop, but instead of being reprimanded or ordered out on to the street, as I fully expected, the only tangible result was that the service improved enormously. There was probably a subversive lesson tucked in here somewhere, which my father would not have wanted me to learn.

As I walked in I thought of Patrick for a moment. I remembered him standing in that same doorway, checking the room with his lazy smile, to see if there were any pretty possibilities seated at other tables. One of the strangest parts of growing older being that ever-increasing Team of the Dead, who stand behind your shoulder and take it in turns to jump in and out of your head. A picture, a shop, a street, a clock that someone gave you, an ornament that came from this dead aunt or a chair from that dead uncle, and suddenly for a second they're alive again, whispering into your ear. There is a religion somewhere in the world that believes we all die twice; once in the normal way and the second time when the last person who really knew us dies, so one's living memory is gone from the earth. I subscribe to that and I thought happily of my old cousin that day, if only to note that the place had changed since he was there. The murals had gone and with them much of the atmosphere, while the sleek panelling, pale and smooth, which had been installed in their place gave the sensation of sitting in a giant cigar

336

thermidor. I suppose these things come under the heading of 'rebranding,' that twenty-first-century snake oil for every ailment. Kieran was already in his seat when I arrived. We waved at a distance, shook hands when I drew near and sat.

As everyone knows, the ageing process never fails to shock when it has not been witnessed on a daily basis. The Kieran I knew had been a fresh-faced oik, with fake hair and a fake tan, who bore almost no resemblance to the elderly, senior man of affairs sitting opposite me. But if his face was a great deal older, nevertheless, as he approached his seventieth year, it was also finer than it had been in his youth, less blotchy, less puffy and infinitely more secure. The too-red cheeks were gone and the glossy highlights, taking with them the true colour of his hair, whatever it may have been, but leaving him a rather distinguished grey, like a model in an advertisement for Grecian 2000. The hair itself had stayed, the lucky stiff, and his eyes were not, as I recalled, small and piggy but curiously kind for someone who had made such killings in the savage world of property.

'This is very nice of you,' I said, as he sent a waiter off in search of two glasses of champagne.

'It is my pleasure.' He studied his menu and I studied his face. He had acquired real stature, that is the only word I can think of to describe the change. He had acquired authority and the authority of the genuinely great. He was polite, relaxed and unstudied, but with that expectation of obedience that marks the powerful apart. The waiter returned with our drinks. 'So,' he said, when we were alone again, 'what's this about?' I murmured about my charity. It was not quite fictional as I felt that if he did wish to make a donation, there might as well be profit in it for someone, but I could see at once he wasn't really interested. 'I might as well cut you off now,' he interjected with a good-natured hand raised to stop the flow. 'I only give to about three things. I've had to ring-fence my interests as I find I get about a hundred applications a week these days. All of them perfectly worthy causes, of course, but I cannot cure every evil in the world. I'll give you a cheque if you like, but not for much and that will be your lot.'

I nodded. He was very compelling. I would have accepted this decision even if my request had been a truthful one. 'Thank you,' I said, but I was puzzled. His secretary had tried to tell me exactly this when I first rang and he could have finished the job without any rudeness when he came on the line. 'Then why are we here having dinner?' The words had not come out quite as I had envisaged and I hurried to qualify them. 'Of course, I'm terribly pleased that we are and it's the greatest treat to see you again, but I'm surprised you have the time.'

'I have time,' he said. 'I have a lot of time for things I want to do.' This was polite, but did not really answer my question, which he saw. 'I find that I spend most of my time these days thinking about the past, and about what happened to me and the life I have led, considering, in short, how I got to where I am.'

'So you always make a special case for people from that past?'

'I like to see them. Particularly if, like you, I have seen very little of them in the meantime.'

'To be honest, I'm amazed you remember me at all. I thought I was going to be greeted by a big, fat *"who?"* '

He gave a silent, little puff of laughter and I noticed, by contrast, how very sad his eyes were. 'I don't think any living human could forget that dinner.'

'No,' I said.

He raised his glass. His years at the top had taught him not to clink it against mine, as he would have done back then. 'To us. Are we much altered do you think?'

I nodded. 'Very, I'd say. I may only be a fatter, balder, sadder version of the young man that I was, but you seem to have changed into someone else completely.'

He laughed more heartily, as if pleased by the notion. 'Kieran de Yong, Designer to the Stars.'

'That's the man I knew.'

'God help you.'

'He wasn't so bad.'

'Drink or depression has made you kind. He was ghastly.'

I did not bother to contradict again since I agreed with him. I could see our waiter lingering nearby, waiting for a break in the conversation to step forward and take the order. Kieran gave him a slight nod and he leaned in, pencil and pad in hand. It is comforting to know that the skill of waiting well is not entirely dead even if these days you have to search, and certainly to pay, for it. I do not in any way dislike the tidal wave of Eastern Europeans whose appointed task is apparently to ask me what I want to eat. They seem cheerful and nice on the whole, and a pleasant contrast to the surly Englishman who always looks as if he is longing to spit in your soup. But I do wish someone would tell them not to barge in when the diner is halfway through a punchline.

The man had garnered all the necessary information and made off to put it into practice. 'What changed you?' I asked and he did not need to be reminded of the meaning of the question.

He thought for a moment. 'Education. Experience. Or are they the same thing? In those days I felt I'd come from nothing, which was obviously not true, as everyone comes from something. I also felt I knew nothing, which was truer but not completely true either, and consequently I felt I had to present myself as the man who knows everything, who is in touch with the universe, embodying the *zeitgeist*. I imagined that I looked like a giant controlling his destiny and not a saddo with a dye job.' He smiled at the memory and shook his head. 'Those jackets, alone. What was *that*?' I couldn't help laughing with him. 'And there you have the reason for why I hated all of you lot.' Which was an unexpected change of direction.

'What do you mean?'

'I felt you were so much more in charge than I was.'

'We weren't.'

'No, I can see that now. But your contempt for me, and everything about me, made me think you were.'

This made me sorrowful. Why do we spend so much of our lives making blameless people unhappy? 'I hope we weren't as bad as that. I hate the word contempt.'

340

He nodded. 'Of course, you're much nicer these days. I knew you would be. Anyone with any brains, gets nicer as they get older. But we were all angry then.'

'You seem to have harnessed your anger to great effect.'

'Someone once said to me that when young and clever men are angry, they either explode or achieve great things.'

The weird coincidence of the words made me sit up. 'How funny. A friend of mine said that about another chap I know, not long ago. Do you remember Serena Gresham?'

'I remember everyone at that dinner.' I raised my eyebrows to acknowledge that this must indeed be the case for all the guests who were present. But he hadn't finished. 'Actually, I remember her more than that. She was quite friendly with Joanna, even after she'd dropped out to run off with me. It was Serena who warned me not to explode.'

I was simultaneously impressed at Serena's generosity of vision in going on with Joanna and Kieran when most of the girls had dropped them and slightly disappointed, as one always is, at the realisation that what had seemed a *bon mot* fashioned expressly for one's own ears is in fact just a slogan for the speaker. 'When she said it to me she was talking about Damian Baxter, another member of the Portuguese Dinner Club.'

'The *founder* member.' He took another sip of his wine. 'In a way, Damian Baxter and I were the two graduates of that year's output from the University of Life.'

Of course they would know each other, these

Masters of the Universe. Damian had told me Kieran avoided him and I was curious as to whether this was really true. 'I suppose you must run into each other from time to time, at gatherings of the Great and the Good,' I said.

'Not really.' And there was my answer.

'That evening will obviously be with us to the end.'

He smiled, with a slight shrug. 'Damian isn't a friend of mine, but not because of that.'

Naturally I wanted to know the reason but I felt it might have an uncomfortable bearing on what I intended to discover before we parted and it didn't seem quite the right time to open that can of worms. 'He's certainly kept his success less secret than you have.' In saying this I found that I already admired Kieran very much. There is always something good in knowing you admire someone without reservation. I enjoyed giving him his due. Particularly as it justified my disapproval of someone I had always disliked.

He shook his head. 'Damian hasn't courted fame. He simply let it happen. I have spent who knows how much money keeping my name out of everything. Which is the more vain and self-important response?'

'Why did it matter to you?'

He thought for a moment. 'A mixture. Part of me believed it was very grown up to avoid a public profile and part of me had had enough. I did quite a lot of first-nighting and glad-handing and the rest of it during my days as a pseudo-posh dressmaker. It was moderately necessary then, though not as necessary as I pretended. But for a property developer, fame gives you nothing that you need and plenty you don't want.' The waiter had arrived with a clutch of appropriate equipment and Kieran waited until the man had finished arming us for the delights to come. 'Fame has its uses. The jumping of queues on to aeroplanes and into hospitals. It gives you good tables in restaurants that were full before you rang. You get theatre seats and tickets for the opera, and even invitations from people you are genuinely interested to know. But money gives you all these things without the hassle. You're not besieged to open this and support that, because nobody knows who you are and it wouldn't help if you did. The newspapers don't comb your background and interview your school friends to see if you kissed someone behind the bicycle shed in 1963. I don't have to put up with any of that. I get requests for large donations and I give some. That's all that is expected of me.'

'Were you surprised when you made money? I mean, proper money?' This seems an odd question to ask of a slight acquaintance after a forty-year gap. I can only tell you it didn't feel odd at the time to either of us.

'Everyone who is very successful will tell you that the initial response is entirely schizoid. One part of you thinks: All this for *me?* There must be some mistake! And the other greets immense, good fortune with: What on earth took you so long?'

'I suppose self-belief is a key ingredient.'

He nodded. 'So they tell us. But it's never quite enough to prepare you for what's happening. I made a lot of money when I sold the shops, but even so, when I did the sums for the projected profit on the first development I thought I'd put in too many noughts. I couldn't believe it would generate so much. But it did. Then there was more and more and more and more. And everything changed.'

'You didn't.'

'Oh, but I did. In those early years I went completely crazy. I was a jackass, a micro-manager to a truly demented degree. My home, my clothes, my cars, everything had to be just *so*. Looking back, I think I must have been imitating some notion of how posh people behaved but I got it completely wrong. I kept complaining in restaurants, and insisting on different shades of towel and different kinds of water in hotels. I wouldn't go to the telephone when people I knew rang.' He paused, bewildered, trying to understand his own remembered lunacy.

'Why not?'

'I thought that important people didn't. It was crazy. Even the President of the United States goes to the telephone if he knows the person at the other end, but I wouldn't. I had armies of assistants, working from sheaves of messages, with endless lists doled out to all and sundry. And I cancelled; boy, did I cancel. Last-minute duck-out. That was me.'

'I've never really understood why people do that.' I haven't. And yet it is an increasingly common phenomenon among the would-be great.

He sucked at his lip. 'Nor me, really. I think I felt trapped the moment I'd agreed to do anything, because the coming event, whatever it was, wouldn't be under my control. Then, as it drew nearer I would begin to panic, and on the day I'd

344

decide I couldn't possibly go, usually for some nonsensical and irrelevant reason, and all the people I paid to kiss my arse would tell me that my host or hostess would understand, so I'd chuck.'

'When did that end?'

'When I'd been dropped by everybody. I still thought I was a sought-after guest, until one day I realised I was only ever asked to celebrity stunts, but never to where anything interesting was happening. Politicians, performers, writers, even thinkers, I wasn't invited to meet them any more. I was just too unreliable.'

This admission fascinated me, since I have known so many film stars and television faces who've gradually removed themselves from society, or at least from the society of anyone remotely rewarding who is not a fan. As a rule they are quite unaware of it, and continue to think of themselves as pursued and desired when they are neither. 'My grandmother used to say that you should never be more difficult than you're worth.'

'She was right. I broke her rule and paid. I was *much* more difficult than I was worth.' His tone had gone through a kind of exasperation and was suddenly full of real pain. I looked at him. 'That was when Joanna left me. It was understandable. She'd married me as a protest against the rules of the Establishment and suddenly she was living with a man who thought it was important to have his shirts made with a quarter of an inch difference in the length of the two sleeves, who could only buy his ties in Rome or have his shoes mended by a particular cobbler in St James's. It was all so boring. Can you blame her?'

I thought it might be time to lighten the mood.

345

'From what I remember of your mother-in-law, I imagine she rather approved of the change in you. That and the money, of course.'

He looked at me, as the waiter brought the first course. 'Did you know Valerie Langley?'

'Not well. I knew her as Joanna's mother, not as "Valerie".'

'She has much to answer for.' His tone was not jocular. I tried to think of something to add to this, but he hadn't finished. 'Did you realise that she only took us out to Portugal to split us up? Can you imagine a mother doing that to her own daughter?'

I could, really, when the mother in question was Valerie Langley, but there wasn't much point in flinging petrol on to the flames, so I decided to move to different shores for a bit. 'I gather you married again after you and Joanna split up. Is your second wife still around?'

He almost jumped, as if my words had distracted him from something he was busy with. 'No. We're divorced. Years ago.'

'I'm sorry. It didn't say that in your biography.'

Again he looked at me as if I were forcing him to discuss a parking ticket that had been issued to somebody else in 1953. 'Don't be sorry. Jeanne was nothing.' Which was a chilling comment, but not just in its cruelty. Perhaps it said too much about his loneliness.

'How is Joanna?' He'd already mentioned her, so there didn't seem to be any reason why I shouldn't ask. 'Are you on good terms these days?'

The question seemed to take him by surprise and return him to the present. My words had told him something beyond their content. 'Why did you

346

want to see me?' he asked.

Suddenly I felt as if I had been caught shoplifting, or worse, putting a school friend's torch into my pocket. 'I'm on an errand, really.'

'What errand? For whom?'

'Damian.' I hesitated, praying for inspiration. 'You know he's ill—'

'And like to die.'

It almost amused me he should quote *Richard III* in this context. 'Precisely. And he finds he's interested in hearing about how his friends from those days . . .' I wasn't at all sure how to end this. 'How they turned out. Whether life worked for them. You know. Rather as you were saying about your own past and how you like to talk about it.' This last was a lame attempt to put them into the same boat.

'All his friends? Or just some of his friends?'

'Just some at this stage, and he asked me to help because he's really lost touch with them and we used to be quite close.'

Which wouldn't wash with Kieran and no wonder. 'I'm astonished that you, of all people, accepted the brief.'

Naturally, this was a perfectly reasonable comment. 'So am I, really. I didn't mean to do it when he first asked me, but then I went down to his home to see him, and I felt . . .' I tailed off. What had I felt that overturned a lifetime of dislike?

Kieran answered for me. 'You felt you couldn't refuse. Because death was pulling at his sleeve and you had only thought of him as young before you got there.'

'That's the sort of thing.' It *was* the sort of thing,

347

although that wasn't the whole reason. Underlying any pity for Damian I may, I admit, have felt I sensed a kind of larger, general sadness growing in me, a sorrow at the cruelty of time. At any rate, Kieran had succeeded in making me feel awkward and undignified with my nosy enquiries and my bogus charity.

'Which "some"?'

'Sorry?' The phrase sounded foreign. I couldn't understand him.

'Which "some" of Damian's friends?'

I listed the women. He listened as he ate his cod's roe, breaking the toast and pressing the pink squidge on to it with the kind of fastidious neatness that seems to tell of a man living alone. Not camp at all, nor fussy, but disciplined and *neat*, like a locker in an army barracks. He finished his plate before he spoke again. 'Has this got something to do with my son?'

Of course, the words were like a punch in the gut. I felt quite sick and for a second I thought I was actually going to *be* sick. But at least I decided to end the dishonesty at once, since it was clear I was as mysterious to Kieran as a sheet of laminated glass. I took a breath and answered, 'Yes.'

He absorbed this, seemingly turning it round and round his brain, looking at it from every angle, like a connoisseur unconvinced by the reputed excellence of a highly priced piece of old porcelain. Then he made a decision. 'I don't want to talk any more about it here. Do you have time to come back to my home for some coffee?' I nodded. 'Then that is what we shall do.' And before my eyes he threw off the intimate, self-

348

deprecating persona he had demonstrated, and replaced it with a mask of smooth and easy sophistication, chatting away breezily about countries he liked to visit, how disappointing he found the government, whether the ecology movement had got out of hand, until we'd finished and paid and he led the way out of the hotel to a large Rolls-Royce with a chauffeur, who was standing by the open door.

Kieran nodded at the magnificent car. 'Sometimes the old ways are best,' he observed lightly and we got in.

We drove to one of those new and, it must be said, unlovely blocks that have recently been built by the side of Vauxhall Bridge. Never having entered any of them, I rather wondered at his choice of dwelling. I think I must have expected him to live in a ravishing manor house in Chelsea, built originally for a cheery gentleman farmer in the 1730s and now on the market for enough to refinance Madrid. But on stepping out of the lift at the top-floor landing, then into Kieran's flat—I always resist the word 'apartment,' but I suspect it would be a more accurate term—I understood at once. At the end of a long, wide hall the whole of one side of the building, about thirty feet deep and who knows how long, was a single, vast drawing room. There were tall windows in three walls, giving a view of London second only to the Millennium Wheel. I looked down at the curling, night-time Thames, with its busy, toy boats, twinkling with coloured lights, at the dinky cars whizzing along the ribbon-roads, at the tiny pedestrian dots, hurrying down the pavements under the lamp posts. It was like flying.

Nor was there less to wonder at inside. The whole place was filled with the loveliest things I have ever seen in a private dwelling. Normally in a family house, even a very grand one, the exquisite pieces are occasionally interlarded with a pair of chairs covered by Aunt Joan and something Daddy brought back from the Sudan. But there was none of that here. Two matching Savonnerie carpets covered the gleaming floor and on it sat furniture so beautiful that it looked as if it had all been removed from one of Europe's major palaces. The paintings were mainly landscapes rather than portraits and, while I usually find them a trifle dull, I could not say that about these spectacular jewels of the genre. These were landscapes by Canaletto and Claude Lorraine and Gainsborough and Constable and other names I can only guess at. There was one ravishing painting of *La Princesse de Monaco*, by Angelica Kauffmann, which caught my eye. Kieran saw where I was looking. 'I don't like portraits as a rule. I find them sentimental. But I bought that because it reminded me of Joanna.' He was right. It was very like her. Joanna wearing a wide, flower-trimmed hat and the looser casual fashions of the 1790s, which seemed so carefree until you remembered that the sitter was less than three years from her hideous death. The unfortunate princess had ridden in the last tumbrel of the Reign of Terror. The officers heard the rioting of the Thermidor *coup d'état* break out as they drove towards the guillotine but, unfortunately for their passengers, they decided to complete the grisly journey, reasoning that no one would blame them if the regime was overthrown, but if Robespierre survived in power, they would all die for sparing the victims. They were probably right.

The picture was above an elaborate chimneypiece, which I admired. He told me it was from the scattered trove of a great house that had been demolished in my time, releasing a flood of doorcases and fireplaces and balustrades and other plunder when it bit the dust during the hopeless years of the 1950s. The family are still there, happily ensconced, these days, in a charming converted orangery.

'Can you burn a fire in a building as new as this? Is it real?'

'Certainly. I wanted the penthouse, so I could construct a chimney. I hate a drawing room without a fire, don't you? They weren't too difficult about it.' He talked as if he'd installed an extra bathroom.

Not for the first time I wondered what it must be like to be astonishingly rich. Of course, we're all astonishingly rich when compared to the inhabitants of enormous parts of the globe and I do not mean to sound ungrateful. But what is it like when the only reason not to do something, or buy something, or eat something, or drink something is because you do not want to? 'It would be *so* boring!' one hears people say. But would it? It's not boring to have hot water every morning, or a delicious dinner every night, to sleep in good sheets or live in pretty rooms or collect a few nice pictures, so why would it be boring to be able to treble all these blessings at a touch? I am fairly sure that I would love it. 'Have you got a house in the country?' I asked.

'No.' He spoke with a slightly tolerant air, as if I

should know better. 'Not now. I've done all that.' He chuckled. 'At one point I had an estate in Gloucestershire, another in Scotland, a flat in New York, a villa in Italy quite near Florence, and a London house in Cheyne Row. I'd arrive at each of them, fret about everything that had been done wrongly since I was last there and leave. I never seemed to stay anywhere for more than three days at a stretch, so I never got beyond the complaining stage. Although I do quite miss the house in the Cotswolds.' A pink cloud of nostalgia hovered over him for a moment. 'The library was one of the prettiest rooms I've ever seen, never mind lived in. But no.' He shook his head to loosen these disturbing, self-indulgent images. 'I'm finished with all that. There's no point.'

This was an odd phrase, but I let it go. Kieran had ordered some coffee while we were in the car and now a discreet manservant brought it in. Once again, I was on the set of a Lonsdale comedy. I wonder now whether I fully realised what I would see of the modern world when I took Damian's shilling. Was it a shock that all this way of life, which we were told so firmly in the Sixties was most definitely dying, was instead alive and well, and not even very unusual any more? I consider myself able to move about pretty freely and I have spent a good deal of my time in enviable houses of one sort or another, but I was beginning to grasp that it wasn't, as it used to be, that there was the odd person still living in an Edwardian way, the occasional millionaire who invented electricity and we should all be grateful to him, dear. Nowadays there is a whole new class of rich people leading rich lives, as numerous as under the Georgians.

The only difference is that now it goes on behind closed doors facilitating the dishonest representation of these things that the media go in for. As a result, the vast majority is largely unaware that there is a new and affluent group who live in this way but do not, unlike their predecessors a century ago, take much responsibility for those less blessed. This new breed feel no need to lead the public in public, but only from the shadows behind the Throne.

I poured myself a cup of coffee and sat in a tapestry-covered *bergère*, fashioned, I would guess, during the middle years of the eighteenth century. I felt we might as well get things started. 'So, how is Joanna?' I said, since that was where we had broken off.

Kieran looked at me quite steadily for a moment. Even he must have realised this was why we were here. 'Joanna is dead,' he replied.

'What?'

'And dead, I'm afraid, in a sad way. She was found in a public lavatory, not far from Swindon, with an empty hypodermic needle beside her. She had overdosed on heroin. When the police got there, they thought she'd been locked in the cubicle for about five days. They were alerted by the smell which, in that setting, as you can imagine, had to be pretty strong before it was noticed.' It was at this precise moment that I realised Kieran de Yong was a man cursed. This horrible, sordid, tragic image was always with him, of a woman I would guess he had loved much more than he believed he would at the start. It was a picture that hovered an inch or two behind his thoughts unless he was asleep, and then I am quite sure it visited his dreams. I saw that he had agreed to meet me because all he ever really wanted to talk about, or think about, was Joanna and I had known her. But when we did meet, he had found he couldn't begin the conversation without this account, and, whatever he may have originally planned, he couldn't give it in a crowded, noisy restaurant. Having acquitted this task, he almost relaxed.

Sometimes one hears or witnesses a thing so shocking that the brain cannot programme it for a second. I remember I was once in an earthquake in South America, and as I watched the ornaments and books jump and leap about, it took a second or two before my brain would tell me what was happening. This was just such a moment. Joanna Langley, enchanting, ravishing Joanna, was dead and in a way more suited to the forgotten, the abandoned and the lost; not to a darling of the gods.

'Christ.' For one tiny instant I thought I was going to burst into tears and when I looked over at Kieran it seemed that he might too, but then he recovered. At last he nodded slowly, as if my exclamation had been a comment. The fact is there are some deaths that have a gentle aspect, that bring a kind of comfort of their own to help the survivors bear their grief. This was not one of them. 'When did it happen?'

'October 1985. The fifteenth. We'd split up a couple of years before, as you probably know, and we didn't speak for a bit, except about Malcolm, because we were having . . .' he hesitated. What were they having? 'An argument. A disagreement.' He was gathering momentum. 'A fight. But then

354

we got the judgement, which was at least a decision, and I felt we could move on, that we were both getting through it.' He gave a gesture of hopelessness with his hands.

'But you weren't.'

'Obviously not.'

'What was the disagreement about?' Again, on paper this seems intrusive, but we had, as they say now, 'bonded' during the evening, or I felt we had, and it didn't seem to be prying when I said it.

'Joanna was having a lot of problems. Well,' he ran his fingers through his enviable hair, 'you can tell that from the way she died. And I wanted to be Malcolm's principal carer. I don't mean I didn't want her to see him, or anything like that.' It was clear that guilt for his first wife's death coursed through his veins so hotly he could still feel it twenty-three years later. 'I just thought he would be better off living with me, rather than trailing round after his mother. I had more money than she did by then—'

'Jeepers.'

He shook his head. 'Alfred went down in a property crash a few years earlier, so there was nothing much left in that quarter. Their whole life had changed from when you knew them. They were really quite broke, living in a flat on the edge of Streatham.' I had a sudden, vivid vision of Mrs Langley, sparkling with gems and watching from the edge of a ballroom like a shifty ferret to spy any interest in her daughter from Viscount Summersby. I never liked her much but I was sorry all the same. At that time nobody would have imagined the future waiting for her. 'It wasn't only the money. Joanna was very disappointed in the way the world had turned out. She thought by then we'd all be living in some kind of spiritual Nepal, smoking dope and mouthing the lyrics from *Hair*. Not taking out pensions in Mrs Thatcher's Britain.'

'A lot of our generation thought that. Some of them are in government.'

But I couldn't staunch the flow. Kieran had to tell his story. As the television quiz show has it: He'd started, so he'd finish. 'And of course, looking at it from her point of view I was at the peak of my madness, screaming if there was a crease on my collar, sacking staff because the knives and forks weren't tidy enough in the kitchen drawer . . . None of that side of it was her fault.' His effort to be fair to his late wife was more than commendable, it was heartbreaking. He sighed again. 'Anyway, we fought about the boy like a couple of cats. She said I'd poison his mind and make him a fascist. I said she'd poison his body and make him an addict. On and on we went, tearing at each other's throats. Until finally she dropped the bombshell. We were having breakfast one morning in that weird, angry way of two people who are still living together but know they won't be for long. We were sitting there in silence, until she looked up, preparing to speak. I knew some insult was on its way, so I deliberately made no enquiries. After a bit she got bored and just said it.'

'What?'

'That Malcolm wasn't my son.'

'How did she say it?'

'Like that. "Malcolm isn't your son." '

He stopped now to let the words sink in. So was

356

this where my quest was to end? It felt strange to have reached my destination, and yet also satisfactory in a way that Joanna's death should be partially redeemed by the boy's father at last acknowledging his blood child. Even if there was an anticlimactic element in the thought of Damian's fortune going to the only family in England who wouldn't notice it.

Kieran hadn't finished. 'You mentioned the house party in Portugal.'

'Yes.' I knew Portugal would come into it.

'She said she'd met up with "the boy's father" there and that she'd slept with him when we were back in London. That night, in fact. As soon as we got home from the airport we had a row about why we'd gone at all and she walked out . . .' He shrugged. 'It was obvious she was talking about Damian.' He must have caught and mistaken my response to this news, and hurried to undo any possible hurt. 'She was always very fond of you, but . . .' How was he to phrase it?

I helped him out. 'She wasn't interested in me.'

We both knew she wasn't, so why should he argue? 'Not like that,' he said, accepting my own verdict. 'And Joanna couldn't have cared less about the Tremaynes. It had to be Damian.' He paused. However often he went over this territory, it obviously still hurt. 'So I sat there, with a piece of toast in one hand and a coffee cup in the other, while she blew my life out of the water. And I minded when she told me. I minded very much.'

'Of course you did.'

'It wasn't just the boy. She was unravelling our life. This was retroactive legislation. We'd only been married a year at the time she was talking

357

about and I'd thought we were happy, then. I'd been against the damn holiday anyway, because I dreaded her being pulled back into a crowd that I didn't believe was any good for her.'

'But you went because her mother made you. And when you got back she slept with Damian.' At least I now understood his visceral dislike.

'That's about it. And by this stage of the battle she was glad to talk about it, because it was going to save her son from the vile Leona Helmsley world of mad indulgence that I was living in. She thought it would settle matters. That I would give up and back off, and Malcolm would go with her, and I would be left alone to count my money and weep.'

'But that didn't happen.'

'Of course not. My name was on the birth certificate for God's sake. I was married to her when he was conceived, never mind born. I loved him. He was my son.' He almost shouted this assertion, back in the grip of the row, but seeing my startled face he recovered, repeating the words in a gentler tone, which touched me as it would have touched anyone who heard him. 'I loved him. He was my son. I could have made my claim on that basis alone.' I sat up. I'd assumed he *had* made his claim on that basis alone, if he'd kept in contact with the boy. Which, from the way he was talking, he obviously had.

'But you didn't?'

He shook his head. 'I had a paternity test done. I wanted to know how tough the battle was going to be.' He looked at me again quite fiercely, and for a moment I rather sympathised with Joanna when I saw what she'd taken on. I suppose nobody can be as successful as Kieran had been without having some steel in them somewhere. 'When the results came back they showed Malcolm was mine after all.'

All my sense of matters being resolved deserted me on the instant. 'How did she take it?'

'How do you think?' He rolled his eyes at me. 'She wasn't thinking straight by then. She said she didn't believe me. It was exactly the kind of thing I would fix, blah, blah, blah. You can imagine.' I could. 'So we ran another test under her team's supervision and obviously the result was the same again, and by then she was coming apart at the seams . . .' He was standing, staring out of one of the windows, silhouetted against a dark-blue velvet sky studded with stars. He continued talking, facing on to the night, hardly aware I was there. 'As you might expect, she hadn't helped her case as a rational woman with all this screaming carry-on, so it wasn't a huge surprise when the judge gave me full custody, with visiting rights for her, which was much more than I'd asked for. We got the decision in September eighty-five.'

'And the following month she killed herself.'

'She killed herself, or she took an accidental overdose. Anyway,' he sighed, wearily, his remembered rage quite gone, 'she was dead. That's how it finished for Joanna. And it was all so unnecessary. Malcolm was fourteen by then. I couldn't have controlled his seeing her even if I'd wanted to, which I didn't, for more than a year or two at the most.'

Some decisions are so difficult to unravel; decisions made by countries and decisions of private individuals can be impossible to explain.

Why did Napoleon invade Russia? Why didn't Charles I make peace when it was offered? And why did Joanna Langley run away and marry this man when he was an anxious and desperate grotesque, but leave him when he was at the beginning of his triumphs? Why did she try to pull their boy in half when he was old enough to make up his own mind about both his parents and their warring philosophies? Why did she spiral into death-dealing depression when she really had nothing to fear?

'I don't understand why we never heard about it. Why isn't it on the Internet?'

'Mainly because I have spent an enormous amount of time and money making sure that no one hears about it. I kept the reporting to a minimum at the time, I will not tell you how, and I have one man who spends his working life combing the Web to get rid of any stories that I dislike, including even a whisper of Joanna.'

'Why?'

'Because I owe it to her. I ruined her life. I won't let her be a tabloid item in death.'

I ruined her life. I was so struck by the unvarnished, stark, merciless guilt in this. He allowed himself no defence at all. 'How sad,' I said. And I meant it with all my heart. I was truly sad. Sad at the ruin that, in a few short minutes, I'd heard engulf the whole House of Langley. In my sorrowing mind, rich, nice Alfred and his scratchy, ambitious Valerie had been suddenly pulled from their golden pedestal, where they had been secure in my imaginings until now and dashed down, like Don Giovanni, back to the place below, from whence they came. While Joanna, my lifelong standard for how lovely a woman can be, lay desecrated and dead, her scabrous wrist pitted with needle marks, her dirty, tangled hair spread out on a urine-stained, concrete floor somewhere in the Midlands. 'How very sad.'

I looked at my watch. It was time to leave. I understood now that Kieran had embraced the chance to talk about the wife who had left him against his will, but who would never leave his head. He had simply wanted to talk about her with someone who'd known her and those opportunities must be getting rare, even for him. He noticed me checking the time. 'I'd like to show you something before you go,' he said, and leaving the magnificent Chamber of Privilege he led me down the passage, past half-open doors revealing delectable rooms for eating and reading and other delights, until we came to the last door in the row. He opened it and ushered me into what was postulated as a study of some sort, with a desk and a comfortable chair. I could sense that Kieran probably did his actual work in it, as opposed to leafing through papers with a scribbling secretary in the glamorous library along the passage. Certainly he spent a lot of time here, as much as he could I would say, but the reason was not because it was quiet or tidy. In fact, its role as a writing room was not its moral purpose. This was a shrine. All four walls were covered with framed photographs, one consisting entirely of pictures of Joanna, Joanna as I remembered her, young and definitively gorgeous; then Joanna a little older and a little older still, but never Joanna old. Joanna at thirty, looking more harassed and careworn and lined than she should have done;

Joanna at thirty-three, pictured leaving the law courts during the divorce, a candid picture of her unhappiness, so generously taken by the snapper of some evening rag but presumably unprinted; Joanna at thirty-five, sitting with her son, laughing. Kieran was looking with me. 'That was taken by a friend of hers. Malcolm was there for lunch or something and this friend took it. It was the last picture of them together. It's the last picture of her. She had less than a week to go. You couldn't have told.'

'No, indeed.' I stared at the smiling mouth and the tired eyes. I found myself hoping it had been a really happy day, that last outing with her beloved child. I glanced around for newspaper pictures of the story. Even after all he'd said, I was surprised there weren't any. 'And there was no coverage at all? I still don't understand how you kept it out of the papers completely. Even the local ones?'

He looked uncomfortable. 'There were a few squibs, but not much.'

'I couldn't find anything on Google. There was really nothing about her at all, once you'd separated.'

Kieran knew why. 'She used my real name after the divorce. That was the name on everything in her bag when they found her. I managed to stop them making the connection.' He hesitated. 'You can read the coverage if you punch in Joanna Futtock.'

'Futtock?' I was so glad to know that I could still find something funny.

He looked rather sheepish. 'Why do you think I never gave up "de Yong"?'

'I did wonder. What was your mother's maiden

name?'

'Cock.' He gave a despairing sigh. 'I ask you.'

'Some people have all the luck,' I said. Then we both did laugh.

I'd started to look round the other walls of this little star chamber. There were pictures of Joanna with Kieran, a young Kieran with his awful blond mop and an apparently endless supply of the ugliest clothes in the world. Then grown-up Kieran; Kieran successful; Kieran shaking hands with presidents and kings; even Kieran in better and better suits. And alongside Kieran, everywhere you looked, there were more and more pictures of the boy. Malcolm in the school photograph from pre-prep; Malcolm swimming; Malcolm on a bicycle; Malcolm on a horse; Malcolm the public schoolboy, with both parents, one on either side of the sulking child, resisting his role at some Speech Day celebration. Malcolm skiing; Malcolm at university; Malcolm graduating with a very serious face; Malcolm backpacking. 'What's he up to now?' I asked.

Kieran was silent for a second, then he spoke in as pleasant a manner as he could manage. 'He's dead, too.'

'What?' I did not know the boy at all and the father only slightly, but I felt as if I were being pistol-whipped.

'Nothing bad. Not like his mother.' This time I could see his eyes filling, even while he remained in admirable control of his voice. 'He was perfectly well, twenty-three, just starting at Warburg's and he couldn't shake off a bout of flu, so we thought he should be looked at.' He stopped to breathe, back in that terrible moment. 'I took him to hospital for some tests and he was dead seven weeks later.' He rubbed his nose swiftly with his left hand, trying unsuccessfully to push back the tears. He talked on, more to steady himself than to give me any information. 'And that was it, really. I didn't quite take in what had happened. Not at first. Not for a while. A few years afterwards I even married again.' He shook his head at life's absurdity. 'Of course, it was ridiculous and it didn't last long. I made a mistake, you see.' He looked back at me. 'I thought I could still go on living. Anyway,' he sighed, as if this at least was understood between us, 'after I'd got rid of Jeanne I sold the houses and everything else, and came here. I did bring a lot of stuff with me, as you can see. I hadn't signed off completely.'

'How do you spend your time?'

'Oh.' He thought for a second, as if this was rather a curious query and difficult to answer. 'I've still got quite a lot of things on the boil and I take a bit of interest in financing research, into cancer, mainly. I'd like to think that it might help to prevent it happening to someone else. And I do worry about education these days, or rather the lack of it. If I'd been born now, I'd have ended up pulling pints in a bar in Chelmsford. I mind about those kids who'll never have a chance, the way things are.' He seemed pleased to think about these issues and glad of his role in them. Which he deserved to be. 'Apart from that I read. I watch a lot of television and I enjoy it, which nobody admits to. You see,' he tried to smile but gave up, 'the thing is, when your only child is dead, you're dead.' He paused as if to mark the rightness of this sentence to himself. 'Your life is finished. You're

364

not a parent any more. You're nothing. It's over. You're just waiting for your body to catch up with your soul.'

He stopped talking and we just stood there in that holy place of love. Kieran was weeping quite openly by this stage, with tears coursing down his cheeks, leaving a dark trail of water marks on his expensive lapels, and I freely confess that I was, too. We didn't say anything more and for a few minutes we didn't even move. It would have been a strange sight if anyone had interrupted us. Two rather overweight men in late middle age, standing motionless in their Savile Row suits, crying.

Terry

ELEVEN

Not very surprisingly, after an evening like that I decided I needed some air. Kieran offered to get his driver to take me home but I wanted to walk, just for a bit, and he didn't insist. So we shook hands in that funny English way, as if we hadn't been through an emotional trauma together, as though the whole thing hadn't really happened and the stains of our tears had some other, more banal and more acceptable explanation. We made the usual murmurings about meeting again, which one always says. Unusually, I rather hope it will happen, but I expect not. After that I set off down the Embankment.

It was a long walk home and quite cold, but it did not seem so. I strolled along, both reliving and then laying to rest my memories of Joanna. I was glad to have had a chance to revalue Kieran, even while I knew he was far beyond help, and I felt that I had been allowed to look into a soul that was worth looking into. Filled with these melancholy thoughts, I had just turned off Gloucester Road into Hereford Square when there was a scream, then laughter, then shouting, then the sound of someone being sick. I wish I could write that I was astonished to hear what sounded like a large Indian takeaway being splashily deposited on to the pavement, but these days it would require a Martian, and one only recently arrived from outer space, to be surprised at these charming goings-on. A group of young men and women in their early twenties, I would guess, were loitering on the

369

corner of the square, perhaps recent refugees from the Hereford Arms on the other side of the road, but perhaps not. One woman, in a short leather skirt and trainers, was throwing up and another, with suspiciously black hair, was tending to her. The rest just stood around, waiting for the next act in their evening's entertainment. Foolishly, I paused to study them. 'Got a problem?' said a man with a shaved head and a whole array of piercings down the edge of his right ear. I wondered the weight didn't throw him off balance.

'My problems seem nothing to yours,' I said and then rather regretted my clever-clogs answer as he took a menacing step towards me.

'Leave him, Ron. He's not worth it,' the girl with black hair and what looked like four different petticoats swaddling her bottom shouted over her shoulder. Happily he appeared to agree and turned away.

As he moved back, he shouted a crisp 'Fuck off' at me, but more as a kind of standard ritual, as one might say good morning in a village street. And so, before he could change his mind, I did.

It's not often that I walk at night, though more from laziness than fear, but when I do I am amazed at the changes that have come about in London during my adult lifetime, the main one being, of course, not the mugging and the general crime, nor even the dirt and uncollected rubbish that swirls and drifts in piles against the railings and the plane trees, waiting in vain for the men to come. It is the drunkenness that has transformed the streets, not just of London but of almost every town, into a lesser hell for lawful citizens. The kind of drunkenness that in years gone by used to be talked of in Siberia at the height of Stalin's iron rule as a reflection of the misery of the oppressed, or it was rumoured to be manifest up near the pole, where the long nights of winter drive strong men mad. Why did it happen here? When did it start? I used to think it was a class thing and somehow linked to the ills of social deprivation, but it isn't. Not long ago I attended a twenty-first party, held in one of St James's smartest clubs. The birthday boy was clever, charming, tipped for success and linked to half the peerage, and I watched as all the nice young girls and young men cheerfully tossed back the booze until they were staggering or vomiting or both. As I left, I heard a tray of glasses go west amid loud laughter, and a girl in a pretty *couture* dress of lilac chiffon pushed past me, hand on mouth, hoping to make it just in time. Outside, a fellow with traces of sick on his evening shirt was urinating against the car parked next to mine. I had escaped not a moment too soon.

Certainly some people drank too much in my day, as they always have, but drunkenness was rare and sad, and made men look like fools. Until as little as ten years ago being drunk was a mistake, a regrettable by-product of making merry, a miscalculation which, the next day, required an apology. Now it's the point. Does anyone out there understand why we let it happen? Because I don't. Of course I can see the charm of the 'café culture' we were said to be encouraging. But how long can a sane person contemplate failure without admitting it? At what point does optimism become delusion? The other day some fat-headed woman on the radio was lecturing her browbeaten

371

interviewer, denying that there was anything wrong with binge-drinking, insisting that the true problem lay with the middle-aged, middle-class drunks, apparently swilling it down in their own houses. He, poor battered fellow, dared not argue that even if this were true, even if all the *bons bourgeois* were lying flat on the carpet, singing sea shanties every night of their lives, they would still not be a problem, because they would not be a problem to *anyone else*. Why do modern leaders not grasp that their job is to control antisocial behaviour but not private activity; to regulate our actions as regards others, but not where they only concern ourselves? At times it is hard not to feel that as a culture we are lost, in permanent denial and spinning in the void.

I turned the key and opened the door of the flat on to the darkness of living alone. I walked into the drawing room and switched on a scattering of lamps from the door. I was only beginning to get used to the notion that every time I returned to my home I would find it just as I'd left it. When Bridget went I will say she went most thoroughly. As I waved her off I suspected that she saw the separation as only temporary and that I would soon find telltale signs that she expected to be back, but I would say now that I wronged her, that in some way she had decided she was as glad to be rid of me as I to be rid of her. These things are peculiar. You agonise for months, or even years, on end. Should you finish it? Should you not? But having made the decision, you're as impatient as a child on Christmas Eve. It is with the greatest difficulty you refrain from packing for them, pushing them into a taxi and shooing them away that very night. You long for them to go, you ache for it, so you can begin the rest of your life. 'You'll miss me,' she said as she walked through the flat, checking for any last-minute items she'd forgotten.

'I know I will,' I said, as one must in such a case. There is an etiquette involved and this comes into the same category as 'It isn't you, it's me.' Actually, I thought at the time that I would miss her. But I didn't much. Or far less than I expected. I can cook quite well when I put my mind to it and I'm lucky enough to have a woman who cleans a few times a week, so the main change was that I no longer had to spend the long, dark evenings with someone who was permanently disappointed in me. And that was nice. In fact, one of the great gifts of getting older is the discovery that the very thing you feared, 'being alone,' is actually much nicer than you thought. I should qualify this. To be old and ill alone, to die alone, is usually a sad thing, and at some point one may want to take steps to avoid this fate if possible. I suppose the prospect of a solitary death is even scarier for the childless, as they have no one they can reasonably expect to get involved with their disintegration, but even for them, and I am one of them, chunks on your own before you hove into sight of the Pearly Gates are simply lovely. You eat what you like, you watch what you like, you drink what you like, whoopee, and all without guilt or the need to hurry in case you'll be found out. If you feel social you go out, if you don't you stay in. If you want to talk you pick up the telephone, if not you don't, and all around is the blessed gift of silence, not the silence of resentment but of peace.

Of course, as a rule this only applies if one has

recently come out of a relationship that was less than satisfactory. For the surviving widow or widower of a happy marriage things are obviously different. I will always remember my father, left on his own, remarking that while others might feel released by the death of their spouse to pursue an interest or a hobby or to get involved with some worthy activity that their marriage had prevented, he had personally gained nothing and lost everything, a very moving tribute, even if my mother deserved it more than he knew. But for the man or woman after a longed-for break-up things are quite different. There are missing bits, of course, the sex for one, but for a long time sex between Bridget and me had been more a question of feeling it was expected of one rather than demonstrating any real interest in the other on either of our parts. I won't deny that the thought of re-embarking on a career of 'dating' to fill the gap is a terrifying one to people in their fifties, but even so, freedom is a word that always shines.

The following morning, as I sat at my desk, I reviewed my non-existent progress in the search for the fortunate child, but I felt I must be approaching its conclusion. There were after all only two women left on the list to eliminate: Candida Finch and Terry Vitkov. After that, my task would presumably be done. When I had contemplated these possibilities, before this time, I had assumed that I would check out Candida first since she was in England. If she proved to be the one we were looking for I would not have to go to Los Angeles, which did seem rather a chore, so it was logical to try her next. But when I dialled her number, clearly printed for me on Damian's list, I was repeatedly treated, for almost the only time in this adventure, to the synthetic courtesies of an answering machine, made worse by my leaving message upon message, so far without tangible result. I wasn't comfortable any more with my bogus charity excuse, not since Kieran had somehow exposed it without meaning to, and instead of formulating another lie I decided just to make a simple request, stating my name, suggesting she had probably forgotten me but that we knew each other once and asking her to get in touch when she had a moment. I then left my numbers, put the receiver carefully back on to its cradle and hoped for the best. But the best was slow in coming and after three weeks of this, plus an unanswered postcard, I wasn't quite sure what to do next to serve my master. We did not, after all, have very long to play with.

'Go to Los Angeles,' said Damian down the line. 'Take a break, stay a few days. You can tick off Terry and do yourself some good. Do you have an agent out there?'

'Only as part of an arrangement with the London ones. I've never met him.'

'There you are, then. Give him a treat. Pick up some girls, take him out for the evening, give him the time of his life. I'm paying.'

Should I resent this attempt to sound generous? Or was he really being generous? 'My agent here says he's gay.'

'All the better. Flirt with him. Make him think he's the only man you've ever found attractive. Ask his advice and tell him how helpful it is when you receive it, then press an unfinished manuscript into his hands and give him a sense of ownership in what you're doing.' Comments like this made me painfully aware of how much more Damian knew about the world than I.

I had spoken to him of my evening with Kieran de Yong, not all of it, not the last bit, but enough for him to know that I had liked him and that the dead boy had definitely not been Damian's child. He was silent at the other end for a minute or two. 'Poor Joanna,' he said.

'Yes.'

'She had every gift she needed for the era that was coming.'

'I agree.'

'If only she'd been a cynic. She died of optimism, in a way.'

'Like a lot of sixties children.'

'I'm glad you liked him,' he said in an unusually generous tone. 'Of course, he can't stand me.'

'And we know why.' I hesitated, wondering whether I wanted to return to that troubling episode, yet conscious that every uncovered detail of this journey insisted on taking me there. 'Did we all know what you were up to? That time in Estoril? Are the accounts I'm getting truthful? Or are their memories playing tricks on them? Because it's starting to sound as if you slept with every woman in the world in the space of a few days.'

'I was young,' he replied and we both laughed.

*   *   *

I first met Terry, as I have said, at the ball given for Dagmar of Moravia. Lucy Dalton had disliked her on sight and so did some others, but I did not.

376

I don't mean I was mad about her but, to invert Kieran's chilling phrase, she wasn't nothing. She was full of energy, full of what was once called pluck, and I did like her determination, and her mother's, to have first and foremost a very good time. Her father, of whom we would never see much, had made a killing with an advertising agency, first based in Cincinnati and later on Madison Avenue, at just the hour when the world was discovering quite what advertising could really do. Right through the 1950s, there had been a sense in many quarters that it was enough to say 'Use this! It's *Good*!' And that would do the trick, launching the product on a grateful public, until the moment, and it was in my teens, that the world of marketing would change forever and begin its remorseless campaign to take over civilisation. Jeff Vitkov spotted this coming era sooner than most. He was a simple, unpretentious soul, brilliant in his way but not, or so we thought, complicated in his wishes or his needs, the last man on earth to wish to climb the social ladder. Even after the move to New York he continued to regard Cincinnati as his home and he would possibly have left the family based there, flying back on the weekends, enjoying vacations in some modest but comfortable resort hotel, if his wife, Verena, had not made the unwelcome discovery that even the vertiginous improvement in their finances had not brought the social recognition she craved and, reasonably enough, felt entitled to. There is a fantasy one often hears voiced in England that America is classless, which, as any traveller will know, is arrant nonsense and never more so than in the provincial towns, whose social arrangements

377

can be impressively resistant to the ambitious newcomer. Someone remarked, not all that long ago, that it would be easier to gain entreé to the King's chamber at Versailles than to break into the inner gang of Charleston, and much the same could be said in all the cities of the true, US *Gratin.*

This was always so. One of the main reasons for the great invasion by American heiresses in the 1880s and 1890s, the so-called Buccaneers, was that many of the daughters of those newly rich papas grew tired of having doors shut in their faces back home in Cleveland or St Louis or Detroit, and preferred instead to enjoy the deep and genuine warmth with which the well-born English have always welcomed money. It is hard to deny that the careers of girls like Virginia Bonynge, Viscountess Deerhurst, who began life as the daughter of a convicted murderer from the Middle West, would seem to confirm that things were much easier this side of the pond. Needless to say, this would often lead to sweet revenge, as the mothers of the Duchess of Manchester or the Countess of Rosslyn or Lady Randolph Churchill, or many, many others would sweep home in triumph to the place where they'd been snubbed, to rub their sisters' noses in it. I suspected at the time that this thinking, or something like it, was behind the plan, forming in Verena Vitkov's mind towards the end of 1967, to put her daughter through a London Season.

There were options open to mothers, in those days, to defray some of the expense if necessary. Things were already less abundant than they had been before the war, when there were three or four balls in London every night. Until the end of presentation there were half a dozen each week; by my time there were two or three; and fifteen years later it was down to less than ten in the whole Season. Even in '68, some girls gave only cocktail parties and no dance, others would throw both but share the ball, and there was no shame in this. Serena Gresham shared her coming-out ball with her cousin, Candida Finch, although this was of course because Lady Claremont was funding them both. But from the start, Terry Vitkov was anxious to cover every base and I have no doubt she was more than encouraged in this by her mother, the unsinkable Verena. In the event the drinks party, held early in the proceedings before they'd quite found their feet, was a standard affair at the Goring, but for the ball they were determined to make the evening memorable. This they undoubtedly achieved if not quite in the way they had intended, but that comes later and, to be fair, it was an original location. Mrs Jeffrey Vitkov, so ran the invitation, would be At Home, 'for Terry,' on such and such a night at Madame Tussaud's Waxworks in the Euston Road.

I do not know if you can still hire the waxworks for a private party. Not just a room, or a special chamber set aside for 'entertaining,' but the whole edifice and all it holds. I doubt it, or if you can, I imagine the price would be prohibitive to all save the super-rich, but forty years ago you could. There was less danger in it for them, of course, than there would be today. Apart from any other reason we were a more law-abiding lot. We took more care. Crime, as it might touch the middle and upper classes, was rare. People may groan when they hear that houses in the country were not locked, but they weren't. Not if one had just gone shopping. In central London we walked home alone at night without a qualm. Shoplifting was not considered cool by anyone. It was just stealing. I don't think mugging was sufficiently common even to qualify for a special name. And again, as I said, we were much less drunk. This did not mean, of course, that every party went without mishap.

I dined very well on the night of Terry's ball because my hosts for the dinner beforehand, had forgotten all about it. I turned up at the door of a rather smart house in Montpelier Square, joined on the step as I waited for the occupants to respond to my ring of the bell by Lucy Dalton and a man I hardly knew, who later became the head of Schroder's, or some such spangled operation, although you couldn't have told his future held such promise then. The three of us stood, shifting our weight from foot to foot, until the door was at last opened by Mrs Northbrook (for that was her name), who stood there in jeans and a jersey, with a gin and tonic in her other hand. At the sight of us the blood drained from her face and we were greeted with the telling words, 'Jesus Christ, it's not *tonight!*' The result of this was that Mr Northbrook was summoned with a scream and had to book a table for ten at an excellent place just across from Harrods, in that funny little triangle which I think used to have a grass bit in front of it, or have I made that up? As we waited, we all sat in their pretty, untidy and unready drawing room, swilling down some rather good Pouilly Fumé, which Laura Northbrook (we had moved on since the doorstep moment) had providentially found in the fridge before she joined her husband upstairs to struggle into their clothes. After such a welcome they could hardly stint with these frightful strangers wished upon them and the result was one of the best dinners I had eaten all year.

Our group was therefore in a jolly and convivial mood when we arrived at the famous entrance at about eleven that night. I suppose there must have been bouncers or someone similar to admit us, but, as I've already said, I have no solid memory of cards to be taken, or lists to be ticked off. The main party space had been arranged in what was then, and maybe is now, known as the Hall of Kings. The wax images of England's Royalty had been moved back into a circle round the dance floor, cleared at the centre, but the figures were still sufficiently spaced apart for us to be able to stroll among them and photographs would later appear in the press—though not in the *Tatler*, which had originally been the plan—of debs and their escorts apparently standing next to Henry VIII or Queen Caroline of Anspach. I was myself snapped with a girl I knew from my Hampshire years after my father's retirement from the diplomatic. It never, mercifully, appeared in print, but for some reason now forgotten I still have a copy of the picture. We look as if we're talking to a startled and offended Princess Margaret.

As we know, every waxwork ever made appears to be either under sedation, or recently arrested for criminal assault and in this respect almost uniquely, the last four decades have seen little change. Except perhaps in their subject matter. We certainly all knew far more history then, that is the whole nation did, not just the privileged, the

381

educational establishment having not yet broken the link between teaching and the imparting of knowledge; so figures like Wellington and Disraeli and Gordon of Khartoum still had a resonance that spread far beyond the elite, the only group today who might have heard of them. Nor, when it came to waxworks, was there the modern, pusillanimous terror of causing offence and I can bear witness that the Chamber of Horrors in those days was really horrible. That night it had been set aside for a discothèque, and when Lucy and I went downstairs to explore it was quite clear the authorities were a long way from worrying about whether or not someone might get hit by a falling basket of nasturtiums or a stray conker.

There were stone pillars dividing the space and at the top of each, on a little ledge, was a severed head, disfigured with some hideous atrocity. Eyes hung out of sockets, flaps of skin revealed whitened bone, one even had an iron bar thrust right through it, causing the face to look very surprised, as well it might. A long glass case held miniature examples of every torture known to man, some quite new to me, and we walked slowly down it, wondering at human cruelty. Then there were the serial killers, although I don't believe that term was yet in use, but we certainly had them, if by some other title. George Smith, who drowned several unfortunate brides, presided over a bathtub which, we were told, was the actual one in which he had perpetrated his crimes, Dr Hawley Crippen was there and John Haig, who had met his chief victim in the Onslow Court Hotel, which I knew well since it was just down the street from where my grandmother used to live. Haig selected

Mrs Durand-Deacon from among the diners in the restaurant and worked his way into her affections before he took her off to the country somewhere and plunged her into a vat of acid. Lucy and I stood, silenced by the sight of these drab and ordinary men who had caused such untold misery. Today these displays tend to have a comic, even camp, element to them which somehow protects one from the reality that what you are witnessing is true, that all these terrible things did happen, but then there was a counter-impetus, to make it as real as possible and the result was curiously haunting, even remembered now, after so long.

At last, in the very centre of the chamber we came upon a dingy curtain with an instruction not to pull it open without preparing well. I think it was forbidden to anyone under sixteen or something similarly enticing. It was the curtain that fascinated me. It was old, threadbare and dirty, like a curtain in a garden shed to hide the weedkillers from sight, and in a way this made it much more sinister than some self-advertising veil of scarlet satin. 'Shall we?' I said.

'You do it. I don't want to look.' Lucy turned away but did not, of course, move. People say things like this, not because they intend not to look but because they do not wish to take any responsibility for the horrors that will be revealed. It is a way of enjoying base pleasures while retaining their superiority.

I pulled back the curtain. The shock was immediate and stark. Even if it was not prompted by the young woman who was hanging from an iron hook that had penetrated her vitals and on which she was apparently writhing in vivid, screaming agony. This, I could handle. What almost made me cry out in pain was the sight of Damian holding Serena in a fierce embrace and quite obviously plunging his tongue so far into her mouth that she must have had trouble breathing. Although I cannot pretend that she looked, even to me, as if she were resisting his advances. Far from it. She clawed at his back, she ran her fingers through his hair, she squeezed her body against his, until she seemed to be attempting somehow to crush the pair of them into one single being. 'No wonder the curtain carried a warning,' said Lucy and they froze, then looked across at us. I desperately searched for a phrase that would contain my rage at Damian, my disappointment in Serena and my contempt for the new morality all at once. It was too ambitious. I might have been able to make up a combination word in German, but English has its limitations.

'You're busy,' I said. Which didn't exactly hit the mark I was aiming at.

They had broken apart by now and Serena was straightening herself up. Her body language told so clearly that she was longing to ask both of us, Lucy and me, not to say anything, but of course she felt the request would be demeaning. 'We won't say anything,' I said.

'I don't care if you do,' she replied with immense relief.

Damian, meanwhile, was carrying on with his usual insouciance. 'I'll see you later on.' He gave Serena a swift hug and wiped the lipstick off his mouth with a handkerchief, which he replaced in his pocket. Without a word to us he slipped through the curtain and was gone.

The sound of an O. C. Smith record, which was much in demand that summer, *Hickory Holler's Tramp*, suddenly filled the space, making an odd cultural contrast with all those severed heads and murderers and the luckless victim swinging on her hook, but the three of us still stood there. Until there was a noise and the unwelcome face of Andrew Summersby poked round the curtain. 'There you are,' he said, ignoring us, 'I've been looking everywhere.' He took in our grotesque, waxen companion. 'Ooh er.' He laughed. 'Someone's going to wake up with indigestion.' And he gave the figure a push, as if she were in a child's swing. The hideous thing moved slowly back and forth at the end of its rope.

'Let's dance,' said Lucy, and without another word to Serena we left her to the noble dullard, and made our way to a dark little dance floor in the shadow of a guillotine, on to which a French aristocrat in a jacket of cheap-looking wrinkled velveteen, was being strapped by two burly revolutionaries. From a draped alcove to one side the entire Royal Family of France looked on serenely.

'Are you all right?' To my bewilderment, Lucy appeared to be on the edge of tears. I couldn't imagine why.

She was irritated by the enquiry. 'Of course I am,' she said sharply, bobbing fiercely in time to the music for a bit. Then she looked up at me apologetically. 'Don't mind me,' she said. 'I had some bad news just as I was leaving home and it suddenly came back.' I looked suitably solicitous. 'An aunt of mine, my mother's sister. She's got cancer.' This was quite clever of her, I can see now. At the time I am writing of, the English had just about begun to move on from referring to cancer as 'a long illness bravely borne,' but there was still something dread in the word, still something, if not exactly shameful, at least to be avoided at all costs. In those days the diagnosis was generally considered a death sentence, and when one heard of people taking treatments one almost despised them for not being able to face the truth, although I suppose logic tells us some of them must have survived, mustn't they? Anyway, the point is it wasn't at all like today, when you really do have a reasonable shot, if not quite as reasonable in every case as non-medicos tend to assume. For Lucy to say the word at all was bound to distract me. Still, looking back, I admit I am slightly embarrassed that I completely believed her explanation.

'I am sorry,' I said. 'But there are all sorts of things they can do now.' One mouthed these clichés at the time, they were as routine as 'How do you do?' but one never thought they contained a grain of truth. She gave a routine nod and we danced on.

For some reason, an innocent one I am certain, Terry or more probably her mother had decided to cut a cake at the peak of the evening. This was not generally done. As I have observed, in those pre-don't-drink-and-drive days, we ate before we arrived and we did not generally eat again until the breakfast was served towards the end of the dance. There might occasionally be some sort of speech and a toast, although by no means always, at a mid point in the festivities, but this usually consisted of some old uncle just standing and saying what a marvellous girl so-and-so was, and we would all raise our glasses and that was that. There were dangers involved in this departure from the norm, but quite honestly, when there was no speech, which was usually the case, there were times when the proceedings fell a bit flat. We arrived, we drank, we danced, we went home and there had never been what my mother would refer to as 'A Moment' in the evening that really registered. The father of the deb in question would have the bitter knowledge that he had paid out thousands upon thousands for a night that no one would remember. On the other hand the danger of a speech and a toast is always that it may in some way feel rather naff. At least, when the occasion is not a wedding or something where speeches are generally expected. Anyway, on this particular evening, perhaps because neither Terry nor Verena was absolutely at ease with the rules, they decided to have cake and a toast, as if it had indeed been the wedding it was not.

I gather people wandering throughout the waxworks were summoned by a kind of tannoy, which would obviously have been installed in that building anyway for crowd control, but by then Lucy and I were back in the Hall of Kings, seated rather wearily at a table with Georgina Waddilove and Richard Tremayne, an unlikely couple if you like, overlooked by some of the duller members of the Hanoverian dynasty, one of whom was responsible for Richard's predecessor, the first Duke of Trent, in what I suspect must have been an uncharacteristic night of merriment. I have forgotten why Richard was with us, probably because he was tired and couldn't find anywhere else to sit. At all events Jeff Vitkov, who had come over from New York especially for the ball and was obviously determined to make his mark, took the microphone from the band singer and announced that he was going to propose a toast to his 'young and beautiful daughter, and her even younger and more beautiful mother.' This is the kind of thing that makes the English cringe, of course, and we were only just recovering when he added that we were all going to eat some genuine, American brownies, to mark the 'debut,' ugh, of a 'genuine, American girl.' Quite apart from the toe-curling sentimentality of all this, to most of us in those days 'Brownies' meant young Girl Guides, just as 'Cubs' meant young Boy Scouts, so there was a certain amount of hilarity released by the announcement that we were going to eat some, but we listened on as Jeff praised his daughter, Terry, who then seized the microphone for herself, paying tearful tribute to her wonderful 'Pop and Mom,' which made us freeze even more solidly in our chairs. Taking up a large knife, she sort of slid it through a mound of the brownies in question, and after that a mass of waitresses appeared, carrying decorated trays full of the little sticky brown cakes we now all know so well but didn't then. I hate chocolate and I remember so did Georgina, so, alone at our table, we didn't eat any, but they must have been good, because more or less everyone else did, and across the room I could see Damian absolutely piling in.

The events that followed a little while later seemed to start almost as a rumour, a sense of strangeness spreading through the gathering, before anyone was aware of the source. I recall that I was dancing with Minna Bunting, although our little walkout was over by that stage, and there was suddenly the sound of someone being violently sick. Which, then, was very startling. People on the dance floor began to look at each other, as there were more odd sounds, men and women started to scream with laughter, not ordinary amused laughter, but a shrill cackling like a witches' coven at work. In what seemed like no time at all we could hear shouting and singing and yelling and crying coming from every corner. I looked at my partner to share my puzzlement, but even she didn't look too clever. 'I feel incredibly ill,' she muttered and walked off the floor without another word. I hurried after her, but at the edge she suddenly clutched her head and ran off somewhere, presumably to a distant but welcoming cloakroom. Somehow the dancers themselves had maintained a kind of order, but once we had left them, the crowd filling the rest of the rooms and swirling around us felt slightly—or, before long, *very*—mad. One of the mothers rushed past me, with her bosom hanging out of her dress and I saw Annabella Warren, Andrew Summersby's sister, screaming and lying flat out, with her skirt hitched above her midriff, displaying some thoroughly unusual-looking underwear, possibly recycled by her nanny. Not far away a young man in the corner was in the process of pulling his shirt over his head. In the mêlée I had soon lost sight of Minna, but someone caught my arm.

'What the hell's going on?' Georgina was by my side, her impressive bulk providing me with something to shelter behind. A girl tripped and fell, spreadeagled at our feet, laughing.

389

'Come on, everybody! Clap your hands!' The voice, amplified by the microphone, was only too familiar. We turned and registered that the boy undressing was now revealed as none other than Master Baxter, who had shed the rest of his clothes, and was cavorting wildly round the stage in his underpants and looking in grave danger of losing even those.

By now the ballroom was bedlam. Some people must have escaped at the first signs of trouble, with that marvellous instinct that the British upper classes generally display in such a situation, but those who were not at the exits already were finding it increasingly hard to get to them. Suddenly I caught sight of Terry, in the midst of the demented crowd. Her hair had collapsed and a separate arrangement of ringlets had detached itself from her head and somehow got caught on a zip or hook fastener behind her neck, leaving a kind of mane to sweep down her back, making her look faintly feral as she attempted to claw her way through the ranks of her guests. I reached across a weeping man with his regurgitated dinner down his front and caught her wrist, pulling her through the crowd towards us. 'What is it? What's happening?'

'Somebody spiked the brownies. They were full of hash.'

'What?' Is it to be believed that the word was not immediately familiar to me? Or was it just the shock of discovery blocking my concentration?

'Hash. Marijuana. Dope.' Terry was altogether more at home with the topic, if angrier than Genghis Khan.

'Why? Who would do such a thing?'

'Someone who wanted to ruin my party and

pretend to themselves it was a joke.' This was, I have no doubt, a completely accurate diagnosis. She was rich, she was good-looking, she was an outsider. That was more than enough to ensure enmity in several quarters, although this seemed an unusually unpleasant way of demonstrating it. Then again, the perpetrator may not have been aware of the level of mayhem that would ensue from their jolly prank. We were not all experts then.

'You seem OK.'

'I'm OK because I'm on a diet.' She said it snappily and it was almost funny, if we had not been in the middle of such desolation. At that moment a weeping Verena Vitkov claimed her daughter from the other side. Someone had trodden on her dress, and it had torn away from a seam at the waist, leaving not her legs but her roll-on exposed, which was of course much worse.

'Let's get out of here,' I said to Georgina and she nodded, but then two things happened. The first was that I could see Serena Gresham had climbed on to the stage with a dinner jacket, presumably Damian's, which she was trying to wrap round him despite his protests. She also had his trousers over her arm but obviously that task was a bridge too far and she didn't even attempt it. The second thing to catch at our attention was the sound of a police whistle, which echoed through the chamber like the shrill tolling of Doom. At once, what had already been chaos was transformed into a panicking stampede. It is easy now to think, almost calmly, of the notion of a drugs raid. In the forty years that have elapsed since these events, drugs themselves have ceased to seem extraordinary. Regrettable, I would hope, and something to be avoided for most of us even today, but no longer weird. In those days the vast majority of this crowd were strangers to the very notion. Whatever the impression that pop stars and Channel Four like to give of the Sixties, if their tales are true, which I often doubt, they were operating in a different world from my bunch. Obviously the bad boys among us were starting to experiment and by seven or eight years later a lot of us would have been introduced to the whole trendy culture of drugs and damn-it-all, but not by then. After all, most of what came to be called 'the Sixties' happened in the following decade. Yet here we were, debutantes and beaux, plus many of their mothers and fathers, in a full-scale drugs raid, which would provide, as we were only too aware, a perfectly wonderful story for the papers the following day. Out of family loyalty, if nothing else, all those nice, young sons and daughters of earls and viscounts, of high court judges and generals, of bankers and heads of corporations, had to get out of that room unseen and unapprehended, to stop their blameless daddies being soaked in the spray of public ridicule that was even then being loaded up, ready to flow. If the room had been on fire there couldn't have been a more urgent dash for the door.

I too would have headed in the same direction as the crowd, but Georgina held me back. 'It's hopeless,' she said. 'They'll be waiting for us on the pavement.'

'Where, then?'

'This way. There'll be a service exit for the group. And the maids must have been bringing the drinks up from somewhere.'

Together we pushed against the crowd. I glimpsed Candida Finch, green-faced and at the end of her tether, leaning against the opposite wall but she was too far away for me to help her. Some girls were dancing a sort of reel, accompanying themselves with alternating screams, in the middle of the floor between us. Then Candida was swept away and I didn't see her again. 'This is a nightmare.' Serena was nearly upon me when I realised who it was. She had an arm round Damian, who was still ranting and calling out to everyone to clap their hands. 'I'll clap *your* hands if you don't shut up,' she said, but it didn't seem to have much effect. Damian fell, and others surged over him, until I really began to wonder if he would be seriously injured. 'Help me get him up.' Serena was down among the lunging feet and I knew I had to do my best. Together we managed to hook our arms under his and literally drag him to the edge of the room.

'Why are you all right? Didn't you eat any either?'

Serena wrinkled her nose. 'I wasn't hungry.'

'Here we go!' The enterprising Georgina had found a service door at the back behind a curtain that a few people, but not many, were taking advantage of. Behind us, the whistles and general shouting had increased in volume, and it was clear that those who had tried to leave in a more orthodox manner were being subjected to hideous humiliations before they were allowed to do so.

'My God, the press is outside!' This from Lucy, who had started down the main stair, only to make this unwelcome discovery and beat a retreat whence she had come. 'If I get in the paper my father will kill me.' It's funny. We were so much more governed by these considerations than our equivalents are now.

Following our leader, Georgina, we came to a landing at the top of a stone, service staircase. Guests in various stages of dishevelment were hurrying down it. One girl broke her heel and fell the remainder of the second flight with a scream, but without pausing she scrambled up, tore the shoe off the other foot and plunged on. Unfortunately, Damian seemed to be getting worse. He had now ceased his requests for us to clap our hands and had decided instead simply to go to sleep. 'I'm perfectly all right,' he murmured, his chin sinking deeply into his chest. 'I just need a little shut-eye and then I'll be as right as rain.' Down went his chin even further, followed by his eyelids, and he began to snore.

'We'll have to leave him,' said Georgina. 'They won't kill him. He'll just have his name taken, and a warning or something of the kind, and that'll be the end of it.'

'I'm not leaving him,' said Serena. 'Who knows what they'll do? And what happens afterwards? If he has his name on a list at a drugs raid, he might never get a passport or a security rating or a job at an embassy or anything.' This string of words, flooding out as they did, created a rather marvellous contrast to the life we were leading at that precise moment, cowering on a dingy, back stairway, on the run from the police. It conjured up images of embassy gatherings at which Damian would shine, and foreign travel and important work in the City. I found myself wishing that

Serena had voiced such fragrant worries about my destiny.

But Georgina was unconvinced. 'Don't be ridiculous,' she said. He's not newsworthy. That's the only thing we have to worry about. You're a headline. She's a headline. Even I'm worth a mention. He's not. Leave him here to sleep it off. Maybe they won't come up this far.'

'I'm not leaving him,' said Serena. 'You go without us if you want.'

I remembered her defence of Damian at Dagmar's ball, when she stood up for him alone and all the rest of us were silent. I decided I was not prepared for a repetition. 'I'll help,' I said. 'If we balance him between us we'll manage.' She looked at me. I could tell she was pretty grateful not to have been taken up on her suggestion of facing the Mongol hordes alone. So we did just as I said. Hoisting him up, and against a low chorus of Damian's mumbled protests about just needing a little shut-eye, the group of us somehow got him to the bottom of the stair. We hurried past the ground floor, since we could hear the shouted protests of indignant adults being stopped and questioned, as well as screams and yells and singing coming from the young. Eventually we found ourselves in a basement, searching for a door or window that would open.

We were alone, a little club against the world, in a very murky passage, when a side door opened and a girl stuck her head out. 'There's a window here that seems to lead out to an alley,' she said and ducked back inside the room. I did not know her well. Her name was Charlotte Something and she ended up a countess, but I forget which one it was. Nevertheless, I shall always remember her with real gratitude. She had no obligation to come back and tell us of her useful find, instead of just climbing out and running for it. That kind of generosity, when there is nothing in it for the giver, is what always touches one most. Anyway, we followed her into what must have been a sort of cleaning cupboard because it was full of brushes and dusters and tins of polish, and sure enough there was an unbarred window, which had been forced open for what looked like the first time since the Armistice.

Here, as before, the problem was Damian, almost comatose by this point, and we wrestled with him for a bit until finally Georgina, who was stronger than any of us, bent down and threw her shoulder beneath him in a sort of fireman's lift and, with an exasperated sigh, flung him at the open space. Serena had already climbed out and was able to grab one arm and his head, and with her and Lucy pulling, while Georgina and I pushed, we did succeed in getting him through, although it was too much like assisting at the delivery of a baby elephant for my taste. There were men's voices in the passage outside, as Georgina squeezed out, and I would guess I was probably the last to make it to freedom by that route before it was sealed off by the enemy. We pulled down the window as quickly as we could, then raced to the end of the alley, Georgina and I dragging Damian between us. You will understand that to be pulling a largish young man, naked except for underpants and a dinner jacket, was unusual to say the least of it, and we could not consider ourselves out of danger until Serena, waving us into the shadows, had managed to stop an innocent taxi driver, who had no idea what he was letting himself in for.

'Where shall we take him?' she hissed over her shoulder and even I could see that this would be a large mouthful for the Claremonts to swallow on an empty stomach. I imagine he had originally planned to drive himself back to Cambridge, after a cup of coffee or two, as I blush to say we did in those days, but clearly that was now out of the question.

'My flat. Wetherby Gardens,' I said. My parents were there, but after nineteen years of me they were not entirely unequipped for this sort of escapade. Serena gave the address and, opening the door, she climbed in ready for Georgina and me to rush Damian across the pavement and into the welcoming darkness of the cab. We made it, clambering in with puffing and sighing, and Lucy hurried in behind us. It may sound as if the taxi was overloaded and so it was, but you must understand we thought nothing of that, neither passenger nor driver, and nor did the powers that be. They weren't concerned with micro-managing our lives, as they are today, and in this I think, indeed I know, that we were happier for it. Some changes have been improvements, on some the jury is still out, but when it comes to the constant, meddling intervention by the state, we were much, much better off then than we are now. Of course, there were times when we were at risk and the smug, would-be controllers will tut-tut at that, but to encourage the surrender of freedom in order to avoid danger is the hallmark o f a tyranny and always a poor exchange.

'Should we put his trousers on?' Serena had somehow managed to keep the flapping items with her. We all looked down at Infant Damian curled up like an unborn child and the thought of the task defeated us.

'Let's not,' said Lucy firmly.

'What about your poor parents?' asked Georgina. 'Suppose they're still awake?'

Another glance confirmed the earlier decision. 'They're strong,' I said. 'They can take it.' With its distinctive rattle, the taxi started off, but as we came back out on to the Euston Road we could see that the police were still there with a host of cars and vans, and there was that now familiar, but then rare, accompaniment of the popping of cameras, blinding the poor wretches caught in their glare, all destined for unwelcome fame on the morrow.

My parents were philosophical, as they stood, blinking, in their dressing gowns, staring down at Damian slumped in a chair, still in his lively and distinctive costume, but now with his trousers deposited in a crumpled pool at his feet, like a ritual offering. 'He'll have to sleep on the floor in your room,' said my mother, without the possibility of any disagreement. 'I have a committee meeting in here at ten tomorrow morning, and there is *no* guarantee he'll be up and about by then.'

'No,' I said. And together we dragged Damian down the passage, depositing him on a folded eiderdown with some blankets on top.

'Where are the rest of his clothes?' asked my mother. I looked at her blankly. 'His shirt and so on.'

'At Madame Tussaud's, I suppose.'

'From where he had better not reclaim them.'

Her voice was, I thought, unnecessarily severe. 'He could have got you all into a great deal of trouble.'

'That's rather unfair,' I said. 'It wasn't his fault.' But my mother paid no attention to my attempted defence. She was only displaying the behaviour that I have since discovered was absolutely endemic to her and to many like her. When they approve of someone in their children's lives, and when it is because of the social position of said individual, they will never admit it and will find endless excuses for no matter what bad behaviour. But when, instead, they *dis*approve, again for social rather than more meaningful reasons, rather than concede this, everything *else* about the unwanted friend must be condemned. This falls into the same category as when they give directions. If it is desirable that you should attend an event, it is 'easy-peasy, straight down the M4 and you're there,' but when they do not believe you should go, the same journey becomes 'quite endless. You trudge down the M4 forever and when you get off it there's an absolute maze of roads and villages to be negotiated. It's not worth it.' My mother was not a snob in any normal sense, she would have been shocked at the notion that she might be, but that didn't stop her being offended when she felt I had been 'latched on to' (her phrase), and this is what she felt about Damian. There was some truth in her analysis, of course.

Damian woke in the early hours of the following morning, I would guess at around three. I know this because he woke me, too, by whispering 'are you awake?' into my ear, until I was. He was completely sober. 'I'm starving,' he said. 'Is there anything to eat?'

'Couldn't it wait? You'll have breakfast in a minute.'

'I'm afraid it just can't. I can go and look for myself if you like.'

This seemed like a worse option, so I pulled myself to my feet, pulled on a dressing gown over my pyjamas, all of which garments date the incident, since, like almost every other male, I have abandoned traditional nightwear at some point during the subsequent decades, and I set off through the flat, with Damian following. With difficulty I persuaded him against a fry-up, and he settled for a bowl of cereal followed by some toast and tea. I joined him in the last, as we sat hunched over the tiny kitchen table. He started to laugh. 'What's so funny?'

'The whole evening. Lord only knows what they'll put in the papers.'

'Not us, which is the main thing. Poor Terry.' Nobody seemed to feel at all sorry for the ruin and waste inflicted on our hostess. I felt it was time someone did.

But Damian shook his head. 'Don't worry about her. She'll get a big story out of it. It'll probably be the defining moment of the Season before she's finished.'

'Perhaps it is.'

'Perhaps.' Looking back, that party did come to represent a moment for a lot of us, when the past, present and future fused together in some kind of crazy way. When the anti-authority, destabilising counterculture, which would win eventually (although not in the way we all then thought), swept in through the doors of our safe little, nearly-pre-1939 world and carried us off with it. Damian put another piece of plastic bread in the toaster. 'I don't know why I'm so hungry. Does hash make you hungry?'

'I'm not really the person to ask.'

He looked at me, hesitating and then deciding to speak. 'I'm afraid you got quite a shock when you pulled back that curtain.' I was silent, not exactly through indignation or a sense of being wronged. I just couldn't imagine what I could say that would convey the right message, because I didn't know what the right message might be. He nodded as if I'd spoken. 'I know you're keen on her.'

'Does she?' I couldn't help myself. Aren't we sad, sometimes? The odd thing was, and I remember this quite clearly, I wasn't sure what answer I wanted him to give.

Damian shrugged as he helped himself to butter. 'If I know, I dare say she does.'

'What about you?'

My question was oddly phrased and he looked up. 'What do you mean?'

Of course, the fact was I wanted to hit him. Right there, smack, in the middle of his face, with a great, heavy, wounding punch that would send him over backwards, with any luck cracking his head against the stove as he fell. I've often wondered what it must be like to live in a rougher world from the one I have always occupied, in a hit-now-ask-questions-later kind of society. One's always supposed to say how ghastly violence is, and of course it *is* ghastly, but there must be compensations. 'Are you serious about her?' I asked.

He laughed. 'Don't be so fucking pompous.'

'I just meant—'

'You meant you are so jealous your face hurts, and you're only assuming a poncy, pseudo-uncle pose so you can patronise me and put me down, and show me I'm a ridiculous interloper, out of my mind for daring to dream so far above my reach.' He put a bit more marmalade on to his toast and bit into it. Of course, I had to admit that every one of his words was documentary truth. If kicking him to death would have made Serena love me, I would have done it there and then. Biff, boff, bang. Instead, I opted for underhand fighting. 'I thought she was going out with Andrew Summersby now.' I was not without a trick or two of my own.

Damian looked up, sharply. 'Why do you think that?'

'He seemed very proprietorial when he came looking for her after you'd gone. Then they went off together.'

He gave a slightly annoyed grin. 'Andrew was at the dinner she had to go to and it is true that right now her parents think she's going out with him. Since Andrew seems to share this delusion, she couldn't be bothered to have it out with him tonight. No doubt, she soon will.'

I thought about this. It sounded to me as if Serena and Andrew were indeed an item, a thought that sickened me, and Damian was trying, for my benefit, to exaggerate his chances with her, when all he had managed was one kiss. We may have been more innocent then, but one kiss didn't mean much. 'Are you going to her dance?' I said.

'Can you ask? I'm staying at Gresham for it.'

I have never been a very confident person,

although I do not really know why this is so. It is true that I was not good-looking when I was young, but I was quite clever and I seemed to get about. My parents loved me, I have no doubt of that, and I've always had a lot of friends. Nor were girlfriends an insuperable problem, if a few may have been on the lookout for something better. I even got on well with my sister before her marriage. Yet with all this, I was not confident and I had to admire Damian for that reason. No castle walls could apparently keep him out and I envied him for it. Even at that moment, when I wished him in chains, his feet encased in blocks of concrete, at the bottom of the sea. Even as I imagined his thick hair waving as the tides pushed it to and fro, fishes swimming across his staring, sightless eyes, in some way, *malgré moi*, I felt admiration. 'Has Lady Claremont invited you?'

'Not yet, but she will. Candida and Serena are sorting it out between them. Serena's going to tell her mother that Candida fancies me.' He looked at me as he said it. As an alibi this was perfectly sensible and Lady Claremont would believe it, since Candida fancied everything male that moved, but as well as this there was a meaning in his words which I could see he had not thought through properly before he spoke them. Their echo in the room annoyed him. Because his speech meant that if Lady Claremont had even a whiff of this man's interest in her daughter he would not be welcome in her house. 'It's OK,' he said in answer to my unspoken query. 'I understand that type. I know I can make her like me.' Obviously he did not understand Lady Claremont's type, nor that of her husband, nor that of any of their world, largely because those people were not then, and are not now, interested in being understood by the likes of Damian Baxter. As a matter of fact I think Lady Claremont might well have liked him under different circumstances. She might have enjoyed his humour and his self-belief, she might even have allowed him into their circle as one of those token Real World Members that such households go in for. But that is all.

TWELVE

I am not an Englishman who hates Los Angeles. I'm not like those actors and directors who insist that every day spent there is drudgery, that it's all so 'false' they cannot besmirch their souls for one more minute and that they shout with joy when the 'plane takes off from LAX. I suppose some of them may be telling the truth, but I would guess not many. More usually, they are just ashamed of their desire for the rewards that only Hollywood will bring, and they disparage the place and all its works in the hope that they will not lose caste among their soulful brethren back in Blighty. I had only been once before the trip in question, many years before, when I was seeking fame and fortune in a fairly disorientated way, but I have visited a few times recently and I always enjoy myself when I am there. It is a resolutely upbeat place and after a long unbroken stretch of British pessimism, it feels good sometimes to look on the sunny side of life. I know the natives take this to extremes. But still, there is something about the up, Up, UP!ness

404

of it all that is a tonic to sad spirits and I am always pleased to be there.

In the forty years that separated my youthful friendship with Terry Vitkov and this, our re-encounter, she had enjoyed what is known as a chequered career. Even her time in London had not gone according to plan. She and her mother had done quite well, all things considered, but Terry had not ended up a viscountess presiding over twenty bedrooms in a house open to the public, which had unquestionably been the target, and they must have been disappointed. Looking back, I think the difficulty may have been that the Vitkovs as a group had made the common mistake of confusing a large salary with having money. A salary may enable you to live well while it's coming in, very well, but it does not alter the reality of your position and no one knows this better than the British upper class. Just as television fame, while it continues, feels like film stardom but seldom survives the cancellation of the series. Naturally, none of this would have mattered if a nice young man had fallen in love with Terry, but she was an abrasive personality, with her big features and her big teeth, loud in laughter, short on humour, and with a kind of unconcealed greed that was rather off-putting even to the worldly. In short she did not land her fish. There was a moment when she might have had an army major who was probably in line to get a baronetcy from an ageing uncle (although the latter was unmarried and these things are never certain), but the young officer took fright and fell back into the arms of a judge's daughter from Rutland. In some ways he might have been better off with Terry, as

405

she would at least have filled the house with people who could talk, but how long would she have stood it, that life of rainy walks and discussing horses over plates of summer pudding, once the title had arrived? So, if the path the Major took was duller, it was also probably smoother for him in the long run.

I last saw her, I am fairly sure, around the time of the party in Estoril, but not because she was there. In fact, she was annoyed that she had failed to secure an invitation. If only I had been so lucky. She may already have been pregnant then, but if so, none of us knew it, only that she had a plain but eager American millionaire pursuing her, divorced but not too old, whom she subsequently married in time for the baby's birth. The millionaire's name was Greg Something and he had been working in Eastern Europe at the time. After leaving there they had returned together to sun-drenched California where he pursued a career with Merrill Lynch and we'd lost them. I never really knew him but I liked him and, judging by our few meetings, I would have said he was far better suited to her than any of her English beaux, and if I had given it a moment's thought, I would have hoped for many years of bliss before Abraham saw fit to part them. Unfortunately, or so the story goes, Terry, a decade further down the line, attempted to cash him in for a much richer banker from Connecticut, before the latter dumped her for a model and left her high and dry, her first husband having made his escape while the going was good and settled down in North Virginia with his second family.

So Terry and her daughter had stayed on in Los

406

Angeles, where she pursued a career of some kind as a television presenter, dealing, or so I have been told, in something called the infomercial, where women chat about hair products and kitchen utensils and different types of luggage in a natural, unstudied way, as if it were remotely believable that they would do so were they not trying to sell you something.

I had rung from London, just to make sure she was still there, and she had been quite receptive to the idea we should catch up. I knew she was not one to be touched by charity, so I told her there was some interest in my latest book from a film studio and predictably that caught at her imagination. 'But that's wonderful!' she trilled. 'You must tell me all about it when we meet!' I had done a little homework and I suggested we might dine at a restaurant on the shore in Santa Monica the night after my arrival.

I knew her at once, when she came in and stood for a moment by the maître d's desk, as he pointed me out to her, and I waved. She started to make her way through the tables in that old no-nonsense way of hers. She was dressed as an American, East Coast, rich woman, which is a different costume from the jeans and chains favoured by workers in the Showbiz Industry, more Park Avenue than footballer's wife, which I found interesting. A neat, beige shirt-waister, a well-cut jacket over her shoulders, good, discreet jewellery. It was all less flashy and in better taste than I'd been expecting, but still unmistakably Terry. And yet, if I knew her, I also did not know her, this woman with the lacquered hair advancing towards me. I could see that the familiar chin was still too prominent, and

407

the eyes and teeth too large, but other elements of her face had changed alarmingly. She appeared to have had her lips stuffed with some kind of plastic filler, in the way that American women often do now. As a practice it fascinates me, because I have yet to meet a man who doesn't profess to find it quite repulsive. I can only suppose that some of them must be lying or the surgeons wouldn't do such a roaring trade. Maybe American men like it more than European ones do.

Thankfully, if Terry's mouth had become bulbous and mildly unsettling, it was not yet actually disturbing. But it wasn't alone in betraying the telltale signs of tamper. Her forehead was so smooth she might have been dead, since no expression or mannerism seemed to make it move above the eyebrows, and the eyes themselves had become very fixed in their orbit. Of course, more or less all this stuff, carrying with it, as it must, horrible images of the pinning and stretching and sawing and sewing of bloody skin and bruised bone, has come about in my lifetime and I can't be alone in finding it an odd fashion to have developed alongside the supposed liberation of women. Cutting their faces about, presumably to please men, does not strike one as a convincing mark of equality. In fact, it feels uncomfortably insecure, a Western manifestation of female circumcision or facial disfigurement or some other dark and ancient method of asserting male ownership.

Plastic surgery is better now than forty years ago, when it was largely reserved for actresses and foreign ones at that. But even today, when the results can be spectacular, there is a high and ironic price to pay, because for most men it's a turnoff to end all. The knowledge that a woman has been sliced about diminishes to nothing one's desire to see her without her kit. Although here I admit that women pay less high a price than men. Women who have 'work done' lose their sexual power over men. Men who resort to it lose everything.

Terry had reached my table. 'My God! You look—' She hesitated. I think she had been planning to say '*exactly* the same!' but, having come nearer and actually seen me, it was obvious that my appearance had altered so completely that I should carry a passport to prove my identity to anyone who has not met me since the sixties. '*Fantastic!*' she said instead, which did the work perfectly acceptably. I smiled. I had already got to my feet so I leaned over and kissed her on the cheek. 'Now, you *do* look fantastic,' I said and we sat, jovial and comfortable in our generous dishonesty.

A bland and pleasant-looking waiter stepped in briskly to tell us that his name was Gary and he very much hoped we were going to have an enjoyable evening, a hope I shared, even if I can never really see why it should matter much to the Garys of this world either way. He poured out two glasses of ice cubes, with a little water, and explained the specials, which all seemed to be frightening and hitherto unknown kinds of fish, and then, after promising to bring us some Chardonnay, he left us to our own devices. 'So, how is life in California?' This wasn't a very original opener, but I had by this stage of the Damian Mission, acquired the habit of going in gently, knowing that I would be investigating the paternity of their young before the night was out.

She gave a bright, generalised smile. 'Great!' she said, which was what I expected. I knew that with Californians this first act of any conversation is obligatory, where all decisions they have ever made are the right ones. Later, in some cases, the truth level may improve, but even for those rare individuals who long to unburden themselves of their pain they must still observe this ritual. Rather like having to eat the bread and butter before Nanny will give you cake.

'You never felt the need to go back to Cincinnati?'

She shook her head. 'It wasn't what I wanted. Not really. Greg's business was here.' She smiled and waved her hand towards the window. We could just hear the sounds of the sea under the restaurant hubbub. 'And there are no complaints about the weather.'

I nodded, mainly because one is always supposed to agree with this, but I can't be the only Englishman who finds those endlessly sunny days rather dull. I like our weather. I like the soft light of its grey days and the smell of the air after rain. Most of all I like the sudden changeability. 'If you're tired of the weather in England,' goes the old adage, 'just wait for five minutes.' I know it makes it hard to arrange outdoor events and no hostess with a brain would plan anything that was completely weather dependent, but even so . . . Anyway, I let it go.

Nice Gary had returned and poured out some wine, while we took a final glance at the menu. 'Is it possible to have the seafood salad but without

410

the shrimp or the calamari?' Terry had begun the dismemberment of the official suggestions that is part of eating out with a West Coast resident. 'And what exactly is in the dressing?' Gary answered as best he could, but he did not achieve a sale. 'Is there chicken stock in the artichoke soup?' He thought not. But did he *know?* No, he wasn't completely sure. So he went to the kitchen and returned with the happy news that the stock was vegetarian friendly, but while he was away, Terry had moved on. 'Is there any flour in the tempura batter?' I looked at her. She smiled. 'I'm allergic to gluten.' It was something that obviously pleased her. Gary, of course, was used to this. He was probably a West Coast boy himself and had grown up in the certain knowledge that only people of low status order off the menu as it is printed. However, I think we were all coming to realise that Terry was approaching the moment when, even in Santa Monica, a decision might be required. 'I think I'll start with some asparagus, but no butter or dressing, just olive oil. Then scallops, but hold the mixed salad. I'll take hearts of lettuce, plain.' Gary managed to write all this down, relieved no doubt that his release was on the horizon. He turned to me. Too soon. 'Can I get some spinach?' Why do Americans say 'get' in this context? They are not presumably planning to go into the kitchen and fetch it themselves. 'Mashed but not creamed. Absolutely no cream.'

She turned to me, but I spoke first. 'You're allergic to dairy.'

She nodded happily. Meanwhile, Gary had noted every detail on his little pad. She still hadn't finished. 'Is the spinach cooked with salt?' With infinite and, I thought, admirable patience, Gary ventured that yes, the spinach was cooked with a little salt. Terry shook her head, as if it were hard to believe in this day and age, 'no salt when they cook it.' I could not imagine how, even under this provocation, Patient Gary kept his cool. He hoped that would be possible. 'It's possible,' said Terry. 'No salt.' By now I could see that even Gary, that laid-back boy from sunny California, was ready to sink his pencil deep into Terry's neck and stand by, watching, as the blood oozed out around its tip. But he nodded, not trusting himself to give a vocal response.

He turned to me and we exchanged eye contact, recognising our alliance in that strange way that one can befriend a total stranger who has been a co-witness to impossible behaviour. 'I'll have the artichoke soup, a steak, medium rare and a green salad.' He seemed almost bewildered that the process had been so speedy.

'That's it?'

'That's it.'

With the hint of a sigh, he was just moving away, when Terry spoke again. 'Is there mayonnaise in your coleslaw?'

Gary paused. When he spoke again his voice had acquired the super-softness of a doctor's when dealing with a potentially dangerous patient. 'Yes, madam,' he said. 'There is mayonnaise in our coleslaw.'

'Oh. Then forget it.' She dismissed him with a slight, insulting flick of her hand and picked up her glass for another drink.

In justice, having been a silent witness for so long, I felt the need to intervene. 'Terry.' She turned, surprised perhaps that I should have an opinion. 'There's always mayonnaise in coleslaw.'

Again that little shake of the head in wondering disbelief. 'Not in our house,' she said and Gary made his escape.

Obviously, what this little vignette had told me was that Terry's life in California was not *Great!* These bids to be different, this insistence on the power to change, to inflict absolute governance in the captive situation of a restaurant, are the recourse of those who feel no power to change anything elsewhere. Los Angeles is a town where status is all and status is only given to success. Dukes and millionaires and playboys by the dozen may arrive and be glad-handed for a time, but they are unwise if they choose to live there, because the town is, perhaps even creditably, committed to recognising only professional success, and nothing else, to be of lasting value. The burdensome obligation imposed on all its inhabitants is therefore to present themselves as successes, because otherwise they forfeit their right to respect in that environment. How's the family? Great! The new job? Best decision I ever made! The house? Terrific! All this, when the man in question is bankrupt, facing repossession, his children are on drugs and he is teetering on the brink of a divorce. There is no place in that town for the 'interesting failure,' or for anyone who is not determined on a life that will be shaped in an upward-heading curve.

'So, what happened to Greg? I heard you split up.'

This seemed to buck her up. 'They talk about me, then? Over there?'

413

'Oh, yes,' I said, although it had in fact been thirty years since anyone I knew had mentioned her name—before Damian, that is.

'I guess they still remember my party.'

They didn't, but even I could see they might have. 'Did you ever find out who did it?'

'Not until a long time later. Then someone said it was that guy who married Lucy Somebody. Your friend. He knew the girl who was making the brownies and he mixed it in when she wasn't looking. That was her story, anyway.'

Philip Rawnsley-Price. Much good did it do him.

She was back on track. 'Greg's OK. I don't really see him now.' She shrugged and poured another glass. We were nearly through the bottle and the first course hadn't arrived. I wondered if she'd like to change to red. She would. My old pal Gary arrived with some food and scuttled away to fetch more wine before Terry could question him about the contents of her plate. She moved some items around disdainfully with her fork. 'Jesus, I hope they don't use cornflour on these.'

'Why would they?'

'Sometimes they do. The next morning I look like a racoon.' How tiring it must be to live in an atmosphere of permanent danger. She started to eat with a certain amount of gusto, despite the risks. 'Greg's done pretty well, actually. He saw what was coming with the whole silicone thing and left Merrill Lynch to get into it. He understood the potential before most people did. Really. I should have stayed with him.' She laughed wryly with, I detected, a certain amount of real feeling.

'Why didn't you?' I was curious to know if she would tell me about the flighty millionaire who

414

had tempted her from her vows.

'Oh, you know.' She gave me an inclusively immoral grin. 'I met a guy.'

'And what happened?'

Terry shrugged. 'It didn't work out.' She shook her hair back with a soft, mirthless laugh. 'Lordie, lordie, was I lucky to be rid of *him!*'

'Were you?'

The glance I received in answer to this told me that she was, in fact, very *un*lucky to have been rid of the man in question and that in all probability he represented the Big Plan which would never now reach fruition. 'Let's not talk about him.'

Of course, I probably shouldn't have probed this bit of her story. It was, after all, the failed part and therefore anti-Californian. I wondered how often she had regretted leaving Greg, now clearly as rich as Croesus. 'How's your daughter?'

'Susie?' She seemed quite interested that I had this information. 'You remember Susie?'

'Well, I remember you got married and had a baby straight away. And all much sooner than most of the rest of us.'

She was drunk enough by this time to grimace at the memory. 'Damn right she was born straight away. Boy, I took a gamble there and, I may tell you, I very nearly lost.' This was rather intriguing, so I said nothing and hoped for more. Which I got. 'Greg was a big mixture back then. His growing up was completely Troy Donahue and Sandra Dee, going to the prom, dancing to the Beach Boys, you know the kind of thing.'

'I do.' In fact, the Americanism of my youth was powerfully evocative of a cleaner, more innocent world, when in Hollywood movies the whole world

415

wanted to be American and the big issue, not only for Greg but for everyone, was who wore your pin. Yes, it was blinkered, but it was also charming in its fathomless self-belief.

Terry continued, 'His parents were religious, very Midwest, and that was their existence. But Greg was also a Sixties boy, talking the talk, walking the walk. Smoking the dope. You know how it was.' Of course I knew how it was. A whole generation waiting to see which side of the wall the world was going to jump. And half at least of them pretending that things were no longer important to them, when of course they were. 'Anyway, he kept saying he was too young to settle down and couldn't we just have fun . . .'

'And couldn't you?'

Her eye narrowed for a moment. 'I needed a life. I needed to move on.' The alcohol was making her honest. 'I needed money.'

'Your father had money.'

'My father had a salary.' The distinction, as we know, was not lost on me. 'And I liked Greg. I thought we'd be happy. And I knew he'd never let his parents find out he had an illegitimate child.' She paused.

'That was the gamble.'

'As I said. We'd been living together for a few months, which was, if you remember, pretty wild at the time. Then Greg's bank posted him to Poland and he asked me to go with him. So I did. And he still couldn't make up his mind. So I got pregnant.'

'While you were there?'

'Sure. We married and she was born out there. In Warsaw.'

'How romantic.'

416

'It wasn't as romantic then as it might be now. Believe me.' I did.

'What did your parents think about it?'

'They were glad. They liked Greg.' She thought for a moment. 'They split up, you know.'

'No, I didn't know. I'm sorry.'

'It worked out. They're both fine. Mom got married again.'

'Give her my love.' She nodded. 'What happened to your father? Did he marry?'

She shook her head. 'Not yet. He's decided he's gay. Of course, he could still marry, I guess. These days. But he hasn't.'

'Is he happy?'

'I'm not sure. He hasn't got anyone . . . special. But then he hasn't got my mom yelling at him either.'

We both smiled at our joint recollection of the formidable Verena. But I was struck, for the millionth time, by the personal convolutions required by our new century. Would it have occurred to Jeff Vitkov, nice, boring, old Jeff, the brilliant entrepreneur and family man, to question his sexuality when he had got well into his fifties, in any other period but our own? If he had been born even twenty years earlier, he would just have taken up golf, seen a bit more of the chaps at the club and not given the matter another thought. Would he have been any worse off? I doubt it. Although this is not a topic that supports nostalgia. Even if I am not a fan of change for change's sake, nor indeed of most change if it comes to that, I am fairly sure that in the end we will all be better off for living in a world where any kind of sexuality is compatible with the twin notions of decency and commitment. But I suppose I just wish the whole subject could drop into the background again where it used to be, and not be compulsorily worn around society's neck day in, day out.

I didn't see I could contribute much on the subject of Jeff and his trials, so I just smiled. 'Anyway, you're all right. That's the main thing.'

'Yeah,' she also smiled, but hers stopped short of her eyes. 'Donnie's OK.' Donnie was obviously the new husband. I wasn't sure that 'OK' quite sold him with any strength of purpose, but I suppose they'd been together for a few years by then.

'Does he get on with Susie?' I was naturally much more interested in getting back to my quarry.

'Yuh.' She shrugged. 'I mean, Susie's a grown woman now. But yes, they get on, I guess.'

'I guess' ranked somewhere alongside 'OK' when it came to degrees of ecstatic joy. Try as I might, I couldn't read this as a household drenched in sunbeams. 'What does she do?'

'She's a producer.'

Of course, in Los Angeles this doesn't mean much more than 'she's a member of the human race.' Later, after this visit, when Damian's mission had resulted, perhaps ironically, in my opening up an American career for myself, I would be much more familiar with the ways of the city, but I was an innocent then. 'How exciting,' I said. 'What's she produced?' As I have observed, if I had known more I would not have asked this question.

Terry smiled even more brightly. 'She's got a lot of very interesting projects. She's working on something for Warner's right now.' She nodded as

418

if this brought the subject to a close, which of course it did.

'Is she married?'

'Divorced. And fucked up with it.' The remark had slipped out, loudly, and now she regretted it. 'To be honest, we don't see a lot of each other. You know how it is. She's busy.' She shrugged. I can't imagine that she thought she was concealing her pain, but maybe she did.

'Of course.' I know I am sounding increasingly feeble in my report of this interchange, but Terry's volume was rising and I was becoming uncomfortably aware that the people on both sides of our table were pretending to talk and had in fact tuned into our conversation.

Gary the Wary now returned to our table, bringing huge, Californian, mounded platefuls, draining my appetite away, and Terry ordered another bottle. 'Do you see anyone now?' she muttered between sips. 'Anyone from the old crowd?' I was not convinced that Terry had ever really been in our old 'crowd,' if crowd there had been, but it seemed a good moment to bring up the subject of Damian, so I did. For once, Terry was genuinely interested in what I was saying. 'How is he?' I explained and I could see that even her flinty heart had been mildly touched. 'I'm sorry to hear that.' But then her mind flew away from sticky sentiment and back to its natural climes. 'He made a lot of money.'

'He did.'

'Would you have guessed he would? Then?'

I thought for a moment. 'I was always pretty sure he was going to do well.'

'Even though you hated him?'

So she had remembered quite a bit about the old days. 'I didn't hate him all the way through. Not at the beginning.' She acknowledged this. I thought we might as well get on with the matter on hand. 'You had a thing with him, didn't you?'

The question made her sit up with an amused snort at its impertinence, although I am not convinced one can be impertinent to someone like Terry. 'I had a "thing" with a lot of people,' she said. This was, of course, quite true, unusually true for the era we'd lived through, and came better from her than from me. She accompanied the sentence with a sideways glance, as well she might, since one of those no doubt fortunate people who had enjoyed a 'thing' with her was me. It had only been a one-night 'thing' but it happened. Sensing my moment of recall, Terry raised her glass in a toast. 'To good times,' she said with an unnerving, secret smile making me even more aware of that curious, semi-detached sensation, when you are talking to a person you once slept with, but the incident is so far away from your present life that it feels as if you are discussing completely different people. Still, as I say, it did happen.

*　　　*　　　*

I was staying at a house in Staffordshire and the couple I had been billeted on were in the middle of a furious, poisonous row when I arrived. I'd been sent there for the ball of that same Minna Bunting with whom I had enjoyed my momentary and entirely virtuous walkout. Our time together was over and, since there was nothing to 'forget,' we had remained friends. Strange as it may seem, this was completely possible in those days. In 1968, to introduce someone as a 'my girlfriend' did not automatically translate as 'my mistress' in the way it does today. Indeed now, if she were *not* your mistress you would feel you were implying a lie. But not then. Anyway, I had received the usual postcard—'We would be so pleased if you would stay with us for Minna's dance'—and I found myself parking outside a large, pleasant, stone rectory, which I think I remember was somewhere near Lichfield. The card had told me my hostess was a 'Mrs Peter Mainwaring' and she had signed herself 'Billie,' so I had all the information I needed as I climbed out of the car. That said, those names that are not generally pronounced as they are written can pose a problem. Would she be posh and call herself 'Mannering' or not posh and say it as it was spelled? I decided that, rather as it is better to be overdressed than under, I would go for Mannering. As it transpired I needn't have worried, since she clearly couldn't have cared less what I called her. '*Yes?*' she said, glaring at me, as she wrenched open the door. Her face was red with rage and the veins were standing out on her neck.

'I think I'm staying with you for the Buntings' dance,' I muttered.

For a moment I thought she was going to hit me. 'Oh, *for Christ's sake!*' she snarled and turned back into the hall. I confess that even now, older and wiser as I hope I am, I always find this kind of situation pretty trying, because one is hamstrung by being a stranger who cannot respond in kind. In those days, young as I was, I found it impossible. I remember wondering whether it would be more polite and, in truth, better all round, just to get straight back into the car and drive to a local hotel and arrive at the dance from there. Or would that make matters even worse? But Mrs Peter Mainwaring, aka Billie, had not finished with me. 'What are you waiting for? Come in!'

I picked up my suitcase and stumbled forward into a large and light hall. It was a brilliant, sunflower yellow, which seemed at variance with the cloudy scene being played out in it. The paintwork was white and a really lovely portrait of a mother and child by Reynolds hung against the back wall. A tall man, presumably Mr Peter Mainwaring, was standing halfway up the wide staircase. 'Who is it?' he shouted.

'It's another one of the Buntings' fucking guests. How many did you tell them? This isn't a fucking hotel!'

'Oh, shut up! And show him to his room.'

'You show him to his fucking room!' I was beginning to wonder if she had any other adjective at her command.

Throughout this unloving exchange, I may say, I stood there in the centre of the pretty hall quite still, motionless in fact, frozen with nervous terror, like a cigar store Indian. Then I had the bright idea that I should try to act as a soothing agent. 'I'm sure I can find my own way,' I said. This might be categorised as a mistake.

She turned on me like a ravening beast. 'Don't be so fucking stupid!' I could see that Billie's irritation at my arrival was now developing into an active dislike. 'How can you find your own way when you don't know the fucking house!'

At this point, and were I older and more

422

confident, I would probably have told her to keep her anger to herself, basically, to employ her own language, to fuck off, and left. But part of youth is somehow to assume blame, to think that every problem must be in some way down to you, and I was no different. I'm sure most of the young of the late 1930s thought the Second World War was their fault. Anyway, as I stood there, blushing and stuttering while our hosts snarled at each other, by some heavenly miracle Terry Vitkov appeared on the landing above Peter Mainwaring and waved to me. I cannot think of a time when I was ever more pleased to see anybody. 'Terry!' I shouted, as if I had been in love with her since I was fourteen, and hurried up the stairs, past my angry hostess, past my host, to reach her. 'I'll show him where he's sleeping. It's next to mine. Right?' And before they could do much more than nod I had been rescued.

Terry and I became a unit of mutual support through the hours that followed. Apparently the husband, Peter, had bought a house, or a villa, somewhere in France without telling his wife, and Billie had heard the news for the first time about twenty minutes before Terry had got there. She'd come by train, I can't remember now why I didn't give her a lift. Maybe I was driving from somewhere else. The point was she arrived about an hour before me. In that time the fight had apparently escalated from quite a slow-burning start, until Billie was standing in the hall, screaming names that would be shocking even today and threatening a divorce that would cost him 'every fucking [naturally] penny he owned.' I never completely got to the bottom of quite why his crime was so terrible. I wonder now if there wasn't someone else involved. Either that, or Billie had made plans for the money that had been subverted by the very act of purchase.

My room was pleasant enough and much as I had come to expect during these sojourns with unknown hosts in the lesser houses of England: The pretty paper, with a faint, pseudo-Victorian pattern, the interlined curtains in not-quite-Colefax, and some flower prints framed in gilt with *eau de Nil* mounts. I had my own bathroom, which was by no means standard in those days; better still it did not boast too many earwigs and woodlice, and there was a perfectly decent bed. But no amount of comfort could offset the surreal quality of the shouting that continued below, amplified no doubt by the fact that they were once more alone and free to tear out each other's throats without interruption.

There were two more arrivals. The first was a boy called Sam Hoare, whom I recall better than I might normally have done because he was going to be an actor, a really extraordinary ambition at the time. In my social group, at least, wanting to go on the stage seemed not so much doomed to failure as requiring treatment. He was a tall, good-looking fellow and ended up, I think I'm right in saying, as quite a big wheel in television production, so in a way he was right to persevere, however annoying it was for his parents. The last guest, who was staying in the house and not just coming for dinner, was a nice girl called Carina Fox, whom I always liked without ever knowing especially well. We heard the dogs barking and some talk in the hall and, as Terry had done earlier with me, we sneaked along the gallery to the top of the staircase and rescued them. The Mainwarings transferred the pair into our custody without a backward look. Not for Peter and Billie any worry about whether their guests were tired after the journey and needed some tea. As we know, these incidents are very bonding. The four of us sat in my bedroom, comparing notes and wondering how we were going to get through the evening ahead, until in some way we felt we were friends, and not at all the semi-strangers we might have been in more normal circumstances.

Dinner started moderately well. They had, after all, had some time to simmer down, and there were two outside, local couples, nearer our hosts in age, who had been invited to join the party, so, after an uneventful glass of champagne in the garden, the ten of us sat down at about a quarter to nine that night and at first made small talk as if none of the earlier episode had taken place. Indeed, I'm sure the newcomers, an army general with a nice wife and a nearby landowning couple, had no idea that their dear friends, Peter and Billie, had been playing out a touring version of *Who's Afraid of Virginia Woolf* until just before they broke up to have their baths. The dining room was quite handsome, with excellent china and glass on the table and again, surprisingly good pictures. I would guess that Peter came from a family that had lost its estates but held on to a lot of the kit, which was quite common then. Or now, really. But I'm not sure there was limitless money left and I imagine Billie had cooked the food. In ungrand, rectory-type houses, even where the owners belonged to what used to be called the

Gentry, there wasn't nearly as much pulling in of temporary catering staff in the Sixties as there is today and most hostesses felt compelled, perhaps by some lingering war ethic, to do the work themselves. I have said before that the food was seldom much good and would often depend on ghastly magazine-printed receipts, as women then would cut these out and paste them into kitchen scrapbooks, printed especially for the purpose. The cooking done, it was quite normal to ask a couple of local women to come in and help serve it and wash up and so on, which was exactly what had been arranged on this particular night. We'd got through the first course easily enough, the obligatory salmon mousse that appeared in those days on almost every dinner table with taste-numbing regularity. It was followed by some sort of escalope in a glutinous sauce, covered in sprinklings of this and that, and with carrots cut into terrifying rosettes, which again we survived. But before the pudding made its appearance came the first rumblings of trouble. I was about halfway down the table, in my usual, junior position, when I saw the soldier's wife, Lady Gregson, turn to Sam Hoare who was sitting on her right, as the maid removed her empty plate. 'Wasn't that delicious?' she said, which could hardly be considered contentious.

Sam opened his mouth to agree, but before he could do so his host, on Lady Gregson's other side, cut in, 'It was more delicious than it was original, but that's not saying much.'

'*What?*' Billie Mainwaring's voice sliced through the atmosphere, silencing most of the rest of us, even those who didn't know what was going on.

426

Lady Gregson, who was a nice woman but not an exceptionally clever one, now took the measure of the situation and spoke before Peter could answer. 'We were just saying how much we enjoyed the last course.'

But Peter had been tucking into his excellent claret for quite a while by this time and clearly some sort of dam within him had at last given way. 'Yes,' he said. 'I always enjoy it. Every time you produce it. Which is more or less every time anyone is unlucky enough to dine in this house.' At which moment, with slightly unfortunate timing, one of the maids arrived at Lady Gregson's left, which placed her next to Peter's chair. She was holding a platter of what looked like white cheesecake. 'Oh God, darling.' He rolled his eyes. 'Not this again.'

'I *love* cheesecake.' Lady Gregson's tone was now becoming harder, as if she, sensing a whiff of rebellion, were determined to impose order on the gathering whether we liked it or not. She was the kind of woman who would have been very useful at Lucknow.

'What about the strawberries?' Peter was now staring straight at his wife.

'We're having cheesecake.' Billie's voice had all the animation of the Speaking Clock. 'I didn't think we'd want the strawberries.'

'But I bought them for tonight.'

'Very well.' There was a quality of tension in the air that reminded me of one of those films, so popular in that era, about the threat of nuclear war, a universal obsession of the time. The Big Scene was always centred on whether or not the President of Somewhere was going to press the button and start it. Having let the moment resonate, Billie spoke again: 'Mrs Carter, please fetch the strawberries.'

The poor woman didn't know what to make of this. She looked at her employer as if she couldn't be serious. 'But they're—'

Billie cut her off with a raised palm, nodding her head like a fatal signal from a Roman emperor. 'Just bring the strawberries, please, Mrs Carter.'

Of course, there are times when this sort of thing comes as a relief. As most of us know, there is nothing that will cheer a dreary dinner party more than a quarrel between a husband and wife. But this incident seemed to have acquired an intensity that made it slightly inappropriate as guest-pleasing fare. It was all too raw and real. At least we did not have long to wait for the next act. In the interim the rest of the company had taken the disputed cheesecake, but nobody had begun to eat. I saw Sam give a quick wink to Carina and, on my left, Terry's chair was beginning to shake with smothered giggles. Apart from these slight diversions we just sat there, divining that, in the words of the comic routine, we ain't seen nothing yet. Mrs Carter re-entered the room and went to Lady Gregson's side with a bowl of strawberries, but as she began to help herself it was absolutely clear to everyone present that the fruit was completely frozen, like steel bullets, and had just been removed from the freezer. The wretched woman dug in the spoon and put them on to her plate, where they fell with a metallic noise like large ball bearings. Mrs Carter moved to Peter, who carefully spooned out a big, rattling helping.

428

Clatter, clatter, clatter, they sounded as he heaped them on to his plate. On went Mrs Carter to the next guest and the next, no one was passed by, no one dared refuse, so the hard, little marbles fell noisily on to every plate in the room. Even mine, although I cannot now think why we didn't just refuse them, as one might refuse anything in the normal way of things. With a puzzled look Mrs Carter retired to the kitchen and then began the business of eating these granite chips. By this time you may be sure there was no conversation in the room, nor anything remotely approaching it. Just ten people trying to eat small round pieces of stone. At one stage the General seemed to get one lodged in his windpipe and threw his head up sharply, like a tethered beast, and no sooner were we past this hazard than the landowner's wife, Mrs Towneley, bit down with a fearsome crack and reached for her mouth with a cry that she'd broken a tooth. Even this did not elicit a Governor's Pardon from our hosts. Still we crunched on, particularly Peter who bit and chewed and sucked and smiled, as if it were the most delicious confection imaginable. 'You seem to be enjoying them,' said Lady Gregson, whose destiny that night was to make everything worse, just when she sought to do the opposite.

'It's such a treat to eat something unusual,' said Peter. 'At any rate in this house.' He spoke loudly and clearly into the silent crunching room. Inevitably, all eyes turned to his wife.

For a moment I thought she wasn't going to respond. But she did. 'You fucking bastard,' said Billie, reverting to her standard vocabulary when enraged, although actually this time she spoke quite softly and the words were rather effective despite their lack of originality. Next, she stood and, leaning forward, picked up the bowl holding the remainder of the icy inedibles. With a gesture like throwing a bucket of water on to a fire, she flung what was left of the frozen fruit at Peter, in the process spraying the rest of us, as well as the table and the floor, with sharp, bouncing, painful little missiles. She finished by lobbing the bowl at him which missed since he ducked and shattered against an attractive George IV wine cooler in the corner. In the pause that followed you could hear only breathing.

'Shall we get our coats?' said Lady Gregson brightly. 'How many cars are we taking to the dance?' In a commendable effort to bring matters to a conclusion she stood, pushed back her chair, stepped on a frozen strawberry and fell completely flat, cracking her head on the edge of the table as she went down, and with her evening frock riding up to show a rather grubby petticoat and a ladder in her right stocking, although that might have been a product of the moment. She lay totally motionless, stretched out on the floor, and for a second I wondered if she were dead. I suspect the others did too, since nobody moved or spoke, and for a time we were enveloped in a positively prehistoric silence. Then a low groan ameliorated this worry at least.

'I don't think we *all* need to drive, do you, darling?' said Peter, also standing, and the dinner party was at an end.

All of which goes to explain why I ended up in bed with Terry that night. We stayed together when we finally got to the dance, as it felt odd not to be with someone who had witnessed the previous events of the evening. Sam Hoare and Carina seemed to be similarly motivated and were soon dancing. In fact, they began a romance that was to take them through marriage, three children and a famously unpleasant divorce, when Sam ran off with the daughter of an Italian car manufacturer in 1985. At any rate, from our house party that only left Terry for me and I wasn't sorry. From then, somehow, as the night progressed it all seemed to become inevitable, in the way these things can and do. We jigged away while the music was brisk, but when the lights lowered at around one in the morning, and the DJ put on *Honey* , a sickeningly sentimental hit of the day, one of those ballads about dead loved ones, we moved into each other's arms without a question and began the slow, rhythmic clinch that passed for dancing in the last phase of these events.

In a way those mordant, melodic dirges were one of the hallmarks of the period, although the fashion for them has entirely faded long before now. It was an odd phenomenon, when you think of it, songs about husbands, wives, girlfriends, boyfriends, all being killed in car crashes and train smashes, by cancer and, above all, on motorbikes, the last scenario combining several pet crazes of the time. I suppose there must have been something in their facile, tear-soaked emotionalism that chimed with our largely false sense of trailblazing and 'release.' They ranged from the tuneful and robust *Tell Laura I Love Her* to those like *Terry* or *Teenangel* and, while we're on the subject, *Honey*, which were soppy beyond endurance, but the stand-out example, the

431

exception that proved the rule, a song which, like the more recent *Dancing Queen*, must have been performed in more bathrooms than any other hit of the day, was definitely *The Leader of the Pack* by the Shangri Las. There is a verse in it, which has always fascinated me: 'One day my Dad said "find someone new"/ I had to tell my Jimmie we're through/ He stood there and he asked me why/ All I could do was cry/ I'm sorry I hurt you, the Leader of the Pack.' No prize for guessing who's in charge here: Dad. This tough leather biker boy with his shining wheels, this girl in the grip of passion, both know better than to argue when Dad puts his foot down. 'Find someone new! *Now!*' 'OK, Dad. Whatever you say.' What would the lyric be changed to were it re-recorded today? 'I had to tell my Dad to get stuffed'? I cannot think of another vignette that tells of the collapse of our family structure and our discipline as a society more economically yet more vividly. No wonder so much of the world laughs at us.

At any rate on that evening the sad refrain did its work, and by the time Terry and I were helping ourselves to breakfast in the large marquee, rather imaginatively decorated with farming tools and sheaves of corn, we both knew where we were headed and I was glad of it. As most of us can remember, there is something sweet, during the early, hunting years particularly, in the knowledge that one's next amorous partner has been located and is willing.

I drove us back to the Mainwarings' house in my car, drunk as I was, with Terry nudging me to keep my mind on the business, and we let ourselves in through the unlocked front door as we had been

432

directed. How would such arrangements work in these more fearful days? The answer, I suppose, is that they wouldn't. Then we climbed the stairs, attempting to make as little noise as possible. I do not think we even hesitated for form's sake as we approached our separate chambers. I am pretty sure that I just followed Terry into her bedroom without either explanation or permission, closed the door gently and began.

Of course, one of the problems of being male, which I suspect has never changed nor will it, is that young men tend to operate on an Exocet-type imperative to seek bed larks no matter what. This was perhaps especially true in those days, when a great many of our female contemporaries were having no such thing, with the result that the moment there was a possibility of scoring, the faintest breach in the wall of virtue, one simply went for it without pausing to consider whether this was something one really wanted to do. Unfortunately, that realisation, that questioning of purpose, sometimes came later. Usually, when you were already in bed and it was far too late to back out. My generation was not, including the men (whatever the ageing trendies like to imply), nearly as promiscuous as those who came after us, even before we reached the complete sexual mayhem of today. But it was beginning. The male in his early twenties who was still a virgin, a comparatively normal type for my father's generation, had become strange to us and the goal of achieving as many conquests as we could was fairly standard. And so from time to time, inevitably, any man would find himself in bed with a woman who might be termed unlikely.

Usually when this happened he would just bang on, and the dazed query, *What was I thinking of?* did not surface in the front of his brain until the following morning. But inevitably there were occasions when a Damascene moment would suddenly strike mid-action. The scales would fall from your eyes and the whole event would be rendered completely and indefensively *insane* as you lay there, naked, with another, unwanted, body in your arms. So it was that night with me and Terry Vitkov. The truth was I was not in the least attracted to her; I didn't even like her all that much in the normal way of things, and without the Mainwarings' battles and the near hysteria of the evening we had lived through I would never have been in this position. If events had not created a sense of artificial closeness in our hearts I would have gone to sleep, happily alone. But now that I was in bed with her, now that I could smell the faintly acrid scent of her body and feel her wiry hair and spongy waist, and handle the rather pendulous breasts, I knew with an awful clarity that I wanted to be anywhere but there. I rolled back on to the pillow, heaving my body off hers as I did so.

'What's the matter?' said Terry in her now grating voice.

'Nothing,' I said.

'There'd better *not* be.'

Which, naturally, sealed my fate. I had a momentary vision of becoming a funny story, a fake who couldn't deliver, a joke to be sniggered over with the other girls as they wiggled their little fingers derisively, all of which I knew Terry was perfectly capable of delivering. 'Everything's fine,'

I said. 'Come here.' And with as much resolution as I could muster on the instant I did my duty.

*   *   *

The dinner was not going particularly well. Gary had almost given up on us and Terry was, by this stage, airborne. We were staring at the menus for pudding and when Terry started to heckle over the ingredients of some sort of strudel it was clear from Gary's expression that we had reached the city limits. 'I'll just have a cup of coffee,' I said in a feeble attempt to push Terry forward to the next part of the evening. Inevitably, this gave her ideas.

'Come to my place for coffee. You wanna see where I live, don't you?' Her drawl was beginning to stretch out to positively Southern proportions. Inexplicably, really, since I knew she came from the Midwest. It reminded me of Dorothy Parker's description of her mother-in-law as the only woman who could get three syllables out of 'egg.'

'Shall I bring the check?' volunteered Gary eagerly, seizing at the chance of ridding himself of this potential troublemaker before the real storm broke. Not many minutes later we were standing in the car park.

Here we faced a dilemma. I had drunk little, knowing I would be driving back, but Terry had sunk the best part of three bottles. 'Let me drive you,' I suggested. 'You can send someone for your car in the morning.'

'Don't be so boring.' She laughed as if we were engaged on a teenage prank, as opposed to committing an offence that might very possibly include manslaughter. 'Follow me!' We then began

435

one of the most hair-raising experiences of my entire life, shooting first up towards Beverly Hills, then skidding round the wide curves of the LA mountain roads, until we had somehow—don't ask me how—reached Mulholland Drive, that wide ridge, the spine that divides Los Angeles proper from the San Fernando Valley. There is a thriller, *A Portrait in Black*, a Lana Turner vehicle I think, which involves a woman who cannot drive being told nevertheless to get behind the wheel and follow her lover, i.e. the murderer, in a car. She weaves about and is almost undone when it starts to rain, since she has no idea how to work the windscreen wipers. From side to side she veers wildly, up, down, all over the place, weeping hysterical tears (or is that from *The Bad and the Beautiful*?). Anyway, this was more or less my experience the night Terry Vitkov took me home. Except that in my version I was following the crazy woman who was out of control of the vehicle, instead of her following me. I do not even now know how we arrived alive.

The house, when we got there, was perhaps a little more modest than I had been expecting, although it wasn't too bad. A large open hall, a bar that was pretending to be a library on the left and a big 'living room' that was glass on all three sides to make the most of the sensational view of the city below, a million lights of every colour, a giant's jewel box, twinkling below us. It felt as if we were coming in to land. But the rooms had a cheap and dingy feel, with dirty shagpile carpets and long sofas covered in oatmeal weave, going slightly on the arms. A couple of pretend antiques and a sketch in chalks of an artificially slimmed-down

436

Terry by what looked like a pavement artist from outside the National Portrait Gallery completed the decoration. 'What'll you have?' she said, lurching towards the bar.

'Nothing for me. I'm fine.'

'Nobody's fine if they haven't got a drink.'

'Some whisky then, thank you. I'll do it.' This seemed more sensible if I were not to end up with a tumblerful. Terry poured herself some Bourbon, rummaging for ice in one of those ice-makers that loudly produce their chunky load at all hours of the day or night. 'Is Donnie here?'

'I don't think so.'

Again, her lack of enthusiasm made it hard to feel this was a union where their fingers were permanently on each other's pulse. I sipped my drink, wondering if I was glad to find we were alone, although whether I was fearful of a sexual advance or alcoholic poisoning I could not tell you. Either way it was time to start inching back to the story of Greg and the woman, Susie, which had to be done by Donnie's return. 'So, how long have you been married this time?'

'About four years.'

'How did you meet?'

'He's a producer. In television,' she added quickly, to differentiate this man as a working producer as opposed to simply a resident of LA. 'I make these programmes where we discuss what's on the market—'

'I know. Infomercials.' I smiled, thinking to show how up I was in the jargon of modern television.

Instead, she gave me a look as if I had slapped her across the table. 'I hate that word!' But the

437

restaurant food wars had tired her out and she wasn't looking for another fight. Instead she just sipped her drink and then said in all seriousness, 'I prefer to think of myself as an ambassador for the buyer.' She spoke the words with great gravitas, so I can only suppose she expected me to take them at face value. After a suitable pause she continued, 'I went out with Donnie for a while, and then he proposed and I thought "what the hell".'

'Here's to you,' I said and raised my glass. 'I hope you're very happy.'

She sipped again, leaning back against the cushions. Predictably, her relaxation had brought down her guard and soon I learned that, as I had already surmised, she wasn't very happy. In fact, I would be hard put to it to testify that she was happy at all. Donnie, it seemed, was a lot older than her and since we were both at the upper end of our fifties, he can't have been much less than seventy. He also had less money than she'd been led to believe, 'which I find very hurtful,' and, worst of all, he had two daughters who wouldn't 'get off his back.'

'In what way?'

'They keep ringing him up, they keep wanting to see him. I know they're after his money when he goes.'

This was quite hard to respond to. There was nothing unreasonable in their desire to see their father and *of course* they expected his money when he went. It didn't make them unloving. 'At least they don't want it before he goes,' I volunteered.

She shook her head fiercely. 'You don't understand. I *need* that money. I've *earned* it.' She was extremely drunk by now, as she ought to have been, given how much Chardonnay, Merlot and Jack Daniel's had passed down her capacious throat that evening.

'Well, I'm sure he's planning to give you a fair share. Why don't you ask him?'

'He's planning to give me a life interest in half his money, which reverts to them on my death.'

What made this odd was that it was delivered as if she were describing a crime against nature, when it seemed eminently sensible, even generous, to me. I didn't dare go that far, reasoning that while I knew Terry, Donnie was a stranger to me so he could not feel justified in relying on my help. I settled for: 'That's not what you want?'

'*Damn right!*' She reached across me for the bottle and filled her glass. As she did so, she caught sight of a framed photograph among a group of them arranged on the shelves behind the bar. It was of an elderly, white-haired man with two young women, one on either side. They were all smiling. 'Those bitches,' said Terry with soft malignity and reaching out with the hand that was not holding the glass, smashed the picture forward, face down. It hit the wood with a loud smack, but I couldn't quite tell whether the glass had broken.

'And you've been married four years?' I asked tentatively, attempting to row for shallower water, but unable by the very nature of my task to leave her private life alone.

'Yuh.' More Jack Daniel's poured down her ever-open gullet.

'Then maybe he'll alter things when you've been together for longer.'

'Four years with Donnie is a lifetime, believe me.' What always fascinates me about people like

439

Terry, and I have known a few, is their absolute control over the moral universe. You and I know that she had been approaching desperation while making her dreadful infomercials and wondering if her life would ever begin again. Then along comes this nice, lonely old man and she decides to marry him, in the hope of inheriting everything to which she had no right whatever, and the sooner the better. She then discovers that he intends to leave his fortune to his two daughters, whom he loves and who are obviously the very people he ought to leave it to. They are affectionate and close to Donnie, and apart from no doubt *loathing* their new stepmother they are, I'm sure, normal, sensible women. Yet Terry, and others like her, are able to take this kind of simple tale and turn and twist it until, with a glass splinter in their eye and through some kind of tainted logic, they recast the universe making themselves the ones who have the right to complain. They are the deserving put-upon victims of a cruel system. They are the ones to be pitied. I tell myself that they must know they are living a lie, yet they display no sign of it, and usually their friends and associates give in eventually, first by pretending to take their side and often, in the end, by actually believing they are in the right. My own value system had, however, survived the assault and in fact I wanted to write to Donnie with my support there and then.

My ruminations were interrupted when Terry's shrill voice brought me back to the present. 'Get this!' she shouted by way of introduction. Clearly, I was going to be treated to another example of Donnie's outrageous choices, with most of which I was sure I would agree. 'He's even planning to leave a sum to Susie. Outright.' She paused, to punctuate this unbelievable injustice. 'But not outright to me. For me, it's a "life interest".' She spat out the words, nodding almost triumphantly, as if at the end of a hilarious anecdote.

I was starting to like Donnie more and more. So much more than I liked his wife. 'She is his stepdaughter.'

'That's funny!' She rocked with artificial laughter.

'Where is Susie? Is she in Los Angeles?' With this question, as I should have seen, I had overplayed my hand. It was late and I was still faintly jet-lagged and perhaps, by this stage, a bit drunk and, anyway, I just wanted to get on. My words seemed to echo in the room, altering its atmosphere.

Terry was many things, but not stupid. 'Why are you here?' she said, and her voice suddenly sounded completely sober and absolutely reasonable.

You must understand that I was nearly at the end of my search. There were only Terry and Candida left, and so there had to be a fifty per cent chance that Susie was the Holy Grail Baby. In a way, I confess to hoping, for Damian's sake, that it would be Candida Finch's child, but there was no reason why it shouldn't be this one. I felt I might as well just ask the question, far away from home as we were. I had no intention of telling Terry about the list and after all, Damian wouldn't be especially newsworthy in this neck of the woods if Terry wanted to make a story about her infidelity to her first husband, which I doubted. 'You said you'd been with Greg for quite a while when you got pregnant.'

'Yes.'

'Damian remembers that he had an affair with you around that time.'

She smiled, not immediately making the connection. 'We didn't have an "affair," not then, not ever. Not what you'd call an affair.' She had relaxed again and was once more drawling her words. In some way I thought she was rather enjoying herself. 'We had a funny on-off thing for years. We never quite went out, we never quite broke off. If you're asking if I was unfaithful, I never felt it counted with Damian.'

'Anyway, the point is'—this was it—'he wonders if Susie is really Greg's daughter.'

I had expected at least token indignation but, unpredictably, Terry threw her head back and roared with laughter. This time it was completely genuine. For a while she was quite unable to stop and she was still wiping her eyes before she could answer. 'No,' she said at last, shaking her head, 'she's not Greg's daughter.' I said nothing. 'You're right. I had been sleeping with Greg for a long time by then, for quite a long time since I decided to get pregnant. I was taking no precautions and I began to wonder if he could have children. If he was, you know, fertile.'

'So you revived things with Damian, to see if you could get pregnant that way.' I could easily see how this had happened. She wanted to bring Greg up to the mark and the whole paternity issue was much muddier in those days. It was a scheme that might easily have worked. Obviously, it did work. It just didn't quite fit with the original letter that had started all this, given that the whole thing had

442

been planned by her. Damian could hardly be accused of seduction or 'deceit.' The charge would more properly be levelled the other way. Still, we could clarify that later.

'Yes. I guess that's exactly what I did.' She was defiant now, made brave and even brazen by the liquor. She tilted her face as if to challenge me.

'I'm not here to judge you. Only to find out the truth.'

'And what does Damian want to do about it?'

So, I had reached my goal. We had arrived. With this in mind I thought some modest helping of honesty would not now go amiss. 'He's dying, as I have told you. I believe he wants to make sure that his child is well provided for.' That seemed enough.

'Would Susie have to know?'

This was an interesting question. I would have thought that Susie would have wanted to know, but would it be a condition? Then again, was it up to her mother? Susie was in her late thirties, after all. 'That's something I'll have to check with Damian. There'll be a DNA test, but I dare say we can come up with some other perfectly believable reason for that if we have to, or it could be done without her knowledge.'

'I see.' From her tone I could tell at once that my words had changed things, but I couldn't quite understand why, since I was not aware I had made any very stringent conditions. She stood and walked towards the glass wall, taking what I could now see was the handle of one of the panels and sliding it back to let in the night air. For a moment she breathed deeply. 'Damian isn't Susie's father,' she said.

443

I hope I can convey how totally inexplicable this seemed. I had sat all evening and listened to a woman who was rapacious for money, other people's money, any money that she could lay her hands on; a woman disappointed by life and everything it had brought her; a woman trapped in an existence she hated and by a husband she cared nothing for, and now, here she was, on the brink of the luckiest break anyone living has ever heard of, the chance to make her daughter one of the richest women in Europe, and she was turning it down without the smallest argument. 'You can't know that,' I said. 'You say yourself she isn't Greg's. She must be someone's.'

She nodded. 'Yes. She must be someone's. But she isn't Greg's and she isn't Damian's.' She paused, wondering, I now realise, whether to go on. I am glad she did. 'And she isn't mine.'

For a moment I was too astonished to say an obligatory 'What?' or 'How can that be?' or even 'Oh.' I just looked at her.

She sighed, shivering suddenly in the draught, and moved back into the room towards the dingy sofa. 'You were quite right. About what I was trying to do. I wanted to be pregnant, because I knew Greg would marry me when I was. I'd been sleeping with Damian every now and then for a couple of years so I was sure he wouldn't mind. And he didn't. It was just after you all went on that crazy holiday in Portugal.'

'I thought he said it was before.'

'No. I called him and his flatmate said he was out there, so I left a message. He rang me the day he got back and I went round. It's funny. When we got together for the last time . . .' She had become

444

wistful, a nicer person momentarily, in memory of her younger dreams, 'I thought we might go on with it. He seemed different when he got home, less . . . I don't know exactly, less unreachable, and for a day or two I thought that maybe it would be Damian and not Greg after all.'

'But it didn't happen?'

'No. He'd run into that beautiful girl out there, and he met up with her again when she was back in London.'

'Only once I think.'

'Really? I thought it was more than that. What was her name?'

'Joanna Langley.'

'That's it. What happened to her?'

'She died.'

'Oh.' She sighed, saddened by the inexorable process of life. 'The point is that when he got back, Damian was in a strange mood. I heard about what happened.' I nodded. 'I think the truth is he was sick of all of us. I lost touch with him after that.'

'So did we all.'

'Joanna Langley's dead. Wow. I used to be so jealous of her.' I could see that the news had made her stop in her tracks. For anyone, hearing of the death of a person you had thought alive and well is a little like killing them because suddenly they're dead in your brain instead of living. But with the Sixties generation it is more than this. They preached the value of youth so loudly and so long that they cannot believe an unkind God has let them grow old. Still less can they accept they too must die. As if their determination to adopt clothes and prejudices more suited to people thirty, forty, fifty years younger than themselves would act as an elixir to keep them forever from the clutches of the Grim Reaper. You see television interviews and articles in papers expressing shocked amazement whenever an old rocker pops his clogs. What did they think would happen?

At last, with a philosophical nod, Terry resumed her story. 'I slept with Damian two or three times before we finished. There were no hard feelings.' She paused to check that this squared with my information.

'I'm sure there weren't. But nothing happened?'

She shook her head. 'Nothing happened. Then Greg went to Poland and I followed him, and I slept with *him*, but still nothing happened and nothing happened, and finally I went to see a doctor while I was out there and guess what?'

'It wasn't him, it was you.'

She smiled, like a teacher pleased with my attention. 'It was me. All the time it was me. Some tubes were missing or something . . .' She raised her eyebrows, trying to control her delivery. 'You know the first thing that occurred to me? Why the hell had I wasted so much time worrying about getting pregnant? My late teens should have been a ball.'

'You didn't do badly,' I said.

Which made her laugh. 'Anyway, I knew that once Greg learned I could never have a child, once his mother heard about it, the whole thing would be over and it'd be back to square one. So I bought a baby.'

It seems strange now, but this sentence took me completely by surprise. Why? I cannot tell you. There was no such thing as surrogacy in those

446

days, or if there was we knew nothing of it. She'd admitted she'd had a baby to get Greg to marry her and she'd told me she couldn't have children. What did I imagine she had done? Even so, I was flabbergasted. What I came up with was: 'How?'

She smiled. 'Are you planning it?' But she was far too deep in to telling the story to back out now. 'I was doing some social work then, with a group sponsored by the embassy. This was 1971, long before the end of Communism or anything else. There was no Solidarity. There was no hope. Poland was an occupied country and the people were desperate. It wasn't hard. I found a young mother who already had four children and she'd just discovered she was pregnant. I offered to take the baby, whatever it was, whether or not there was anything wrong with it.'

'Would you have?'

She thought for a moment. 'I hope so,' she said, which I liked her for.

'But how did you manage the whole thing?'

'It wasn't difficult. I found a doctor who could be bribed.' I must have looked shocked at this because she became quite incensed. 'Jesus, most of the time he was prescribing drugs to teenagers. Was this worse?'

'Of course not.'

'I didn't "show" until I was about five months "gone." I told Greg I didn't feel comfortable with sex, and with his puritan background he didn't either. Then I asked if he'd mind not being at the birth, as the thought made me uncomfortable. Boy, you should have seen the relief on his face. These days, if the father isn't there peering up your flue as the head appears, he's a bad person,

447

but in 1971 it wasn't compulsory.'

'How did you manage the birth itself?'

'I had a stroke of luck when he was called to New York just before the baby came. The dates I'd given him were three weeks behind the true ones, to leave some room for manoeuvre. I did have a plan of checking into a different room. I think it would have worked but in the end I didn't need it. She went into labour and I took the mother to the nursing home where, thanks to the doctor, she just gave my name. The baby was delivered and the registration was perfectly routine. When Greg got back, I was waiting for him at home with little Susie. We cried a river. Everyone was happy.'

'And nobody ever found out?'

'Why would they? I told him I loved him, but I couldn't have sex until I got my figure back. He suspected nothing. Nobody was worse off. Including Susie. I mean that.' Clearly, she did mean it and I would say it was probably true, although one can never be quite sure about these things. Even if I do not endorse the present fashion for leaving babies with mothers who are clearly quite incapable of caring for them, rather than finding them decent homes. Terry was nearly finished. 'For a while I thought the doctor might blackmail me, but he didn't, so that was that. Maybe he was scared I'd blackmail him.'

'And there were never any tests that gave it away?'

'What tests? They're both blood group O, which was kind of a relief actually. But who runs a DNA test on their own daughter?'

'Did Greg have any more children?'

'None of his own. Two steps. He adores Susie

and she adores him.' She sighed a little wearily. 'She much prefers him to me.'

I nodded. 'So he'll take care of her.' For some reason I was rather glad of this. Susie had missed a larger fortune which, in my fevered mind, she had possessed for maybe two or even three minutes. It was good to feel she would never know want.

'Oh yes. She's safer than I'll ever be.'

I had to ask. 'Would you have gone on with it if I hadn't mentioned the test?'

She thought for a moment. 'Probably. The temptation was too great. But of course there would have been some hurdle by the end of it, so I'm glad you did. Before I got too excited.'

It was once more the hour to depart and this time I knew for certain we would not meet again. Since, even if I were back in the town, I wouldn't look her up. But something in the story she had told had won me round a bit. I was reminded of the haunting words of Lady Caroline Lamb: 'With all that has been said about life's brevity, for most of us it is very, very long.' Terry's life had already been very long and very frustrating, with scant reward to show for it. That this had largely been her fault was no consolation, as I knew well. She had thrown away her only chance of a decent future with Greg and never replaced him with anything like an equal opportunity. Now she had lost even the child she'd invented to be with him. We kissed at the door. 'Please don't mention this to anyone.' She shook her head. I had something more to say. 'And please don't ever tell them.'

'Would I?'

'I don't know. If you got too drunk and too angry you might.'

She did not resent this, which was commendable, but she was confident in her denial. 'I have been drunk and angry many times since we last met and I haven't told them yet.' This, I am sure, was true. All of it.

'Good.' Now I really was going. But I had a last wish before we parted. 'Be kind to Donnie,' I said. 'He doesn't sound a bad chap.'

The evening had made me sentimental in my estimation of her. I should have been more clear-sighted. The truth was, with the sole exception of her feeling towards her not-daughter, the old Terry Vitkov was quite unchanged. 'He's a bastard,' she replied and shut the door.

Candida

THIRTEEN

Which only left Candida Finch.

I stayed on a few days in Los Angeles, in Beverly Hills to be precise, at the very comfortable Peninsular Hotel—a haven for the English, since it is the only one where you can actually walk out to the post office or get something to eat without having to stand and wait every time for a crisply suited 'valet' to fetch your car. I'd enjoyed meeting my agent who turned out to be charming, and if I did not quite follow Damian's instructions to the letter, still we got on very well and he sent me round the town to meet a few people while I was still out there. Since I was allowed the untold luxury of first class travel back to London, I felt quite relaxed and invigorated when I got home. How strange it is, the way enough sleep and the resulting physical energy can make one feel as if one's whole life is going well, while the lack of them has the opposite effect.

However, when I finally returned to the flat, if I was expecting to find a series of messages from Candida answering those I'd left before I went away, I was disappointed. There was nothing. Accordingly, I recorded yet another on her machine which was still not picking up, and settled down to a day or two of work on my latest novel, a tale of middle-class angst in a seaside town, which was approaching what I would hesitate to call its climax and which I had, understandably, recently neglected. It was on the morning of the following day, when I'd finally managed to get some way

453

back into the rhythm of my troubled, marine triangle, that the telephone on my desk started to ring.

'You called Candida Finch yesterday,' said a female voice and, for a moment, quite illogically, I thought it must be Candida herself who was speaking. I can't think why, since it obviously wasn't.

'Yes, I wondered if I could see you, which I know sounds odd.'

'It does sound very odd, and I'm not Candida, I'm Serena.' A thousand bags of sherbet exploded in my vitals.

'Serena?' Of course it was Serena. It was her voice, for God's sake. What had I been thinking of? But why should Serena ring me? How could that have happened? I pondered the question without speaking, silently wondering, earpiece clamped to my ear.

'Hello?' Her voice had gone up in volume.

'Yes.'

'Oh, I thought you'd been cut off. It all went quiet.'

'No, I'm still here.'

'Good.'

I suddenly worried that I could hear in her voice a querying sound, as if she were afraid that the person she was speaking to was in fact a nutter and it might be dangerous to continue the conversation. I trembled lest she might act on this subconscious warning. All of which illustrates the fevered level of my imagination. 'How can I help?'

'I was talking to Candida this morning and she said she'd had a message to ring you, that you wanted to see her.'

'She's had more than one message from me, I'm afraid. I thought she must have emigrated.'

'She's been in Paris and she only got back last night.'

'It's rather wonderful that you're still in touch.' As the words left my mouth, I could hear their senselessness. Why did I say this? Why was it wonderful? Why shouldn't they be in touch? Was I mad?

'She's my cousin.'

Which I should have known. In fact, I must have known it. In fact, I *did* know it. Perfectly well. They gave a ball together, for God's sake. I was present at it. What kind of fool forgets something like that? What kind of stupid *moron*? 'Of course,' I said lightly. 'Of course you are. I should have remembered.' Where was this twaddle leading? To some International Idiots' Convention? Why couldn't I say anything that didn't sound illogical and inane?

'Anyway, I wondered if it was all part of Damian's search.'

My heart stopped. What had I said to her? Had I been so surprised by her presence at Gresham that I'd given it all away? Could I have? What had I told her? My thoughts were flying about like a crowd of ravens with nowhere to settle. I couldn't seem to remember anything about that evening, yet I thought I'd remembered every moment. 'Search?' I said, feeling this was the best way to flush out information.

'You said Damian wanted you to look up some of his old friends. You told me when we met up that time in Yorkshire. I wondered if Candida was one of them, since she couldn't think of any other reason you'd want to see her again.'

'She's rather hard on herself. I can think of lots of reasons.'

'But was it? Is it?'

'As a matter of fact yes, it is. I thought I'd buy her lunch and get her news. That's all he wants, really.'

'Well, I've got a much better idea. She's coming down here next weekend, so I wondered if you could join her. Join us. We'd love it.'

My despair at my own stupidity was suddenly and totally replaced by a chorus of angels' wings. 'That's incredibly kind. Do you mean it?'

'Absolutely. Come on Friday, for dinner. And you can leave at some stage on Sunday afternoon.'

'As long as we've got that settled.'

She laughed. 'Andrew always needs to know he'll have the house back by dinner on Sunday.'

I'll bet he does, I thought, the mannerless toad. 'What about clothes?'

'He wears a smoking jacket but no tie on Saturday night. Apart from that we'll be in rags the whole time.'

'Well, if you're sure . . .'

'Completely sure. I'll e-mail you directions. We're very easy to find, but you might as well have them, if you'll give me your address.'

So I did. And it was settled. I wondered if I ought to ring Candida, but I never heard back from her, so presumably Serena had filled her in.

After this conversation I sat at the desk for several minutes, quite unable to resolve exactly what I was thinking. Naturally, as I have observed, the invitation had set off a peal of chiming, silver bells in my heart, ringing and singing with joy at the prospect of two whole days when I might look upon her face to my heart's content. But there is also the old proverb that it is better to travel hopefully than to arrive, and now that I was faced with a real prospect of having the Blessed Serena back in my life, paradoxically, I wasn't completely convinced it was a good idea. Of course, all this was Damian's fault. It was Damian's fault she had left my life thirty-eight years before. At least I dated the beginning of the end from that dinner. Now it was Damian's fault she had come back. That she had been, would always be, the love of my life, was clearly established, to my satisfaction anyway, and, if I was honest with myself, it was her return to my conscious mind that had spelled curtains for poor Bridget, as I had more or less told my father. The reminder of what love is, of what it could be, made the thin facsimile that I had been living feel rather pointless.

But then Serena was content with the way her life was, and if she wasn't she would never leave her husband, of that I was quite sure, and if she did it wouldn't be for me, and if it would I had nothing comparable to offer her, and . . . so on. I was equally certain she was not the type for any extra-marital activity, and if even this too were wrong, I would certainly not be her chosen co-adulterer. I knew well enough that while maturity and some success had transformed me into a marriage possibility for various, lonely divorcees who were not quite clear as to how they would finance their latter years, still I was not the sort of man who tempts a girl to sin. I had neither the looks nor the chops.

No, the future that was on offer, or at least a

possibility since nothing at all was yet on offer, would simply be as a friend, a walker, a companion. The literate ally that fashionable women married to fools or workaholics sometimes need to buy them lunch or carry their coat at the theatre, who might join a party at the villa in Amalfi and make the other guests laugh. Did I want this? I had done enough of it in the past, of course, and sung for my supper a thousand times and more, but did I want it with the added twist of pain? To sit and watch the woman I would have died for, as she chattered on about a weekend in Trouville or a play at the Almeida or her latest purchases? No. A man has his pride, I thought, my mind clearly still running on empty. I would go for the weekend. I had anyway to question Candida, or that was my excuse, but that would finish it. I was nearly at the end of the quest that had taken me through my old stamping ground of long ago. But once the search was done, Candida's child would get the money and Damian would die, and I would go home and write my books again, and say hello to Serena when I saw her at Christie's Summer Party. And it would be enough to know that she was well. Or so I vowed.

Waverly Park sounds a little more romantic than it is. The original seat of the Earls of Belton, Mellingburgh Castle, left the family when the senior line died out in an heiress during the 1890s and is now buried beneath the station car park in Milton Keynes, for much of which its walls supplied the hardcore. But the title had jumped sideways to a junior branch and they celebrated its arrival with marriage to a well-endowed American and the purchase of Waverly in Dorset, not far from the Jurassic coast. The estate had shrunk, after both wars and then again quite recently as when old Lord Belton died it turned out his provisions had been drawn up quite wrongly, making it impossible to prevent half the estate being divided between Andrew's siblings. I believe there was an expectation that they would gamely hand this back to their older brother, but as so often with these things, it didn't happen. To make matters worse, the sister, Annabella, had turned out a gambler and she sold her share within three years of getting it, leaving a gaping hole in the centre of the farms, and the other son, Eustace, married to an even worse bully than his mother, had divided his between four daughters, none of whom would stay long term. I was told later that the whole mess had occurred because Lady Belton insisted on using the son of a cousin as their lawyer, instead of someone who knew what they were doing. I cannot swear to the truth of this, but it sounds very likely. The net result was that Andrew was left with far too little land to support the house, a situation exacerbated by his almost chemical lack of brainpower, which ensured that no outside income would come to his aid. Serena may have had something to look forward to from her father, but families like the Greshams do not stay rich by enriching all the siblings and it would never have been much.

The house itself was a fairly large but unremarkable pile. There had been a dwelling there since the 1660s but all that remained of this period was the cantilevered staircase, the nicest thing to look at in the place. The entire building had been enveloped twice, well in the 1750s and badly in the 1900s, by the newly arrived and gleeful Beltons. A burst of optimism in the late 1940s on the part of Andrew's grandfather had swept away the service wing, relocated the kitchens to the site of a former morning room and converted the great hall to a library. The effect of this was to pull the entrance round the corner, away from the main portico, so the existing front door led one through a sort of tunnel towards the stairs, arriving at them from the back, at a slightly peculiar angle. It never works to fight a house's architecture and Waverly was no exception to the rule. The rooms had been tossed this way and that in the changeover, swapping their roles as they went, ending with dining rooms full of sofas and drawing rooms stuffed with tables and chairs. Huge fireplaces found themselves warming tiny studies, and dainty bedroom detailing adorned the walls of a semi-ballroom. None of which was improved by the timing of the work, during those post-war years when building materials were rationed, so almost everything had been contrived from plywood and painted plaster. Not all of it was bad. The loss of the hall was hopeless and dislocated the whole ground floor, but the library that replaced it was a great success, and the breakfast room was pretty, if too small. In truth, the house had a lost, bewildered feel, like a private home too quickly changed to a hotel, where the rooms have not been allowed a period of adjustment to get used to their new jobs. Naturally, Andrew thought it a palace and every visitor as lucky as a peasant from Nan Cheng allowed entry for a few, sacred moments to the glories of the Forbidden City.

The drive out of London on Friday afternoon

was as murderous as ever, and it was after six when I finally arrived and staggered down the passage with my case. Serena emerged from a doorway and stood there in welcome, dressed in a shirt and skirt, casual and marvellous. 'Dump that there. You can go up later. Come and have some tea.' I followed her into what proved to be the library and a few faces turned to look at me. There were others besides Candida and what I perceived was an already grumpy Andrew, making a great show of being absorbed in *Country Life.*

One pair, the Jamiesons, I'd met a few times in London and the others, a sporty couple from Norfolk called Hugh and Melissa Purbrick whose life seemed to consist of farming and killing things and not much else, were some sort of connections of an old friend of my mother, so I didn't anticipate much trouble. 'Do you want tea? Or a drink to take upstairs?' said Serena, but I refused both and sat on the sofa next to Candida.

'I feel very guilty,' she said. 'I came back to my answering machine flashing like the Blackpool illuminations. I thought I must have won the Lottery. Either that, or somebody was dead. But they were all from you.' She had not aged well, certainly nothing like as well as Serena. Her hair was grey and her face was rough and lined and even redder than it used to be, although I would not speculate as to the cause. On the whole, unlike her cousin she looked her age, but her manner was very different from what it had been when I knew her and at first encounter considerably improved. She seemed much calmer, no, not calmer, calm. As the French say, she was *bien dans sa peau,* and as a result I found myself warming to her in a way that

461

I never really had done when we were young.

'I'm afraid I was a bit eager. Sorry.'

She shook her head to free us from the need to apologise. 'I should switch it off when I go away. At least people would know I hadn't got the message instead of having to deduce it.'

'What were you doing in Paris?'

'Oh, just larking about. I've got a grand-daughter who's mad about art and I persuaded her parents to let me take her to see the Musée d'Orsay. Of course, once we were there we spent about three minutes in the museum and the rest of the time shopping.' She smiled, curious now to get to the bottom of it. 'So what's the big thing? Serena said that you were coming as an envoy of the mighty Damian.'

'In a way. No, I am.'

'You're looking up his friends from the old days.'

'I suppose so.'

'I'm rather flattered to be included. Whom have you seen?' I told her. 'Now I'm less flattered. What a peculiar list.' She pondered the names again. 'Weren't they all in Portugal that time?'

'All except Terry.'

She thought for a moment. 'Of course, that evening was another story.' She stretched her eyes silently at me, sharing the memory. 'Have we ever talked about it?'

'Not properly. We've hardly met since we got back.'

'No. I suppose that's right.' Again she thought over what I'd been telling her. 'Terry Vitkov . . .' she grimaced. 'I'm quite surprised she was a pal of Damian's. I thought he had better taste.'

462

'Ouch.' I was amused by this as plenty of people from those days would probably have said something similar of her.

'Is she the same as ever?'

'She is the same, if you add the effects of forty years of disappointment.'

Candida absorbed this for a moment. 'Do you remember her dance?'

'No one who was there could forget it without medical intervention.'

She laughed. 'It was the first time I'd been in the papers since the announcement of my birth. My grandmother wouldn't speak to me for weeks.' I considered Candida's subsequent career of sexual profligacy, illegitimate motherhood and the more recent tragedy of 9/11, and pondered what the grandmother in question would have made of any of that. Presumably death had spared her. Candida was still at Madame Tussaud's. 'I know she did it. Whatever she said at the time.'

'She says not. She says it was Philip Rawnsley-Price.'

'He might have helped her. He was stupid enough. But she must have known. The choice of brownies for a start. We were all so innocent.'

'Quite innocent.' I didn't bother to defend Terry, although I didn't think the accusation true. I suppose I didn't care.

Candida was staring at the fire. By this time I knew the process of what I had to put these people through. I'd arrive and suddenly the woman of the week would be plunged back into a world of four decades ago, which she hadn't thought about in ages. 'Golly, we had some funny times that year. Do you remember Dagmar's dance?'

463

'Who could forget?'

'When Damian gatecrashed and had a fight with—' She put her hand to her mouth. She'd suddenly remembered the identity of Damian's opponent. Our host shook out the pages of his magazine sharply.

'I remember it well,' I said. We shared the moment and tried not to look at the bump on the bridge of Andrew's nose.

Candida sighed. 'The main thing I recall is just how young we were. How little we knew of what was coming.'

'I think we were great,' I said. Which she took no exception to and smiled. 'What's your son doing now?'

'I have two sons and a daughter, in fact.' She flashed me a slightly defensive glance. 'But I know you mean Archie.' Perhaps sensing I meant her no ill, she relaxed. 'He's got his own property company. He's frightfully rich and successful.'

Not half as rich and successful as he's going to be, I thought. 'Is he married?'

'Absolutely. He's got a wife called Agnes and two kids, the shopaholic daughter, who's ten, and a son of six. Funnily enough, Agnes's mother is a girl you used to hang about with, Minna Bunting. She married a chap called Havelock, who was in the army. Do you remember her?'

'Very well.'

She pulled a slight face. 'That's the thing. I don't. I never really knew her at the time, but of course now we pretend we were terrific friends and we've almost convinced each other it's true.'

Was it comforting or smothering, this constant interlocking of the old patterns? Revolutions in morality might flare up, Socialism in all its indignant fury might come and go, but still the same faces, the same families, the same relationships, are endlessly repeated. 'I like the name Agnes,' I said.

'So do I. Quite,' she added, telling me more of what she thought of her daughter-in-law than she intended.

'Was it very hard with Archie?'

Candida was silent for a moment. She paid me the compliment of not pretending she didn't know what I was asking. 'It was easier in a way than it would have been for some. Both my parents were dead and so was my grandmother by then. Just. I hated my stepmother and couldn't have given a monkey's tiddly what she thought about anything. I was terribly broke, of course. My stepmother wouldn't give me a penny and by the end she didn't have much to give, but at least I didn't have to feel I was letting everyone down. Actually, Aunt Roo behaved very well, given that she thought I was out of my mind.'

'But?'

'Same as the earlier answer. My parents were dead and I hated my stepmother. I had no close family, no backup, beyond Aunt Roo and Serena, and they thought I'd gone mad. So did my friends, to be honest, but they were a little bit more circumspect about showing it.'

'I know you married in the end.'

'I did. A chap called Harry Stanforth. Did you ever come across him?'

'His name seems familiar, since I first heard it, so maybe I did, but if so I can't remember where. I was terribly sorry to hear what happened.'

465

'Yes.' She gave one of those twitchy smiles of bleak acceptance. 'It is difficult when nothing's ever found. I always used to feel for mothers of sons killed in foreign wars, who never got a body back to bury, and now I know just what it's like. I don't know why exactly, but you need a proper funeral with something there, something more than a photograph, which is what I had, in order to feel it really is the end.'

'The Americans call it "closure." '

'Well, I wouldn't, but I do know what they mean. You keep imagining that he's in a coma somewhere or struggling with amnesia, or he escaped and had a nervous breakdown in Waikiki. Of course, you tell yourself to accept it, not to believe anything different, but you can't help it. Every time the doorbell goes unexpectedly, or the telephone rings very late at night . . .' she smiled gently at her own foolishness. 'You do get over it in the end.'

'Awful.'

'But you mustn't think I'm a sad person. Please don't.' Candida's tone had changed and she was looking straight at my eyes. I could see that she was keen to convince me, and I think she was telling the truth. I suppose it was somehow a case of being loyal to his memory. 'I'm not at all sad. Really. I was sad before I met Harry, and trapped at the end of a cul-de-sac with a boy half my family felt uncomfortable with. I know you all thought me ridiculous in those days.'

'Not ridiculous.'

'Ridiculous. A loud, red-faced bed-hopper who was embarrassing to have around.' This was all true so I didn't contradict her, but as with almost

466

all of the women I had visited I had that revelation of how much better we would have got on forty years before if we had only known each other's true natures. Candida shrugged off these memories with happier ones. 'Then Harry arrived one day and just saved me. He saved us. I don't know to this day what he saw in me, but we never had an unhappy hour.'

'He loved you.' Funnily enough I meant this. I could sort of begin to see what he had loved in her now, which came as something of a surprise.

She nodded, her eyes starting to glisten. 'I think he did. God knows why. And he took us both on. He adopted Archie, you know, completely legally, and then we had two more, and when he . . .' I could see that despite her strictures her eyes were filling, and so were mine. 'When he died it turned out he'd left some money equally to the three of them. Just split three ways. He made no distinction. And that meant so much to Archie. So *very* much. Did you know that all their mobiles worked, when they were trapped in the tower?'

I nodded. 'I read about that.'

'And what was so extraordinary, what was wonderful really, was that they didn't, most of them anyway, ring to yell for help. They rang the people who were nearest to them, their wives and husbands and children, to say how much they loved them. Harry did that. Of course I'd turned mine off—typical—and when I tried to call him back I couldn't get through, but he left a message saying how marrying me was the best thing he'd ever done. I saved it. I've got it now. He thanks me for marrying him. Can you imagine that? In the midst of all that fear and horror he thanked me for

467

marrying him. So you see, I'm not sad at all in the greater scheme of things. I'm lucky.'

I looked at her coarse, ruddy face and her brimming eyes, and I knew she was absolutely right. 'So you are,' I said. I had arrived prepared to pity her, but in fact the time she'd spent since we last really talked had been infinitely more satisfactory than that same period in Terry's life or Lucy's or Dagmar's or, heaven knows, Joanna's. By anyone's reckoning Candida Stanforth, née Finch, was the luckiest of the five on Damian's list. In all the standard categories reckoned important among these people she had started at the back of the field and ended up way out in front. 'Did you ever get into publishing? You used to say you wanted to.'

She nodded. 'I did. But proper publishing. Not the vanity stuff I thought would be my only way in. Harry made me. He pulled a string and got me a job as a reader at a small outfit that specialised in women writers. But I stuck at it and they kept me on. Eventually I edited quite a few books.'

'But not any more?'

'Not at the moment. I felt I needed to take time off, when . . .' I nodded, anxious not to return her to that dreadful day. 'But I'm thinking of going back. Actually, I was rather good at it.' In this simple phrase I knew what her debt to Harry Stanforth was and why she still fought for people to appreciate her luck in finding him. This Candida had self-worth, of which there'd hardly been a trace when I had known her in her ugly, angry, unhappy youth. In those days her childhood was too recent for its ill effects to have been set aside. 'The fact is I had twenty-three years with a

468

terrific, honourable, lovely, loving man.' It was a simple, moving tribute and I had no difficulty in liking Harry enormously on the strength of it. She leant towards me and lowered her voice to a whisper. 'I'd rather be in my shoes than Serena's.' And we laughed, which brought things to an end. Not long afterwards, we went upstairs to change.

I was sleeping in a panelled, corner room, painted off-white, with large windows on two sides, and far-reaching views across the well-wooded park. There was a pretty, canopied bed, upholstered in good, if old, chintz and some Audubon prints of birds around the walls. It was all reasonably attractive, if unoriginal, but the faded colours of the material and the bright shocking pink of the mounts on the pictures made the whole effect feel very 1970s, as if no money had been spent anywhere in its vicinity for thirty years at least. I had my own bathroom, with more of the same colour scheme and a hot tap that made distant, gurgling noises full of intent but the water, when it came, was less than tepid. I sponged myself down as best I could and pulled some clothes out of the case.

The posh English love to sound informal. 'Nobody's coming,' they say. 'It'll just be us.' Which it seldom is. 'You won't have to do a thing,' when of course you will. Most of all, when they say 'don't change' they don't mean it. They do mean you are not to put on a dinner jacket, but not that you are to stay in the same clothes. It's funny in a way, because all you are doing, for an 'informal' dinner in the country is putting on another version of exactly what you wore at tea, particularly the men. But the point is that when you come down it

469

must *be* another version. The only thing to steer clear of for a weekend is the dark suit. Unless there is some charity function or a funeral or something which has its own rules, a gentleman will get no use out of a city suit in the country, where, increasingly, it seems that there are two costumes for the evening, grand or tatters with nothing in between.

The re-rise of grand is rather interesting in this context as well, or it is to me. Contrary to the expectations of only a few years ago, dinner jackets, having known a lean period, and even more, smoking jackets, are once more on the rise. Of these I am more fascinated by the smoking jacket, a garment whose rules have entirely altered in my own time. Not all that long ago it showed the depth of ignorance to wear one in any house where you weren't at least sleeping and preferably living. But now that's changed. More and more country dinners are enlivened by a myriad of velvet shades stretched tight across the broad backs of the chaps. Usually without ties, an unfortunate fad for the middle-aged, whose red, mottled necks do not show to advantage. But having fought the fashion for a time, protesting it was 'quite incorrect,' I rather like it now; putting men into colour, as it does, for the first time in two centuries. As for the rag rules, the one imperative, as I have said, is that they should be different rags when you come down the stairs from the rags that you went up in. To me, the business of pulling off a shirt and jersey and a pair of cords, in order to bathe and put on another shirt, another jersey and another pair of cords can be a bit comedic, but there we are. You can't fight Tammany Hall. Anyway, on this particular evening I did my stuff and I was ready to go down to the drawing room, when I caught sight of a framed photograph on a chest to the right of the carved and painted chimneypiece. It was Serena and Candida, standing side by side in what must have been the receiving line for their Coming Out dance at Gresham. I could make out the portraits in the hall behind them and in the picture Lady Claremont was just turning to one side, as if her attention had been caught by an arriving guest. Then I saw the figure of a young man a few paces back, behind the girls but with his face fixed eagerly on them as if he couldn't look away. Which I knew at once that he could not. For it was me.

*   *   *

As far as anything can be in this mortal setting, the ball at Gresham Abbey for Serena Gresham and Candida Finch was more or less perfection. For some reason it was held quite late, after the summer break, at a time of the year leading up to Christmas that used then to be labelled 'The Little Season.' We were fairly jaded by that stage, having been doing the rounds since the end of the spring and there was not much that a hostess could produce to surprise us, but Lady Claremont had decided, perhaps because she was aware of this, that she would not surprise, she would merely perfect. For some strange reason I kept all my invitations for quite a long time but I have lost them now, so I forget whether it was held in late October or early November. It was definitely a winter ball and we all knew it would be the last really big, private one before the charity balls took

471

over and the whole rigmarole wound up, which in a way gave the evening a kind of built-in romance.

I had stayed at Gresham a few times by that stage and of course I had hoped to be included in the abbey house party, but the competition was predictably stiff and I was not. As it turned out, my host was a fairly dreary one but not insultingly so, a retired general, with his nice, typical army wife, who lived in a small manor house entirely decorated in that sort of non-taste that such people can go in for. Nothing was actually ugly or common, but nothing was charming or pretty either, except for the odd painting or piece of furniture they had inherited through no merit of their own. A couple of the ones who were staying qualified as friends, Minna Bunting and that same Sam Hoare who had featured as another witness to the Battle of the Mainwarings before Minna's dance, and the others were all quite familiar as well, since we had been performing this ritual together for six months by then. As usual, some local couples came for the dinner, a blameless concoction of salmon mousse (*comme toujours*), chicken à la king and crème brûlée, a menu more suited perhaps to an aged invalid with no teeth than a bunch of ravenous teenagers, but we made the best of it and chatted away quite sociably. There was nothing wrong with any of this, but nor was there anything of much interest in it and it was certainly no distraction from the main purpose of the evening: To get to the dance. Sometimes the dinners and house parties could be so entertaining that one lingered and arrived at the dance a little too late to enjoy it. But there was certainly no chance of that on this occasion. After a polite

472

interval had passed we drank up our coffee, slid away to the loo and clambered into the cars.

There was a kind of general excitement in the air when we entered the hall, though I did not then know why. Serena and Candida and the Claremonts were standing there receiving. 'I'm so glad you could come,' said Serena and kissed me, which nearly winded me, as usual. 'I wish you were staying here,' she added in a whisper, as a compliment rather than because she meant it. I had become a bit of a Gresham regular by the end of that year, having been billeted with them for a couple of northern dances and staying once on my own on the way down from Scotland, and I was in danger of succumbing to that awful smugness of trying to demonstrate that one is a welcome guest somewhere enviable, but I did not suspect at the time, what I know now, that the welcome I always received was a reflection of Serena's enjoyment of my being in love with her. I do not mean she was interested in me romantically, not in the least, only that she wanted me to go on being in love with her until it wasn't fun any more. The young are like that. I can now remember when the photograph was taken. I was still reeling in bliss from her comment and I was unable to make myself move out of the room where she stood, even though I knew I had to give place, so I stepped behind them, where I could linger a little longer; then a flash went off and I was caught forever, like a fly in amber. Lucy Dalton rescued me, taking my arm and walking me away. 'What's your house party like?'

'Dull but respectable.'

'Sounds like paradise compared to mine. There

473

doesn't seem to be any running water. Literally. Nothing comes out of the taps except a dirty trickle of what looks like prune juice. Doesn't Serena look marvellous? But of course you're not the man to disagree with *that*. I hear the discothèque is *fabulous*. It was done by someone's boyfriend, but I forget who. Come on.' All this was delivered in one spurt without pause or breath, so I couldn't hope to come in with a comment.

The discothèque *was* fabulous. It occupied a large section of what must normally have been a basement servants' hall or even a section of the no doubt extensive wine cellars. A doorway under the main staircase was surrounded by synthetic flames and a sign read 'Welcome to Hell!' While on the other side of the door the entire space, including the walls of the staircase leading down, was covered in foil and flames made of tinsel and satin, blown with fans and lit by a spinning wheel, making them flicker and leap, so they really did feel quite real. At the bottom the hell theme embraced the entire area, with huge copies of the grimmer paintings by Hieronymus Bosch lining the walls with images of suffering, while the fire and flames played over the heads of the dancers. As a final detail the DJ and two of the waitresses had been put into scarlet devils' outfits, so they could attend to the guests while maintaining the illusion. The only discordant note came from the music, some of which seemed very out of place in Hades. When we came down the steps a popular ballad by the Turtles, *Elenore*, was playing. Somehow the lyrics, 'I really think you're groovy, let's go out to a movie,' didn't quite chime with the Tortures of the Damned.

We danced and gossiped and said hello to other people for a bit until, round about half past eleven or maybe midnight, a sudden rush for the staircase told us that something was happening we wouldn't want to miss.

Lucy and I struggled up to the hall in our turn and found we were carried along in the crush towards the State Dining Room, which had been designated the main ballroom of the evening. The space had been cleared of furniture and somehow, unlike most of the other houses I had penetrated, the stage erected at one end for the band and, more unusually, the lighting looked entirely professional. This put a spin on the proceedings from the start, even before we knew what was happening. I don't quite know why, but there was always something satisfactory in dancing inside a great house and not in a marquee with wobbly coconut matting and a portable dance floor, and Gresham Abbey was the very acme of a great house. Stern, full-lengths of earlier, male Greshams lined the walls of the enormous room, in armour and brocade and Victorian fustian, in lovelocks and perukes and periwigs, extending their white, stockinged legs to display the garters that encased them. Above the marble chimneypiece a vast, equestrian portrait of the first Earl of Claremont by Kneller dominated the chamber, a loud, impressive statement of self-congratulation, and the contrast between the rigid splendour of this symbol of high birth and high achievement and the crowd of teenage young writhing away below it was almost startling.

At this precise moment, the door opened that on ordinary days led to the servery and, further below, to the kitchens. Tonight it revealed a group of young men who came bouncing through on to the stage, and started to play and sing. With a kind of group sigh we suddenly all realised that this, incredibly, was Steve Winwood, lead singer of the group formed and named for the man who ran up on to the stage after him, Spencer Davis. This was the real live Spencer Davis. No sooner had this information penetrated our skulls, than they started to play their song of a couple of years previously, *Keep on Running*. It is hard to explain now what this felt like then. We are a jaded people, these days. We see film stars and singers and every other permutation of fame wherever we go, indeed sometimes, judging by the magazines, it seems that more people are famous than not. But this wasn't true in 1968 and to be in the same room as a real-live band playing and singing its own hit number, which most of us had bought anyway two years before and played ever since, was to be inside a fantasy. It was astonishing, mind-searing, completely impossible to take in. Even Lucy was silenced, if not for long. 'Can you believe it?' she said. I couldn't. We were so sweet, really.

It was then that I saw Damian. He was standing inside one of the window embrasures and so half in shadow, looking at the world-shaking sight but without any outward sign of excitement or even pleasure. He just stood there, listening, watching, but watching without interest. My own attention was taken back by the band and, to be honest, I forgot all about him until much later on, but I still have that image, a melancholic at the carnival, lodged in my brain. After that, I was back in the party, dancing and talking and drinking for hours,

476

and finally, at about half past two, going off in search of breakfast, which I found in the conservatory. This was a huge glass-and-cast-iron affair, what was once called a winter garden, built for one of the countesses in the 1880s, and on this night it had been cleared and filled with little round tables and chairs, each one decorated with a pyramid of flowers. A long buffet stood against one end, and the exotic climbing flowers on the stone wall behind it formed a kind of living wallpaper. What made it even more unusual was that the whole space had been carpeted for the occasion in bright red, cut close round the stone fountain at its centre, and the route of access, normally a short walk along a terrace from one of the drawing rooms, had been covered in with a passage, fashioned in wood for that one night only, but as an absolute facsimile, in every way, of the room it connected to, with dado, panels and cornice, and the very handles on the windows made as exact reproductions of the originals. In short, there is a level, perhaps in all things, where the object or activity is of so exquisite a standard that it becomes an art form in itself, and for me that little, constructed passage achieved it. Like everything else that evening, it was extraordinary.

I walked down the table, helping myself to the delights, then sauntered around, chatting with assorted clutches of guests. Joanna was there and I talked to her for a bit, and Dagmar, finally alighting at a table with Candida, which was in itself a bit unusual as normally by this stage of the evening she would be laughing like someone with terminal whooping cough and I would give her a wide berth, but on this evening, at her own dance which made it odd, she was curiously piano, so I sat down. I seemed to have shed Lucy by that time and I know I didn't fix myself up with a partner for the evening, as one usually did at these things, although I cannot tell you why. Certainly it did not in any way lessen my enjoyment. I think, looking back, that maybe it would have felt awkward and dishonest to have had to flirt and concentrate and pretend that some other girl was the centre of my attention for the evening when I was in Serena's house and at Serena's party. 'Have you seen anything of your friend Damian?' said Candida. Again, she seemed quite unlike her normal self and positively thoughtful, not an adjective she would generally attract at half past two in the morning.

I had to concentrate for a moment. The question had come out of nowhere. 'Not recently. I saw him in the dining room when we were listening to the band earlier. Why?'

'No reason.' She turned to one of the Tremayne boys who had arrived at the table with some pals and a plate of sausages.

I'd finished eating and Carla Wakefield wanted my seat, so I left the conservatory and wandered back through the emptying house. For no reason, I turned into the little oval anteroom, outside the dining room, where the music was still echoing through the rafters. There was a little group of paintings depicting the five senses that I found intriguing and I leaned in to see more of the detail, when an icy blast hit me and I stood to see that a door leading out to the terrace was open and Serena was coming in from the night. She was alone, and while she was, for me, as lovely as

478

anyone can imagine a woman could be, she looked as if she were shivering with cold. 'What were you doing out there?' I said. 'You must be freezing.'

For a second she had to concentrate to work out both who I was and what I was saying, but having regained control of her brain, she nodded. 'It is a bit chilly,' she said.

'But what were you doing?'

She shrugged lightly. 'Just thinking,' she said.

'I don't suppose you want to dance,' I spoke cheerfully, but without any expectations.

I quite understand that, in this account of my relations with Serena Gresham I must seem pessimistic and negative to a tedious degree, but you have to understand that at this time in my life I was young and ugly. To be ugly when young is something that no one who has not experienced it should ever claim to understand. It is all very well to talk about superficial values and 'beauty of character,' and the rest of the guff that ugly teenagers have to listen to from their mothers, the 'marvellous thing about being different' and so on, but the plain truth is you are bankrupt in the only currency with value. You may have friends without number, but when it comes to romance you have nothing to bargain with, nothing to sell. You are not to be shown off and flaunted, you are the last resort when there's no one left worth dancing with. When you are kissed, you do not turn into a prince. You are just a kissed toad and usually the kisser regrets it in the morning. The best reputation you can acquire is that you never talk. If you are good company and you can hold your tongue, you will see some action, but woe betide the ugly suitor who grows overconfident and brags.

Of course, things change. In time, at last, some people will start to see through your face to your other qualities and eventually, in the thirties and forties, other factors come into play. Success will mend your features and so will money, and this is not, actually, because the women concerned are necessarily mercenary. It is because you have begun to smell differently. Success makes you a different person. But you never forget those few, those very few, Grade A women who loved you when no one else did. In the words of a thriller, I know who you are and you will always have a place in my heart. But even the least of these did not come along before my middle twenties. When I was eighteen, ugly and in love, I knew I was in love alone.

'Yes. Let's dance,' said Serena, and I can still remember that strange mixture of butterflies and feeling sick that her answer gave me.

Spencer Davis had left by then. Presumably they were already racing down the motorway, or the equivalent in those days, having more than earned their wedge and made the evening legendary. God bless them all. I hope they know what happiness they gave us. It was three o'clock by this stage and nearly the end of the ball. A disc jockey had taken over again, but you could hear in his voice that he was winding down. He put on a slow record I rather liked, *A Single Girl*, which had been a hit a year or two earlier, and we moved closer. There is something so peculiar about dancing. You are entitled to slide your arm round the waist of a woman, to hold her closely, to feel her breasts against your chest through your shirt and the thin silk of an evening dress; her hair brushes against your cheek, her very scent excites you, yet there is no intimacy in it, no assumption of anything but politeness and sociability. Needless to say I was in paradise as we shifted our weight from foot to foot, and talked of the band and the party, and what a complete success the evening had been. But although she was obviously pleased to hear it, still Serena seemed thoughtful and not as elated as I had expected her to be. As she was entitled to feel. 'Have you seen Damian?' she said. 'He was looking for you.'

'Why?'

'I think he wants to ask you for a lift tomorrow.'

'I'm going rather early.'

'He knows. He has to get away first thing, too.' I was so absorbed in the wonder of dancing with her that I didn't register this much, although I remember it did occur to me that I should find any excuse to linger, were I lucky enough to be staying at Gresham.

'Have you enjoyed yourself?' I asked.

She thought for a moment. 'These things are such milestones,' she said, which was an odd answer really, even if it was true. These events *were* rites of passage to my generation and we did not much question their validity. It may seem strange in our aggressively anti-formal age but then we saw the point of ritual. The girls came out, the men came of age. The former happened when the girl was eighteen, the latter when the man was twenty-one. This was because the upper classes entirely ignored the government's altering the age of seniority to eighteen for many years, if indeed they recognise it now. These events were a marking of adulthood. After they had been observed you were a fully fledged member of the club, and your membership would continue to be parsed by ceremony: Weddings and christenings, parties for our offspring, more weddings and finally funerals. These were the Big Moments by which we steered our course through life. That's gone now. There are seemingly no obligatory events. The only thing that really marks an aristocratic upbringing apart from a middle-class one today is that the upper classes still marry before giving birth. Or, when they don't, it is exceptional. Apart from that many of the traditions that once distinguished them as a tribe seem largely to have melted into the sand.

The song came to an end and Serena was claimed by her departing guests, while I wandered off through the house, reluctant, even now, to call it a day. I left the dancing and crossed the anteroom, where a girl in pink was asleep on a rather pretty sofa, before poking through the half-open door into the Tapestry Drawing Room which lay beyond. At first I thought it was empty. There were only a few lamps lit and the room was engulfed in gloom. The Empress Catherine's clock caught the eye as one lamp was so placed to make the glass on the face shine, but otherwise it was clearly a room that had done its work for the day. Then I saw that it was not in fact empty, but that one chair beneath a vast tapestry reaching to the cornice was occupied and the sitter was none other than Damian Baxter. 'Hello,' I said. 'Serena told me you wanted to ask me something.'

He looked up. 'Yes. I wondered whether you could give me a lift home tomorrow, if you're driving straight down. I know you're leaving early.'

I was interested by this, because I had never heard Damian speak of his home before. 'Where is home?' I said.

'Northampton. I imagine you'll drive straight past it. Unless you're not going back to London at all.'

'Of course I'll take you. I'll pick you up at about nine.'

That seemed to be the end of it. Mission accomplished. He stood. 'I think I'll go to bed,' he said. There was something curiously unembroidered about his manner, which I had come to see as endlessly calculated. But not tonight.

'What did you think of the party?'

'Amazing.'

'And did you have a good time?'

'So-so,' he said.

As promised, I arrived back at the abbey at approximately nine the following morning. The door was standing open so I just went in. As I had expected, the house party might still have been in their rooms, but the place was a whirl of activity. A great house on the day after a party is always rather evocative. Servants were wandering about, collecting missed glasses and things, and carrying furniture back to their proper places. The table was being assembled at one end of the dining room, while the huge carpet was unrolled in front of me, and when I asked after the house party's breakfast I was nodded through to the little dining room beyond it, a simple room, if not as little as all that, enlivened by some paintings of racehorses, with their riders in the Gresham colours. Lady Claremont had broken her usual rule and there were three tables, a bit jammed in, set for about twenty-four. Damian was alone, finishing off a piece of toast. He stood as I entered. 'My case is already in the hall.'

'Don't you want to say goodbye to anyone?'

'They're all asleep and I said goodbye last night.' So, without further ado, we loaded up his bag and left. He didn't say anything much as we drove along, beyond a few directions, until we were back on the Al heading south. Then, at last, he did speak. 'I'm not going to do that again,' he said.

'We're none of us going to do much more of it. I think I've only got another two dances and a few charity things, then it's over.'

'I'm not even going to them. I've had enough. I should do some work, anyway, before I forget what it is I'm supposed to be studying.'

I looked at him. There was something resolute and glum about him, which was new. 'Did anything happen last night?' I asked.

'What do you mean?'

'You seem rather disenchanted.'

'If I am disenchanted, it has nothing to do with last night. It's the whole bloody, self-indulgent, boring thing. I've had enough of it.'

'Which of course is your privilege.'

After that, we drove more or less in silence until at last we reached Northampton. It is not a town I know, but Damian took me safely to a row of perfectly respectable semi-detached 1930s villas, all built of brick with tiles hung above the waistline, and each with a name on the gate. The one we stopped outside was called 'Sunnyside.' As we were unloading, the door opened and a middle-

484

aged couple came out, the man in a rather loud jersey and worsted slacks, and the woman in a grey skirt with a cardigan over her shoulders, held in place by a shiny chain. The man came forward to take the case. 'This is my father,' said Damian and he introduced me. I shook hands and said hello.

'Pleased to meet you,' said Mr Baxter.

'How do you do,' I said in return, deliberately blocking his cheerful welcome by not answering in kind, with what I foolishly imagined, in my youthful fatuity, to be good breeding.

'Won't you come in?' said Mrs Baxter. 'Would you like a coffee?' But I didn't go in and I didn't have any coffee. I regret it now, that refusal of their hospitality. My excuse was that I had an appointment in London at three o'clock and I wasn't sure I'd make it as it was. I told myself it was important, and perhaps it was, but I regret it now. And even if I couldn't bring myself to say it, I was pleased to meet them. They were nice, decent people; the mother went out of her way to be polite and the father was, I think, a clever man. I learned later that he was the manager of a shoe factory with a special interest in opera and it saddened me in a way that I had not met them before. That they had not been included in any of the year's frolics, not even at the university. Looking back, I realise it was a key moment for me, though I wasn't aware of it at the time, in that it was one of the first instances when I came to appreciate the insidious poison of snobbery, the tyranny of it, the meaningless values that made me reject their friendly overtures, that had made Damian hide these two, pleasant, intelligent people because he was ashamed of them.

485

On the morning in question, I realise now, Damian was making a kind of statement of apology, of non-shame, by bringing me here. He had hidden them behind a barrier because he did not want me to judge him, to look down on him, on the basis of his parents, with whom there was nothing wrong at all, and in this he was right. We would have looked down on him. I blush to write it and I liked them when I met them, but we would have done, without any moral justification whatever. He had wanted to move into a different world and he felt part of that would be shedding his background. He'd managed the transition, but on this particular morning I think he was ashamed of his ambition, ashamed of rejecting his own past. The truth is we should all have been ashamed in having played along with it without question. At any rate, with avowals to meet again the following Monday at Cambridge we parted and I got back into my car.

We did meet again, of course, several times, but we did not meet alone for the rest of my time at university. Essentially my friendship with Damian Baxter ended on that day, the morning after Serena Gresham's dance, and I cannot pretend I was sorry, even if my feelings for him were less savage then than they would be when we did next find ourselves under the same roof. But that was a couple of years later, when we were out in the world, and quite a different story.

FOURTEEN

The weekend passed pleasantly enough. We ate, we talked, we slept, we walked. Sophie Jamieson turned out to share my interest in French history and the Purbricks were great friends of some cousins of mine who lived near them, so it all went very smoothly in the way of these things. I must say Andrew had not improved with the years. Having inherited the earldom and the savaged remnant that the family lawyer's depredations had left of the estate, it was as if the last vestiges of self-knowledge or self-doubt had been flung to the four winds. He was king, and a very angry king at that, raging at the gardeners and the cook and his wife about almost everything. Serena took it all in her stride but once, when I was on my way downstairs before dinner on Friday evening, I found him haranguing her in the hall about a frame that should have been mended or something. I caught her eye as I was on my way to the library door and she did not look away but raised her eyebrows slightly, which he would not have seen and which I took as more or less the greatest compliment an English toff can pay: to include you in their private, family dramas.

After lunch on Saturday, when we'd finished drinking our cups of coffee in the drawing room, Serena proposed a walk by the river and most of us stuck up our hands to join her. 'You'll need boots,' she said, but there were masses of spares for people who'd forgotten them, so we were soon equipped and on our way. The gardens at Waverly were pretty and predictable, the usual Victorian layout that had been calmed down by the restriction of only having two gardeners instead of twelve, and we walked through them, admiring vocally as we went, but they weren't the main pleasure ground event. Serena led us out of a gate and on down an avenue through a paddock and into a wood, until finally we came out on to a grassy bank, perfectly placed to allow us to walk along the edge of a wide river whose name I now forget. I admired the wonders of nature. 'It's totally artificial,' she said. 'They rerouted the riverbed in the 1850s and made the walks to go with the altered course.' I could only reflect on the brilliance of that generation in their understanding of how to live.

We were alone in a comfortable pair by then, as the others had lagged behind. I looked around at the view as Serena slid her arm through mine. On the other side of the water a huge willow leaned over, trailing its creeper-like branches on the surface, making ripples in the flow. Suddenly there was a flurry of movement and a heron appeared above the trees, wide wings beating back and forth, slowly and rhythmically, as it sailed across the sky. 'They're such thieves. Andrew says we should shoot them or the river will be quite empty.' But even as she spoke the words, her eyes followed the great, grey bird on its wondrous journey. 'It's such a privilege to live here,' she said after a minute or two.

I looked at her. 'I hope so.'

'It is.' She was staring me straight in the eye, so I think she was trying to be honest. 'He's quite a different person when we're alone.'

Naturally, this was very flattering, as the lack of names or qualifications implied a kind of shorthand between us which I was thrilled to think might exist, and even more thrilled by the idea that she recognised it, but in another way she was registering her guilt at signalling Andrew's preposterous behaviour in the hall the previous evening. Her statement is anyway the standard defence of all women who find themselves married to, or stuck with, men who all their friends think are awful. Often this comes as a revelation after quite a considerable period during which they thought people quite liked their mate, and it must be a disappointment to discover that the reverse is true, but I would guess this was not the case where Serena was concerned. Nobody had ever liked Andrew. Of course, it is an effective defence to claim hidden qualities for your other half, because by definition it is impossible to disprove. I suppose logic tells one that it must sometimes be true, but I found it hard to believe that Andrew Belton in private was sensitive, endearing and fun, not least because there is no cure for stupidity. Still, I prayed that it might be even partially the case. 'If you say so, I believe it,' I replied.

We walked on for a while before Serena spoke again. 'I wish you'd tell me what you're really doing for Damian.'

'I have told you.'

'You're not going to all this trouble just to get some funny stories from four decades ago. Candida tells me you've been over to Los Angeles to see the dreaded Terry K.'

I couldn't be bothered to be dishonest, since we were so near the end. 'I can't tell you now,' I said, 'because it isn't my secret. But I will tell you soon, if you're interested.'

'I am.' She pondered my answer for a bit. 'I never saw him again after that ghastly night.'

'No. Nor did most of the guests.'

'Yet I often think of him.'

She had brought it up and so I thought I would try to satisfy something that had been niggling me. 'When you planned that whole thing with Candida, turning up out of the blue, what were you hoping to achieve? I can remember you now, standing in that vast, sun-baked square, in those terrible black clothes you all had to borrow.'

She gave a snort of laughter. 'That was so crazy.'

'But what did you hope would come out of it?'

This was a big question and years before it would have been unaskable. But she did not reproach me, or even look cross to be put on the spot. 'Nothing, once my parents were on board. I should have given up the whole idea the moment they said they were coming. I don't know why I didn't.'

'But originally. When you first plotted it?'

She shook her head and her hair caught a glint of the sun. 'To be honest, I don't really know what I wanted to come out of it, given how I managed things later. I suppose I felt trapped. And angry. I was married and a mother and Christ knows what, all before I was twenty-one, and I felt I'd been lured into a cage and the door had slammed shut. Damian stood for everything that had been taken from me. But it was silly. We hadn't been honest with each other and that always makes for trouble. It would all have been different if we were young today, but how does that help?'

'Do you still feel trapped?'

She smiled. 'Isn't there a laboratory test where if animals are kept in a trap long enough, they come back when they're let out, because it's home?' We strolled on, listening to the birds. 'Does he ever talk about me?' Despite a Pavlovian irritation, this question interested me. More or less every woman I had seen on my quest had asked this and Serena wasn't even one of the contenders. It was pointless to deny that Damian clearly had qualities that I had been quite unaware of at the time.

'Of course we talk about you. You're the one thing we have in common.' I said it as a joke, although it was truer than I had previously known. I could not tell you how she took it, but she smiled and we walked on.

'Did you see the picture in your room?'

'I did.'

'Classic. I put it out for you. God, weren't we young?'

'Young and, in your case, lovely.'

She sighed. 'I can never understand why you and I didn't get off together at some point, during the whole thing.'

This made me stop in my tracks. 'Can't you? I can. You didn't fancy me.' There was no point in beating about the bush.

She looked a little miffed, perhaps because it sounded as if I were reproaching her, which I truly wasn't. 'You never pressed your case very hard,' she said at last. She was apparently attempting at least to share the blame for our non-romance.

'Because I knew that if I did, our friendship would become untenable and I would drop out of your life. It was fun for you to have me dying for love, as long as it never became embarrassing and I never put you on the spot. You could have had me any day you wished, with a crook of your finger, which you were fully aware of. But you never wanted me, except as a courtier worshipping at your shrine. And I was happy. If that was the best that was on offer, I was glad to oblige.'

She made a slight expression of horror at this perfectly honest account. 'Did you know all that, then?'

I shook my head. 'No. Except possibly instinctively. But I know it now.'

'Oh dear,' she said. 'You make me sound like such a bitch.'

But this wasn't right and I was anxious for her to know I didn't think it. 'Not at all. It worked well for a long time. I was your *parfit knight* and you were *la belle dame sans merci*. It's an arrangement that has been perfectly serviceable for hundreds of years, after all. It only went wrong because of Portugal and that wasn't your fault. It became embarrassing after that evening, so we dropped out of each other's lives, but it would only have happened sooner if I'd made a pass.'

She thought for a time, as we walked on again in silence. There was a rustle of movement in the undergrowth and the distinctive red of a fox's coat flashed through the browns and greens for a moment. As if recognising him, she spoke, 'Damian has much to answer for.'

'The interesting thing is I think he would agree with you.'

The others were closing in on us now and soon the conversation would become general again. But before they reached where we were standing Serena spoke softly. 'I hope you don't hate me.'

Her voice was gentle and, I think, sincere, and when I turned towards her, she was smiling. I don't think she meant it as a serious enquiry, but she was apologising for wounding me in those lost years, when heart pain could be so sharp and was so easily administered. I looked at her and for the millionth time wondered at every feature. A tiny crumb of something from lunch was clinging to the corner of her mouth and I imagined a life where I would have the right to lick it off. 'What do you think?' I said.

*   *   *

Dinner that night was the main event of the weekend and I dutifully bathed, putting on evening trousers, a shirt with no tie, reluctantly, and a smoking jacket. I went downstairs feeling rather cheery but, once in the drawing room, things got heavier with the inclusion among the guests for the evening of Andrew's mother, the now Dowager Countess, who lived not in the real dower house, a smart Georgian villa on the edge of the park, which was let to an American banker, but in a cottage in the village formerly reserved for the head keeper. She was standing stiffly by the chimneypiece when I came in. Lady Belton was a lot older, naturally, than when I had last seen her, but age had done little to soothe her incipient madness. She still stared out of those pale-blue, Dutch-doll eyes, and her hair was dyed to an approximation of the Italianate black it had once been. Nor had her sense of style made much of a leap forward. She wore a curious outfit, a kind of long, khaki nightgown with an uneven neckline. I'm not sure what effect she was aiming at, but it can't have been what she achieved. Her jewellery, I need hardly say, was excellent.

Serena introduced me, observing that her mother-in-law must remember me from the old days. Lady Belton ignored this. 'How do you do,' she said, extending her bony, knuckled hand. Is there anything more annoying than people saying how do you do when you have met them a thousand times? If there is, I would like to know what it might be. I had a recent instance where I was greeted as a stranger by a woman I'd known since childhood, who had grown famous in the interim. Every time I met her for literally years, she would lean forward gracefully and make no sign that we had ever seen each other before. Finally I resolved that if she tried it one more time I would let her have it. But something of my resolve must have shown in my face and all bullies are equipped with an antenna that tells them when the bullying must stop. She read my eyes and held out her hand. 'How lovely to see you again,' she said.

Serena had moved off to get me a drink, so I was left alone with the old besom. 'It's so nice to catch up with Andrew and Serena after all these years,' I said feebly by way of an opener.

'Do you know Lord Belton?' she replied, without a glimmer of a smile. Presumably this was to show me that I should have referred to him by his proper rank. There was a bowl of avocado dip quite near us on a side table, and just for a second I had an almost irresistible urge to pick it up and

494

squish it into her face.

Instead, I opened my mouth to say 'Yes, I know them and I know you too, you silly, old bat.' But there's no point, is there? She would only have hidden behind my 'terrible rudeness' and never have recognised her own. I didn't draw her at dinner, hallelujah, and instead I watched pityingly as Hugh Purbrick battled through her silences, trying to engage her with talk of people she must have met but of whom she denied all knowledge, or on topics in which she made it clear she had no interest. In short, she gave him no quarter.

The young are often told, or were in the days when I was a child, that *parvenus* and other rank outsiders may on occasion be rude, but *real* ladies and gentlemen are never anything but perfectly polite. This is, of course, complete rubbish. The rude, like the polite, may be found at every level of society, but there is a particular kind of rudeness, when it rests on empty snobbery, on an assumption of superiority made by people who have nothing superior about them, who have nothing about them at all, in fact, that is unique to the upper classes and very hard to swallow. Old Lady Belton was a classic example, a walking mass of bogus values, a hollow gourd, a cause for revolution. I had disliked her when I was young, but now, after forty years to think about it, I saw her as worse than simply unpleasant and foolish. Rather, I recognised her as someone who would be almost evil if she weren't so stupid, as the very reason for her children's empty lives. There is much that makes me nostalgic for the England of my youth, much that I think has been lost to our detriment, but sometimes one must recognise where it was wrong and why it had to change. Where the upper classes are concerned, Lady Belton was that reason made flesh. She was an embodiment of all that was bad about the old system and of absolutely none of its virtues. I do not like to hate but I confess that, seeing her again, I almost hated her. I hated her for what she represented and because, ultimately, I blamed her for Andrew's worthlessness. If I were to be merciful where he is concerned, and I find it hard, I would acknowledge that with a mother like the one he had he never stood a chance. Between them, these two pointless people had wasted my Serena's life. Andrew was in fact Lady Belton's other neighbour at dinner that night, since she had been placed, in accordance with precedence, on his right. They did not exchange one word from soup to nuts. Neither could be judged a loser by it.

Afterwards, some of the party made up a table for bridge and a few of them sneaked off to watch a late film on television in some chaotic children's cubbyhole where Andrew had banished 'the foul machine,' so after the locals had gone home and the rest of the house party had taken themselves off to bed, I found myself with Candida in a corner of the library, hugging a glass of whisky, gossiping as the fire died. Serena had looked in and made us free with the tray of drinks but she was taken up with settling the others, and for me it was enough just to see her operating her existence, charting her course through the commitments that made her days real. And I was pleased to be left alone with Candida, since it meant that I was able to continue my investigations. I had told Candida about finding the picture in my room the night before, but now we were alone we fell to discussing that party of so long ago, how it went and how it ended. I reminded her that I had driven Damian home in rather a glump, and that it marked the finish of his career as a deb's delight. 'Poor Damian,' she said. 'I've never felt sorrier for anybody.'

This was an unexpected comment, since I had no idea what she was talking about. 'Why?'

My query was clearly as much of a surprise to her as her statement had been to me. 'Because of the whole drama,' she replied, as if this must be quite obvious.

'What drama?'

She gave me a quizzical look, as if I might be teasing and leading her on, but my gaze was as innocent as a newborn child's. 'How amazing,' she said. 'Did he really never tell you?'

Then I asked and I listened.

Candida knew Damian well, long before that night. She had flirted with him in her frightening way, she had danced with him, even, I suspected as she talked, slept with him and generally befriended him as the season had progressed. And she had managed to get him included in the Gresham house party, without drawing attention to Serena, and—

'But I don't understand. Why did you? I thought you fancied him yourself.' I remembered that other, different Candida rolling her eyes at Queen Charlotte's Ball and almost shuddered.

She shook her head. 'That was all finished long before. And by that time he and Serena were in love with each other.' Again she spoke as if I must surely have had some suspicion of these things at

497

the very least, and it was precious of me to pretend that I did not. 'That is, I thought they were in love with each other. Serena was in love with him.'

'I don't believe it.' Of course, I didn't want to believe it and in truth I hadn't seen much evidence. They'd kissed. But if we were supposed to be in love with everyone we'd ever kissed . . .

She shrugged as if to say believe what you like, I am telling you the truth. 'She wanted to marry him, absurd as that sounds, and as you know, she was eighteen at the time and Damian was nineteen and still at university, so they needed her parents' consent.'

'Why? When did the law change?'

'At the beginning of 1970. It was still twenty-one in Sixty-eight.'

'But the Claremonts would never have given their consent if he'd been the Duke of Gloucester.'

'Yes, they would. They did. They pushed her into marrying Andrew the following year, and she was still only nineteen.' Which was true. 'Anyway, Serena had got it into her head that if they could only get to know Damian they would fall for him and in time give their permission, which obviously I can now see was a hopeless idea.'

'Worse than hopeless. Insane.'

My intervention was not soothing to her. 'Yes. Well, as I say, I know that now, but at the time I had convinced myself, or Serena had convinced me, that it might work. It wasn't that she wanted to plunge into obscurity with him. She was sure that Damian would do incredibly well in his career and history has, after all, proved her right a thousand times over.'

I nodded. This conversation was having an

498

uncomfortable effect on me. I was feeling numb and strangely tingly, as if I were coming down with 'flu. I am not pretending I didn't know they were attracted to each other, they were both good-looking and on the circuit and, as I've admitted, I'd seen the kissing incident at Terry's ball. That was enough to make me jealous and angry and indignant, but this . . . this was something entirely different. This was when I learned a lesson I will not now lose, although it has come too late to do much good. Namely, that just because you start people off, you do not control them thereafter, nor do you have the right to pretend that you do. However Damian began that year under my aegis, however he met those people initially, he was living a life among them, in that world, by the end of it, that was as valid as my own. I had brought him out from under his stone, but at the finish he'd held the promise in his hands of what would have constituted my whole life's happiness. I was so jealous I wanted to kill almost anybody.

'Well, somehow her parents got wind of the whole plan. I thought later it might have been Andrew who had tipped off his mother, the dreaded Lady B. Wasn't she ghastly tonight?'

'Ghastly.'

'Well, she was desperate to catch Serena for Andrew and she might have deliberately put a spoke in the works, but we'll never know. On the day, Damian and Serena drove down together from London. I was coming from somewhere or other, but I got here at about five, after most of the house party, and they were all having tea in the drawing room. Of course, Aunt Roo was being very charming—'

'Why is she called Aunt Roo?'

She thought for a moment. 'I'm not completely sure. I think it's something to do with *Winnie the Pooh*. Remember the mother kangaroo was called Kanga and the baby was called Roo?' I nodded. 'It was some game they used to play at Barrymount, when they were growing up in Ireland. Her real name's Rosemary, but she was always Roo in the family.' Somehow Lady Claremont's nickname only reinforced the iron walls of the culture that Damian, in his youthful ignorance, took on all those years ago.

'Anyway, when I came in, Damian was trying very hard. Too hard. He smiled and chatted and giggled and flashed and flickered, and Aunt Roo laughed and asked him about Cambridge and so on, but I remember thinking Uncle Pel was very quiet—which he wasn't usually in those days—and I could tell by the look she gave me, that Serena knew it wasn't going as well as Damian obviously thought. The guests who were staying did that silent thing, of not quite laughing and not quite letting him in. My other aunt was there, and as Damian was rabbiting on, Aunt Sheila and Roo kept swapping quiet, sisterly glances, which seemed so unkind and disloyal. I can see that's not terribly logical for me to say, but I felt infuriated for Serena, for both of them really.' She paused, breathless with the memory. 'I suppose that was when I realised it wasn't going to work.'

She stopped for a moment, as if this was the first time she had ever fully registered this salient point. 'So. We all went up to change and I was sitting at my dressing table, doing my best with my hair. I remember I'd forgotten to have it done,

500

which seems a bit mad for your own dance, but at this precise moment there was a knock and Roo and Pel came into the room. They were already changed and Roo was covered in diamonds, and it should all have been rather merry and gay, but somehow it wasn't. Then Uncle Pel said, "How long has this been going on?" And we were all quite quiet, as if someone was supposed to ask what he was talking about, but of course we all knew what he was talking about, so there wasn't any point. Then I started a defence of Serena and Damian, of both of them, but even as I was talking I could hear that it all sounded so childish and ridiculous, as if I were suddenly seeing it through their eyes. I'd never been with Uncle Pel when he was so angry, in fact I'd never really seen him angry at all, but that night he was bulging with anger, blazing with it. "She wants to run off with this smarmy, little oik?" he said. "This greaser, with his oily hair and his dodgy vowels and his 'pleased to meet you' and his clothes from Marks and Spencer?" I've never forgotten that. *"His clothes from Marks and Spencer."* And I looked at Roo and she said "Watson unpacked for him," and that was that. Then it was her turn. "Of course we want Serena to be happy," she said. "It's all we want. Truly." Which it obviously wasn't. "But you see, we want her to be happy in a way we understand, in a way that will last." '

'I said I thought that this would last, but even as I spoke the words I felt like some little, preppy, Sandra Dee figure asking to be allowed to stay out late.' Candida sighed. 'I'm afraid I wasn't much use.'

'Did Damian really say "pleased to meet you"?'

501

'Apparently. It just shows how nervous he must have been.'

'Poor chap. Was that it?'

She shook her head. 'By no means. Uncle Pel hadn't finished. He was absolutely fizzing and he sort of waved his finger at me, right under my nose, like a teacher in a situation comedy, as if I were the guilty one, which I now think he must have believed, since he knew I'd connived in getting Damian up there. "You tell Serena to get rid of this little social-climbing, money-grubbing shit," he said. "You tell her to dump him, if she doesn't want to leave it to me to manage. That kind of chap comes into this house by the servants' entrance, or not at all." '

I couldn't help interrupting. 'That sounds rather vulgar for the Lord Claremont I remember.'

Candida nodded. 'You're right. It wasn't him at all. I think he was just so angry that his mental, editing machine had switched itself off. In fairness to Roo, it was too much for her, too, and she slapped him down. She said, "Really, Pel, don't be so idiotic. You sound like a period drama on television. You'll be telling him to get off your land next." When she said that I smiled. I couldn't help myself, but Roo saw it as a breach in the wall and she turned to me in the most coaxing way. "We have nothing against this young man, Candida," she said, and she spoke very calmly, but in a way her calmness was more deadly to Serena's hopes than Pel's fury, as I could tell it was not a mood that might blow away in the morning. "Honestly we don't. He is making an effort to be nice and he is perfectly welcome as a guest. But you must see it's out of the question. The whole thing is simply

502

ludicrous and that's all there is to it." She paused, I assume to let me nod. Which I didn't, so she ploughed on. "Just find a way to tell Serena that we don't think it a good idea. It'll come much better from you. If we tackle her it'll blow up into a hideous production. She's a sensible girl. I'm sure she'll see the wisdom of what we're saying when she's had time to think.' I asked her if they wanted me to tell Serena that night, but she shook her head. "No. Don't spoil the party," she said. "Tell her tomorrow or the next day, before you leave. When you have a quiet moment." Then she waited for a response and I suppose, by being silent, in a way I'd agreed.'

'So did you?'

Again Candida shook her head. 'I didn't have to. That's the point. After we'd all stopped hissing at each other we could hear the sounds of the first batch of people arriving for dinner, and Pel and Roo went down to greet them. I was still sitting in front of the glass, feeling a bit bludgeoned to tell the truth, and I heard a voice. "That's me told." I looked over and Damian was standing there.'

'In your room?'

'Yes.' She nodded, scrunching up her eyes for a second at the memory. 'He was next door, which maybe I'd forgotten, if I even knew. There was a pair of interconnecting doors, those doors that were so useful to the Edwardians, with a space between them, a couple of feet wide, which formed a completely effective sound barrier, and neither Pel nor Roo had shouted, so I wasn't worried. The door was shut and since there was an armchair in front of it I must have assumed that it was locked, that they both were, but they weren't. I suppose he'd been standing in the space between the two doors and now he'd opened the one into my room and come through it. The whole thing was so terrible I can hardly frame the words to describe it. I remember it now, forty years later, as one of the most horrible moments of my entire life, which, believe me, is saying something. We just stared at each other, then eventually I muttered about their not understanding his feelings, and hoping that he wouldn't hate them and all that sort of thing. But Damian shook his head with a brisk little chuckle, and said, "Hate them? Why should I hate them? They've found me out." And I didn't understand him at first, because I'd been so convinced by Serena that he really did love her. So I couldn't believe that he was telling me it wasn't true, that all the time he'd been out to catch her for her money and whatnot. I didn't want to believe him, but that's what he said. He told Serena later on that night, so I didn't have to. She and I talked about it, but only once. And I don't think they saw each other again—except for that one ghastly evening in Portugal, of course. They might have run into each other at some gathering over the years, I suppose, but I never heard her mention it, if they did. He wasn't at any more of the parties that year. He seemed to give us all up after the incident and I can't say I'm surprised.'

'Nor me. When did he tell her?'

'Right at the end. I'm sure he wouldn't have wanted to spoil the evening, but he couldn't have borne for her to hear it from anyone else and I think he'd already decided to leave first thing the next day. I seem to remember that he got her into the Tapestry Drawing Room just before it all

504

folded, but I may have made that up.'

'And he told her it had all been his plan to advance himself and that he didn't love her?'

'I suppose so. I mean yes. Although, even now, I don't think it was ever the whole truth. He might have seen her as a ladder in some way, but I'm sure he was genuinely fond of her.'

'I doubt it was true at all. If he said he loved her I'm sure he did.'

She looked at me, surprised. 'I thought you disliked him.'

'I hated him. I hate him now, really, if marginally less than before. That doesn't mean I think him a liar, which I don't, except under extreme provocation.'

She grimaced. 'As we know.'

But I didn't want to drift away to that other, cursed evening. I wanted to stay with the night of the ball. 'He was lying to you to save face. I wonder that you couldn't see that. She was never going to have much money anyway. If he was after that, he'd have gone for Joanna Langley.'

She blushed. 'You don't think he wanted a grand wife with a title?'

'He wouldn't have cared about it. Not then. Maybe at the beginning, but not by that stage. He turned down Dagmar of Moravia. He could have had a princess for a wife if he'd wanted.'

She thought about this. 'Well, I must have agreed with you at the time, or the whole Portuguese adventure would never have happened. I suppose the years have made me more cynical than I was.'

'Poor Serena. So she'd made her decision to defy her parents and marry her true love, and then, in one short evening, it was finished and there was nothing left for her to do but to go out on to the terrace for some fresh air and to come up with a new life scheme.'

'Did she? You know more about it than I do.'

'Yes, she did. And then she came in again and found me waiting in the anteroom, and we danced together just before I left.' I thought of Serena's blank eyes and her muttered 'these things are such milestones.' She might have said millstones. It would have been just as true.

'I see. Well, perhaps you're right about Damian. I hope so. But he's had his revenge in a way. He ended up a figure of far greater significance than any of the rest of us. I wonder if Pel and Roo ever think about that.'

'You did have a soft spot for him, then?'

'Damian? Oh, absolutely. I adored him. As I told you, we did have a bit of a thing, but it was earlier in the year than all this. Once Damian and Serena got together, I don't remember him being involved with anyone else in our crowd.'

'Until after.'

She blushed, slightly. 'Oh, yes. After. But you know how it is during the lonely years. Before life settles.'

'Can I ask an impertinent question?'

She smiled. 'I think after the talk we've just had I can hardly prevent it.'

'Who was Archie's father? Did I know him? Was he one of the gang from that era? Or was it someone you met when it was over?'

'It's hard to say.'

Which seemed a peculiar reply. 'Do you ever see him now?'

506

'I don't know.' I stared at her, looking, I imagine, fairly puzzled and she laughed. 'These days I'm an old, respectable banker's widow, but it was not always thus. You must know that everyone has some parts of their life that are hard to reconcile with their present.'

I nodded. 'I know it better than most.' And I certainly already knew it about her.

'The truth is I'm not quite sure who Archie's father was. I bounced around a fair bit at that time. I think my excuse was that I'd lost my way or I was trying to find myself, or some other Sixties cliché that allowed me to do as I pleased without feeling guilty, and I took full advantage of the philosophy. Then, one day I woke up pregnant. Every single entry in my address book wanted me to get rid of it, of course, friends and family alike, but I wouldn't and I am terribly grateful now.'

'But you never tried to find out?'

'I didn't see the point. What would I have gained? Someone poking their nose in where it wasn't wanted? Some emotional cripple who felt he had the right to lean on me because I'd carried his child? At one stage I thought it might be George Tremayne. I was pretty sure later that it wasn't, but imagine what it would have been like having him getting sloshed at the kitchen table.' I grimaced. 'So, no. I decided to battle through it alone.'

'How were you sure? That it wasn't George?'

She thought for a moment. 'I heard that he was having trouble getting his wife pregnant. That rather chubby girl whose father made cars. She'd got two children by a first husband, so it couldn't have been her.' She nodded, satisfied with her own

507

conclusions. 'Anyway, having Archie put me back on the straight and narrow. It was a bumpy road for a bit, even if it was straight, and God knows it was narrow. But it led me to Harry.'

'So there was a happy ending.'

She smiled. 'That's so nice. To hear Harry described as my happy ending. These days everyone who says his name bursts into tears. But they're wrong and you're right. He *was* my happy ending. And now,' she stood, stretching herself, 'I really must go to bed or I'll die.'

* * *

I was deep in a dream involving Neil Kinnock and Joan Crawford and a woman who used to work for my mother as a cleaner called Mrs Pointer. We were all trying to have a picnic on Beachy Head, but the tartan rug kept blowing up and spilling everything, and for some reason we couldn't weight it down. Until we decided to lie on it to hold it steady, but how can that have worked and what did we do with the food? Which didn't seem to matter much, as Joan was squeezing into my back and she slid an arm round my waist, letting her hand slide down as she did so, and . . . I woke up. Except I hadn't woken up, because although it was fairly dark and I wasn't at a picnic any more, I could still feel Joan's body pressed into mine and a gentle hand enfolding my erect penis, and then a voice said 'are you awake?' very softly, and it didn't sound at all like Joan's. Not a bit. It wasn't even American. I thought about this for a moment, because the voice was familiar and I felt I should know it but I didn't recognise it until it spoke my name, and suddenly I knew beyond any doubt . . . it was Serena's. It was Serena Belton's voice and she was here beside me, with her hand on my penis. And then I still couldn't believe I wasn't dreaming, because this, after all, was my lifelong dream, and I began to wonder whether I was in a dream within a dream, when you think you've woken up but you haven't. And I might have gone on thinking this for a bit longer if her lips had not nestled into the side of my cheek and I turned, and she was there.

In the flesh. In my arms. In my bed.

'Is this really happening?' I whispered, afraid that if I spoke too loudly the whole mirage would shimmer and disappear. It was very early dawn and the soft, dim, grey light had begun to creep in through the cracks in the curtains, lightening the room just enough for me to make her out, her shining, sacred head on the pillow next to mine.

'It is if you want it to.'

I smiled. 'Do you make a habit of stealing into men's rooms at night?'

'Only when they're in love with me,' she said.

I still could not accept this gift from heaven. 'But why? I know you don't love me. We had a long discussion about it this very afternoon.' Of all things, I didn't want to frighten her away, but I did want to understand.

'I love your love,' she said. 'I don't pretend to share it, and when we were young I doubt that I was much more than amused. But as the years went on and bad things happened, I always knew one man in the world at least loved me. And that was you. Seeing you again reminded me of it.'

'Is that why you got me down here?'

'You make me feel safe. When we met up in Yorkshire I felt glad to see you and that was why. I am safe in your love. I wish we saw more of you. I don't know why we drifted out of each other's lives.'

'I thought it was because of what Damian said.'

She shook her head. 'I knew it was nonsense. I knew it straight away but even more as time went on. He was in pain, that's all.'

'So was I by the end of that dinner.' For the first time in my life, I could envisage a day when I would find it funny.

She stroked my hair, or what was left of it. 'You should have stayed. You both should have stayed on afterwards and laughed.'

'I couldn't.' She did not argue, and together we let the bitter memory go and returned to the glorious present. Suddenly I felt the freedom to touch her surge through me, like a child who finally lets himself believe that it really *is* Christmas morning. I reached up and traced the outline of her lips with my finger.

She kissed it gently as I did so. 'You may not know it, but you have seen me through some dark times and this is your reward.' As she spoke she moved closer and brought her mouth to mine, and we began, as the phrase has it, to make love. And while many times in my life those words have not been an accurate description of the activity they refer to, on that occasion they were as true as the Gospel. What we were making in that bed on that blessed morn was love. Pure love. Nor was there the slightest diminution of passion because the woman in my arms was a matron in her fifties rather than the lissom girl I had hungered for so many years before. She was my Serena at last. I held her in my arms and, for this one time perhaps, I was hers. I had finally arrived at my yearned-for destination. And although I was so aroused by her presence that I thought I would explode at one more touch, still, when I entered her, the sensation that filled me with a hot glow like molten lava was not just sexual excitement but total happiness. It sounds sentimental, which I am not as a rule, but that moment of being inside Serena, of feeling myself held by her body, for the first and presumably the only time in my life, after waiting for forty years, was the single happiest moment I have ever known, the climax, the very peak of my existence, nor do I expect to equal it before the grave claims me.

I do not seek recognition as a skilful lover. I assume I am no better and no worse than most men, but if ever I knew what I was doing that was the day. I dare say I should have felt guilty, but I didn't. Her husband had the gift of her whole, adult life and he would never know the value of it. I did, and I felt that I deserved my hour without enraging too many of the gods. I am glad and relieved to relate that my tired, fat, flabby body rose to the challenge of the chance of paradise and never have I been so entirely engrossed in the present to the exclusion of all else. For those minutes I had no future and no past, only her. We made love three times before she slipped away, and when I stared at the gathered silk canopy above my head I knew I was a different man from the one who had lain down to sleep. I had made love to a woman I was absolutely and entirely in love with. The woman who held my heart had opened her body to the rest of me. There is no greater joy allowed us. Not on earth. And, in echo of Candida, I knew, because of that single episode, because of this one hour in a life of many years, because I had known real, unconditional bliss I could never again be a sad man. I thought it then, I think it now, and I am grateful. If Damian's search led me to this, then I was paid in full and far in excess of any mortal man's deserts.

Portugal and After

FIFTEEN

As it happened, the fateful invitation to Portugal came right out of the blue. One day the telephone rang in my parents' flat—where I was, on the principle of Hobson's choice, still living—and when I picked it up a familiar voice asked for me by name. 'Speaking,' I said.

'That was easy. I thought I was going to have to track you down through ten addresses. It's Candida. Candida Finch.'

'Hello.' I could not keep the surprise out of my voice entirely, since we had never been all that friendly.

'I know. Why am I ringing? Well, it's an invitation, really. Is there any chance I could tempt you to join a gang of us in Estoril for a couple of weeks at the end of July? An old friend of mine has got a job in Lisbon, in some bank or other, and they've given him this huge villa and no one to put in it. He says if we can all just get ourselves out there, we can stay as long as we like for nothing. So I thought it might be fun to mount a sort of reunion of the Class of Sixty-eight, before we've all forgotten what we look like. What do you say?' My surprise was not lessened by any of this, as I wasn't aware that I'd ever been a favourite of hers while the Season was going on, let alone why I should be chosen for a special reunion.

I had not seen Candida Finch much after the whole thing came to an end and by the time of the call almost two years had passed since the events I have been revisiting. It was in the early summer of

1970, when my days as a dancing partner were long behind me. I had left Cambridge that June, with a perfectly respectable if not overwhelming degree, and the perilous career of a writer beckoned. Or at least it did not beckon, because I soon realised that I was trying to push through a solid, brick wall. My father was not hostile to my plan, once he had got over his disappointment that I wasn't going to do anything sensible, but he declined to support me economically. 'If it isn't going to work, old boy,' he said genially, 'we'd better find out sooner rather than later,' which was, of course, in its way, a direct challenge. Eventually I got a job as a kind of super office boy in a publishing group for children's magazines, which would begin in the following September and for which I would be paid a handsome stipend that would have comfortably maintained a Yorkshire terrier. I did go on to do the job, for three years in fact, finally clambering up to some sort of junior editing post, and somehow I managed to make ends meet. My mother used to cheat, as mothers will; she would slip me notes and pay for clothes and pick up my bills for petrol and car repairs, but even she would not actually give me a regular allowance, as she would have felt disloyal to my father. Let us say that during this period of my time on earth I lived, I survived, but it was essentially a life without frills or extras. All of which harsh reality I knew would be my fate at the end of that summer and it made Candida's suggestion seem rather inviting.

'That's incredibly kind of you. Who else is coming?' Of course, I knew as I said this that I had to accept, because you can't ask who is coming to some event and then refuse. Inevitably it sounds as if you might have accepted if the guest list had been of a higher standard.

Candida knew this. 'I think we'll have fun. We've got Dagmar and Lucy and the Tremayne brothers.' I wasn't mad about the Tremaynes, but I didn't actually hate them, and I was actively fond of the other two, so the idea was growing on me. I knew there wasn't the smallest chance I would otherwise have a proper holiday that year before I started what I liked to call my 'career.' 'I've found a charter airline where they almost pay you, so the tickets will cost about sixpence. Can I definitely include you in?'

I am ashamed to say this settled it. I was confident I could get my dear mama to sub a cheap ticket, so all I would need was pocket money and a couple of clean shirts, and I would have ten days of luxury in the sun. I was pleased by the idea of seeing Lucy and Dagmar, and even Candida too, for that matter, all of whom I had not caught up with for a long while. 'Yes. I'm in,' I said.

'Good. I'll make the reservations and send you the bumph. There is one thing . . .' She tailed off for a brief pause, as if choosing her words, and then continued, 'We're a bit short of men. The trouble is so many of them have already started working and it's hard for them to get away without notice. I have been slightly scraping the barrel.'

'As witness the inclusion of the Tremaynes.'

'Don't be unkind. George is all right.' This made me wonder briefly if Lord George was planning to take advantage of Candida in some way, but I couldn't think how.

'But if I come, won't we be three of each?'

Obviously, she hadn't done her maths and this

momentarily threw her. 'Yes. I suppose we will . . .' She hesitated. I could almost hear her sucking her teeth.

I decided to help. 'But you'd rather have extra in case someone drops out.'

'That's it. I hate it when the men are outnumbered.'

'What about Sam Hoare?'

'Working.'

'Philip Rawnsley-Price?'

'Ugh.' She laughed and began again. 'The fact is I was wondering if you might ask, you know, what's his name, Damian Baxter. Your pal from Cambridge who used to come to all the dances.' The studied casualness of this request told me it had been a long-term part of the scheme. I didn't answer at once and she came in again. 'Of course, if it's a nuisance—'

'No, no.' I had, after all, nothing specific against Damian then. He had been more successful than I with Serena and I resented it. But that was all I knew at the time. The worst I could have accused him of was enjoying a flirtation with her. More to the point, neither of us had got her in the end. To our, I assume, joint horror she had married Andrew Summersby in April of the previous year and in the following March, three months before this conversation, she had given birth to a daughter. In other words she had moved far, far away from us by now. 'All right, I'll try,' I said.

'You don't think he'll want to.'

'I don't know. He dropped out of the Season so completely that there might be a principle involved.'

'You haven't discussed it?'

518

'We haven't discussed anything. I hardly saw him after your dance.'

'But you didn't quarrel?'

'Oh, no. We just didn't see each other.'

'Well, you haven't seen me either and we haven't quarrelled.'

I didn't know why I was putting up such resistance. 'All right. You're on. I'll give it a go. I'm not sure if the numbers I've got still work for him but I'll do my best.'

'Excellent. Thanks.' She seemed a little brighter. 'OK. Let me know what he says and we will take steps accordingly.'

Things were more complicated in the years before mobiles. Whenever anyone moved you'd lost them, although one hoped only temporarily. Nor did we have answering machines, so if people were out they were out. Then again, we managed. However, when I looked in my old address book I found I still had Damian's parents' number and they were quite happy to provide me with the new number for his flat in London, which he'd apparently just moved into. 'I'm very impressed,' I said. And I was, actually.

'So are we,' I could hear that his mother was smiling as she spoke. 'He's on his way, is our Damian.'

I repeated this to Damian when I dialled the number and he picked up. 'I'm sharing a rented flat at the wrong end of Vauxhall, even supposing there's a right end. I am still some way from Businessman of the Year.'

'It all sounds quite advanced to me. Have you found a job already?'

'I fixed it before I left Cambridge.' He

mentioned some dizzying, American bank. 'They were recruiting and . . . they recruited me.' I was suitably awestruck. One thing I have learned in life: Those who get to the top tend to start at the top. 'I begin at the end of August,' he said.

'So do I, but I suspect in less style.' I explained about my lowly job as whipping boy in the magazine offices. We fell silent. I suspect that for both of us the exchange had only served to underline the extent to which we had lost touch while still at university. Damian had not only dropped out of the Season, but also out of my life, and I don't believe I had fully appreciated it before that moment.

I explained the reason for my call. 'I don't know.' He didn't sound keen.

'I told Candida I thought you might have had enough of us.'

'I always liked Candida.' I was quite surprised by this. I never took notice of their friendship at the time, but then, how much had I noticed? Although I couldn't help feeling that if Candida had known how she was remembered she would have rung him directly and not bothered with me. He spoke again. 'OK. Why not? After paying my deposit here and buying the clothes I need to work in I haven't a penny left, so there's no chance of any other holiday this year.'

'My position entirely.' I was a little surprised by his acceptance, maybe, but on the whole pleased. It seemed to offer an opportunity to take us past the slightly odd end to our friendship and to give us the chance to go our separate ways after the summer more peacefully.

'Did you go to the wedding?' he said.

I'd wondered how long it would take him to ask. 'Yes.'

'I didn't.'

'I know.'

'I was asked.' He needed me to hear that his absence had been his choice, not hers. 'Have you seen the baby?'

'Once. She's the image of Andrew.'

'Lucky girl.' He snorted derisively, trying to make a joke out of the sorrow we shared but did not admit. 'Right. Send me the arrangements when you've got them and I will see you in the sun.' The conversation was over.

The villa, when we arrived, was on the coast, wedged between Estoril and Cascais. I dare say it is much more built up now but then, thirty-eight years ago, there were only rocks below its terrace, leading directly to a wide and glorious, sandy beach and, beyond it, the sea. It couldn't really have been better. The house was built, along with two or three others stretching along the coast in those pre-planning days, during the 1950s and it consisted of a large, main room—one cannot call it a drawing room, full as it was of rattan furniture and the like—as well as a dining room/hall, which took up the whole of the entrance front, with a mass of kitchens behind. These we hardly penetrated, since they were full of busy, Portuguese women who always looked cross whenever we went in. The bedrooms were arranged on two floors, ground and first, in a long wing that stretched away from behind the main block at a rightangle. Each room had its own bathroom and high French windows opening upstairs on to a balcony with an outside staircase leading down, and on the ground floor directly on to a wide, balustraded terrace overlooking the sea.

Our host was a genial fellow, John Dalrymple, something of an egghead who would later play a role in Mrs Thatcher's government, but I never knew what, exactly. Given his straightness, his girlfriend was a little unlikely, a neurotic, American blonde with snuffles, complaining constantly of a sore throat. Her name was Alicky, which I assume was a shortening of Alexandra, although that was not confirmed. I remember her better than I might have, because she was the first person I knew to be in a permanent state about the poisons being put into our food by the government and how the whole world was about to implode. At the time we thought her a five-star whacko, but looking back, I suppose in a way she was ahead of her time. It was she who had decided that for reasons of security, although few people thought like that in those days, the girls would sleep upstairs and the boys down below, giving us the advantage of the French windows that opened on to the terrace and the wonderful view of the sea. My bedroom, at the far end of the wing, had that familiar, clean, sea-smelling feeling, with the pale tiled floor, the wicker furniture, the white covers and curtains, that always tells you this is a summer place. I sometimes wonder why attempts to reproduce this room back in England are invariably a failure. Probably because it does not work in the northern light.

I had flown in on the same plane as Candida, Dagmar and Lucy, but in the event, Damian had not travelled with us. He was already there and in his room, changing, when we arrived so we all set off to do the same. The Tremaynes had been staying in Paris and had driven across Spain in order to continue their holiday for nothing. They too were recovering in private, which meant that it was not until we all gathered on the terrace an hour or two later, the girls in their splendid, summer colours, me in my underwhelming, Englishman's 'summer casual wear,' which always makes us look as if we're aching to get back into a suit (which most of us are), that the party finally assembled, and it was a very nice way to begin. John had arranged for us all to be given glasses of champagne, while he explained the plan for the first evening, which was for the whole party to jump into cars and head for the Moorish ruins at Cintra, a little way along the coast, and have a picnic dinner there. It seemed a very appropriate, opening adventure.

Cintra is a magical place, or it was then. I have not seen it since. At some point in the nineteenth century a presumably unbalanced Bragança king had built a huge, turreted castle on the hilltop, more suited to Count Dracula than a constitutional monarchy, while a little way beyond, making the place even more special and strange and complementing the Disneyesque splendours of the Royal palace, there was a long extended ruin of a fortified, Moorish stronghold, running from hill to hill, which had been abandoned by the retreating hordes during the Middle Ages. On that summer night this pair of monuments to two forgotten empires made richly cinematic outlines against the sky, as the sun sank in the west.

What I had gathered since our arrival was that John Dalrymple was very bored in his posting, though whether this was the bank's fault or, more probably, because of his choice of romantic companion I could not say. Either way, he was only too delighted to have some people to entertain. He and Candida seemed to go back quite far, though as friends not lovers, and it was clear from this, our first 'moment' of the stay, that nothing was too much trouble. A table had been set up beneath the castle walls among some trees—olives, perhaps? I picture them in my mind as twisted and scraggy, seemingly clinging to life in the dusty soil. Candle lanterns had been hung among the rather threadbare branches, and rugs and cushions strewn about, making the whole thing into the feast of some Arab emperor. We took our drinks and walked about among the outskirts of the ruins, where stray blocks and lumps of stone had rolled over the centuries. The Tremaynes were there, a little improved, I thought, from when I'd known them, poised as they were on the brink of City careers that had been conjured up out of nothing by some friends of their papa, and they were hovering attentively round Dagmar. Lucy was talking to Alicky and John.

A little way away, Damian walked arm in arm with Candida. When I glanced across at them, with a sinking heart I could see a trace of her terrifying, Gorgon-like, flirtatious manner beginning to surface. He made some no doubt blameless remark, which was greeted by her roar of a laugh, which made everyone look up to see her eyes rolling in her head in what I suspect she thought a beguiling and intriguing way. As usual, when it came to matters of this kind, her taste let her down. Damian began to give telltale glances to

524

anyone who'd pick them up, seeking an escape route. Even so, it seemed very peaceful, as if we were all in the right place at the right time. Which would prove quite ironic before we were finished. At that moment a bell was rung, announcing that we were to help ourselves to the first course, so we drifted up to the table, and, laden with plates, glasses and all the rest of the paraphernalia, we found our way over to the cushions. Lucy plonked down next to me. 'What are you up to now?' I asked. I hadn't heard much about many of the girls and nothing at all of her.

She made a slight mouth movement as she paused in her eating. 'I'm helping a friend with a gallery in Fulham.'

'What does it show?'

'Oh, you know. Stuff.' I wasn't convinced this was the language of complete commitment. 'Our next thing is to launch some Polish guy, whose pictures look to me as if he'd stuck a canvas at the end of a garage and thrown tins of paint at it, but Corinne says it's more complicated than that and they're all to do with his anger against Communism.' Lucy shrugged lightly. I noticed her clothes were more hippie'ish than when I saw her last, with an Indian shirt under a worn, embroidered waistcoat and different layers of shawls or stoles or something, leaking out over her jeans, until it was quite hard to know whether she was wearing trousers or a skirt. Both, I suppose. 'What about you?' I explained the dismal job awaiting me. 'I do think you're lucky. Knowing what you want to do.'

'I'm not sure my father would agree with you.'

'No, I mean it. I wish I knew what I want to do. I

thought I might travel for a bit, but I don't know.' She stretched and yawned. 'Everything's such a palaver.'

'It depends what you want from life generally.'

'That's the thing. I'm not sure. Not some boring husband going in and out of the City, while I give dinners and drive to the country on Friday morning to open up the house.' She spoke, as people do when they make this sort of statement, as if her low opinion of the life she outlined was an absolute *donné* among right-thinking people, when the reality is that for women like Lucy to live a very different life from the one she had described is hard. They may do a hippie version of it, with bunches of herbs hanging down from the kitchen ceiling and unmade beds and artist friends turning up unannounced for the weekend, but the difference between this and the arrangements of their more formal sisters, who meet their guests off preordained trains, and make them dress for dinner and come to church, is pretty minimal when you get down to it. Apart from anything else, the guests of both types of parties are almost always closely related by blood. But Lucy hadn't finished. 'I just want to do something different, to live somehow differently and never to stop living differently. I suppose I'm a follower of Chairman Mao. I want to live in a state of permanent revolution.'

'That's not for me.' We had been joined by Dagmar, who settled down on a nearby, paisley cushion and dragged a rug over her knees, before she got down to her food. The night was beginning to hint that it would not stay warm forever. 'In fact, I don't agree with Lucy's definition of the fate

526

to be avoided above all others. I wouldn't mind going to the country to open up the house on Friday. But I want to do something in the world myself, as well. Something useful. I don't just want to be a wife, I want to be a person.' In this one may gauge that the 1960s philosophies had begun to get into their rhythm in the last years of the decade and that they had done their work on the princess from the Balkans. She'd caught the classic disease of the era, that of needing permanently to occupy the moral high ground. As a philosophy it could be exhausting, and it would be for most of us, when every soap star and newsreader would have to prove that all they cared about was the good of others, but here, on that Portuguese night, I didn't see much harm in it.

'What?' I said with fake astonishment. 'A princess of the House of Ludinghausen-Anhalt-Zerbst with a proper job?'

She sighed. 'That's the point. My mother doesn't want me to work, but I've started doing things for various charities, which even she can't object to, and I'm hoping to build from there. And when Mr Right comes along, always assuming that he does, I know he won't fight my having an identity of my own because I won't marry him if he does. I don't want to be a silent wife.' She had been a pretty silent debutante, so I was quite touched listening to her. 'I want to feel . . . well, I'll say it again: Useful.' Then I noticed, to my amazement, that as she was outlining this scenario of modern certainties her eyes were following Damian. I saw that he had managed to unload Candida on to our hosts, John and Alicky, where she was trapped by her own good manners, while he helped himself to some more food at the table under the trees. He finished heaping his plate and turned, surveying the company, and at that moment both Dagmar and Lucy raised their hands and waved. He saw us and came over, making our group into a foursome.

'We're discussing our futures,' I said. 'Lucy wants to be a wild child and Dagmar a missionary. What about you?'

'I just want my life to be perfect,' he replied with complete sincerity.

'And what would make it perfect?' asked Dagmar, timidly.

Damian thought for a minute. 'Well. Let me see. First, money. So I mean to make plenty of that.'

'Very good.' This was a chorus from all of us and we meant it.

'Then a perfect woman, who loves me as I love her, and together we will make a perfect child, and we will live in high state and be the envy of everyone who sets eyes on us.'

'You don't want much,' I said.

'I want what is due to me.' I remember this sentence quite distinctly because, while there are many people who say such things in jest, there are very few who seem really to believe them. In this case time would bear out his pretensions.

'What constitutes a perfect woman?' This again from Dagmar.

Damian thought. 'Beauty and brains, of course.'

'And birth?' I was surprised to hear Lucy ask that.

He considered this. 'Birth, inasmuch as she will have style and grace and sophistication and knowledge of the world. But she will not be

528

hemmed in by her birth. She will not be oppressed by it. She will not allow her parents or her dead ancestors to dictate what she says or does. She will be free and, if necessary, she will break with every human being she has ever loved before me and cleave to my side.'

'I never know what "cleave" means in that context,' I mused. But nobody was interested in my query.

The two girls, both of whom I could now see were vying for the vacant position in Damian's mind, at least as far as this conversation went, pondered his words. 'She certainly should, if she's got anything to her,' said Lucy, which gave her an immediate advantage.

'It's hard to throw off everything of value,' countered Dagmar, but then she faltered. 'I mean, if you think it has value.' Damian seemed to nod, as if giving her permission to continue. 'And it's hard to throw off people you love, people who may deserve your love. Would your perfect woman be true to herself if she broke away from her roots, entirely?'

'I am asking a lot,' he said thoughtfully. By considering his answer, Damian was treating Dagmar with respect and Lucy thereby lost the initiative. 'Nor am I defending my demands, which may be thoroughly unreasonable. But I am telling you what I would need to know she could do if it came to it.'

Then Dagmar said, 'I think she could if she had to, but I'm just pointing out it would be hard.'

'I never said it wouldn't.'

Obviously, I missed the significance of all this at the time because, as we all now know, I was almost completely ignorant of much of what had gone on over the Season two years before, but I have since learned that this interchange was the preamble to Dagmar's last night of fantasy that she could be Damian's dream woman. I hope she enjoyed it.

Over the next couple of days we drifted, getting up late, swimming, eating at long tables set out on the terrace under a line of umbrellas, and going for walks in the village—doing, in fact, what people like us do best: Taking advantage of other people's money. But then, the following Monday, 27 July to be precise, we awoke to hear the startling news that Antonio de Oliveira Salazar, ex-Prime Minister of Portugal, founder of the Estado Novo—which, with Spain, had been the last Fascist state of Western Europe—had died in the night at the age of eighty-one.

'This is incredible,' I said as the party began to gather for breakfast on the terrace, pulling fruit from great piles set out for our delight, pouring coffee, buttering toast. I had thought the announcement would have stilled the table. Not so.

'Why?' asked George Tremayne.

'Because the last of the dictators, who shaped the middle of the century, who fought the war, who changed the world, is dead. Hitler, Stalin, Mussolini, Primo de Rivera . . .'

'Franco's still alive,' said Richard Tremayne. 'So now he'll be the last of them to die.'

Which was, of course, a point. 'Nevertheless, it is extraordinary that we should be in Portugal, just outside Lisbon, when he went.' I was not going to give up easily. 'The newspapers say he's going to lie in state in Lisbon Cathedral for a few days.

Obviously, we must all queue up and go.'

'To do what?' said George.

'To walk past his body. This is a historic moment.'

I turned to Damian for support, but he just helped himself to some more milk for his cornflakes.

I am not sure quite what it tells us about the battle of the sexes but in the event all the girls came and none of the other men. Naturally, they didn't have anything suitable to wear, and they borrowed black skirts and shawls and mantillas from the furious women in the kitchen, but they all came, including Alicky, despite her continuing complaints throughout the pilgrimage about her swelling and painful throat, of which we had heard more than enough by this point.

That said, the advantage of having Alicky with us was that she was able to be very stern with the driver, one of John's perks from the bank, who deposited us on the edge of the huge piazza in front of the cathedral, telling him exactly where he was to wait and, no, she couldn't give him an idea of how long we were going to be. In the lengthening shadows of the late afternoon we took up our positions in the endless line of shuffling, morose men and weeping women. Apart from anything else, I was impressed, or intrigued, or something, by the sorrow on display. I had been accustomed to think of Salazar as the last of the wicked old buffers who had plunged Europe into bloody turmoil, and here was a wide cross section of the Portuguese, from nobles to peasants (the last constituting the people who might have had the greatest right to complain against his rule), all openly sobbing at his departure. I suppose it's always hard to give up what you're used to.

'Candida?' The voice cut through me like a bacon slicer. I knew it as well as I knew my own without turning round, and I could not believe I was hearing it, in this ancient sea capital so far from home. 'Candida, what on earth are you doing here?' At this we all turned to greet Serena as she walked across the square, dragging a rather hot-looking Lady Claremont and the dreaded Lady Belton in her wake. In their party too the men were not interested in politics. Seeing all our faces, Serena let out a short scream. 'My God! What is this? I don't believe it! Why on earth are you all here?' We then embarked on an explanation and it turned out that, by an unbelievable coincidence, her own parents had taken one of the other villas in the development where ours lay, that they had invited Andrew's parents, that they'd arrived the day before and they would be staying for the coming week, and . . . wasn't it *amazing?*

I need hardly tell you that, as it turned out, it was not amazing. It was not in the least amazing. It was not even a coincidence. The scheme, which I did not uncover for some time after this and then only because I ran into George Tremayne at a race meeting three or four summers later, had originated with Serena, who wanted to see Damian again. Even when I heard the truth from George I didn't understand quite why (although I do now), but it was anyway important to her. John had been asking Candida to bring out a group of friends for some time, that bit was true, and they decided that if Candida could get Damian into the group, Serena and Andrew would, by coincidence, take a villa nearby. Obviously, Damian would not come if Serena were to be in the party, nor would Andrew if Damian was, so the subterfuge was necessary, once you accepted the intention. Where the plan might be said to have gone awry was that Serena's parents, perhaps suspicious in some way, had announced they would bear the cost of the trip and join them. This Andrew would not allow Serena to refuse, since it was such a saving. The final button came when Lady Belton suggested that she and her benighted husband also come along, as she would 'welcome the chance to know the Claremonts better.' I never found out what would have happened if Damian had refused when I asked him. I imagine the whole thing would just have been cancelled. However, at the time, I suspected nothing. I thought the chance meeting was genuine chance, a heaven-sent miracle that Serena Gresham—correction, Serena *Summersby* —should be standing in a sun-drenched, southern square, also wearing ill-fitting, borrowed black and waiting to pay homage to a dead tyrant alongside me. I allowed myself to wonder at her properly. 'How are you?' I asked.

'Frazzled and worn out. Take my advice. Don't travel with your parents, your in-laws and your two-month-old baby, in the same party.'

'I'll remember that.' I looked at her. She was quite unchanged. That my golden girl was now a wife and mother seemed more or less impossible to believe. 'How are you getting on?'

She glanced swiftly across at Lady Belton, but the old trout was busily snubbing some tourist who'd attempted to strike up a conversation and enjoying it too much to notice us. 'All right.' Then, sensing that her answer had not sounded like the voice of love's young dream, she smiled. 'My life's terribly grown up now. You wouldn't believe it was me. I spend the whole time talking to plumbers and having things covered, and asking Andrew whether he's done the sales tax.'

'But you're happy?'

We did not need to exchange a glance to know that, with this question, I was pushing my luck. 'Of course I am,' she said.

'Where is Andrew?'

She shrugged. 'Back at the villa. He says he's not interested in history.'

'This isn't history, it's history in the making.'

'What can I tell you? He's not interested.'

To the fury of the people behind us, we stuffed Serena, her mother and her mother-in-law into our group, and together we all staggered up the cathedral steps. From there we passed into the cool, shadowed interior of the great church, where the sounds of crying were more audible and, as they echoed through the aisles and cloisters, curiously haunting. Grief is always grief, whether or not the deceased deserves it. At last we walked past the coffin. The head was covered in some sort of scarf, but the hands, waxy and still, were pressed together as if in prayer, raised and resting on the chest of the corpse. 'I wonder how they do that,' said Serena. 'Do you think they've got a special thing?'

I stared at the body. It was dressed, as are all dictators in death apparently, in a rather nasty, lightweight suit that looked as if it had come from Burton Tailoring. 'What I can never get over,' I whispered, 'is the way the moment people are dead, they look as if they've been dead for a thousand years. As if they were never alive.'

Serena nodded. 'It's enough to make you believe in God,' she said.

Once outside again the plan was made. The Claremonts, the Beltons and the Summersbys would go home now to change, and they would all join us for dinner in a couple of hours back at the villa. Full of this pleasant scenario, we climbed into the waiting vehicles.

I now think I must share a little of the blame for what happened later as, for some reason which in retrospect seems completely inexplicable, I never mentioned to Damian that we had run into Serena. In my defence, I knew very little, if anything, of what I have since learned had gone on between them. I knew they'd kissed once and I genuinely thought that was about it, but even so it does seem odd. I did not consciously conceal it, because when we got back Damian was nowhere to be seen. He had not, we heard from Lucy, slept well the previous night and he'd retired to catch up so as to be on form for dinner. 'Don't let's wake him,' said Dagmar firmly and we didn't. Clearly, I should have gone to his room, propped his eyes open and told him what I knew, but I was not aware of the urgency and I suppose I imagined I would catch him before the others arrived. Then, a little later, Lucy volunteered to go and tell him, and before we could discuss it she'd vanished, leaving Dagmar biting her lip. At the time I did suspect Lucy's ultimate purpose in going to Damian's bedroom, but not that she would make no mention of the meeting at the cathedral, the dinner that was planned for that evening, or Serena. Which proved to be the case.

There was one more surprise in store, on this most surprising of all days—before the Big Surprise later that is—which John greeted us with when we got back. 'There was a call from a friend of yours,' he said as we walked out on to the terrace. Naturally I, and presumably the rest, thought this would be from Serena, making some change to the evening's schedule. John disabused us: 'Joanna de Yong? Is that the name?'

Candida was astonished. 'Joanna de Yong?' she said. 'Where was she ringing from?'

'She's here. She's staying with her husband and her parents quite nearby. They arrived today.' He was smiling as if he were bringing us glad tidings, but the response was not what he'd anticipated.

We all looked at each other in silence. Wasn't this too mad? Was Estoril the only holiday destination of choice? It was developing into a Russian play. I do vividly remember the oddness of all this, which later got buried beneath the horror. Dagmar commented at the time that it seemed as if we had arranged a modest reunion, and Fate had decided to get in on the act and bring everyone of significance from that period on to the stage at once. In other words she was as innocent as I was about what was taking place behind the scenes. At last Lucy spoke. 'What did she want?' She was always less a fan of Joanna than some, as I remembered well.

John was clearly a little undermined by the response to his news. 'Only to see you all. I've invited her and her husband over for dinner. I hope that's all right. She asked who was staying and she seemed to know every name, so I thought you'd be pleased.' He stopped, hesitant, afraid he'd made a boo-boo.

'Of course we're pleased,' said Candida. But she wasn't very, and now I know why. The planned, and morally dubious, dinner for Serena to re-meet Damian already had to absorb Serena's parents and in-laws, which was less than ideal. Now it was beginning to expand into a state banquet.

'She's bringing her parents,' said John.

Which put the tin lid on it. 'Jesus,' said Lucy and she spoke for most of the company.

Naturally, as you will have surmised, the de Yong arrival had nothing to do with chance either, and I learned about this strange turn of events much sooner than I did the other. I was still changing when there was a knock on the door and without waiting for permission from me Joanna came in. Without a hello, in fact without a word, she lay down on the bed with a loud sigh. 'I don't know what we're all doing here,' she said.

'Having a lovely time?' I had not seen her since the end of 1968's festivities but she was still a miracle to look at.

'You wish.' She stared up at me, rolling her eyes, as I waited for her to explain herself. 'My mother fixed the whole thing without any reference to me, you know.'

'Obviously, I don't know. What are you talking about?'

'I'd rung Serena—'

'Do you keep up with her?'

She caught my surprise and smiled. 'Not everyone's dropped me.'

'I'm sure not.'

She received this with a quizzical expression,

537

suited to humouring the slow witted. 'Anyway, she told me she was going to Portugal with her parents. And that Candida would be here at the same time with some friends, including you and Damian.'

'Really?' This didn't quite square with the scene we had just enacted in Lisbon outside the cathedral, but before I had time to investigate it Joanna ran on. The silly thing is I recall her remark now, clearly, but I forgot it at the time, so I still failed to add two and two and get to four.

'For some unexplained and foolish reason I relayed all this to my mother and, lo and behold, a week ago she informed me that she'd planned a surprise for me and she'd taken a villa in Estoril. Obviously, I told her it was quite impossible.'

'But?'

'But she blubbed and blubbed, and sighed and fell about, and asked why I hated her, and hadn't she tried to help me since the marriage, and now they'd paid a fortune for the villa because they'd jumped the queue and all the rest of it, and I gave in.' She was holding a bottle of Coca-Cola, the old, rather pretty, glass type, and she took a long, lazy swig.

'I'm glad you did. It's nice to see you.'

She shrugged. 'She thinks I'm bored with Kieran. She thinks she can wean me off him with all of you as bait. You're here to remind me of the fun I'm missing. That's why she's brought us. She even asked if I would be glad to see Damian again.' She threw back her head and laughed out loud. 'Damian. Two years ago she wanted to commit suicide when she thought I was serious about him.'

And still I didn't put the information together: Serena knew Damian was coming all along. What was the matter with me? 'Poor Kieran,' I said. I had in fact met Kieran de Yong by that stage, as some weeks after the sensational elopement there was a cocktail party at the Dorchester for the newly-weds in an attempt by Valerie Langley to normalise the situation. I admit I didn't quite get the point of him then. But I was young and anyway I don't remember thinking any the worse of Joanna for her choice. There is, after all, no accounting for taste. 'How is marriage?'

'It's OK,' she said. But then, after a pause, 'It does go on a bit.' Which sounded uncomfortably eloquent. I said nothing.

'Have you seen Damian yet?'

She shook her head. 'He's still in his room. We were far too early. My mother's impatience wouldn't let us wait. This is the world she always wanted for me and she thinks Kieran is the reason I've dropped out of it. According to her I'm drowning. Socially. She wants to pull me back to the shore. She wants a divorce as soon as it can be arranged.'

'You can't be serious.' It's hard to explain how outlandish this seemed in 1970. Even ten years later it would have been perfectly believable.

'Oh, but I am. She thinks if I dump Kieran now, everyone will forget about him. We've had no kids, despite going at it like rabbits.' She paused to register that I was a little shocked. It's odd to think one could be by such references when they came from a woman, but lots of us were. Having registered my blushes with a blush of her own, she continued, 'The point is, if she can prise me free

539

now, there'll be no baggage that can't be safely hidden inside the identity of my second husband, whoever he may be.'

'And she'd be happy with Damian?'

'After Kieran, she'd be happy with a passing Chinese laundryman.'

I smiled. Although, to be honest, in a way I was rather impressed with Valerie Langley's commitment. I knew that in similar circumstances my own parents would just have shrugged and sighed, and occasionally allowed only *very* old friends to commiserate, but it would never have occurred to either of them actually to *do* anything about it. It wasn't that I approved of the plan. Joanna had, after all, taken her vows and in those days that meant rather more than it does in these. But still, it certainly didn't make me dislike her parents. 'What does your father feel about it?'

'He quite likes Kieran, but he wasn't consulted.'

'And Kieran is here?'

She nodded. 'And he knows exactly what she's trying to do.'

'Yikes.' Of course, we hadn't touched on the nub of the matter. 'Are you going to allow yourself to give him up?'

She thought about my question, but I don't think there was any real doubt in her mind. 'No,' she said. 'I wouldn't give her the satisfaction.'

Kieran de Yong was the first person I spotted when I finally emerged to join the thrash. It would have been hard to miss him. His hair was dyed a particularly virulent shade of pinkish blond and he was wearing tight jeans under a kind of military jacket, which looked as if it had once graced an officer in the Guards, but the cuffs were now turned back to reveal a pink satin lining. His densely patterned shirt was wide open at the neck, to reveal two or three thick chains. The overall effect was not so much hideous as pathetic and, given what I had just heard, I felt very sorry for him. 'Do you know Portugal at all?' I asked, trying to make it sound as if I were interested in the answer.

He shook his head. 'No.'

Lucy had joined us and she tried next: 'Where are you and Joanna living now?'

'Pimlico.'

We were both rather flummoxed, since obviously we could not simply stand and ask him questions, receiving one-word answers, until the end of the evening. But then he said something that indicated he was a little less dense than we had all assumed: 'I know what this is all about. She thinks I don't, but I do. And I'm not leaving.'

Naturally, Lucy hadn't a clue as to the meaning of this, but I did and I rather handed it to him for agreeing to come at all. It was the decision of a brave man. I couldn't very well comment without getting myself into a mess, but I smiled and filled his glass and attempted to establish that I was not an enemy.

There was still no sign of Damian. I registered that his windows remained tightly shut, just as I heard a flurry of arriving cars, followed by voices and doors opening and shutting, and out on to the terrace issued the whole Claremont/Belton party. Serena had brought the baby girl and there was a certain amount of fussing attendant on her arrival. I suggested they put the cot in my room, since it opened directly on to the terrace where we would

541

be eating, and this was generally reckoned a good idea. It saddened me to see that the infant, Mary, was still the living image of Andrew. Not only did this seem like thoroughly bad luck for her, but it also gave rise to painful images in my semi-conscious mind.

To mark his distance from all this 'women's business,' Lord Claremont hailed me in his vague and cheerful way. I think he was relieved to find a familiar face and also to have escaped from the exclusive company of his daughter's in-laws, since I could tell at once they weren't at all his type, however he may have urged the marriage. He started to walk towards me, but the temptations of Joanna and Lucy soon drew him in that direction for a little flirtation over his sangria, or whatever the Portuguese equivalent is called. The Beltons clung together, staring out to sea, she too difficult and he too tired to talk to anyone else. Lady Claremont walked across. 'How are you?' She smiled. I told her. 'So you're forging off into an artistic life. How exciting.'

'My parents don't approve either.'

This made her laugh. 'It's not that. I rather like the idea. It just seems so terribly unpredictable. But if you don't mind a few years starving in a garret, I'm sure it's the right thing to do. One must always try to follow one's heart.'

'I quite agree. And there are worse things than starving in a garret.' By chance, as I said this my eyes were resting on Serena, who was talking to Candida by the balustrade. Now this was purely because I couldn't find anywhere more satisfactory to rest my eyes than on her, but I could see at once that Lady Claremont had taken my comment as a

542

criticism of Serena's life choices, for which she no doubt felt extra responsible, as well she might. Her face hardened a little as she looked back at me and her smile became fractionally taut.

'You must go down and see Serena and Andrew. They've got the *most* marvellous set-up, a simply lovely farmhouse on the edge of the estate. Serena is all geared up to decorate it, which she loves, and the village is within walking distance. It's ideal. Do you know Dorset?'

'Not really. I used to go to Lulworth when I was a child.'

'It's *such* a beautiful place, really enchanting, and still almost a secret from the outside world. She's too lucky for any words.'

'I'm glad,' I said. It was somehow important for me that Lady Claremont should know I didn't want to make trouble. 'I'm very fond of Serena.'

She laughed again, more easily, relieved to have passed the sticky corner. 'Oh, my dear boy,' she said, 'we all know *that*.'

It was then that I heard the doors open behind me and I looked round to find Damian standing there, the darkened room behind him throwing him into a kind of high relief. He was completely motionless, but I did not need to be told where his gaze had fastened. Some of the others had registered him too. Not least Lord Claremont, whose brow visibly darkened. If he'd had any suspicions as to what this was all about, his worst ones were in this instant confirmed. He shot a glance at his wife and I noticed her give a tiny, almost indiscernible shake of her head. Damian's silent stillness was becoming a little embarrassing, so I walked over. 'Isn't it extraordinary?' I said.

543

'Serena's parents have taken more or less the next-door villa. We all ran into each other this afternoon outside the cathedral. Wasn't it weird? You should have come.'

'Obviously,' said Damian, remaining completely stationary.

I pointed out Joanna and briskly explained the second not-coincidence. He smiled. 'Oh, brave new world, that has such wonders in it,' he said. But still he did not step forward into the party, or indeed alter his position at all. During this, Serena had been watching, waiting, I can only suppose, for him to make the first move, but if so, she was obviously going to be disappointed, so she decided it was time for her officially to register his presence. I admired her manner in doing it. A lifetime of emotional concealment can sometimes have its uses. She walked up briskly with a wide smile. 'Damian,' she said, 'what a treat. How are you?' Andrew had followed her across the terrace, and now stood, almost threateningly, as he locked eyes with the man who had after all knocked him down in front of us all at Dagmar's ball. She, Dagmar, perhaps recalling the same incident with shame, left her own conversation and drew near. 'You remember Andrew,' said Serena, as if this whole thing might be happening on any street in any city.

'Yes,' said Damian. 'I remember him.'

'And I remember you,' said Andrew.

I think the idea crossed several minds in that second that we might be about to witness a rematch, but Candida, sensing danger, came over, clapping her hands. 'Let's all have a walk before dinner. There's a path down through the rocks,

544

directly onto the beach. Don't you agree?' And before Serena could mention it: 'Your mother-in-law says she'll stay here and watch out for the baby.' Behind her Lady Belton had parked herself in a chair, with the expression of one of the accused at Nuremberg hearing his sentence read out.

In a way it did seem a solution and nobody raised any objection, so we broke away in groups and followed Candida, who had collared her uncle, Lord Claremont, as her personal guide. He didn't put up much resistance and set off by her side, after refilling his drink and carrying it with him. We all pottered down on to the sand and I must say it was a marvellous sight, the wide, blue sea, shining and glinting in that pellucid, evening light. We loitered, listening to the waves for a while, but when we set off for our walk down the beach I realised with a faintly sinking heart—although why? When she was a married woman, and so no concern of mine—that Serena and Damian had slipped to the back of the group. With her marvellous instinct for avoiding trouble Lady Claremont had also taken this in and made a beeline for her son-in-law, sliding her arm through his, and involving him in some apparently intense flow of talk, heaven knows what about—what would one talk about when trying to interest Andrew Summersby?—as she dragged him down the beach with her. But I could see her husband watching his daughter and Damian at the end of the trailing line, and it was not hard to tell that the sight was becoming more and more disturbing to him.

Joanna had joined me, and now she whispered:

'Do you think we're going to see some fireworks?'

'I bloody well hope not.'

'My mother's furious. She thought I'd have Damian all to myself, but it's quite clear he couldn't care less whether I live or die. Not when Serena's around.' Of course, at the time I thought she was exaggerating. That's how slow I was.

At this stage Andrew drifted away from his mother-in-law. He cast an angry look at the pair who were now quite a long way behind us on the sand, but Lucy came to his aid. I think that by this stage we were all, by unspoken agreement, working together trying to avoid a collision. Andrew had left Lady Claremont walking on her own and I could hear Pel Claremont as he drew alongside his wife. 'Do you see who that is?'

'Of course I do.'

'Did you know he was here?'

'Obviously not.'

'What's he talking to her about?'

'How should I know?'

'By Christ, if he's trying something . . .'

'If you say one single word you will only make things worse. I want your promise. You will say nothing contentious, not one word, before you close your eyes on your pillow.'

Lady Claremont hissed the phrase 'not one word' like a giant, angry snake and it was easy to tell she meant business, but whether she got the answer she required I couldn't say, since I had to crane forward to catch the last of these muttered exchanges and her husband's reply was lost beneath the sounds of the surf. Not knowing most of the facts, I couldn't understand their hostility to Damian. I turned back to Joanna, on my left. 'Did you hear any of that? If so, what's it about?'

But she shook her head. 'I wasn't listening,' she said.

I noticed we had been joined by Dagmar on the other side. 'What about you?' I asked, but she'd also missed it. In fact, she seemed rather quiet that night and uncharacteristically thoughtful. I looked at her, raising my eyebrows to signify a question, but she shook her head and gave a sad smile. 'Nothing. I'm just pondering the rest of my life.'

'Heavens.'

She waited until Joanna had dropped back to walk with George Tremayne. 'You started it, last night,' she said. 'You and Damian.' With her moist mouth twitching she was at her most poignant. 'All I want is a nice man who loves me. It sounds so tragic but that's it. I don't care how I live, really, as long as it's not in a complete hutch. I just want a nice man who loves me and treats me with respect.'

'He'll turn up,' I said. How baselessly optimistic one is when young, although I did not then guess how completely her request for even a tolerable future would be denied.

Dagmar nodded, sighing softly. I did not understand why this melancholy had gripped her, but of course now I know. The previous night, after their final tryst, Damian had told her she would never have him, she would never have the one above all others whom she loved and wanted. Any of us who have lived through a similar dismissal will feel for her. At last she gave a wistful smile. 'Maybe. Que sera sera.'

'Well, no doubt everything will work out for the best.'

'But I do doubt it,' she said.

At last Candida, sensing or praying that the danger had passed, turned us around, and slowly we made our way back to the villa. The light was failing, now, and the maids had arranged lit candles down the table and turned on the lamps that threw their beams against the house, so we seemed to be climbing up the path through the rocks, towards a fairy palace made of jewels.

We started peaceably enough. The first course was a sort of Portuguese version of *Insalata Tricolore* with olives added for good measure. I forget what the proper name was but it was good and we ate of it freely, which was just as well since it was destined to get us all through until the following morning. The trouble began when the main course arrived, some sort of fish stew, which looked and smelled delicious although I never got to swallow any, brought by the angry women in the kitchen. They did not hold it for us, but instead put three large, white, china bowls, filled with the steaming mixture, onto the table at intervals, leaving it to us to help ourselves and others. Meanwhile, and perhaps inevitably, Lord Claremont had been tucking into the drink since he arrived. In fairness to him, and again I did not know it then, he was simply livid to have found Damian at this house where, as he saw it, he and his wife had been lured by artifice. Once there, and presented with this bounder, which was bad enough, he found himself sitting next to a very common woman whom he did not know and who kept trying to engage him in a conversation about things and people of whom he had never heard. On the other hand, Valerie Langley was only too

548

thrilled by her *placement,* since one of her main goals in coming out of England had been to catch the Claremont family for herself and for her daughter, and was quite unaware that it was not working well.

To get things straight, to trace the source of the explosion, one must bear in mind that Pel Claremont thought Damian Baxter a liar and a cad, who'd attempted to seduce Serena into a marriage that would have ruined her life, all in an attempt to promote his own slimy and ill-bred interests. This was not my reading of the matter at all, but it was his and he did not understand why he had to sit at dinner with the author of his misfortunes. The plain truth is that neither Serena nor Candida had thought this through. The whole thing was as doomed as their original plan that exposure to Damian, at Gresham, would bring her parents round. Clearly, once the Claremonts had invited themselves on this expedition, Candida should have cancelled, or at the very least made a totally different plan as to how Serena and Damian would meet, because, given my new and greater understanding of the situation I now think Serena was incapable of turning down the chance to see him when it was offered. Unfortunately.

Damian was silent as we returned from the walk, and he had been fairly monosyllabic all evening since then. I saw Serena make an attempt to sit next to him, but he deliberately placed himself in a different, empty, chair, where the seats on either side were already taken by Candida and Lady Claremont, who may have been a little surprised when he chose her as his neighbour, but who contained it. After that, Damian talked to

549

Candida exclusively and of course it would have been to everyone's benefit if he had continued to do so, but Lady Claremont lived by certain rules and one of them was that at dinner, when the course changed and the next one was brought, it was time to turn to your other neighbour. Accordingly, she resigned George Tremayne to the claims of Dagmar and turned to Damian on her other side. 'So, what are you doing now?' she asked pleasantly. 'Have you made any plans for the future?'

Damian stared at her for a moment, long enough for most of us to register his deliberate insolence. 'Do you really want to know?' he said. Now, as I am happy to testify, this was very unfair. At the time it was completely bewildering to the rest of the party as we could not imagine what on earth Lady Claremont had done to deserve it, but even if I now accept that she had been an accomplice in wrecking his life, I still don't think it was fair. In this context she was just trying to get through dinner. Just trying to allow Candida or John or Alicky to feel that the evening was a success. What's wrong with that?

With something like a deep breath she nodded. 'Yes, I do,' she said, as steadily as she could manage. 'I'm very interested to know what lies ahead for all Serena's old friends.' Honestly, I would swear she meant this in a friendly way. She did not want Damian to marry her daughter it is true, but I don't believe she wished him ill beyond that. This may not have been true of her husband, but it was true of her. For a second Damian looked slightly ashamed. He seemed to gather himself and he opened his mouth to speak, presumably to talk about the bank or something.

But before he could utter a word, Lord Claremont cut in. 'Well,' he said as he reached for a bottle of red that required him to stretch right across the table, 'we *are* interested in a way. But only really to be sure that if you do have any plans they won't involve us.' The effect of this was electric. In an instant every conversation was dead. Lady Claremont slowly shut her eyes and held them closed against the tidal wave that she probably guessed was coming. John and Alicky were just puzzled as to why their guests had suddenly chosen to be so rude to each other. The Langleys looked shocked, as did the younger group including me, while Lady Belton assumed her usual expression of indignant disdain. In the silence, Lord Belton took a huge slug of wine.

'They won't,' said Damian easily. 'What makes you think I'd make a mistake of that magnitude twice.'

'Stop this!' Suddenly Serena was as angry as I had ever seen her. 'Stop this right now!' Her eyes were blazing, but of course it was too late.

Lord Claremont quietened her with a sharp gesture of his hand, then looked his opponent in the eye and took another sip. Next, slowly and with some style, he lowered his glass and smiled before he spoke. In truth, his languor was not enough to conceal that he was very drunk. 'Now, you look here, you little shit—' This actually made half the people at the table jump, like mice they all jigged up and down in a row. Lady Claremont gave a sort of low groan, which sounded like 'Oh, no,' but might have just been a sound of mourning, as she leaned forward with one hand raised, and Valerie

551

Langley let out a kind of wailing 'What?' to no one in particular.

But, by now, Damian was standing. 'No,' he said. '*You* look here, you pompous, ridiculous, boring, idiotic, unfunny, pretentious, ludicrous *joke*.' There were seven adjectives employed in this sentence and I was fascinated by them, because I cannot imagine that seven words could do more to change a life. When Damian had first got to his feet, he was part of a minor incident, which a few apologies and a 'have a drink, old boy' would soon have fixed. By the time he'd finished his speech, less than a minute later, he was out of this world for good and there was no possibility of return. The gates of the drawing rooms of 1970s England had clanged shut against him and the air was thick with the smoke of burning bridges.

Lord Claremont himself appeared stunned, as if he had been hit by a car and was not quite sure as to the extent of his wounds. 'How dare you—' he started to say.

But Damian was having none of it. We were way past that stage, by now. 'How dare I? *How dare I?* Who *on earth* do you think you are? What insanity gives you the right to talk to me in that manner, you *stupid old man?*' Now this was a curious moment, because to most of us present these words could easily have been said in their entirety except for the final insult by Lord Claremont to Damian, so the reversal of their direction created an odd sensation. We may be absolutely sure that never in Lord Claremont's fifty-eight years had he been addressed in anything even approaching this manner. Like all rich aristocrats the world over, he had no real understanding of his own abilities,

552

because he had been praised for gifts he did not possess since childhood and it is hardly to be wondered at if he did not question the conclusions that every suck-up had fed him for half a century. He wasn't clever enough to know they had been talking bunkum and that he had nothing to offer in any normal market. It was a shock, a horrid shock, for him suddenly to feel that, rather than a universal figure of dignity and poise and admiration, he was in fact a fool.

At this point, most ill-advisedly, Lady Belton decided the time had come to intervene. 'You disgraceful boy.' She spoke loudly, addressing the company as well as Damian to make her point, but unfortunately in an imperious, fluting manner more suited to a farce than a real argument. I imagine she thought it lent her majesty, when in reality she sounded like Marie Dressler in *Dinner at Eight*. 'Stop it this minute,' she trilled, 'and apologise to Lord Claremont!'

Damian spun round and in the blink of an eye, to our universal horror, he suddenly snatched up a knife from the breadboard on the table. It was a large, wide kitchen knife that might be used in a butcher's and certainly lethal. The whole episode was now turning into a full-blown nightmare, which none of us felt able to control. Please don't misunderstand me. I was perfectly sure at the time that he would not use it to harm anyone, that wasn't in him. We weren't in any danger. But he knew how to play with it, flicking it about to punctuate his movements and speech, to make the moment tingle. In this he judged correctly. If we were still before, we were paralysed now.

Slowly and sedately Damian stalked Lady

Belton down the table. Seeing him approach, she gripped the side arms of her chair and forced herself hard against its back. For this one and only time I felt a bit sorry for her. 'You pathetic, old harridan, you scarecrow, you freak, what possible business is it of yours?' He waited for an answer, as if this were a reasonable question. She looked at the blade and said nothing. 'You insane piece of wrinkled baggage with your demented snobbery and your ugly dresses and your even uglier pseudo-morality.' He was level with her by now and he stopped, leaning in slightly as if to get a better look at this sad object of his curiosity. 'What is it about you? Wait a minute. It's coming back to me.' He touched his bottom lip with the tip of the knife as if tussling with a knotty problem. 'Wasn't your father a bit dodgy? Or was it your mother?' Again, he stopped as if she might answer and confirm his diagnosis one way or the other. Instead, she stared at him, a bright glimmer of fear twitching beneath her hauteur. I must concede that this was a brilliant stroke, a real rapier thrust, that would have gone right up under the ribs. The truth was Lady Belton's mother had not been *tellement grande chose*, but she thought no one knew. Like many people in her position, she believed that because nobody ever gave her their true opinion, they literally had no knowledge of the things she wished concealed. But we did know it. We all knew it, that her mother had married up and then been left with a baby girl when she was abandoned by her noble spouse, who took off for green fields and pastures new, and never came, or looked, back. Doubtless this went some way to explaining Lady Belton's unhinged snobbishness. 'Don't worry,' said Damian. 'Nobody would know you're a mongrel. Just a laughable and imbecilic bully.' She listened to him, but still she said nothing. She seemed to be breathing heavily, as if after a long run; her cheeks were palpitating and appeared to be more red and blotchy than when he started. I wondered if she might be about to have a stroke.

I could not let it continue. However inflated Lord Claremont might be, however insane Lady Belton, this just wasn't cricket. I stood. 'Come on, Damian, that's enough,' I said. I could feel a slight sigh of relief among the group, as if I had marked the limits and we would now return to sanity. It was not to be.

Damian turned. Facing him, I at last understood that his anger had made him mad. Temporarily mad maybe, but mad. It cannot be much different for a traveller to find himself in a forest glade and suddenly to spy a wolf walking slowly towards him. I saw his grip on the handle of his weapon and I was frightened. I admit it. I was afraid. 'What? Is it your turn to tell me off?' he sneered. 'You sad, little, grubbing nonentity. You piece of dirt. You filth. You coward.'

'Damian, for pity's sake, he's your *friend*—' This came from Dagmar. I was touched that out of all of them she alone should try to defend me in the face of this onslaught. Perhaps Serena might have, but one glance told me she was in her own private hell.

Damian looked first at Dagmar, then at all of them. 'What? You think he's my friend? You think he's your friend? He's not your friend.' He shook his head, continuing to walk up and down the table like an armed panther. I could see two of the maids hovering in the shadows, watching, but no one at the table moved. They had seen the treatment of Lady Belton and they had no wish to be next before the guns. 'He despises you. Do you think he finds you funny?' He directed this at Lord Claremont. 'Or stylish?' He waited in vain for a response from Lady Claremont. 'Or interesting in any way?' That was aimed at the whole table. 'He thinks you're stupid and dull, but he likes your life. He likes your houses. He likes your titles. He likes the pitiful sense of self-importance he derives from knowing that people know he knows you.' He hit all the 'knows' in this with equal strength, so it sounded more like a song than a sentence. 'He likes to creep around after you and kiss your arses and brag about you when he gets home. But don't ever think that he likes you.'

Through all this Serena had sat completely still, her head bowed, and I could see now that she was crying. A steady stream of tears ran down from both eyes, leaving dark marks of mascara across her cheeks as it travelled south. 'And you think he's in love with you, don't you?' He was standing by her now and she did look up, but she did not answer. 'Your little swain, who sticks by you through thick and thin, and you laugh at him—' She had made the beginnings of a protest at this, but he silenced her with a raised palm, 'You laugh at him, you've laughed at him with me, but you tolerate him because he loves you and you think that's sweet.' Serena now looked across at me. I think she was shaking her head to distance herself from what he was saying, but I had gone into another place, a numb place, a hollow, lonely place, where I tried but failed to hide. 'He doesn't love you. He loves what you are, he loves what he can boast about, your name, your money.' He paused to take a breath, to be fresh again for the final strike. 'You should hear what he says about you, all of you, when we're alone. He's just a regular little toady, a Johnny-on-the-make, creeping and crawling like a bumboy round you, to worm and lick and slide his way into your lives.'

Lord Claremont probably spoke for the rest of them, when he let out a loud and disgusted 'Good God!' Damian had chosen well the right mud to throw at me if he wanted it to stick.

He hadn't finished with Serena. 'You idiot. You fool.' He spoke with an undiluted contempt that made the company shudder. 'You could have escaped. You could have lived a life. And instead, you chose to spend your days with this . . . *oaf!*' He clipped Andrew's shoulder as he passed. 'This *twerp!* This *blob!* And for what? To live in a big house, and have people you don't like pull their forelocks and grovel.' Dagmar was crying out loud by now and Damian stopped when he got to her. Oddly, when he spoke next his voice was momentarily quite kind. 'You're not a bad sort. You deserve better than anything that will come to you.' But by then he had moved on and now he was standing almost next to Joanna, who was watching him with the fascination of a rabbit faced by a stoat. 'You might have escaped, without your vixen bitch of a mother. Keep trying.' What made all this so surreal was that everyone was here, all the objects of his attack were sitting in front of him. Mrs Langley let out a yelp, but her husband held her arm to keep her silent.

Damian was starting to run down and you could

tell it, because Richard Tremayne rose from his chair and even Andrew looked ready to move. His grip was loosening. 'I hate you all. I loathe your false values. I wish you ill in everything you say or do. And yet, even now, I pity you.' The others, sensing from this that the tirade was coming to an end, began fractionally to relax. Maybe he saw this, or maybe he had always planned it, but the fact is that Damian was not quite finished. 'I'm going now but I must give you a moment to remember me by.' He smiled.

'I think we've already had it,' Candida re-entered the fray.

'No. Something more colourful,' he said, and in one sharp, astonishing movement he threw down the knife and grabbed the first bowl of fish stew, smashing it over the end of the table where the steaming mass of boiling sea life was sprayed over Lady Claremont and Lucy and Kieran and Richard Tremayne. At this there was anguish and cries of anger and pain as the burning liquid covered them, but there was no real physical reaction beyond shock, and before anyone could move, Damian had snatched up the middle bowl. Crash! Down it went, this time catching Candida, Lord Claremont, Dagmar, George and Joanna. But as he lunged for the third and final bowl the others snapped awake and made a dive for it themselves. Alfred Langley stood with both hands on the rim. Unfortunately for him, Damian had the strength of a tiger and with one wrench it was out of his hands. Seizing it, Damian raised it high above his head, like a pagan priest with an offering for a savage and unforgiving deity, and for a moment everything and everyone was motionless. Then he brought it down hard

558

against an edge, ensuring that the mass of the bowl's contents covered Lady Belton, who received her anointing with a sickening scream. There was a thick tomato sauce involved in whatever the recipe had been and by now the table looked like the end of the battle of Borodino, with everyone at it covered in a sticky, smelly, steaming mess of fishy gore. The shards of china had shot about, too, and Lucy was nursing a cut on her forehead, while George was bleeding quite heavily from his right cheek. It's a miracle that nobody was blinded. 'I'll say goodnight, then,' said Damian, and without another word he walked across the terrace, through the open doors into his bedroom and closed them behind him. Once and forever, he was out of their lives.

After he'd gone we sat, all of us, not moving, in total shock. Like victims who have survived an air crash but are not yet sure of it. Then Serena and Dagmar started to cry quite loudly, and Lady Belton, who resembled nothing so much as a red-nosed clown in the *Cirque du Soleil*, with tendrils of lobster and crab stuck in her hair, began to scream out orders to her dazed and equally fish-festooned husband. 'Take me away from here! At once! Take me away!'

At this point Valerie Langley cried out that we should call the police, but Alfred did not need the quick, startled looks from the others to know this would never happen. They were not going to finish the evening by providing the press with the best gossip story they had printed in years. With silent understanding and a nod, Alfred steered his wife away from the very idea.

To say the party broke up soon after that would

be a significant and major understatement. The party shattered, splintered, exploded, fell into ruins, with the Claremonts and the Langleys running to their different cars as if a gunman were on the loose and training his weapon from a window. Those of us who remained sat, stinking of fish, waiting to see what would happen next. George Tremayne poured himself a drink and brought one over to me, which I thought was decent of him, even if it confirmed the horrid sense that they were all pitying me, pitying and despising me, which they obviously were. They may have varied in the degree to which they believed Damian's words, but they all believed some of them and I understood what the consequence must be. Others back at home would hear the story, endlessly embellished, and I would thenceforth be tarred in London as a creeping toady, a social climbing greaser, a speck of smarmy, contemptible dirt. I felt my reward for taking up Damian and forcing him upon them had finally arrived. I was finished in the world of my growing-up years. I was an outcast. I was a pariah.

Candida approached, perhaps to offer sympathy, but before she could speak, I took her to one side. 'I'll leave tomorrow.' I spoke in a low voice, because I didn't want to become a *cause célèbre*, and, worst of all, have others feel obliged to take my side. 'First thing.'

'Don't be silly.'

'No. I must. I introduced him to everyone. He's my fault. I can't stay. Not after that.' I was grateful for her attempt at support, but it was true. I couldn't stay among these people for a minute longer than I had to. Andrew Summersby came alongside and Candida appealed to him to persuade me not to go. He shook his head. 'I should think it's the only course open to him,' he said in his most ferociously pompous manner. It was lucky the maids had removed the knife.

Candida did not argue any more that night. 'Well, sleep on it,' she said. 'See how you feel in the morning. We all know he was talking rubbish.' I smiled and kissed her, and slipped away to my room.

Knowing Candida better now, I think it's possible she had genuinely dismissed the charges against me but I did not believe it then. And later that night, when I was bathed and smelling a bit less like a welk stall in Bermondsey Market, I asked myself was Damian truly talking rubbish? In some ways I think he was. Most of all in what he said about Serena. Certainly every word was deliberately chosen to damage me irretrievably among those people. To finish me with them. As he was going to vanish from their sight, so, he vowed, would I. It was a cruel attack, and I am sure the best part of it for him was that it would ruin and diminish me in front of her. He wanted to make my love seem a petty and paltry affectation, a device to get invited to dinner, instead of the engine that turned my life.

Even so, it was not quite all rubbish. The funny thing was that there were times when I had envied Damian. I envied his power among these men and women. I had known many of them all my life but within a matter of weeks of their meeting him he had more power over them than I had ever achieved. He was handsome, of course, and charismatic and I was neither, but finally it wasn't

561

that. Newcomer as he was, he did not allow them to dictate the rules of the game, but I . . . maybe I did. Had I not given more leeway to the jokes of Lord Claremont and his ilk than I would have done to those of a social inferior? Did I not pretend, by never arguing, that the fatuities I'd listened to after dinner in a series of great and splendid dining rooms were interesting comments? I had sat up late with fools and laughed and nodded and flattered their fathomless self-importance without revealing a trace of my real feelings. Would I have bothered with Dagmar were she not a princess? Did I not maintain civilities with someone like Andrew, a man I despised and would have actively disliked even if Serena had never been born? Would I have given him the little respect that I did if there weren't a faint impulse within me to bow down before his position? I'm not sure. Were my mother alive and able to read this, she would say it was all nonsense, that I was brought up to be polite and why should I be criticised for that. One part of me thinks she would be right, but another . . .

At all events the evening finished me in that world for many years. Damian was gone from their sight, but so, to a large extent, was I. With a few, a very few, exceptions, I dropped out of their round, at first because of embarrassment, but later in disgust with my own self. Even Serena seemed to back away from me or so I thought. For a time I would still drop by occasionally, once or twice in a year, to see her or to see the children or, I suppose, because I could not stay away but I felt that the shadow of that evening was always with us, that something had died, and at last I accepted it and severed all connection.

Of course, today I am older and kinder and, looking back, I judge that I treated myself harshly. I do not think Serena was responsible for my exile. Nor do I blame any of the others because I think I did it to punish myself and I was wrong. The truth is that Damian spoke that night out of anger and a desire for revenge, although I am still not quite sure why I was the target for such heavy, apparently unprovoked blows. It may simply be that he blamed me for pulling him into the unholy mess in the first place. If so, with the wisdom of hindsight, I'm inclined to think he had a point.

SIXTEEN

I rang Damian when I got back from Waverly and told him everything I'd learned. And I voiced a thought I hated to find in my brain. 'This is a silly question, but you're sure it's not Serena?'

'I'm sure.'

'Because I know now there's so much more to your story than I'd seen.'

'I'm glad, but no, it's not. I wish it were in a way, but it can't be.' I could hear that he really was pleased to hear that I'd come some way towards understanding what that year had been for him. 'I last slept with Serena in the autumn of 1968. She married in the spring of 1969 and there was no baby in between. I only saw her one more time after her dance, and that was for the evening in Portugal when she wasn't staying in the villa and she had her dreary husband, silly parents, horrible

563

in-laws and a baby girl in tow. Besides, even if I'd muddled all the dates it would have to be that child, Mary, who I hear is still the spitting image of her ghastly daddy Andrew.' All of which was true. The missing mother was not Serena Belton.

'Then it's Candida. It must be.'

'Did you talk to her about me?'

'A bit. She mentioned that you'd gone out together, but it was quite early on in the Season.'

'Yes. But we never fell out. We were always friends and we picked up again when it was finished, just once or twice, for old times' sake. I know you weren't all that keen on Candida, but I liked her.'

I was very interested by this. With all these women he seemed to have been so much more aware of them, so much more clear-sighted as to their true natures, than I had been. 'She did imply there was a little hanky-panky when the year was over. Is that when the baby might have begun?'

'No, it wasn't then. That was finished a long time before the holiday.' There was a short silence at the other end of the line. 'She came to me, after that dinner, when everyone was asleep. I woke in the night and she was with me, naked in my bed, and we made love. Then, when I woke up in the morning she was gone.'

'Did you see her the next day, before you took off?'

'Nobody had surfaced when I went. I just called a taxi and disappeared. But she left a note in my room, for me to find, so we parted on good terms.'

'Did you meet up afterwards? In London?'

'I never saw any of them again. Including you.'

'No.' I too had gone to the airport at dawn, but

564

somehow we managed to avoid each other. On my part consciously. And no, like all of us I had not seen Damian from that day until my summons.

He interrupted my thoughts. 'That is, I did see Joanna. Just once, but we know it wasn't her.'

'And Terry.'

He was puzzled for a second, and then he nodded and smiled. 'You're right. I'd remembered it as being before we left. But you're right. It was when we got back. Poor old Terry.'

'What did the note say? From Candida?'

' "I still love you" and she signed it with that funny scrawl of hers. I was very touched. I don't think I have ever been unhappier than I was that night.'

'Which goes for everyone who was there.'

'I used to pray that I would never be so unhappy again. Since I have minutes left, I can presumably be confident of achieving that at least.' He chuckled softly at the hideous memory. At least, I say he chuckled, but the sound was more like the rattling of old and disused pipes in a condemned building. 'I lay on my bed, listening to you talking outside and everyone leaving, and I wished I were dead. For a while I thought they were going to send for the police.'

'That lot? No chance. They do not care to make column inches. That's one thing that hasn't changed.' We were nearly at our destination. There seemed to be nothing left to do but tie up the loose ends. 'Shall I go and tell her about her son's good fortune?'

'Why not? Then come down here. I want to hear what she says.'

Candida was quite content to get my call this time
and equally content to let me invade her for a cup
of coffee that very morning. She lived in the same
old Fulham-type house that so many of her tribe
have come to occupy since I was young. Harry had
obviously made a decent living and she had fixed
the place up very attractively. She greeted me with
her usual, if to me newfound, calm, good manners,
and took me into a pretty, chintzy drawing room,
carrying a tray of coffee things. On the table
behind a sofa was a large, framed photograph of, I
assume, the late Harry Stanforth. He had a bluff,
chunky, smiling face, rather an ordinary one really,
but that is the great and timeless miracle of love. I
saluted him silently, as Candida poured cups for
the pair of us. Then she looked at me. 'Well?' she
said.

I explained about Damian's search and my part
in it. 'I didn't want to do it but even I could see he
didn't really have a viable alternative.'

She sipped her coffee. 'I knew it was something.
Though I'm not sure I guessed it was that. So, how
do I come into it?' Then she just sat, patiently
waiting for me to continue. I couldn't understand
why she wasn't making the connection.

'We think it's you. We think Archie is Damian's
son.'

For a moment she said nothing but just looked
puzzled. Then she gave a little snort of laughter.
'How? I'm not an elephant.' It was my turn to look
puzzled. 'I last slept with Damian almost two years
before Archie was born.'

'But, when we talked, you implied that you had

566

a fling with him after the end of your affair.'

'And so I did. In the summer of 1969. I felt rather sorry for him, the way things had finished with Serena, and when she sent out the invitations to her marriage I looked him up to see how he was coping. We met a few times after that. But then I lost touch with him. That's why I used you to get him to Portugal a year later. I wasn't completely sure he'd want to hear from me again, although I don't now think I need have worried.'

'But you slept with him on that night.'

'What night?'

'When Damian went mad and covered us all with fish stew. Surely you remember?'

'Are you nuts? Of course I remember. Who could forget? But I didn't sleep with him.'

'He woke up in the middle of the night and you were there next to him, in his bed.'

'And this isn't an extract from a novel bought under the counter?'

'You left a note in his room saying you loved him.'

This did bring her up sharp, as she concentrated. She nodded briskly. 'I did do that. I thought he must be feeling so ghastly after what he'd put us through and I scribbled a note saying . . . I forget now. "I forgive you," or something like that—'

' "I still love you".'

'Was it? Anyway, that sort of thing, and I pushed it under his door before I went to bed.'

'Are you sure you didn't sleep with him?'

I could see she was on the edge of becoming indignant. 'Well, I know I've been a bit of a slapper in my time, but I think I'd have remembered if I'd gone to bed with Damian Baxter on that ghastly evening. I cannot believe I would have forgotten any detail about that particular night.'

'No.' I stared at my cup. Was I back at square one? It didn't seem possible.

My words were still running round her brain. 'He woke up and found a woman in his bed, making love to him?' I nodded and she threw back her head, laughing. 'Trust Damian. Just when life couldn't get any lower, he finds himself in the middle of a scene from a James Bond film.' Her mirth had subsided into chuckles.

'But it wasn't you.'

'I can assure you I would remember if I made a habit of that sort of thing.'

And then I knew.

*   *   *

Lady Belton was upstairs, apparently, but she would be delighted to see me if I wouldn't mind waiting in the Morning Room since, rather illogically to my mind, this was apparently where her ladyship always had tea. I would be delighted.

The Morning Room was one of the prettier rooms at Waverly, cosy rather than grand, but with some of their best pictures and a really beautiful, ladies' desk by John Linnell, which I would say was currently used by Serena, since it was covered in papers and letters and invitations waiting to be answered. The nice woman from the village who had let me in was settling the tea things as Serena arrived. 'Thank you so much, Mrs Burnish.' She had already acquired that slightly heartless charm that is assumed by the well-bred to ensure good

568

service, rather than because of any touching of their heart strings. In fact, I could see in her poise and her clothes and even in her smile, that Serena was well on the way to being what is still sometimes called a great lady. 'How lovely to see you again so soon,' she said and kissed me on both cheeks. The fact that the last time we'd met we had made love, and not just love but the most passionate love of my entire life, was somehow, in a way that I cannot exactly define, boxed up and removed to a safe distance by her manner and tone. She was warm and friendly, but I knew then it would never be repeated.

'I can't believe you don't know why I'm here.'

She had poured herself some tea and now she sat, carefully smoothing the folds of her skirt as she did so. She took a sip, then looked at me and gave rather a shy smile. 'I bet I do. Candida rang to tell me what you'd said.' Unusually, she seemed embarrassed, an emotion I would not naturally attribute to her. 'I don't want you to think I always go around sliding into the beds of sleeping men.'

'You told me yourself it was only with men who are in love with you.'

She nodded. 'Thank you for remembering that.'

'I remember everything,' I said.

She started to talk again. It was obviously a relief finally to let it out. 'I wasn't sure at first, because I felt, if he were interested, he would have done something when I sent that idiotic letter. But he did nothing. Nothing at all and I know, because in those days, twenty years ago, I was still in touch with quite a few of the girls who might have written it. What's changed?'

'He's dying.'

569

Which brought her down to earth. 'Yes. Of course.' She looked at the ceiling for a moment. 'I want to explain. About that night in Estoril. I've felt guilty for so many years, particularly over you.'

'Why me?'

'Because you were the one who got it in the neck. All you'd done was ask him to a few parties, and suddenly you were labelled a crawling, social-climbing toady and Christ knows what. It must have been awful.'

'It wasn't great.'

'More to the point, it wasn't true. Most of all what he said about your feelings for me. I know that. I knew it then.' Serena gave me a slightly secret smile, the one open acknowledgement of what we had enjoyed together, and I was rather glad of it. It wasn't much but it was better than nothing. 'How much have you heard about what went on at my ball?'

'Most of it, I think. But only now.'

'Damian told me he'd used me, he wasn't in love with me, I was better off without him, all of it. And I just stood there because I couldn't believe the words he was saying. The music was still playing and some girl was laughing in the anteroom just beyond the door, and I remember thinking how can you be laughing when I'm in here having my life shattered? I loved him with every fibre of my being, you see. I wanted to run away with him, to be with him, to love him to the end of my days and if it meant breaking with everyone I would have done it. But when he started to talk I just froze. I suppose I was in shock, as they say now, but I don't think we had "shock" in those days. I think you were just supposed to go for a walk and get on with

570

it. Anyway, he stopped and he waited for me to speak. And after a bit I looked at him and said, "Well, if you really think it's for the best." And when I was silent he nodded and he gave a funny little bow. I've thought of that so often. I can picture it now. A little bow, like a waiter or some assistant at the embassy who's been sent to make sure you change trains properly, to escort you from the *Gare du Nord* to the *Gare d'Austerlitz* or something. Then he left. And I went out on to the terrace, and after a bit I came in again and danced with you.'

'And I was so glad of it.'

But this time she wanted to tell me the whole story. 'After that I didn't really care what happened to me. I suppose I must have had a sort of nervous breakdown, but again, in those days people like us didn't have nervous breakdowns. That was the sort of thing actresses did, and men who'd embezzled their customers' money. I think people like us were just a bit under the weather, or getting out of the rat race or taking a break. Mummy and Daddy were pushing me and pushing me at Andrew, and he was keen.' She stopped, catching my expression. 'No, he was keen. I know you don't like him, but he isn't as bad as you think.' I made a sort of accepting expression to cover myself. 'And I didn't know what else to do. We weren't trained for anything, then.'

'I know.'

'It seemed a way out. I knew Damian didn't want me, and since I thought of him morning, noon and night, I didn't see what else to do. Anyway, the point is . . .' She shrugged, helplessly. 'That's what happened. That is what happened to me.' She stopped and sighed. Then, suddenly she shivered and, looking up, caught my eye. 'Somebody walked over my grave.' What a strange and haunting saying that is. We sat for a moment in silence until Serena said brightly, 'Do you want some more tea?'

'Please.' I held out my cup.

But she hadn't finished. 'So I got married and I was pregnant fairly soon and you know, all of that stuff is quite exciting when it's going on, and there's lots to do and lots to buy and lots of people making a fuss of you, and I sort of forgot how unhappy I was for a while, and then, when Mary was born, Candida came to see me and we started to talk. And she said something like it wouldn't have worked with Damian, not when my parents were so against him, or words to that effect, and I hadn't known they were against him. I mean, I could guess they weren't *for* him, I knew that from the dinner, but I didn't think they'd had a chance to be against him in any thought-out way, because he'd confessed his base motives and dumped me before they'd got to know him. And then I heard what had gone on. Do you know about that?' I nodded.

Serena was getting angrier. I could see it. Even though all her training was to keep such emotions under wraps, still she could not prevent a trace of her rage from seeping out. She put down her cup and stood, fiddling nervously with the ornaments and invitations that littered the mantelshelf. 'The more I thought about it, the more furious I felt at what had been done to me. Because now I understood why I'd been bundled up with Andrew. And eventually I decided I had to see Damian again. I had to.' She was almost panting. I would doubt she had gone over this ground in any detail for quite a time. 'You know the next bit.'

'I do.'

'Of course, once my parents had pushed in, let alone my ma-in-law, I should have cancelled, but I was so desperate just to set eyes on him, just to touch his hand, just to smell him that I didn't. In retrospect, I suppose they must have been afraid something of the sort was going on.'

'It certainly sounds like it.'

'But after I heard you were bringing him it was more than I could do to back out. I knew I should but I couldn't make myself. So that evening we arrived at your villa and we set off for the walk down the beach. And I asked him about what he'd said and he admitted it had all been a lie. None of it was true. He was in love with me, he said. He would always love me. And I told him that if he'd only told me the truth and not lied at the dance, I would have come away with him that night. I would have packed and left and married him the minute I was twenty-one, and we would have been together for the rest of our lives. He said that he thought he'd done the right thing, the honourable thing.'

'He had.'

She turned on me, her eyes flashing with fury. 'Had he? Then fuck your honour! Fuck his stupid honour! I don't care what his motives were. He lied to me and he ruined our lives!'

'That was the "deceit" you mentioned in the letter, I thought it was something else.'

She frowned for a moment, trying to make sense of this. 'Oh, you mean promising love to get me

573

into bed?'

'Yes.'

'Well, he was the opposite. He feigned indifference. That was the lie.'

'Why didn't you leave Andrew? When you knew?'

Serena's anger appeared to be settling. 'That was my weakness,' she said sadly. 'That was the weakness I wrote about.' She returned to her chair and sat again. 'Damian asked me that. He said if I felt as I did it was the only thing we could do. He begged me to. But it was a different time. You know what they say: The past is a foreign country; they do things differently there. I had a baby. I had family coming out of my ears. The scandal would have been huge, even in 1970, and while my parents were responsible in a way—'

'In a way?'

She nodded. 'All right. They were responsible, but they thought they were acting in my best interests.' She caught my expression. 'Well, they thought their best interests were my best interests.' She paused. 'And I was tired of being pushed and pulled, this way and that, but . . .' She almost groaned and I could feel her breath as it left her body. 'Of course, if it happened today I would have gone with him. I should have gone. I should have done it, but my nerve failed me when it came to it. Damian was half the reason for the waste of our lives. But I was the other half.'

'And later that night?'

Now she almost smiled at the memory. 'We were back at the house we'd rented, which wasn't very far, and of course everyone was absolutely reeling. They helped themselves to huge drinks,

574

even Lady B., and staggered into the many bathrooms to de-fish themselves, and so did I. And after that we all collapsed. But when Andrew went off to bed I said I wasn't tired. I wanted to stay up. I waited until I knew he'd be asleep, then I walked back.'

'You walked?'

'I know. One wouldn't do it now, would one? Or perhaps you would, if you were young and in love and desperate. Perhaps some things never change. I knew which Damian's room was, lord knows, as we'd all seen him flounce into it. I'm not sure exactly what I'd have done if the door had been locked. These days it would be locked, wouldn't it?'

'You'd have woken him up.'

'Yes. I suppose so. But it wasn't, so I slid in, climbed into bed and made love to him in the pitch dark for what I knew would be the last time. He was sort of awake after a bit, but not very, even then. I didn't mind. I was saying goodbye to the life I should have had. It was a private moment, really.'

'But why was it the last time? Even if you weren't prepared to divorce, you could have gone on with the affair.'

She shook her head. 'No. I couldn't have been his mistress, making up lunch dates with girlfriends and pretending to miss the train. That wasn't for us. That wasn't who we were. We should have formed a union that bestrode the world and frightened anyone who stood in our way. We weren't a backstreets number, with telephones being put down when the hubby answers. Absolutely not. Once I'd decided not to leave

Andrew, from that second it was over.'

'I hope Andrew has some inkling of what he owes you.'

'No, but if he did it would wreck everything for him, so it would be rather self-defeating. Anyway, that night I got up and dressed and left, and I never saw Damian again. Finis.'

'How did you know that Peniston was his? Presumably Andrew put in an appearance occasionally.'

'Rather an unfortunate turn of phrase.' Then she smiled, tenderly this time, as she thought of her son, the lovechild. 'I knew because when he was born he was so like Damian. It was mainly gone before he was two. Isn't there some theory that newborn babies resemble their fathers, so they'll be looked after and provided for? His nose, his eyes . . . I used to thank God that no one noticed, although I did see my mother giving him an odd look right at the beginning. But I always knew.'

'Why did you write the letter? Why didn't you just go and see him?'

'I don't know. I was feeling sorry for myself. Andrew was being more tiresome than usual, so I'd come up to London to finish off the Christmas shopping on my own and I was drunk. I don't why I wrote it at all. I wouldn't have posted it if I'd waited until the next day, but someone picked the letters off the hall table before I got up and that was it.'

I laughed. 'Exactly what Damian thought had happened.'

Now she was serious. 'So what's next?'

'I tell Damian. He changes his will. Your son is

576

very, very rich. The House of Belton rises in splendour.'

'Eventually.'

'I can assure you Peniston won't have long to wait.' I remembered one detail, which I supposed we should observe. 'We'll probably have to run some sort of DNA test. Would you mind?'

Without a word she went to her desk, opened a drawer and took out an envelope which she handed to me. On the outside of it was written: 'Peniston's hair. Aged three.' 'Will this do?' she asked. 'Or do you need a newer piece?'

'I'm sure it will be fine.'

'Don't use it all.' But I could see something else was on her mind. 'Does Peniston have to know? Is that one of the conditions?'

'Don't you want him to know?'

She looked around the room. Over the chimneypiece was a portrait of a Victorian, female forebear of Andrew's, 'The Third Countess of Belton' by Franz Xavier Winterhalter, painted with chestnut ringlets and a good deal of bosom. Serena sighed. 'If he knows, he has to choose between living a lie or spoiling his father's life by cutting himself off from the Beltons' history and feeling a fool in front of everyone he's grown up with.'

'A rich fool.'

'A rich fool. But a fool.' She took a breath. 'No. I don't want him to know. I would like him to know that Damian was a wonderful man, I will happily say that we were in love. I want to. But I think that's enough.'

'I'll tell Damian.'

Serena had one more request. 'I'd like to tell him myself. Can I? Would he allow that?'

I looked at this woman, still healthy, still lovely, still in the middle of life, and I thought of that scarcely breathing corpse. 'I doubt it,' I said. 'You could always write him a letter. You've done it before.' We both smiled at this, but I could see that her eyes were starting to fill with tears. 'I'm not sure he's up to seeing anyone. Particularly anyone who hasn't seen him since he was . . .' I tailed off. I couldn't quite find the right word.

'Beautiful,' she said, as the first droplet began its journey down her cheek.

I nodded. 'That's it. Since he was beautiful.'

I spoke to Bassett as I left, giving him the facts of the case and, on his advice, I drove straight from Dorset to Surrey. By the time I got there, two and a half hours later, there was already a lawyer in attendance who told me that a new will favouring the Viscount Summersby had been drawn up and signed. I was glad, even if it felt peculiar for a moment to take such pleasure in a name that I had hated for so long. Damian had asked for me to be shown up as soon as I arrived, and when I entered his bedroom I realised that we were racing against the clock. Damian lay in his bed, with a fearsome array of tubes and bottles, and leaking things on stands, all of which seemed to be connected to some portion of his emaciated, shrivelled carcase. Two nurses hovered around him, but at the sight of me he waved them away and they left us alone.

'It's done. I've signed it,' said Damian.

'The lawyer told me. You didn't want to wait for the results of the test?' I pulled out the lock of hair, taking it from its envelope and handing it to him. But he shook his head. 'No time. And it'll be positive.' I could see the hair itself was much more important to him. He pulled two or three strands from the twisted gold wire holding it together and gestured for me to take them.

'Give them to Bassett. Now. That's all they need.' I rang and the butler came and collected the precious filaments. When I turned back towards the bed I could see Damian holding the rest of the child's curl as, very slowly, he brought it to his lips. 'So we made it,' he said.

'We made it.'

'Not a moment too soon.' His thin lips drew back in a kind of laugh, but it was painful to witness. 'Tell me the story.'

And I did. He made no comment except when it came to the account of his interview with Serena at the ball. I told him I thought his behaviour had been honourable, but he shook his head. 'You are supposed to think it was honourable,' he said. 'But it was proud. I wanted them to want me. And when I drove down there with her I thought I could make them want me. But they didn't, and I wasn't prepared to be the family's *mésalliance*. That was just pride. I spoiled our lives through pride.'

'She thinks she spoiled your lives through fear on the beach at Estoril.' For some reason this almost cheered him. 'She's wrong. But I'm glad, even now, to think she feels it as I do. That's selfish, of course. If I loved her less selfishly I would want her to forget me, but I can't.'

'She doesn't want the boy to know. That is, she wants to tell him about you, but not that you're his father.' He nodded, but without complaint. I could see he was prepared to abide by this. 'She asked to come and see you, to explain.' This produced something like alarm in the rheumy eyes on the pillow, but I shook my head at once to comfort him. 'I told her no, but she sent you a note.' I sat on a chair placed for visitors near the head of the bed and took the thick, cream envelope from my inside pocket. He nodded for me to open it. Beneath the embossed address in deep blue, Waverly Park, she had written in that thick, italic writing that I remembered well, 'I have loved you since I last saw you. I will love you to the end of my life.' It was signed with one word only: 'Serena.' I held it for him and he read it, again and again, his eyes flicking back and forth across the paper.

'You must tell her you were in time for me to see it and that I feel the same,' he muttered. 'Just the same.' And then, 'Will you stay? They can sort out what you need.' I can hardly believe that I hesitated, my head full of those ridiculous, irrelevant things that fall off the shelves into the centre of your brain at the most unsuitable moments, a dinner party I'd said I'd go to, lunch the next day with some friends over from Munich. What gets into one at these times? Before I could answer he reached for my hand, which was resting on the surface of the counterpane, 'Please. I promise I shan't detain you any more than this one time.'

I nodded at once, ashamed it had taken me so long to speak. 'Of course I'll stay,' I said.

And I did stay. I was given dinner, together with the lawyer, a Mr Slade, who invited me to call him Alastair, and we made stiff conversation about global warming in the fourteenth century and the Curious Case of Gordon Brown, as we sat playing with our food in the splendour of the lifeless

580

dining room below, until I was shown back into the bedroom I had occupied on that first visit, in what seemed like another era and was in fact only a couple of months before, where Bassett had found me things to shave with, and brush my teeth with, and wear in bed. 'I'll collect your shirt and the rest of your laundry and have them back with you for the morning, Sir,' he said. In truth, Damian had spent his last years in Fairyland, but a lonely Fairyland. That I did know.

It was Bassett who shook me awake in the early hours of the morning. 'Can you come, Sir? He's on his way.' I looked into his face and I saw that his eyes were full of tears, and it struck me that when a man is dying, if his butler cries then some at least of his life must have been well done. I snatched up the brand-new dressing gown provided, and hurried along through the passages to the chamber of death. It seemed quite full when I got there, with both nurses and a doctor and Alastair Slade on hand, who had clearly been ordered to attend in case of any last-minute alterations, but he was not needed. The atmosphere was stuffy and anxious, and I thought of Louis XVI plunging his fist through a pane of glass to give his wife some air at her *accouchement*. They all turned to look when I appeared, then fell back so automatically, clearing the way to the bed, that I assumed this had been yet another preordained plan in this most ordered of departures.

Damian was only just alive, but when he saw me his lips began to move, so I knelt down and leaned over him, holding my ear as near to his mouth as I could. And I did hear him quite clearly. 'Please tell her I feel the same,' he said. Then it was over.

The test was positive, as he and I had known it would be, so there was no doubt that justice would be done when Damian's affairs were settled. Alastair gave me a copy of the will before we left and invited me to read it through, in case there were any immediate queries he could satisfy, but it was all pretty straightforward, if overwhelming in its sheer magnitude. As I knew, Damian had no surviving close relations and so there was never any chance of a challenge to his some would say eccentric dispositions, and the document was clear enough. I discovered I had been allotted the onerous task of executor. This had been made slightly more bearable in two ways, the first being that I was sole holder of the office, so every other manager, banker, committee member, financial advisor of Damian's vast empire had to defer to me. The second sweetener of the unwieldy pill was that Damian had left me a large amount of money 'in gratitude for his kind execution of a tedious task,' which I had not looked for, but for which I was, and am, extremely grateful. I have no hesitation in saying that the bequest altered my life enormously for the better.

He had also set aside what seemed to me a huge sum to be disposed of by me between, and I quote, 'the others on the list, as he shall see fit. He will understand this designation. I make no recommendations as to how this should be done, since he is the philanthropist, not I.' I was shamelessly partisan in the distribution, giving Dagmar the lion's share which, I am happy to relate, resulted in her leaving William almost at once. I could not forget that she alone had been treated kindly by Damian during his terrible tirade, and I decided this must mean that her happiness was in some way important to him. I gave a sizeable lump to Candida, which she was very grateful for, and another to Lucy, which Philip lost within three years on ill-judged business ventures. Terry, surprisingly perhaps, invested her share well and now enjoys the proceeds. I did not give money to Kieran, since he didn't need it, but I saw him as the legitimate heir to Joanna's goodwill, so I purchased the Turner seascape, which I had admired in the library on my first visit, out of the estate and gave it to him. He was pleased, I think. The only other bequest for which I was personally responsible, but which, as executor I was fully entitled to make, was a substantial sum to Peniston's sister, Mary. This was partly because I felt a twinge of guilt, knowing that she, in truth and unlike Peniston, had the blood of the Beltons running in her veins and partly to substantiate the anodyne notion, helped by the lesser legacies to the other women, that Damian had decided to split his money between those he had loved and their offspring. There was so much money that none of the above made more than the faintest dent in the whole, and the gifts helped the legend that Serena was happy, indeed eager, to foster and promote. Naturally, I needed the promise of silence from Candida and Terry, the only other two who knew, but Candida was Serena's cousin and was never a risk. I was more concerned at having been indiscreet with Terry and I did think of somehow tying the money to a gagging clause but there was a risk this could prove insulting and counter-productive so I decided to rely on what remained of her decency. Thus far, at least, I have not been disappointed.

The funeral was small and simple, and Damian's body was laid to rest in the graveyard, fittingly, of the Church of St Teresa of Avila, which had benefited so much from his benevolence during his lifetime. A few months after that, we had a grander and well-attended memorial at St George's, Hanover Square. The will was public knowledge by this time, and had provided a good deal of conversation in London drawing rooms and at London dinner tables, so there were many faces from the past among the crowded pews, I hope not entirely because the luncheon afterwards, for all the attendees, was to be held at Claridge's. Serena was very helpful with the arrangements and at her suggestion Peniston read a piece. It was that one about death being 'nothing at all,' which I always find rather irritating, but apparently it had been specified. He spoke about his mother's admiration and love for Damian, which I thought rather courageous and good, and I must admit I was also impressed that Andrew turned up and maintained throughout both service and reception a grave, pompous solemnity, which I assume was the nearest he could come to any manifestation of sorrow. Given the circumstances, even the little he was allowed to know, he could hardly be expected to feel much of the latter. Of course, the enormous inheritance had propelled his dynasty overnight to a place among the top twenty families in England, so it behoved him not to look ungrateful, but still, good manners may never be counted on under any circumstances and I was glad of them from him.

Lucy was there, in a peculiar approximation of mourning dress, with a black, silk evening coat and a huge, plastic, purple flower pinned to its collar. Candida arrived with Dagmar, both of them looking elegant and genuinely upset, which warmed my heart, so far had I come in my estimation of the deceased. And even Kieran turned up, though it might have been to confirm that Damian really was dead. Terry did not make the journey from California. That would have been a lot to ask, but she sent a bunch of those fashionable and hideous flowers, beloved of urban florists, that look as if they feed on flies. One woman rather interested me. She was tall and large, but rather chic in her way, wearing a beautifully cut suit and one of the best diamond brooches I have ever seen. She looked at me and smiled and nodded, so clearly I knew her, and in case she came over to say hello I sought the assistance of Serena as to who she might be. Serena was rather surprised by the question. 'Surely you remember Georgina Waddilove,' she said.

'Fat Georgina?' I couldn't keep the astonishment out of my face. 'What happened?'

'You have been out of the great world.' She smiled. 'She married the Marquess of Coningsby.'

I had been out of the great world indeed. 'When?'

'About fifteen years ago. I can't believe you never heard, although they are in Ireland a lot of the time. It was her first and his second, but the miracle was that he only had girls before and

585

Georgina whacked out two boys, the first when she was forty-three, and the second a year later. So she's the mother of the heir *and* the spare.'

'And is he nice?'

'Lovely. Exactly like John Thaw to look at and *so* grateful to Georgina for rescuing him. Number One took off with a friend of his, and he was very cast down when they met, but now he's as happy as a sandboy.'

Actually, this was a really joyful moment for me. I looked at the smiling and almost quite attractive Marchioness of Coningsby, and I knew that gloom is not universal, even in this misery-memoir age. For some people things do come right. 'How wonderful,' I said. 'I hope her mother was alive to attend the wedding.'

'She was. But if she hadn't been, I expect she'd have risen from the tomb to get there.' Serena laughed and so did I, before the other guests at the party claimed her.

So Damian's quest was done and I was not unhappy at the outcome, nor, in the end, about what I'd learned on my travels through my lost youth. I had thought that the secret love story of 1968, had been my own hidden and one-sided worship, which had ended in my exile, but I had discovered instead that Serena Gresham and my betrayer had been the lovers of choice for any true romantic. Even so, I cling to my belief that in rediscovering and recognising the workings of my own heart, and in having finally made love, albeit once, to the object of my passions, I had endorsed my life, in retrospect and for the future, to the end of my days. Whatever may yet come to me, something or nothing it remains to be seen, I have

586

known what the poets write about and I am duly grateful.

I was standing in the hall of the hotel, with its wonderfully vivid, black-and-white marble floor, when Peniston Summersby touched me on the arm. Together we walked out on to the pavement, into the still bright, autumn day, as we discussed what had to be done next, since an estate like Damian's is bound to be a work in progress for many years, but then he hesitated and I knew he wanted to say something to show me that he was aware of his good fortune. 'It's a wonderful opportunity. I mean to try to be worthy of it,' he came up with at last.

'I'm sure you will be.'

'And I want to go on with the things that mattered to him. Then there's cancer research, of course, and I thought we might look at setting up some new scholarships in his name.'

'To be honest, I don't think he'd really care much about perpetuating his name, but I agree with you. Let's do it.'

It was time to part, but I could see he hadn't quite finished. Poor fellow, he looked rather awkward, and in the last analysis there is something a bit odd about being left a kingdom worth more than the National Debt because some bloke was in love with your mother forty years ago, which is all he would ever hear about it. 'Mummy says he was a marvellous man. She wishes I'd known him.'

I considered this for a moment. 'I think he was a brave man,' which I truly do. 'He was unafraid of the rules that frighten people. He made up his own and one must always admire that. I suppose he was

587

an original. It's something so many of us strive for and so few of us achieve.'

With that we shook hands and I walked away down Brook Street.